far-right-wing politicians, is a tour de force in Europe's dark literature. Convincing, gripping and utterly realistic, Eekhaut populates his book with characters and situations which will stay with you long after you've finished."

—Alan Gold, author of the internationally successful
The Jericho Files and the bestseller *The Lost Testament*

"A Belgian detective worthy to follow in the footsteps of Poirot! Political intrigue, an atmospheric venue, and rollicking action from beginning to end!"

—Paul J. Heald, author of *Death in Eden* and *Cotton*

"A subtle, engaging, and very timely thriller."

—Michael Marshall Smith, author of *The Intruders*

"The surprise of this spring. It is original and shows considerable stylistic skills."

—*De Standaard*

"Intelligent and exciting."

—*Crime Zone*

"Eekhaut presents us with lifelike characters, not heroes in the hard-boiled tradition, but human detectives plagued by doubt."

—*Knack*

ABSINTHE

A THRILLER

GUIDO EEKHAUT

Skyhorse Publishing

First English-language Edition

Originally published in the Netherlands under the title *Absint* by Mynx

This is a work of fiction. Names, places, characters, and incidents are either the products of the author's imagination or are used fictitiously.

Skyhorse Publishing books may be purchased in bulk at special discounts for sales promotion, corporate gifts, fund-raising, or educational purposes. Special editions can also be created to specifications. For details, contact the Special Sales Department, Skyhorse Publishing, 307 West 36th Street, 11th Floor, New York, NY 10018 or info@ skyhorsepublishing.com.

Skyhorse® and Skyhorse Publishing® are registered trademarks of Skyhorse Publishing, Inc.®, a Delaware corporation.

Visit our website at www.skyhorsepublishing.com.
Visit the author's website at www.eekhaut.com.

10 9 8 7 6 5 4 3 2 1

Library of Congress Cataloging-in-Publication Data is available on file.
Library of Congress Control Number: 2018943494

Cover design by Erin Seaward-Hiatt
Cover illustration: iStockphoto

Print ISBN: 978-1-5107-3067-0
Ebook ISBN: 978-1-5107-3069-4

Printed in the United States of America

ABSINTHE

Prologue

PARNOW DIDN'T SPEAK DUTCH. He didn't have to. He had no need of that bizarre, guttural language. Nor did he speak much English, apart from a few basic phrases and a limited vocabulary. He knew just enough to get by in daily life and do a few things. Even then, he didn't have much use for it. The handgun with the big black silencer sufficed to show people he meant business. Why go through all the trouble of learning a foreign language when all you needed were some universal gestures that everyone understood? There was no need at all for words and interpreters and such. In his business, people were fast enough on the uptake.

A gun pressed against your head, for instance. That tells you more than enough about the intentions of the one holding the gun. He's clearly not here for fun and games. He wants you to cooperate. Especially because the gun has that nasty silencer. People everywhere watch movies and television and know what a silencer is for. It tells them: you are about to get wasted, and nobody will notice. Not a soul will care.

The young man at the other end of the barrel seemed to know a lot about guns and silencers and universal symbols. His face was contorted with fear. His hands were shaking. He was living his final minutes. Parnow had only one real concern: that the guy was going to pee in his pants. That did occasionally happen to people who were confronted with their last moment on earth. It would be annoying because Parnow would have to endure the stench after the guy was dead.

The young man didn't wet his pants, but he seemed close. The universal symbol was clear and well understood, the message was received.

His life was about to end. Maybe he could avert that by providing answers. The right answers, the ones Parnow expected. That was the message of the gun. "Van Boer," Parnow said. "Where is Van Boer?"

He was at the right address. Someone had slipped him a piece of paper with a name, address, and brief directions for how to find the place. Everything checked out, except that this young man wasn't Van Boer. He knew that at once because this kid was black. Well, not really black, but Surinamese or something, Moroccan maybe, although Parnow was a bit vague about the difference.

It didn't matter. Van Boer wasn't supposed to be black. The picture he'd been given of Van Boer wasn't very sharp, but this certainly was not him. So Van Boer had given out a false address. Parnow had crossed a considerable part of Amsterdam on his way to the wrong place. He didn't like that. He was pissed off, because Amsterdam wasn't the kind of city that he enjoyed wandering around. Too many insolent kids and too many fat tourists. He didn't enjoy this at all. So he pushed the gun a bit harder against the black kid's skull. It might make a dent. He didn't give a shit because the kid wouldn't live long.

"He doesn't live here," the kid said in English, with some difficulty, mostly because it's not easy to talk with a gun to your head. And a silencer attached to the gun. And the end of your short life in sight.

"Where?" Parnow hated this sort of conversation. Surely the situation must have been clear as far as the kid was concerned. He, Parnow, was looking for a man named Van Boer. So he wanted to know where the man lived. Why wouldn't the black kid cooperate? Would be easier all around. How difficult could it be? Van Boer lives on so-and-so street. Easy as pie.

"On Leidsestraat, eighty-four, one flight up," the kid said.

Parnow growled. He let go of the kid, who tumbled to the floor. "Paper," Parnow said. "Write." He hadn't completely understood what the kid said—he needed the address written down. He didn't know his way around Amsterdam either; he didn't know which street the kid meant.

The young man got up, averted his eyes, grabbed a sheet of paper and a pencil, and wrote two lines. Parnow snatched the paper from his hands. "Liedsestrait," he said.

"*Leidsestraat*," the kid corrected him. As if anybody fucking *cared* how the name was pronounced. Telling *him* how the street was called. *Fucking wiseass nigger.* "It's not far from here."

"Oh," Parnow said. Playing tour guide now as well. Telling *him* what to do. *Not far from here.* He raised the gun and shot the kid between the eyes. Parts of his skull and brain splattered the wall behind him. Parnow stepped back and left the apartment. Chaos, the stench of heroin, the stench of sweat, and now the stench of death as well. *Amsterdam! A corrupt and decadent metropolis. Thick with black people and people not capable of holding down a decent job.*

He removed the warm silencer from the gun and stuffed both in his small black backpack. Moments later, after consulting a map, he was on his way to Leidsestraat. Nobody took notice of him. He had dragged the kid from his bed after kicking in his door. It had been easy so far, but frustrating nevertheless. The wrong address. They had given him the wrong address. He glanced at his watch. Half past eight. With some luck, he would find the real Van Boer in his bed as well. That would be fun.

"And what do you plan to do with it?"

Eileen Calster lay on the unmade bed, wearing only a pair of panties. Pink panties, not her best. Under other circumstances, Pieter would have made some remark about them and about her not being properly dressed yet, despite the hour. She couldn't care less. What did it matter that she was still in bed? She had other things on her mind. Such as Pieter's insane plan.

A plan that wouldn't stand a chance in the real world. That much she knew. He was determined to go through with it anyway, now that he had his hands on that famous list. The list of contributors to the Partij Dierbaar Nederland, the PDN. Who invented these party names anyway? Beloved Netherlands Party? You've gotta be kidding. Anyway, this was a list of private citizens who had donated money to Van Tillo's party, including the amounts contributed. Every ambitious CEO of a midsize company in the country who favored the right-wing politics of Van Tillo. Pieter had stolen the list the previous night from the carelessly guarded party headquarters. Politically speaking, the Netherlands would be in turmoil if this list appeared in the press. Too many big names, people who wouldn't want to be associated with this party.

Pieter was far from happy about it. He was worried that his coup of grabbing the list had brought with it a heavy burden, which was indeed the case. He hadn't counted on that. And so he had done nothing with the list yet.

"If they catch you with those documents, you'll go to prison." Not the first time she'd told him that, but he wasn't impressed and hadn't been in the past. She knew how stubborn he was. He was convinced that his sense of justice gave him a license to do as he pleased and made him invulnerable to boot.

"It had to be done," he said. He'd been saying that all day yesterday, trying to convince her, but in vain. "We have to show the world how the PDN practices politics. Where they get their money from. The kind of people who finance them. We all know how important this is."

She stretched slowly in the warm bed. When she first met him, she'd admired his drive. He had been a sort of hero to her. Now she understood he was just plain stubborn, which made him ignore the dangers involved. He was driven by his desire to pursue his ideals, nothing else.

"And you're willing to run such risks? What about the police and the press? Why don't they play their part? They should be intervening if something illegal has happened."

He shrugged. He shrugged more often than before. It wasn't nonchalance—merely a sign he didn't intend to share his motives with her.

She got up and stood at the window. In the street, a pedicab, a cobbled-together vehicle that even tourists sneered at, rolled by. She wanted a cigarette, but Pieter didn't allow smoking in the apartment. Of course, she often ignored him. She'd learned to do her own thing even when Pieter was around. Later she'd go down to the pub, but she wanted to freshen up first. And eat something.

"I have to give all that some very careful thought, Eileen," he said. "I'm not going to flaunt this list in the streets. And do put some clothes on. The whole neighborhood is watching."

"Goddamn, Pieter, this is Amsterdam. Not that provincial shithole you were born in. People see more tits in this street than you probably will in your whole life. Grow up! You're thirty. What are you going to do now you have that list?"

Why was she angry with him? She too came from some shithole, far from the big city. At least he'd grown up in a modern provincial town.

He tried to do something about his hair. Needed a cut, surely, but no time for that. He hadn't slept well last night. He'd been worried, had made plans, had been making plans for the past twenty-four hours. He still didn't see a way out. "There's really no hurry, Eileen. They're not going to miss the list all of a sudden. Their offices are a mess. I can talk to a journalist, but I'll have to figure out who. Most of the newspapers just go along with those right-wingers. So I have to choose wisely. I need a journalist with integrity. One who also works for the major dailies."

"Why not do it sooner? Today, even. Or go to the police. I have a bad feeling about this."

"Nothing concerning the list is illegal. All of it is pretty much within the law. The police won't do anything with it, but the press might. Public opinion is very sensitive about these matters. Money and politics combined, that's very suspect for most people. Getting this list published in the right newspaper may do a lot of damage to certain people. But I want to be careful as to whom to approach. This is dynamite. Is that so hard to understand?"

"You've been working on this for over a year. Why didn't you go public earlier? You're impossible, Pieter! You're naïve. You're the most disorganized conspirator I know." She didn't know any other conspirators, but that didn't matter. He was simply out of his depth.

"Just leave me alone, Eileen!"

She shrugged. Pieter was an idealist. And to her, idealists were the most dangerous kind of people. Guided by inspired ideas but not practical. Rarely focused on lasting results. That's how Pieter was. A year ago, he'd managed to infiltrate the headquarters of the Partij Dierbaar Nederland. For a year, he had worked there without them suspecting anything. Right-wing nationalists of the worst sort, he called them. They seemed respectable, but they were only that on the outside. A party for middle-class xenophobes. A party for anyone who wanted a "livable Holland." Not overtly racist, not overtly fascist, but they did appeal to the most narrow-minded prejudices in society while keeping their extremist views behind closed doors. The Netherlands for the Dutch only. For the white-skinned Dutch. Those sorts of ideas. And it seemed to work well for them. They'd been successful in recent elections, a couple of seats in the upper and lower chambers, two ministerial portfolios in a previous government, but now in the opposition.

"Organizations like these can't raise enough money on donations from ordinary members alone," Pieter had told her. He followed the left-wing papers and bloggers with great interest. Sometimes he even wrote for them. "They wouldn't get very far on that sort of money. Much more is coming in from the business community. From the midsize companies. The self-inflated populist right-wing elite of hardworking Holland."

And Pieter had resolved to prove his theory.

Now he had evidence he needed. It had taken him the better part of a year.

"Well," Eileen said, turning her slender back toward the street, "I hope you don't leave that list lying around here too long. I don't feel safe, if you want my view. Which, I'm sure, you don't." She went in search of a sweater. The outside air was crisp.

"They're not going to send a gang of thugs after me, Eileen," Pieter said. "They don't even know where to find me. I made sure of that."

"These people creep me out."

"They want to protect the Netherlands, sweetie. Against all that is sinister and dark and *alien* in the big, bad world outside. At least that's what they claim, and a lot of people are willing to believe their rhetoric. The same people who want to give up their freedom in order to feel more secure. It just shows how uncritical they are."

"This sweetie doesn't need that sort of protection. This sweetie is tired of oppressive, patronizing ideas. Have you taken a good look at Hendrika Van Tillo yet?"

"I see her almost every day."

"Lucky you. I certainly don't need that woman's protection."

"Neither do I. But a lot of Dutch think they do. The ones who are afraid."

"What should they be afraid of? Islam? Terrorists? People with skin darker than their own? What's the sense in that? Van Tillo is only good at peddling fear. The only thing she's good at."

"I couldn't have said it better, sweetie. That's why I'm doing this."

"Oh," she replied, wanting to tease him now. "And as a reward for your courage, I should pop off to the store so your eminence can have his tea with milk. And maybe your eminence would require a baguette and some Boursin cheese too? Buttermilk, croissants, fresh-squeezed juice? A full English breakfast in bed?"

"That would be a nice start," Pieter said. It sounded as if he expected more from her than breakfast. Not that he had anything to complain about regarding Eileen or the attention he got from her. He was usually the one neglecting her.

She glanced at her body in the mirror. Too skinny, no doubt. Some boys liked that. Boys like Pieter. Boys? Pieter was thirty. He was almost ten years her senior. He still had his boyish looks, just as she liked, but his age had begun to show. A few wrinkles, some gray hairs.

He possessed a careless sort of charm she'd grown fond of. That, and the improbably chaotic way he dealt with the rest of the world—his brilliant but often too focused mind, which made it difficult for him to bring complex projects to a successful close.

But what did *he* see in her? She wasn't sure. A lot of things he didn't share with her. He loved her, she was sure of that, but in what way? She knew so little about his life. He never mentioned previous relations. He never spoke about his past. He only looked forward. Sharing a life with her, that much he had promised. And that seemed enough for her, at least for right now. So why ask difficult questions?

She looked at her cheap Swatch. Almost nine. She had classes soon. Oh, well, she could skip them. She skipped classes more often recently. Anthropology. Who liked anthropology?

She didn't, for sure.

But she had to study. Prepare for her exams. Her parents supported her financially, assuming their daughter would get a diploma. On what

Pieter earned, they could barely afford this apartment. Her parents didn't know they lived together. They assumed she had a student room in Amsterdam, which was what they paid for. They assumed their virtuous daughter had her head in books all the time.

But now Pieter was out of a job. He had pulled that stunt, as he said he would do. Stealing that infamous list from the offices of the politician he worked for. How foolish could you get? He could make money out of selling the list to a newspaper, but he didn't intend to. He wasn't going to get money for it. He was an idealist. Someone would have to pay the rent, but who? Not Pieter, who couldn't even get public benefits of any sort now. Should she consider a part-time job?

She shrugged, glancing at her ass in the mirror in those panties as she pulled on jeans.

"I'll be back, you spoiled brat," she said.

Pieter, under the covers, didn't respond.

She went out, in sneakers without socks. It was chilly outside but dry.

She didn't notice the man watching their building from the doorway on the other side of the street.

He focused on Eileen for a moment and then looked up at the windows of the apartment. He had seen Eileen through the window. He'd seen her without her T-shirt. Decadent world. Skinny girls, just like in Moscow or Chechnya. Girls with bad habits. Not eating, just shooting up and snorting. He knew that sort of girl well. Would do anything for cash. He knew where they got their money. Pieter Van Boer. A pimp.

No mercy, then. A pimp and a thief. He knew the appropriate punishment for that sort of person, and he enjoyed the privilege of doling out the punishment. He didn't even have to invoke God. He had a contract with a more earthly power. That was enough.

A last look at the girl. Long legs and a firm little ass. He didn't know how long she would be away, but it didn't matter much. What he needed to do would take him only a few moments.

He crossed the street and pushed open the door of the building. He'd noticed that the front door did not latch. Careless people!

He walked up the stairs. At Van Boer's apartment, he paused for a moment. No name, no bell. He knocked on the door.

He heard a muffled voice from inside. "Eileen? Is that you?"

Parnow, though he didn't understand the Dutch, could still tell by the tone of the young man's voice that he wasn't on his guard. He pushed the door. It opened easily enough. He stepped inside, the gun with the silencer in his right hand. The black backpack in his left. He let the bag slip slowly from his hand until it rested by the door.

There seemed to be nobody.

Then he noticed the outline of Van Boer under the bed sheets.

"You brought croissants?" the muffled voice asked.

"Pieter Van Boer?" Parnow asked. He made no effort to pronounce the name correctly. After all, this was no social call.

The sheets were jerked back. The confused and startled face of Van Boer appeared. This was definitely the kid from the photo. Parnow was now sure of his victim.

"Who are you?" Pieter asked, in Dutch.

"Where is the list?" Parnow asked, in English.

The young man's gaze wandered to his left for a brief but significant moment. Parnow looked in the same direction. A small, rickety desk with letters, papers, pencils, a laptop, and an antique desk lamp.

Yeah, that's where the list would be.

"I don't know what you mean," Pieter said.

Parnow raised the gun.

Pieter attempted to get up while holding his hands in front of his face.

Funny, Parnow thought, *how they all assume they can stop a 9mm bullet with their hands or arms. As if they're Superman or whatever.* He knew about Superman from the movies. Superman could fend off bullets and even heavier projectiles with so much ease. Typical American bullshit.

Well, Pieter Van Boer couldn't, obviously. No way. He wasn't Superman.

Parnow pulled the trigger twice.

The weapon made a coughing sound. As if someone in the room

had a cold. Van Boer's body fell back. His blood covered the wall in a fan-like pattern.

Parnow lowered the gun. He stepped toward the desk. Pushed pencils and letters aside. A cardboard file. A list of names and amounts. Exactly as he had been told. He folded the file and tucked it into his jacket. Noticed the laptop. Maybe he should take that as well. Maybe his clients would be interested in whatever information it contained. And wasn't there a smartphone around as well?

A subdued cry and a dull thud sounded behind him. He turned.

The girl stood halfway in the room. She had dropped the baker's bag when she saw Van Boer's body. She held both hands in front of her mouth. A paragon of shocked horror.

Parnow stepped toward her. Two steps. The apartment wasn't large. He swung the gun upward again, the barrel facing her.

She had seen him. She didn't step back. She didn't panic. He would have to admit he hadn't expected that. A brave, thin, spindly, startled girl who understood right away the situation as it presented itself to her. Understood the danger she was in. He had known brave girls like her in Russia. And in Ukraine. He had met them in Moscow when he settled scores with dealers. He had seen them under all circumstances. They were the kind of girls that happened to live somewhat longer than the others. Not much, but long enough to enjoy a decent stretch in life.

The girl kicked him in the groin.

Which he hadn't expected at all.

The blow hit him hard. He doubled over.

She whacked him on the cheek with her hard, closed fist.

It hurt, but he also felt shame for not anticipating her reaction. Not being ready for it. He had become old and slow. He couldn't even handle a young girl anymore.

She wanted to hit him again, but she had lost the advantage of surprise. He rammed his fist into her ribs but lost his balance. His jacket fell open and the file fell out.

She kicked him again, rather ineffectively, grabbed the file, and managed to flee the apartment.

In the time it took him to recover and get up again, neither his body nor his honor intact, she was gone. Worse yet, she had disappeared with the list.

He limped to the window. Leaned out. She was running on the other side of the street. He hobbled downstairs, taking the backpack with him. He slid the gun into the backpack. By the time he reached street level, she'd disappeared. He ran in the direction he'd seen her last. But he couldn't spot her anywhere. She knew the city better than he did. He could search up and down streets, but it'd be pointless. He wouldn't find her. At least not today.

He kicked a wall. He wanted to blow off more steam but that would be too conspicuous. So he zippered the backpack with the gun inside, swung it onto his shoulder, and went back the way he had come.

A MONDAY IN SEPTEMBER

Amsterdam

1

"HE'S A TRULY INSUFFERABLE man who only wants to impose his own opinion and isn't going to listen to what other members of the team have to contribute. He ignores his superiors as much as he ignores their orders. He doesn't take them seriously. All this leads to conflicts. His methods are unconventional at best and border on illegal at times. And his opinion of women, well, I won't go into that topic."

This was what Superintendent Teunis had said only a few weeks earlier about Chief Inspector Walter Eekhaut. Or words to that effect. Excepting Teunis herself and the man sitting on the other side of her desk at the time, there had been no witnesses who could, at any later point, repeat exactly what had been stated.

"I assume," the man had said, "that you'd rather get rid of Chief Inspector Eekhaut?"

"And I assume," Teunis had replied, "that I was clear enough on the subject."

The man smirked. He had a name, but it wasn't relevant, because he worked for the Ministry of Foreign Affairs and was high enough up the official ladder to exert influence on the Superintendent of the Brussels Federal Police. "It seems, in a certain way, that he's best suited for the mission we have in mind."

"You've been very vague concerning that mission," Teunis said.

"I have, because this is a delicate assignment. So delicate and at the same time so—how should I put it—so absolutely meaningless, that we want to entrust it to someone outside of our own circle."

"Yes, I understand."

"You do. All this concerns the growing influence of Russian financiers in our banking sector. By *our*, of course, I don't mean those puny banks this kingdom still has left, my dear. What I'm referring to are the really large players in the Benelux market, specifically Fabna Bank."

"Oh," Teunis said, sliding her ballpoint across the surface of her desk, tracing the chaotic pathways of international banking politics.

"Precisely. Our Dutch colleagues of the AIVD, the General Intelligence and Security Service, are the ones who set this whole . . . affair in motion. Interventions of this sort are nothing new, as you probably know. Arab and Japanese companies already own large portions of Western European and American corporations. But that's legitimate financing. White money, as you might say. The Russians, however . . . well, let's say there's much reason for concern. Deep concern. Matters didn't usually get out of hand in the past, but that's changed. You saw the papers. We learned that one single financier in particular is about to acquire around five percent of Fabna. And he's coming to Amsterdam soon. The AIVD wants to keep an eye on him and the whole operation. They're asking for our assistance since Fabna is a Dutch-Belgian company. And they're playing the whole thing by the book. I'm sure you understand why."

"So they need a specialist. But then we're not talking about Eekhaut. He's not a financial specialist in any respect."

"True. And he has a number of deplorable professional habits. But nevertheless, he has a solid reputation as an investigator. At the same time—and I'm counting on your discretion here because I shouldn't be telling you this—we're not really that much interested in this affair. Finance has a heart attack whenever the Russians start flaunting their money, but the minister has other worries. So he doesn't really want to play ball with the Dutch."

"Which minister? Who has authority here?"

"There's the hitch. All the ministers who control part of the dossier are passing responsibility from one to the other. They don't want to be bothered with it. That's why mine has finally decided on a symbolic solution."

"In the shape of a recalcitrant senior detective—?"

"Who isn't even an expert, but who can't do much harm either, and of whom we don't mind ridding ourselves."

"I see," Teunis said. "Well, that suits me just fine, as you probably expected."

"I'm glad we're on the same page," the man said.

And so Chief Inspector Eekhaut found himself on a train from Brussels to Amsterdam, with an economy-class ticket, on a Monday morning in September. He had been looking at the passing landscape, although he had a book on the little table by the window. He hadn't read a page yet. The train had just passed Roosendaal, and the landscape—the Netherlands now and no longer Belgium—became even more flat and wet. It had stopped raining for a while, but it had been raining for three straight days. Ditches and streams were swollen. The Netherlands. Laboriously reclaimed from the water. But for how much longer? If the ocean levels were really on the rise, all of this might soon become sea again, and the Dutch would be in trouble.

They should have built their dikes a bit higher, Eekhaut thought. That's what they're good at—building dikes. Soon they'll live on an inverted island.

He observed the low-hanging clouds. There would be more rain soon.

His mood hadn't improved since early this morning. He had taken the seven o'clock train from Leuven. As usual, he had been early. He had a cup of coffee in the station refreshment room along with a collection of temporarily stranded travelers: an old man with a new suitcase and a second cup of coffee, a few cigarette-smoking laborers, two unattractive women on their way to work in Brussels, a good-looking brunette who was reading an Olivia Goldsmith paperback while puffing at her first cigarette of the day.

In Mechelen, he transferred to the intercity train. Ugliest station in a country that excelled in ugly stations. Then directly toward Amsterdam. In the distance, the horizon was the color of old lead. His luggage had been sent ahead. Expenses were paid by the government, as were his train ticket and the apartment where he was to stay for the duration. They were obviously very pleased to get rid of him. To send him packing to Holland. To the unsuspecting Dutch. So be it.

Teunis had had a few things to say to him about the way he'd behaved while under her command. He wasn't surprised. He knew what she thought of him. No love lost between them. Well, he had himself partially to blame for that. He had never cared much about his image. He wouldn't even contradict the rumors that were circulating about him. "You have issues with female superiors," she told him. "No," he'd replied, "I have issues with authority, and hence with all superiors." After that, the conversation had been difficult.

His problem with authority kept showing up in his annual evaluations, too.

A few people had come to say goodbye. Older colleagues he'd worked with and who knew that his methods yielded results. The stubborn ones, who swore by old-school policing. The dying breed. But Teunis had told them, "The federal police are better off without people like Chief Inspector Eekhaut. Today, there is no room anymore for his kind of improvisation. For the past two decades, we've been introducing and using scientific methods for solving crimes. Eekhaut has never grasped that."

And so on.

He was aware of the story. He knew every word of it. Tone and content hadn't changed during recent years.

He had discussed these methods at length with Teunis—whose first name was probably Isolde or something like that. About the failure of those scientific methods of which she spoke so highly. Neither of them had changed their point of view. In the end, she had simply arranged for his transfer. *Transfer.* It sounded ugly, a punishment. And that was what it really was, a punishment. To the Bureau of International Crime and Extremist Organizations, part of the AIVD in Amsterdam. The Bureau was engaged in combating extremist groups and serious border-crossing crime within a European framework. And it appeared he got the job because he was fluent in both English and French. Because not a single Francophone colleague on the force could be bothered to learn Dutch or English.

And, of course, this was the most distant place they could send him. His assignment was clearly defined, Teunis explained: he was to assist the Dutch with the investigation into Adam Keretsky, the infamous Russian financier. The new future major shareholder of Fabna.

She hadn't even bothered to ask him whether he would accept the job voluntarily. As far as she was concerned, the question was irrelevant.

Her first name *had* to be Isolde—though no one, no one at all, seemed to know what her name actually was. A superintendent wasn't expected to have a first name.

The train moved gracefully through the peaceful green landscape, like an electric ghost. The messy architecture of Flanders had given way to the slightly too tidy architecture of the Netherlands, where it seemed the freedom of families was constricted by obsessively erected walls.

Three foreign students, of various origins, seemed to be having a noisy argument in English, the lingua franca of European intellectuals, about the meaning of intelligent design. One of them had a new Sony laptop with him.

Eekhaut had no affinity for the Netherlands.

The question was, however, if he had ever had any affinity for his own country.

What else had Teunis said about him? The same remarks he had read in his evaluations for years. Insufficiently results-oriented. Exceptionally weak in his administrative skills. Poor communication with superiors. Too little respect for them, as well.

Respect!

He had no, absolutely *no* respect for the kind of hierarchy that Teunis represented.

The train made a slight turn and passed through a small town whose apartment buildings denoted modest prosperity and an orderly lifestyle. An orderly country, with clear rules for everybody. He knew Amsterdam would be different. He had been there a couple of times as a tourist. An anarchic city. A very un-Dutch city. A city very unfriendly toward anyone over twenty and, at the same time, stimulating enough for anyone over fifty.

Not that he was stimulated by his new assignment.

He let his gaze wander to the book in front of him. Nabokov, *Look at the Harlequins!* The last book the author wrote. A bizarre pseudo-memoir. He felt as though the title were about him. A harlequin. Someone who had spent thirty years wearing the mask of a police officer, a civil servant, and who could no longer pretend that mask made any sense. He had been a police officer because he believed in justice. These days, police officers—especially at his level—were recruited from the ranks of young academics who weighed the career opportunities of such a proposition.

The train slowed down. Eekhaut looked at his watch. A little after ten. He had spent three hours on the train. Better than three hours in a car. Nevertheless, it had been a senseless waste of time. Passengers got up, gathering their bags and other items. The students were already on their way to the end of the carriage. Eekhaut grabbed his bag from the luggage rack and put the book away. He hoped his clothes and other possessions had been delivered to his apartment.

The train came to a halt and the doors opened. Everyone got out. Air, different from that of Brussels, greeted him. The station was crowded. People were hurrying toward their trains in the underground passageway that led him to the station's exit. Outside, the sun was shining, although the air remained pleasantly cool.

He slung the bag over his shoulder, searched his jacket pocket, and found a folded sheet of paper. Addresses: his apartment, the office of the AIVD, and a name. Dewaal. His contact with AIVD. The night before, he had studied the map of Amsterdam with the tram routes and a colorful, tourist-oriented guide to the city. His apartment was situated in Utrechtsestraat, right by Frederiksplein, on Tramline 4. Wouldn't be difficult to find.

He looked around. The station building was scaffolded to a perilous degree. Noisy work was in progress, railings and metal frames all around him. They meant serious business here, he thought. Then, to his left, he saw the tram stop.

2

"IT'S GONE?" HENDRIKA VAN Tillo said, hands on her hips, glaring at the somewhat less than imposing Kees Vanheul, her long-suffering secretary. He was much more to her than just a secretary, especially on an organizational and ideological level, if the press were to be believed—or at least that part of the press that had no sympathy for Van Tillo, her party, or her world view. The communist press, as she referred to it without much deference to historical accuracy. So different from the tabloids, with which she tried to remain on good terms because many people read them—the people Van Tillo counted as among her supporters, potential or otherwise.

"What happened, Kees?" she repeated. "It isn't here anymore. The list. What are you going to do about that?"

"I'll just print a new one," Vanheul said. "Takes only a moment—I can do it myself. The file is on my computer."

"Kees, that's not the point." Van Tillo pushed her much too large and unwieldy dark brown leather desk chair out of the way, much as she would deal with a political opponent. She had wanted a bigger office, but no larger room had been available on the premises except the two meeting rooms on the ground floor. And Van Tillo wasn't going to have her office on the ground floor! "The point is that yesterday my list, the one on paper, was in that drawer and now it's gone. That means someone took the list. And that's not acceptable."

"No," he said, "that's not acceptable at all."

"Because the list is missing, Kees," Van Tillo continued mercilessly, "and that could mean it's in the hands of someone who's going to use it for his own purposes. Misuse it, as in, you know, *mis-use*. Against the people whose names and many more details are on it and in plain damn sight for anyone. Damn it, it even has amounts on it. This is a disaster, in every respect. How are we going to explain this?"

"Come now, Hendrika," he soothed, "I'm sure things will straighten themselves out. It's probably just some misunderstanding. Not worth the fuss. Maybe you put it somewhere else. Where could it have gone? No one ever comes here, not in this office. Besides, don't you usually lock your drawers?"

"Why would I lock my drawers, in this office? Can't I trust the people I work with anymore? Is trust in our fellow Dutchmen not one of the cornerstones of our Party?" Every time she said it, it sounded capitalized: Party. The capital letter was only fitting, too. Because they were the only party worthy of that name. A real party of the people. The rest was an assemblage of political opportunists.

"I think we can trust every single person who works here, Hendrika. Though a lot of new people joined us recently. Sometimes I don't know what to make of them. We never had anything like a screening process. Perhaps we should."

"They're all Dutch, Kees. Every one of them." Meaning—and he knew very well what she meant—that they were all white-skinned Dutch, all of them of true indigenous stock. Homegrown people of native character. People of pure blood. Dutch blood. Otherwise, you did not get into the Party.

"I'm sure the list isn't gone," he said.

But she wouldn't be soothed. "Yes, it is. And if it's gone, we have a major problem on our hands. Suppose the press gets hold of it? What do you suppose would happen?"

"We can deal with that. We'll go to court and threaten everyone who intends to publish the list . . . or any part thereof. We've used that tactic before. It works every time."

Van Tillo stubbornly shook her head. "By then it's too late. We can only sue when the information is actually published. Then it's all out in the open. We'll get in a lot of trouble with a lot of important people if that happens. You know how discreet we are when raising funds from the business community. We would lose a large number of backers, and even that would be the least of our worries."

Kees was well aware of the implications of such a leak. His main responsibility was fund-raising. He maintained contacts with the business community, notably with the segment that was only too happy to cough up money for the party because they wanted their social and economic agenda implemented by politicians. These people wanted to remain discreet while doing so, for obvious reasons. They wouldn't appreciate finding their names in the papers connected intimately with Van Tillo's Party. Capital P or not.

The work he did was necessary. It needed to be done. Politics depended on money. Parties had unavoidable expenses and almost no income. Getting Party members—Hendrika in particular—elected was an expensive business. And people could be persuaded to contribute only if they perceived future benefits for themselves and their companies. To them, it wasn't a bad idea to have a direct line to an elected politician when, for instance, export licenses were needed. Or when a company came under fire for producing too much dangerous waste—that sort of thing. A few simple problems could disappear when a high-ranking member of the political elite took a closer look at them.

Kees knew all too well that ideology must yield to such pragmatic interests. Politics couldn't depend solely on slogans and philosophy. There were bills to pay.

Politics was an expensive business, with no room for amateurs. He was not an amateur. He had succeeded in getting Hendrika selected as minister of justice, but that had been some years ago, in another administration—and with another party altogether. She had subsequently left that party to found her own and had taken Kees with her.

He'd been grateful to her for doing so. He also knew that without his political savvy and honed diplomatic skills, she wouldn't have gotten where she was now. She knew that, too.

And now there seemed to be a problem with that list.

"You're quite sure . . . ?" he tried again.

But Hendrika was sure. *List. Gone.*

"Have someone look into whether anyone was here in the office last night, Kees. Can someone do that? Discreetly?"

"I'm afraid there isn't much to check. All we have is two cameras, and neither is installed in this room. But I'll have a look at the recordings to see if they registered anything interesting."

"We have cameras?"

"We do, but few people know about them. They're not in use during the day, but they are at night. Just two of them. I'll have a look."

"Who authorized that, Kees? Those cameras? I wasn't even aware—"

"I handled it myself, Hendrika," Kees said. *As if I need your permission for everything.*

She grunted and left it at that. "Just figure it out. I want that list back where it belongs."

He got up and walked down the hall to a small office at the rear of the building that held the two servers that managed the Party's electronic traffic. Every so often, someone on staff came by to maintain the website and install new applications. Hendrika didn't understand the first thing about computers, and she considered anyone who dealt with them a "freak"—though she never used that word in public or within the Party. She had all her emails printed out. She had a secretarial department that scoured the internet for comments about herself and the Party. She voiced her concern about "the big picture" and couldn't be bothered with details, which fit better better with her "feminine intuition," again by her own account.

In the beginning, when he started working for her, Kees had been put off by her attitude. Gradually, he had stopped getting worked up about it, as he considered it a waste of energy. Nobody was going to change Hendrika. She would never have an electronic device as an accessory.

Behind every strong politician, an even stronger team guarded the gates, occupied the towers, provided weapons and ammunition. He was the main player on that team. He saw himself as the perfect party secretary, one who kept an eye on every day-to-day problem and took care of all situations. Who knew everything that was happening. And who now would have to deal with that stupid list. Why wouldn't she simply lock her drawer?

The servers in the small office at the back operated the security cameras and stored the recordings. The cameras were installed in the third-floor hallway and along the facade of the building. The cameras took a picture every three seconds and saved them.

He sat down and opened some files. A few moments later, he was looking at the images of the previous night. His guess was that Hendrika was mistaken. That she had simply misplaced the list herself. Very few people knew about the list and where to find it. The electronic version was encrypted. But Hendrika, with her aversion to anything computer-related, always wanted an up-to-date paper copy.

And she was careless with it.

On the screen in front of Kees, a figure moved along the facade toward the gate.

Opened the gate and stepped into the alley bordering the building where Kees sat now.

A few moments later, that same figure walked down the hallway one floor up, entered Hendrika's office, and immediately stepped out again. He had been in the office no longer than half a minute. Whatever he had done, it had taken him very little time. He knew what he was looking for and where to find it.

He?

Kees replayed the sequence of captured images.

It was a man. No doubt.

Kees enlarged a couple of the images. It was not just any man. Kees knew right away who it was. The tall, skinny build and the long hair—Kees had seen him before. He worked here, in the building, for the Party. Kees would remember his name in a minute.

He printed two of the images and closed the files. He hurried to Hendrika's office. She looked up, frowning. "Someone was here last night," he said. "In this office." He showed her the printouts.

She squinted at the prints. "And do you know who this is?"

"Some guy working here," Kees said. "Has been for some time. I think he writes copy for our press office and for the website."

"Get him in here!"

"Shall I call the police too?"

"Are you out of your mind? The police? Why not alert the press, while we're at it, and reveal that an important document has been stolen from our offices, a document that has all the potential of harming us? I just want my list back! Get his ass in here. I'll have a strong word with him."

As if, Kees thought, that would be all she would do. He picked up the phone and punched in two digits. He got Jurgen, who ran the Party's communications department.

"Oh, *that* young man," Jurgen said. "The skinny youth."

"That's him," Kees said.

"Van Boer."

"Whatever his name is. I want to speak to him right now. Bring him down yourself. Don't tell him anything yet."

"He's not here," Jurgen said.

"What you mean, he's not there?"

"He didn't show up this morning, Kees. Sick, I guess. Not a word so far, no phone call, nothing. Can't even be bothered to—"

Kees put down the receiver.

"Well?" Hendrika asked.

"He's not in."

"He's not?"

"Hasn't shown up today. I think we have a serious problem. We can assume he stole the list and will probably take it to the press. This is not some random action. This was well prepared. We're probably in deep shit."

"Goddamn it, Kees. We bring someone in here to do a job and he ends up stealing our information. How did he get in, in the first place? What kind of operation are we running here if people just—?"

"I'm afraid," Kees said, "we need to have a serious talk with Monet."

Hendrika folded her hands as if she intended to pray to the Elder Gods of her private ideology. It meant, Kees knew, that she was considering the situation very thoroughly. This was not the usual Hendrika Van Tillo, who often acted out of impulse and counted on Kees to slow her down and make her think about the problem first. But when the name Monet came up, there was every reason to stop acting and think first.

The name Monet meant big problems ahead. Probably unavoidable problems.

"Does it have to come to that?" she asked, looking up.

"Suppose that list . . ." Kees said.

"Why can't we find the fucking sneak and have him . . . I don't know. Have someone convince him that he won't get very far with whatever he intends to do with that list?"

"We don't do that sort of thing, Hendrika. Not what you have in mind. And we don't have people to do it either."

"A pity," Hendrika said.

"There may be other people who can do this for us. The problem may be solvable, just not right away. Contacts need to be established first. And in the meantime, we run the risk that this sneak will take action against us."

Van Tillo shrugged. "What is his name? This unfortunate industrious young man?"

"Er . . . Van Boer."

"And meanwhile, we run the risk that Van Boer takes the list to, let's say, *Vrij Nederland* or any of those liberal newspapers, where they'll be all too glad to disclose in their next issue who supports us financially and by how much. Kees, you know—"

"I know."

"You know we're always cast in a bad light there. Because when I was minister, I had a couple of those liberal journalists prosecuted for—"

"That's hardly relevant now, Hendrika. The point is, the list must be intercepted. Which means we have to tell Monet at once. Then he won't be able to reproach us later for having kept the bad news to ourselves."

Van Tillo got up again. "Right. You call him, Kees. At once."

"Me again. The dirty work."

"Yes. You again. You're the man who handles communications with the bankers. Remember? You maintain the list. So it's your call to make."

He could point out to her that she was the one who had lost the list in the first place, but that wouldn't stick. So he was going to make the call to Monet. Who was not exactly famous for his patience or indulgence.

He looked at his watch. It was still early. For a man like Monet, it was still early. Too bad. Kees didn't like to bother someone like Monet this early in the day, certainly not with bad news, but he had no choice.

He retreated to his own office, which was almost as large as Van Tillo's. But his was sparsely furnished. No leather sofa. No framed van Gogh prints on the walls. No Party posters either. Behind his back, colleagues referred to his office as a monk's cell. He knew what they thought about him. He didn't care.

He got Monet's secretary on the line. "Mr. Monet is at breakfast with some gentlemen from finance," the young man said. He sounded vaguely effeminate. Vaguely. Kees knew about Monet's personal predilections. But you did business with anyone who wanted to share money and power.

Monet had both.

"This is extremely important," he said. "Mr. Monet will appreciate hearing from me right away."

Or not, he thought. Mr. Monet wouldn't appreciate learning from Kees Vanheul that the names of a number of prominent Dutchmen and the amounts of their contribution to Van Tillo's party would soon appear in the press. Maybe even that same day.

He would find that deeply disagreeable.

But, Kees knew, he'd better learn it from him rather than read it in the newspaper or see it on his Twitter stream.

"Yes?" came an irritated, gruff voice on the other end.

"Mr. Monet," Vanheul said. "Kees Vanheul. I'm afraid I have some unpleasant news. It might not be a real problem yet and things may work out fine, but someone unauthorized has taken the list of contributors, and we fear it could end up in the wrong hands."

Vanheul had prepared himself for a flood of abuse.

But the other and of the line remained quiet.

3

EEKHAUT WAITED AT THE tram stop for a carriage with the magical number 4. The place was more crowded than he cared for. All sorts of people, inhabitants of this highly cosmopolitan city, were coming and going. The whole neighborhood was a vast construction site for the extension of the subway. He hadn't known that Amsterdam had a subway.

He was annoyed by the fact that he had to take the tram. Why couldn't one of his future colleagues show up and give him a lift? He was working right now, wasn't he? Did they assume he'd come here as a tourist? Why didn't AIVD simply send a car around? Efficiency was the main concern of the Dutch, so why weren't they showing him any? He had been standing here for a quarter of an hour, waiting for a tram that didn't seem to be in a hurry. He hadn't seen any trams at all. It was the middle of a working day and not a tram in sight.

Was there a strike going on?

Not in Holland. Brussels was plagued by the all too frequent strikes, but surely not this efficient country.

Still, hundreds of people passed by. Thousands of people. It seemed the whole of Amsterdam was on the move. And none of them wanted a tram. Still, there was a sign telling him this was the stop for the number 4 line.

Two uniformed police officers approached him. His escort, royally late? Had he not sent a message to the AIVD that he would be arriving at Amsterdam Central Station at ten?

"Waiting for the tram, sir?" one of the officers asked. The other eyed the crowd lazily.

Eekhaut nodded. "I am. Unless you want to give me a ride?"

"The tram stops moved six months ago to the other side of the square, sir. Not very visible from over here, but there they are. Moved on account of the work being done to the station building."

He wanted to ask why this simple fact, this small and insignificant detail, wasn't announced at the old and temporarily redundant tram stop so the incidental visitor, not acquainted with the local situation, would be brought up to date. But the officer simply said, "A good morning to you, sir," and both of them walked off.

Yes, he thought, *and a good morning to you too.*

He grabbed his bag and walked toward the temporary tram stop. Almost at once, a number 4 tram arrived. He bought a ticket and sat down in the middle of the carriage. A handful of colorfully attired kids, in white woolen sweaters and black and white caps, fooled around at the end of the carriage. One of them had a small digital camera, and he was filming the others. They were a noisy bunch. A day out in the big city, Eekhaut assumed. Not unlike him. Except that he was going to stay here for a while. More or less on a permanent basis, even. And if he got bored with Amsterdam, he could always take a train to Belgium for a weekend or so. If he got homesick. Which probably wouldn't happen. He had never felt homesick in his life. He felt more or less a stranger in any place he happened to be.

There was nothing to return to anyway. Dust would gather in his apartment, on his furniture and on his books, and nobody would care. The occasional weekend back in his hometown would be more than enough. Finally, he would end up spending all of his weekends elsewhere. In a forest. At the seaside. In the Ardennes. He kept the apartment because he was sure this assignment wouldn't be forever.

The tram passed the Damrak and the Rokin in the direction of Muntplein, and then along Rembrandtplein, where crowds had gathered on the terraces of the pubs and restaurants and in the side streets, in spite of the mediocre weather. Then the tram turned right onto Utrechtsestraat. He alighted at the Prinsengracht stop and walked the short distance toward his apartment.

He consulted his map. The good people of Amsterdam had never doubted the sensibility of social order and hierarchy. They knew what made the world turn. Therefore, the first canal from the center was called the Herengracht, the gentleman's canal—referring to the rich citizens that had, in Amsterdam's Golden Age and beyond, governed the city and made it rich—and only after that came the Keizersgracht, the Emperor's Canal. Citizens before nobility. To each his own in this orderly society.

The neighborhood seemed likable, in a broad cultural context. There was a literary bookshop on a corner, and down the street he saw a wine merchant—Gall & Gall—Café Bouwman around the corner on Prinsengracht, and a fancy restaurant, Quartier Latin. He wouldn't die of thirst or hunger and wouldn't have to go without books.

The apartment was three flights up above a clothing boutique in a house with a black facade. The shop's window enlightened him on the incomprehensible excesses of youth's fashion. Black leather, nails, crosses, black army boots, chains. Across the street, a computer store sold secondhand digital equipment. A few houses down was a store that sold washing machines and fridges, which might come in handy if he had trouble with one of his own appliances.

He inspected the building. He had no expectations as to what his apartment was going to be like and therefore wasn't disappointed. A tall, square facade without adornment. It probably dated from around early last century. Well-kept, most likely. Like so many buildings in this city.

He entered the shop. A girl in her very early twenties—cut-off red jeans, shrunken T-shirt showing the contours of breasts without a bra, five piercings in one ear—didn't even frown. This was Amsterdam. She was used to a lot more than a fifty-year-old man stepping into a punk shop. "I'm here for the apartment," he announced. "On the fourth floor. You have a key for me."

"Mmm," the girl said as if she wasn't sure about his real intentions. "Fourth floor? Well, yes. I'll have a look." She rummaged in a drawer and appeared again with a key attached to a pink ribbon. "Here it is. Success!"

He accepted the key. "Thanks. Can I assume electricity is turned on and that sort of thing?"

"I think it is. Can't be a problem. I'm Tanja, by the way. Something wrong, you ask me."

He wasn't sure of the real meaning of that last sentence, assumed no hidden message, and thanked her again. There was no elevator, of course, so he climbed the three flights, glad his bag wasn't heavy. The key fitted the black front door of his apartment perfectly. The corridor's walls were painted a gray that bordered on purple, and the whole of the building needed taking care of, but he had seen worse. He entered the apartment. There was only one apartment per floor. He would not be bothered too much by neighbors.

"Neighbor?" a voice inquired from down the stairs. Eekhaut turned. He stepped outside the apartment again. The head and shoulders of an elderly man, seventy or so, had appeared on the stairs. "Neighbor?" the man repeated.

"Yes?" Eekhaut said.

"Van Leers," the man announced. "Call me Toon. Your neighbor one floor down. Heard you moved in today. From Belgium?"

"Ah, yes, indeed," Eekhaut said.

"Oh, that's not surprising. A lot of different nationalities in this city and in this area. At least you are . . . well, nice to meet you. If you can spare the time, do come by for a drink. I'm always at home."

"Right," Eekhaut said. "I will. Later on. Can't today. Unpacking and so on. And an appointment."

"I understand. Busy. Always busy. You're still young, there is plenty of time. Well, see you soon." The head and shoulders disappeared as suddenly as they had appeared.

Eekhaut retreated back into his apartment. The two steel trunks with his things stood in the center of the living room. The apartment wasn't a large one, there wasn't much in the way of furniture, and what there was had been there for a long time, serving many previous occupants. But Eekhaut practiced the belief that his state of mind was so much more important than physical surroundings.

Not that he had been a firm believer of any philosophy or religion.

In the front room next to the windows stood two leather couches and a tall, looming cabinet with an old-fashioned TV set. Around the corner, he found a dark table, four chairs, and another cabinet. A short corridor accessed a small kitchen—strictly utilitarian but with a microwave, a freezer, and a stove. Behind it was a toilet and a bathroom, and at last a large bedroom containing a formidable bed and wardrobe.

He opened the windows. He opened the cabinets. He found bed sheets and blankets. He found towels in a variety of sizes in the kitchen and in the bathroom. Everything was perfectly clean but far from new.

He knew somebody was paying a heap of money for this apartment, whoever that was. But he had stipulated he wanted to live in the center of Amsterdam, not in some far-off suburb.

He opened the trunks and started unpacking. It was close to eleven. He still had time. His new boss wanted to have lunch with him. He knew what lunch meant in Holland. He knew it meant something different (and so much less) than in Belgium.

His main problem concerned his books. He didn't have an extensive library, but what he had was still in his apartment in Leuven. He had brought only a few, and he would probably buy more here in Amsterdam, but there appeared to be no bookcase anywhere in the apartment. What he had brought he stacked next to the TV. He wasn't going to watch much TV anyway. Half an hour later, his trunks were empty, his things stashed away. He set the trunks next to the wardrobe in the bedroom. Not a nice sight, but it bothered no one but him.

He undressed, showered—the water was hot but the pipes gurgled—dried himself and dressed in another outfit. A gray suit over a pale blue shirt, no tie. He seldom wore a tie.

He closed the windows. Lunch was planned, the paper told him, at half past noon in the Krasnapolsky café. It was a bit of a walk from his apartment, but the weather was fine and he wasn't tempted by another tram ride. Cities invited trips on foot; such was his rule. Even in London, a city much to his taste, he rarely used the tube, and never a bus or cab.

He carefully closed the door to the apartment and descended the stairs. Utrechtsestraat was narrow and busy on account of the passing trams and cars. He walked toward Rembrandtplein and then all the way to the Dam. The inner city was crowded, with lots of tourists. Cyclists rode past him, ringing their bells. Was he in their way, or did they have priority everywhere? He wasn't sure about the rules.

He passed the Bijenkorf department store and mounted the stairs of the Krasnapolsky. In spite of its name, it was part of an Italian hotel chain, but it remained the most famous Grand Café in the center of the city. He turned left into the café area and announced himself to the waiter: "My name is Eekhaut. I have an appointment with Mr. Dewaal, at half past twelve."

The man, in his forties with a high balding forehead and sporting a small mustache, searched on a page of an impressive book. His finger followed a line. "Dewaal? That's correct. Your table is number thirteen, sir."

He sat at the designated table, which was set out for two. A young woman dressed in severe black and white appeared out of nowhere. "Can I get you something to drink, sir? While you wait?"

An aperitif seemed appropriate, but his new boss might get the wrong impression. These Dutch did not go all out on food and drinks, not like the Belgians. He wanted to avoid rubbing Dewaal the wrong way. "A fruit juice, please," he said.

"Right away, sir."

In no time, a fruit juice appeared on his table. Real fruit juice, not the sort of stuff you got out of a bottle in a supermarket. Freshly squeezed oranges. With ice cubes. He assumed the new boss wanted to impress him. Lunch in what was probably the most expensive Grand Café of Amsterdam. Or perhaps this was the new style of the Dutch civil servants.

The café was very busy. The upper class came here for tea or lunch. There was ample room for many people, but the acoustics were poor.

A young woman approached his table. She looked very businesslike. Maybe she worked at a high level in a bank. "Mr. Eekhaut?" she said.

"That's me," he said.

"I am Chief Superintendent Alexandra Dewaal. Welcome to Amsterdam. I see you helped yourself to a drink?"

4

NICK PRINSEN RODE HIS bike at considerable speed southward through Spuistraat. It was a quarter to nine in the morning, and this part of Amsterdam was on the verge of waking up. At the moment, it still appeared sound asleep: only a few early strollers and some bold bikers used the streets. The late echo of the night still hung in the air. At the Magna Plaza, Prinsen turned left and then followed Kalverstraat, not because this route was logical but because he wanted to defy common sense. The pedestrian street would be crowded in a few hours, but for now, it was almost silent. It seemed like a nice idea to be the only biker in Kalverstraat. A bit like being the last person on earth—his favorite fantasy.

He ignored the foul smells in the street. From a distance, he noticed the street cleaning machines that moved at the other end of the street. He drove by some early tourists and salespeople. Some of these stores had already opened. Two young salesclerks in jeans and striped T-shirts drank coffee from green cardboard cups.

Why do I bother? he thought. He could have ridden all the way through Spuistraat and then on Kerkstraat, instead of being stubborn and using this damn pedestrian area. But that's what he wanted to do. The unusual route. He never felt sufficiently challenged by the common solutions in life, by the easy way. He was stubborn.

Riding his bike was another of his stubborn habits. The bike was by far the most convenient means of transport within the city limits of Amsterdam—and thus used by thousands of its inhabitants, people of all ages and persuasions. Nevertheless, he could as easily have walked, taken the tram, or whatever. But no, he chose to ride his bike. Not for the most common reasons, but because the fast ride was a refreshing experience, even in summer, although not in the physical sense. His small and cramped apartment at the northern end of Spuistraat was a sort of prison cell to him, where he did little more than sleep. And even after a night and a lukewarm shower, he was in need of really fresh air. So he rode his bike. And fast, too.

He had been working for the Bureau of International Crime and Extremist Organizations for six months now. Its offices were situated in Kerkstraat, separate—for reasons he couldn't fathom—from those of the rest of the AIVD. It probably had something to do with discretion: the Bureau was entrenched in a war against some of its most ruthless enemies, even more so than the AIVD itself. Prinsen had studied the Bureau's archives and had found nothing but histories of infiltration, counterintelligence, blackmail, and physical threats as the means by which large international criminal organizations countered the police and his new employer in particular.

He passed three men in suits, each carrying a black leather computer case—the uniform of the business person and the manager. They spoke some foreign language, he heard in passing. Maybe Romanian, maybe a Slavic idiom. Amsterdam had in recent years become the center of trade and transactions with countries that didn't even exist as independent states before the disappearance of the Soviet Union, or that at least had never been part of the local financial scene. Mostly countries that prided themselves on being European now but at the time had been fully under the Soviet umbrella.

New Europeans, bringing new hopes, and new troubles as well.

He arrived at the Munttoren. He rode across Rembrandtplein and into Reguliersgracht, avoiding tourists who still seemed unaware of the potential danger that bikes and their riders represented for them. He slowed down when he reached the Amstel Church, but only because the pavement didn't allow for speed. He stopped and glanced at his watch. It had taken him only ten minutes. A decent time. For a moment, he rested. If he slowed down like everyone else he wouldn't arrive in a sweat, but he needed the adrenaline surge.

Even after six months, he was still wondering about the building in front of him. It seemed like nothing more than a large, functional house from the early nineteenth century, recently converted into offices. The facade was the only part that still was authentic. The rest had been torn down and completely rebuilt and modernized years ago. An underground parking space had been added, where he could park his bike.

His badge allowed him access to the side entrance. He took his bike to the lower floor where the lighting was functional but no more. He took a deep breath, shoved the front wheel of his bike into the steel brace mounted against a wall, locked the vehicle, and walked toward the lift. Under his arm he had his briefcase containing the files he'd taken home to read at his leisure. He couldn't manage much reading at the office, in spite of the fact that information was their most valuable weapon against criminals.

There was the catch, however: information was a raw commodity, sometimes authentic, sometimes fouled by external sources and as such untrustworthy. Or, to make things worse, partly true and partly a bunch of lies. He lived with every police officer's dilemma: recognizing truth amid a confluence of lies and fabrications.

But he wasn't complaining. He was twenty-five, and he had a job that fascinated him. An inspector already at his early age, thanks in part to his academic degree and his excellent results at the police academy. At least he didn't have to do traffic duty at the Central Station.

And on top of that, he worked for a highly specialized police unit. That meant a lot to him. It made it worth living in a cramped apartment in the center of Amsterdam.

On the second floor, he walked over to his work space. As a newcomer, he didn't occupy a spot at the window, where the veterans had their desks, those who had enough seniority to be allowed some privileges. Not that windows meant that much: the glass was obscured and fitted with a film that kept sound waves inside. The view wasn't grand either: the Amstelveld was no more than a small disorderly square, bordered by trees, with a playground, and benches for the local pensioners who occasionally walked their dog along the central path. Swinging Amsterdam was nowhere in sight.

Van Gils, the eminent senior member of the small group, occupied one of the window desks. He always was the first one present in the morning. Prinsen suspected the man had no private life worth mentioning, didn't sleep, and actually might live on the premises. None of this would prove to be true, of course. "We should call it the new Russian Mafia," Van Gils announced. "To distinguish it from the, well, the old Russian Mafia, as it were."

"It doesn't make any difference to me," Prinsen said, sitting down. They were continuing a conversation they'd had the day before. "I never had anything to do with your old Russian Mafia. That was before my time, obviously."

"We had them all the way back since the fifties," Van Gils said. "The Russian mob. There were more of them in Rotterdam, but those same Russians dropped by in Amsterdam to have fun and drink and fuck their way through the red-light district. Big spenders, especially in those days. It was all about drugs then. I don't know what else they did and what sort of business they were in, but they were a tough lot and you didn't want to meddle with them."

"And they all wore long black coats, hiding a machine gun underneath."

"That was much later, kid. In the eighties. You think you know better than us?" Van Gils grinned kindly. "You youngsters have no idea. You have no grasp on history. You assume all these Russians to be communists, followers of Marx and so on. Well, they weren't. They were all, every single one of them, staunch supporters of capitalism—in their own fashion. State capitalism it was, to them. They loved it. In the end, it just amounted to the same thing everywhere: you grab what you can and hope to get away with it. And when Gorbachev came along and shouted *glasnost*, they saw many new opportunities, and even more when the old Soviet Union fell apart and they could buy the meaty chunks."

Prinsen eyed his desk. It was a desert landscape. Unlike most of his colleagues, he lived by the desert principle: clean desk every evening, the files stored away in the drawers, and the laptop secured in the cabinet.

Van Gils wasn't aware of that principle, or he couldn't be bothered. Van Gils lived by the notion that chaos had to be created in order to foster creativity, or some such idea. Prinsen allowed for the idea but not when it concerned his desk.

"Aren't we expecting that Belgian today?" he asked.

Van Gils glanced outside, watching a bunch of children, probably on their way to school. "Officially, yes. But I expect him to turn up only tomorrow. The chief will have a talk with him first, over lunch somewhere, and he will want to get his apartment in order. So we'll probably see him tomorrow. He came in by train, from Brussels."

"Does he speak French?" Prinsen wasn't at all fluent in French. Always found it a difficult language. He had fewer problems with English and German. Speaking French assumed total control over tongue and lips, much more than in Dutch. If the Belgian turned out to be Francophone, there would be a problem.

Van Gils shrugged. "Don't know."

"Not that I'm worried. Any news from the observation post?"

"The thing is up and running since yesterday. Breukeling is at the spot right now. You want to go as well?"

"In a moment," Prinsen said. He looked at his watch. "Mr. K is now en route in his plane. He'll arrive at Schiphol Airport in a few minutes. I'm curious what the audio will teach us."

It hadn't been easy to install a listening post at the Renaissance Hotel. They had needed a warrant from the prosecutor, and even then the hotel management had protested against this invasion of privacy. They had practical objections too: they didn't like having electronic equipment installed in their meeting rooms because things might get damaged. But most of all, they feared for their reputation if the story leaked.

The story wouldn't leak, Breukeling had promised, waving the warrant at them. He didn't have to bother with excuses, but it was better to keep the hotel management firmly on their side, especially because the wireless mics had to be installed during the night, without witnesses, which wasn't easy in an international hotel of that size. The Bureau had its own dedicated team for that kind of job, so in the end things went smoothly.

Prinsen was convinced the story would leak anyway, though. He had already learned that much in six months.

Adam Keretsky, he thought. *Mr. K.* Businessman, a big player in the new Russia. You would have a considerable diplomatic incident on your hands if the story got out that the Dutch secret service had listened in on conversations between Keretsky and local businesspeople.

He opened his locker with his key, retrieved the laptop, and sat at his desk. Took the files he had been working on from his briefcase. Got his fountain pen from his jacket pocket. All these routine acts were soothing to him. He needed the reassurance of orderly daily routine. He switched on the laptop and started sorting through new messages.

5

Adam Keretsky experienced no difficulties at all with customs at Schiphol Airport, and he hadn't expected any. He had all the visas he needed, and if any problems had arisen, he could easily have phoned some minister or high-ranking civil servant. In life, it was important to have friends, preferably friends at the top of the social ladder. Below you on that ladder, you had no friends, only colleagues.

On top of that, he looked impressive, not the sort of man a customs officer would want to rub the wrong way. He was nearly two inches over six feet and powerfully built without being fat, his hair still dark brown, with the high cheekbones of his Slavic ancestry and pale blue eyes. He clearly was not the sort of man you would want to subject to a lengthy passport control just for the hell of it. He wore a discreetly expensive suit, white shirt, and dark red tie, telling you he had power and money. The gold Rolex around his wrist confirmed the story.

Adam Keretsky didn't lack for highly placed friends, neither here in the Netherlands nor in Russia. Thanks to those friends, he had been treated in a special burn trauma unit in Belgium, arranged for him by the country's minister of defense. That had been two years ago, after the accident with his Aston Martin in Paris. It had nearly cost him his life, but the Belgians got him the best possible treatment, better than anywhere else, even in Russia. That's when friends mattered. The whole deal had led to a Russian contract for helicopter parts with a Belgian company. And he had paid all the expenses for the treatment, including the wages of two specialized nurses.

Keretsky walked toward the main terminal's exit and waved at a man in a black uniform carrying a card that said FABNA. He had asked not to display his name in Schiphol. "Mr. Keretsky," the man said. "Your car is ready and our people have taken care of your luggage." This was the sort of service he paid for. That and a first-class plane ticket. He spent a lot of money on service, but he also kept things discreet. When you have many enemies, discretion is a defensive tactic.

"Excellent," he said, a word he had come to use more often than before. In the West, small compliments were always appreciated, even by members of the staff. In Russia, he didn't need to be so polite. Over there he had a reputation to maintain, of cool calculation and absolute power. Here, in Holland, he wore velvet gloves while handling people and their feelings.

That's what the people of Fabna Bank would soon come to experience: the feeling of velvet gloves. And the power of his hands, deft at slowly strangling unsuspecting victims—so to speak.

The car, a silver Bentley, hurried through dense traffic toward the center of Amsterdam. The driver was experienced and didn't need to be concerned about speeding tickets. The interior was soft, beige leather. There was even a small bar. Keretsky glanced at the collection of English-language newspapers that came with the car. The news cheered him. The price of crude oil was up, as were those of other commodities in which he had invested. He had bought real estate in London and Berlin, where prices rose yearly by some 8 percent. There was trouble ahead in Pakistan, and oil production in Iraq was down again. All good news as far as he was concerned. Russian oil was an even more interesting investment, as was Russian gas. These were the sorts of industrial activities he had bought into. The world showered him with gifts, which he was eager to accept.

The car slowed, went past Central Station, and stopped at the entrance to the Renaissance Hotel. Keretsky had hardly glanced outside during the trip from the airport while he concentrated on the newspapers. Now he flung them aside and got out. He walked into the hotel and checked his aging Blackberry, which he refused to part with. His appointment was in an hour and a half. Ample time for a shower and a coffee. "Has my luggage been delivered?" he asked at the desk.

"It is being delivered right now, Mr. Keretsky," the man behind the desk affirmed. He was around fifty, and he wore a spiffy uniform, but unfortunately, his tie had loosened slightly. His English was also a bit careless, which irritated Keretsky, who had studied at Cambridge. Why couldn't these Dutch learn to speak proper English, like everyone else?

"Get me my room at once," he ordered.

"You have a suite on the eighth floor, Mr. Keretsky."

He received a white plastic card. Like any tourist. Next time he would look for a hotel with more personal service. Maybe Amsterdam was in need of that sort of hotel. Maybe he'd invest in a group that would build such a hotel rather than go through bloody bankers.

But today he would have to talk with bankers. And after that with members of the local business community. And maybe with some politicians too.

Let's not forget the politicians, he thought. *They're the glue that holds this society together. They create the suitable environment for entrepreneurs. Without them, the entrepreneurs have to play that damn democratic game themselves. And they stink at it.*

Two men approached him. "Is everything to your wishes, Mr. Keretsky?" the first man inquired in Russian. His name was Andreï Tarkovski, and he was Keretsky's representative in the Netherlands. Originally from Saint Petersburg, as was Keretsky. Now he was in charge of the small staff in Amsterdam. Late twenties, a pale, narrow face, and slightly uncertain hands. His hair was thinning, and he kept it combed back to cover his incipient baldness. The other was in his late forties, a squat and muscled henchman. Both men had been busy these last few weeks arranging all sorts of things for Keretsky. Tarkovski was the one who had straightened the path for Fabna. The boy showed promise and talent, as Keretsky had noticed previously. Otherwise, he wouldn't have chosen him to lead the Amsterdam operation.

He had done so against the advice of some of his older lieutenants and against the wishes of his correspondents in Rotterdam. Keretsky frowned at the use of that word. They called themselves *correspondents*, as if they worked for a newspaper. Which wasn't the case. And why was it that Tarkovski posed a problem for them? Like them, he'd grown up in Saint Petersburg—in the wrong neighborhood maybe. Nonetheless, Keretsky had silenced them.

"This is Parnow," Tarkovski said, introducing the henchman. Parnow had the cold eyes of an ex-military man who had seen too many corpses. He had probably been responsible for most of those corpses himself. Afghanistan and Chechnya after that, Keretsky assumed. Good. This sort of person would prove useful after dark. When things got out of control. When dead people had to be disposed of in a hurry, and discreetly.

"Make sure my things are delivered in my room at once, Andreï. Meanwhile, I'll take a shower. Parnow will make sure, again discreetly, that I am not bothered."

"Certainly, Mr. Keretsky."

He took a hot shower, and when he walked out of the bathroom, his luggage had been deposited on the bed. He unearthed a small silver vial from one of the pockets in his suitcase, unscrewed the lid, and shook some of the white powder it contained over a small mirror.

Forty-five minutes later, he stepped out of the Bentley and into the Fabna building. Andreï accompanied him, carrying his briefcase. Keretsky knew little about Amsterdam and wasn't interested in the city. Other people were assigned to drive him from one spot to another and to cater to his needs. Local geographies weren't his concern. He knew only Saint Petersburg, where he'd lived for most of his life. Where he'd killed a man for the first time. Where he'd made his first million. Dollars, not rubles. Nobody measured wealth in rubles. Not even today. In euros, yes, and in dollars. Cities didn't mean much to him. Only people mattered. Cities were handy because many people lived in them and they could be easily reached. They were like concentration camps for consumers.

Mr. Prins, the Dutch banker, approached him, hand extended. In his fifties, neat silver hair, slender in his dark blue suit, a gray tie, and white shirt. One banker started to look exactly like any other banker after a while. Keretsky spoke English with the man. "How was your flight?" Prins inquired. "No trouble at customs, I assume? We've prepared a small lunch, Mr. Keretsky, in one of our meeting rooms."

Keretsky smiled. The velvet approach. In the way he smiled, in his handshake. You created goodwill only because you expected goodwill back tenfold. That much he had learned since he'd begun to work on his social skills. Previously, a strong will and unlimited support from the authorities—on his payroll of course—sufficed. It sufficed to have a couple of bodyguards around who could explain to the other parties, in clear terms, the new rules of the game. Keretsky's rules. After that, business was conducted properly. That's how it went down in Russia. Not anymore. The rules had shifted somewhat, and why not? He'd become respectable. His empire had become respectable.

Here in the West, another approach had been needed from the start. These businesspeople and bankers were intelligent and driven, and keen on proper form. They were, however, no match for the typical Russian oligarch, no match for any of the new breed of Russian entrepreneurs. People like himself, who had learned the trade in the latter days of the Soviet empire. When chaos allowed for anything, as long as you had enough funds and no mercy. Westerners still thought in terms of diplomacy. Keretsky and the new breed had only war in mind.

An hour later his affairs were concluded, contracts signed. He, Adam Keretsky, was now one of the major stakeholders of Fabna Bank, even if he had only 4.5 percent of its stock in his hands. A controlling minority, and he would do the controlling. He could have a seat in the board of directors if he wanted. He wasn't interested. He could influence the board's decisions even without being a member. He did control the price of Russian crude for one thing. That gave him enough leverage.

Mr. Prins smoothly wished him a further pleasant stay in Amsterdam. He looked content, having secured a very much needed capital injection for his bank.

"The next meeting, Andreï?" Keretsky said, after they had been left alone.

"Monet," Andreï said.

"Isn't he that entrepreneur who's the spokesperson for a group of businesspeople?"

"A social club, more or less, Mr. Keretsky. Among them, they control a number of important industrial projects in the Netherlands, but they hardly form a unified group. They work on very diverse projects in different industrial sectors. Highway construction, oil, international shipping, textile import, insurance. Hardworking, all of them. Conspirators."

Keretsky smiled in a fatherly way. One of his Western smiles. "An industrious people, these Dutch, Andreï. Don't you forget that. Historically speaking, they influenced the development of Western society and of Russia too. You of all people should know that, coming from Saint Petersburg. The Dutch stood at the cradle of the Russian shipping industry. Therefore, we should treat them with respect. Respect, Andreï! With *égards*." He used the French word.

"Certainly, Mr. Keretsky."

"You have no idea what I'm talking about, you're too young to know much about history, Andreï Vladimirovitsj," he said, using his patronymic. "One day you'll remember this conversation. Now, back to the present. Where do we meet this infamous Mr. Monet? A bit odd, this French name of his, isn't it? A painter, if I'm not mistaken?"

"Possibly, sir. I am not aware of his hobbies. I can try to find that out, if you wish. We have rented a meeting room at the Renaissance. No lunch, this time."

"Two lunches on the same day, that would be too much, even for a Russian. Did you provide the vodka, Andreï? We could use a glass of vodka. What have we to offer?"

"Stolichnaya and Streletskaya, Mr. Keretsky."

"Streletskaya is for women, not strong enough. No Yat?"

"No, sir. Not sold around here."

"Another opportunity, Andreï. You need to think as I do. Looking for opportunities. In three months, these Dutch will all be drinking Yat and even Dovgan vodka."

The Bentley drove them back to the Renaissance Hotel but not without some delay. "Difficult city, Amsterdam," Tarkovski apologized. "Not suited for cars. Too many bikes, too many tourists. No parking space, certainly not for a Bentley. The streets are generally too narrow and there are too many of those useless canals."

Keretsky didn't reply. He consulted his Blackberry. Stock prices danced across the screen. As long as they danced to his music, he was happy. And today he was. Not only because of the stock prices.

The car arrived at the hotel. Tarkovski went in first. They took the elevator to the sixth floor, where the meeting room was prepared. The man on the couch had short blond hair. He rose and shook Keretsky's hand. In English, he said: "Mr. Keretsky, how do you do?" A slender brown-haired woman in her mid-thirties stood by the window. She held a leather folder and a writing pad. Two other men, both younger than Monet, were introduced to the Russian, who promptly forgot their names.

"Linda will keep notes, if you wish," Monet said.

"That will not be needed, Mr. Monet," Keretsky replied. "There is nothing wrong with my memory yet." He snapped his fingers. Tarkovski brought vodka and coffee. "Dutch coffee is superior to Russian, Mr. Monet," Keretsky said. "The inverse is true of tea. Maybe Holland should import Russian tea? How many tons would you care for? And vodka? Have you ever considered taking some vodka off our hands? Are we in business?"

The woman left the men and disappeared behind a discreetly closed door.

"We would have no problem finding distributors for your tea and vodka, Mr. Keretsky," Monet said. "No problem at all. But we prefer to hear about oil. Oil is more important to us than tea."

Keretsky grinned. "Certainly. Oil. The whole world runs on oil. What will we do when the oil runs out? Currently, this is the most important problem mankind is facing, and nobody has an answer."

"Cars will use hydrogen in the future. Or Russian natural gas."

"Natural gas runs out as fast as oil does. Hydrogen? The idea is far from new. Is that what the West hopes for? That their energy needs will be solved by hydrogen? An idea that has been under consideration for twenty years or more? And in which no one has made any serious investments?"

Monet was visibly ill at ease. He drank from his coffee and took a sip from the vodka, not a good idea in his case. At least not if he wanted to stay alert. "Not only the West, Mr. Keretsky. Not only the West. The whole world is faced with similar problems. Everyone is searching for solutions."

"Would you want a few containers of tea?"

"Yes, but only when we can cooperate in other matters. I can't make money on tea alone."

Keretsky nodded and drank his coffee. Then he said, "I heard, Mr. Monet, that your business deals have been less than satisfactory recently. Are you having trouble with politics again?"

"We have learned to live with politicians."

"Really?" Keretsky said. "I think I heard otherwise. I seem to remember hearing that tax inspectors visited you, Mr. Monet. That must have been very painful. And one of your partners encountered a problem with—"

"We live in a democracy, Mr. Keretsky. Sometimes to our disadvantage. Newspapers tend to write unfavorably about us, whenever they can. And the government is more of a hindrance as far as free trade is concerned. They want to flex their muscles, these politicians, certainly when elections come along. You're familiar with the problem."

"I see what you mean. You need a politician like Putin. He has no beef with entrepreneurs such as yourself. And they have no problems with him. All good friends under the same banner. And all are successful in what they do. Even the people are content, except for those foolish and misguided former communists."

Monet smiled. "Putin."

"You consider him a dictator? He is far from a dictator, Mr. Monet. More than any other politician, he understands clearly the needs of the Russian people. The whole of the Russian population, Mr. Monet. Holland is certainly in need of such a leader."

"We are not Russians, Mr. Keretsky. Whatever may be possible in your country can't happen here."

"Well," Keretsky said, "it will soon come to pass. Maybe long before we all run out of oil."

One of the other Dutchmen said, "But Russia's reserves are large enough, surely? For another thirty or forty years or more?"

Keretsky shook his head. "You forget China."

"Chinese oil production isn't going smoothly," said the Dutchman. "They need modern installations, and only the West seems able to provide them. The Chinese—"

"I wasn't talking about their production, sir, but about their consumption. Every Chinese wants his own car. Within ten years, half of their population will own a car. Oil will be more expensive than gold. There will never be enough oil for all, and at some point, the wells will run dry. Where do you get your energy then? This seems beyond the grasp of politicians. Russia has many other things to offer besides oil."

Monet nodded. "Nuclear energy."

"Yes, nuclear energy. Cheap nuclear power stations that can produce a lot of electricity cheaply, directly to your doorstep."

"Local politics wants to get rid of nuclear energy. It is not popular with the population at large."

"A Dutch nuclear project has never been sold well to the public. They'll eventually beg for nuclear energy when their heaters, the ones that run on oil or whatever, stop working and the electricity bill rises as never before. They'll beg for nuclear energy. But by then it will be too late."

Monet shook his head. "If Russia wants to become part of Europe, it will have to limit its own nuclear program."

"Maybe Europe will want to be part of Russia soon," Keretsky said. He emptied his vodka. "Doesn't that seem like a more realistic future?"

Monet remained silent.

"I see you're worried. Not just about energy?"

Monet said, "We have another matter to discuss, Mr. Keretsky. Something embarrassing, for both of us."

"Embarrassing? Really?"

"Yes, I'm afraid so. You have in the past donated considerable sums to one of our political parties."

"Parties? There are many parties in the Netherlands . . . ah, I seem to remember Ms. Van Tillo. Of course. A very nice lady, who thinks along the same lines as we do. How is she? Am I supposed to meet her this time? Andreï?"

"No, Mr. Keretsky," Monet intervened. "You are not supposed to meet her this time. We have a problem. An unfortunate indiscretion.

The list with your name on it, the list with contributors for Ms. Van Tillo's party, has gone missing. Probably stolen. Last night."

Keretsky leaned back. "I'm surprised, Mr. Monet."

"Ms. Van Tillo is very much shocked on account of this unfortunate incident."

"Oh, I'm sure she is," Keretsky said. "I'm certain that Ms. Van Tillo is very much shocked on account of this very unfortunate incident. I personally, Mr. Monet, am shocked as well, by the carelessness Ms. Van Tillo and her staff exhibit when dealing with sensitive information. As if nobody would care to know how much I myself, and you, contribute to her party. In Russia, Mr. Monet, I'm able to contribute considerable funds to the reelection of Vladimir, and the Russians applaud my largesse. But here, in Holland, I'm a foreign intruder, a threat to every Dutch citizen. And that's why, Mr. Monet, I can't allow such an indiscretion to exist. And I'm sure you won't allow it either. Even less than I, because you live and work here."

He looked at the three Dutchmen. "And what, gentlemen, are you going to do about it?"

"We must figure out who the thief is," Monet said.

"Really? And you will ask him nicely to return the list?"

"Well . . ."

"I understand perfectly, Mr. Monet. I think I clearly understand the situation." Keretsky rose. "Andreï, would you be so kind to ask Parnow in? Then, and in my absence, discuss with Mr. Monet what measures have to be taken to retrieve the said list. Russian measures, if you please, Andreï. The real deal. And in my absence."

Andreï nodded and stepped outside.

6

PRINSEN BICYCLED TO THE Renaissance Hotel, passing his own apartment. It was half past ten, and the city was now fully awake, including the tourist population. They managed to get in the way of the cyclists constantly, not aware of the existence of bike paths, not aware of the clearly marked separation between the different users of the public space. They might have heard about the curious freedoms allowed in this city—drugs, prostitution, the gay scene—and assumed this laxness on behalf of the authorities extended to traffic as well. But taxi drivers, tram conductors, and local cyclists begged to differ.

He left his bike across the street from the entrance to the hotel, chaining it to a fence. Then he walked inside. He walked past reception. Nobody paid any attention. He took the elevator to the fifth floor. Took his smart phone from his pocket and pushed two buttons. Room 404, he noticed. He walked down the corridor and found the room. He knocked.

Movement inside. Someone glanced through the peephole and opened the door. "I would like a cup of coffee," Breukeling announced. He was a sturdy man, in his forties, with the agile hands of an experienced technician and the ready wit of a true Amsterdammer. As far as Prinsen knew, he always wore the same brown suit.

Prinsen held up a brown paper bag. "And donuts," he said. "Can't say I'm neglecting you. I don't want that reputation."

"Excellent," Breukeling said. "I've been here since six this morning. Would have been better off if I'd slept here last night. Although the wife would have suspicions if I did."

"She still is suspicious?"

Breukeling shrugged. "Even I can't say she's wrong." Something had been going on between Breukeling and his wife. Prinsen never knew what exactly. As the youngest of the team members, he wasn't allowed into their inner and private circle, the one where marital problems were discussed. But nevertheless, he'd heard things. Breukeling had been all over a junior female employee of the Bureau. Had been away from home too much. And had been seen around seedy hotels in the wrong part of the city.

The room looked like any other room in a four-star hotel, anywhere in the world. Two carefully made-up beds. A wardrobe, a frame for suitcases, a desk, two chairs. Carpet on the floor. Two reproductions of paintings by Bruegel. Indirect lighting. The door to the bathroom ajar. The room looking out over the inner court of the hotel, curtains open.

The only thing that set it apart from other hotel rooms was the electronic equipment on a large folding table by the window: a radio receiver that captured the signal from the mics and a laptop for storing the recording. The setup wasn't very impressive. But Prinsen had seen pictures of the sort of material the AIVD had used in previous decades, unwieldy receivers and reel-to-reel audio recorders and mixing tables. The equipment in this room would fit into two briefcases, and it could easily be carried by one person. Soon, they wouldn't even have to rent a hotel room in situations like this.

Even now, the room was superfluous, he assumed. You stowed the stuff in a car and parked it in front of the hotel, after having set up the microphones. So why was Breukeling here?

He knew why. The prosecutor's office paid for this affair. The people who approved of the surveillance and paid the bills had probably never seen this setup. They thought in terms of hotel rooms. So the Bureau rented a hotel room.

It didn't matter to Breukeling. He preferred working out of a four-star hotel room, not a car. He could have a rest on the bed. Use the toilet, drink coffee brought by room service or Prinsen, and eat his donuts. A car was small and narrow and uncomfortable. As far as he was concerned, the prosecutor was welcome to foot the bill anytime.

"What about the chief?" he asked. "Is she at the office already?"

"She's meeting the new guy," Prinsen said. "Lunch at the Krasnapolsky later."

Breukeling shook his head gently. "Have we ever been invited to the Krasnapolsky? By Alexandra? Ms. Dewaal? Never, as far as I know. We're allowed to wait in stuffy hotel rooms for a Russian, who may or may not turn up. We eat donuts and drink mediocre hotel coffee. We watch the scenery from the window and wait for a sound from the meeting room downstairs. That's what we do, kiddo. No Krasnapolsky."

Prinsen wanted to reply but finally considered silence as the better option.

Breukeling glanced up. "I understand you don't want to comment, Prinsen. New guy on the block and all that. Still finding your way. Take it from me, this Bureau has its own traditions, most of them dating from before Dewaal. But she brings in new ideas. So we adapt. But some of the older officers—which means almost anybody—have a problem with that, the whole new thing. We have a problem with managers."

"I have no opinion on the subject," Prinsen said.

"No," Breukeling said. "Because you're family. I'll just say it out loud, kid. Everybody knows about it. It wasn't even a secret. I don't know if you're going to spill the beans to . . . your aunt, isn't she? You're her nephew?"

"She's my mom's younger sister. But that has had no bearing on the . . ." He couldn't avoid blushing. He was annoyed by the fact that he had to explain his family relations time and time again.

"Don't apologize. We know about your background. You did very well at the police academy. You'll go far in the force, even if it weren't for family relations. Question is: did you have to get drafted into *this* unit? Really? The AIVD is a big operation, with a lot of interesting jobs. Did she specifically ask for you?"

The small speaker on the radio receiver coughed. The laptop started up promptly. "Aha, something's happening," Breukeling said. He had defects and qualities. One of his qualities was being able to concentrate at once on the task at hand. Someone had entered the meeting room where the microphones had been hidden. Prinsen could avoid explaining his personal situation, for the time being.

Two voices were talking in Dutch. They debated the items that would be discussed during the meeting. How many people were expected. When coffee would be served. They seemed to be looking at documents but got no wiser.

"Nothing that concerns us," Breukeling said. He switched off the speaker but followed the conversation through his headphones. "This is the annoying side of these stakeouts. Marking time. Observations, for days on end. I've been through it all. You're on a stakeout for days and nothing happens. You get tired, concentration is slipping. You want something to keep you occupied. And when something really important happens, your attention is elsewhere. You're fucked. Had it happen to me. You miss what you weren't supposed to miss."

"Shit happens," Prinsen said.

"But the chief won't understand. She's never done stakeouts. Doesn't understand why you can't keep your attention focused." He glanced at Prinsen. "You're bound to go far, kid. I can see that. I hope you remember that people are merely people and sometimes fail in doing their job, even if it's not their fault."

He took a few bites of his donut and drank coffee. Prinsen sat down on the couch. He looked for something to read but found nothing. Breukeling read no books. He read newspapers but not the kind Prinsen read.

"Mmm," the older officer said. "These are really *good* donuts. Where did you get them?"

"There's a little bakery down Haringpakkerssteeg," Prinsen said. "You like them?"

"Coffee's good too," Breukeling said. He hardly listened to the sound from the microphones anymore. "Who wants this recording?"

"The prosecutor insisted on it."

"And AIVD gets to do the dirty work. Does this have anything to do with an ongoing investigation? I'm just here for the fieldwork, kid, that's all. They never tell me anything. Not in cases like these. They tell me: keep watch on the material, but I don't see why there should be two of us here. Maybe they want you to get an idea of how exciting this is."

"I guess so."

"It's simple, really. A child can do it. The technicians install the whole thing, including the computer, and the detective watches because some living being has to be there. There has to be a detective present, for legal reasons, I guess. You just push a key and the computer does the rest. I'm sure your generation has learned to push the right key."

Suddenly, Breukeling sat up and listened. "There they are," he said. He knew Prinsen was excluded from the conversation in the meeting room. For the best, he thought. The kid had better stay out of this.

He heard Russian voices first. Then Dutch. Speaking to each other, then switching to English with a strong Russian accent. If they wouldn't mind waiting for just a moment? Mr. Keretsky would be along soon. The meeting with the bank had gone on longer than expected. Wouldn't be long now. A cup of coffee?

The Dutch voices didn't sound amused. Far from it. But they agreed to be patient. For ten minutes, nothing happened. Then new voices entered the room. Breukeling listened intently. A woman was dispatched. Then the conversation took a turn. Real business was conducted. Stuff that could get people in trouble. After the conversation had ended and everybody seemed to have left the room, Breukeling switched off the machine. "Seems we got the whole thing on tape," he said. "Some heavy stuff. Can be used to prove conspiracy and maybe even murder."

Prinsen felt frustrated because he'd heard nothing. "Where do we deliver the recording?"

"I'll have to make a call," Breukeling said. He took his cell phone and punched a number. "Sir," he said, "Breukeling. We're clear with the Renaissance recording. Am I supposed to bring the recording to our offices?"

He listened. Then he said, "Are you sure? Was that the idea?"

He listened again. He didn't seem to like the instructions. "Sure," he finally said. "We'll arrange that." He didn't sound pleased.

He ended the call. "They want the recording on a memory stick, and I have to deliver it to the prosecutor's office. The original recording must be wiped from the hard drive."

"What purpose would that serve?" Prinsen asked. "The prosecutor? Can he insist that a recording be wiped? That doesn't sound right to me."

"I'm just the messenger boy. And you're not even supposed to have a say. You're in training." He sat working on the laptop. "Sorry you've been kept out of this," he said. "But that's the way things drift." He switched off the laptop and pocketed the stick. "I just do whatever is asked of me."

"Do you send Dewaal a written report?"

"I'm not supposed to. Orders of the prosecutor, the man on the phone just said."

Prinsen didn't comment. The whole thing felt wrong. He knew little of how the Bureau operated yet, but even so. A prosecutor intervening in a surveillance operation was unusual. However, police officers had little choice but to comply. "Aren't we supposed to tell Dewaal about this?" he asked. Because to him it seemed they couldn't do anything their chief didn't at least know about.

Breukeling nodded and phoned again. He didn't reach his party, though.

"Looks like we're going to do whatever the prosecutor orders us," he said to Prinsen. "Let's get going, then."

The stowed the equipment in two bags. A few minutes later, they walked out of the hotel. "Fancy a drink?" Breukeling inquired. "I could use one."

Prinsen looked at his watch. "We're still on duty," he said.

"Ah, kid, who cares? An officer of AIVD is always on duty. Can he never have a drink?"

7

"Lunch?" Alexandra Dewaal proposed.

"Why not?" Eekhaut said.

She eyed his fruit juice. "No aperitif? A decent drink before we eat?"

"Well . . ."

She flagged down a server. "I'll have a martini," she said. "And you?"

"Me too."

"You are . . ." She hesitated. "You arrived this morning?"

"Yes."

"And they found you a nice apartment to live in, I assume?"

"It's all right," he said. Not committing himself yet. He eyed her slender hands, the sleeves of her wine-colored jacket, her naturally blond hair, the efficient but discreet makeup. Thirty, maybe thirty-five, he assumed. "It's in the center of Amsterdam, as I asked."

"I don't care much for the center of Amsterdam," she said. "Too crowded, every hour of the day. Never a moment of peace and quiet and no gardens. I live in Zaandam, where there's a lot of green and trams don't drive by your door at all hours of the day and night." She consulted the menu. He considered himself warned. Zaandam was far superior to Amsterdam. There would be no discussion over this matter. "What shall we have?"

The martinis were served in tall glasses with lots of ice and lots of martini. *This is going to be my undoing*, he thought. Too much booze. He avoided alcohol during the day if at all possible. But now he couldn't.

"The *canard à l'orange* is excellent here," she said. She spoke French expertly, he noticed. Unlike most Dutch. "We don't share the culinary culture of the Flemish," she said, "but we're catching up fast." It was a common enough joke, but she said it as if it was a professional secret.

"I'll follow your lead," he said and closed the menu. Something was bothering him. Not the fact that his new boss was a woman—but that she acted and dressed as if she were meeting a man she wanted to seduce. And yet not, for that wasn't really the outfit of a woman set on seduction. Along with the jacket, she wore a neat and uncompromising skirt and high-heeled shoes.

She didn't fit his expectations of what his new boss ought to be. Female or not. For one thing, he could hardly imagine her interrogating a suspect in that ensemble or carrying a gun under that jacket. And she obviously wasn't.

He could picture her in a business office of some sort. A legal firm. A bank.

Not with the police.

At least not the police he knew. But he knew nothing about *her* sort of police, the AIVD, the security services. The police officers he knew didn't go to lunch in four-star restaurants. At least not with him. Except on one occasion, but that had happened a long time ago. And there never was a reprise.

"Two *canard à l'orange*," Alexandra ordered.

In his mind, she already was *Alexandra*. If she had lunch with him, dressed like that, she ought to be *Alexandra*. In her official capacity, however, she still was Ms. Dewaal.

And he had to be careful with his private fantasies.

"And a bottle of Vieux Macon," she added. As if that was what she did all the time—wining and dining with a certain largesse and considerable style. As if she frequented such establishments every day. And perhaps she did. What did he know about her anyway?

And then he wondered: was she doing this for the sole purpose of impressing him? Was this a bit of show? Why have you brought me here, Alexandra, on my first day with your team? Even before I'm *on* your team? Do you want to prove to the Belgian that this Dutch lady is also capable of living the Burgundian lifestyle for which the Flemish are so famous in Holland? Do you mean to prove me that you, the Dutch, have moved beyond the sandwich and buttermilk lunches for which you were so notorious?

Do you want to prove *anything* to me?

"Are you an officer in the federal police?" she asked.

Back to the real world. "I am," he said. "Have been for twenty-two years. Before that, I was with the judicial police and local police earlier on. Different jobs, different functions."

"Nobody should remain in the same place for too long," she said. "I myself prefer a different assignment every four or five years. Keeps you fresh. Why have you come to Amsterdam?"

"Because I was asked to assist in your investigations. And because my boss wanted to get rid of me and my bad temper."

She wasn't surprised. Neither by the facts nor by his frankness. She knew who he was and why he was here. Of course, she knew. She would have read it in the report that very morning.

"Mmm," she said. "I'd understood that much. 'Opinionated' was one of the terms used to describe you, as I seem to recall."

"Oh, that's the least they can reproach me for," he said.

She sipped from the martini. "And 'insubordination.'"

"Depends on the boss. Some bosses can be dealt with only with a mean dose of insubordination."

"You have any experience working for a female chief?"

"Yes, my last commanding officer was a woman. And she suffered no permanent damage from having me on her team, I suspect."

"I seem to have read that she was the one who used the term 'insufferable' most frequently."

"I'm sure she did."

"And 'insubordination.' That came from her as well."

"I'm sure it did."

The waiter arrived with the wine and uncorked it. He offered it to Eekhaut, who reluctantly tasted it. It seemed fine. Lunch was served. Duck, a bit of salad, and a couple of orange parts. The sauce was thick but clear.

"Am I now officially working for you?" he asked. "As of today, I mean?"

She smiled. "Not yet. Consider today a day of transition. Gives you the opportunity to move your things into your apartment. Take the day off, no problem. I expect you in the office by nine tomorrow. Then we'll discuss the details of your assignment. You're not married?"

"Widower. My wife died ten years ago."

She said nothing to that. Lunch was excellent. If his salary permitted, he would lunch here on occasion, but he was sure it wouldn't, as he'd seen the prices on the menu.

"Experience with street crime?"

"In Brussels? Certainly. Speaks for itself. And with intercultural problems, as they're referred to today."

"But you didn't live in Brussels."

"In Leuven. Provincial university town, twenty-five kilometers from Brussels."

"You know we target organizations that threaten our democratic system," she said. She held her glass, considering the wine. She had hardly eaten anything and didn't seem to be interested in the food.

"That's what you call it over here?"

"What?"

"A threat to democracy. We would call it something different."

"What then?"

"Illegal radical organizations that maintain ties with terrorist and other dangerous entities."

"Yes, that would sum it up too. We also investigate extremist political parties, even if they've been democratically elected."

"That too. And we watch sects. Everything from extreme nationalists to Scientology."

"Oh," she said. "Scientology. Them too."

"And I'm here to help you investigate the background of Adam Keretsky. And to strengthen the ties between Belgian and Dutch police forces, including the security services."

"No," she said slowly, "you're here because Brussels considers you a hard-ass, and they wanted to get rid of you."

"That would about sum it up, yes." He'd worked his way through the duck. "Excellent food they have here."

"I notice you fit in quite easily. That's good. Amsterdam is going to grow on you, you'll see. It's not really a big city. Actually, it's a provincial town that made too much money somewhere in the past. Pity, though, about the tourists who come here for the wrong reasons." She drank her wine and refilled both glasses. "But don't assume, Chief Inspector, that this is paradise. This lunch is the exception. This is a treat. Something I do to impress you. Starting tomorrow, it will be sandwiches and buttermilk all the way."

"I'd expected as much," he said.

"What do you know about Russia?"

Not all that much, he had to admit. A few things he'd read in the newspapers or seen on television. A few books he'd read about the country and the people. Very little, actually.

Dewaal nodded. "They managed to send me a criminal investigator," she said, "and that's what I have to work with."

"What did you expect?"

She leaned back. "As to what we're expecting of you, I want to be as broad as possible. Keretsky, that's a low-level investigation. We *know* a lot about him. What we don't know are his intentions. And the problem is precisely those intentions."

"He invests in Western companies. Which isn't against any law."

"No, it isn't. However, the question is: where does the money come from and what will he do once he's bought himself into those companies? At Fabna, they'll offer him a seat on the board of directors. But perhaps you need to be acquainted with recent Russian economic history? These Russian financiers have no problem buying into Western companies, but the inverse never happens. They even have the unhealthy habit of prosecuting their foreign partners if things don't go their way. People are being extorted, threatened, and thrown into Russian prisons whenever they find themselves in disagreement with their Russian overlords. And boards of directors over here in the West are being thinned out and replaced by Russian henchmen. All too often, the name Keretsky comes up in this context. The Russians have large amounts of cash, oil, and gas, so they're on the economic warpath.

They don't need the Cold War anymore, Eekhaut. They don't need nuclear missiles and submarines. And they're being led by an enlightened despot who wants his country to become the world's leader. Meanwhile, it's exporting the things it's good at producing: oil and organized crime."

"And your role here?" Eekhaut inquired.

She glanced past him for a moment. "Our investigations into Russian influence have stagnated. AIVD wanted to map Russian influence in Dutch industrial circles and financial markets. But that proved to be nearly impossible. These Russians have been deceiving their own government and security services for the better part of a century. The new elite know better than anyone else how to deal with officials. And then, after the fall of the Soviet Union, they grabbed the choicest pieces of industry, the banking world, anything worthwhile. All paid for with criminal funds. Then they dumped anything that weren't making a profit or showing some sort of improvement, putting hundreds of thousands of workers and civil servants out of work. After that, they turned to the West for technological innovation and additional capital and any kind of know-how.

"New economic players emerged from the rubble of the Soviet Union, nominally led by the former *nomenklatura* who were the only properly trained managers during the Soviet era. But *they* were linked with organized crime—otherwise, they'd have been put out of work too. Russia is the new world player not because of its military force but for its economic power. You no longer need an army to invade other countries. Google and Amazon and Microsoft don't have an army either, and look at their power. That's the lesson the oligarchs learned from the West. They look abroad, count their money, and go shopping.

"And they've come to the Netherlands too. Interesting place to do some serious shopping, the Netherlands. Center of international trade. Rotterdam, one of the continent's main ports. The world's, even. The Russians want a piece of that cake. So they go shopping. And we Dutch offer them all the freedom to shop. It's no trouble at all to start your own business in Holland. You start up your company, and that starts up another company, and so on. After a while, everything is connected to everything else, but nobody can figure out where the money comes from. The Russians are excellent accountants. Or they hire excellent accountants."

"I guess this has been going on for a while now?"

"It has. But their attention is now shifting toward financial institutions. Ports are nice things to own when you need to move a lot of physical stuff around. But the really crucial game is played where the really crucial commodity is to be found. Money."

"Easy to move," Eekhaut said. "But difficult to intercept. And takes up no space at all."

"Exactly. So now, Keretsky is dropping by in person. The interesting thing is that these Russians, even those at the top of the pecking order, occasionally have to show their faces. The Americans send an army of lawyers and managers. The Russians come in person. That's their criminal ethics for you: when things need to be done right, you do them yourself. So you don't get screwed. And today, Adam Keretsky is arriving here in Amsterdam, where he's scheduled to meet with the board of Fabna Bank."

"He'll be given the premier welcome, I assume. Red carpet and everything?"

"And all that goes with it. He'll become one of their major shareholders."

"Don't they have a problem with his background?"

"What background? As far as anybody who does business with him is concerned, he is a bona fide Russian entrepreneur who has lots of cash and even more influence. They kowtow to him happily."

"And I'm here to . . .?"

Dewaal grinned. "Because your countrymen have as much interest in Fabna as the Dutch. Because some Belgians still consider the bank theirs. Although it isn't, not after the merger. You're here as the symbolic representative of Belgian *haute finance*. Aren't you glad?"

"What exactly do you expect from me?"

"We keep an eye on Keretsky. We look at the people he does business with. We follow him around. As long as he's legit, we do nothing. In any case, we do nothing, but if he goes off the reservation, we report it to the minister. Every time he pees in the wind, we report it to the minister. But we don't clean up his piss—no, that we don't do."

8

FOR THE FIRST TIME since moving to Amsterdam, Prinsen was seriously considering using the tram instead of his bike. It wasn't a matter of distances—it was that during the day you could barely bicycle through the city center anymore. The center was more crowded than ever. He didn't like being around that many people.

The tram wouldn't solve that, but at least the trips would take less time. Less time around so many people. And especially those rude young people who congregated from all over Europe. All the liberties Amsterdam offered attracted them like flies: the freely available soft drugs, alcohol, cheap hotels, and the adventure of everything that was illegal at home. They were drawn by the myth of the city, a free port for vices.

Most of the detectives were out the office. They usually worked in the field, observing suspects, doing research elsewhere. Not everyone needed a permanent work space all the time, so people often switched desks, except the ones who occupied the desks by the windows.

He mailed a concise report about his activities to Dewaal, including the fact that the recording had been sent solely to the prosecutor. He knew she had to be kept in the loop, even more so since he had doubts about the procedure. The prosecutor could hardly object to his initiative: he worked for the Bureau, and as such, he was required to report to Dewaal.

He wondered if Breukeling would file a similar report. To Dewaal. There had been some strife between her and the more senior members of the Bureau, who weren't all too keen on the new procedures she'd introduced. Like direct reporting on everything they did. It curtailed their autonomy, they argued.

"Interesting experience?" Van Gils inquired. He was leaning against the window, his broad back offered to the outside world. To Prinsen, he was a profile backlit by the light from outdoors. A cutout in the form of a human being.

"Routine," he said. He wasn't going to tell Van Gils about the prosecutor's interference. Breukeling could mention it if he wanted to.

Later, after work, he rode his bike back to Spuistraat and a pub where customers drank outdoors. Summer was past, but it was still warm enough. He managed to squeeze inside and order a beer. Five thirty in the afternoon, he noticed. He went back outside with his beer. High clouds were starting to form but still weren't thick enough to obscure the sun. No one noticed him, a discreet and private young man with a beer. He wouldn't return to his apartment right away.

9

"If any of this had happened in my own company, all of you would be out of a job right now, and you'd never find work anywhere else for the rest of your life!"

To say that Dirk Benedict Monet, owner and CEO of a midsize producer of industrial steel wire and other companies, was angry would be, well, an understatement. He spoke these words to Van Tillo and Vanheul in the small meeting room of his company's headquarters, which was barely big enough to contain these three large egos. The steel wire had not been manufactured in the Netherlands for the last fifteen years, but in three more exotic countries where fiscal control meant as little as the value of employees' wages. Monet was a tall and imposing man, with an equally imposing voice.

Van Tillo stood next to the exquisite antique bookcase that was Monet's pride and joy. He kept the old leather-bound company journals there, some of them dating from the time of his father and grandfather. A company he—if his critics were to be believed—still ran with the same paternalistic drive as his forebears. The press seldom wrote about his management style simply because he managed to hide it from the outside world. In certain circles, though, it was known that in his world view, unions were a communist-inspired invention of the devil. Solidarity and social action were horrible concepts, not fit to coexist with capitalism. He was a proponent of Thatcher: each individual chose his own way toward success, or not, and should be rewarded accordingly.

He encouraged competition among his employees, which had the effect of making them all the more vulnerable.

"What you're saying, really, is that one of your own people, some latent hippie type, whom you know almost nothing about, has managed to infiltrate your pathetic little chickenshit operation, has been stalking around for a year, and finally managed to steal one of your most sensitive documents? Took it home, just like that? As if security just doesn't exist, or only as a theoretical concept, but one alien to your organization."

"He broke in last night," Vanheul admitted. It sounded like the lame excuse it was.

"Oh!" Monet replied, raising his volume even higher. "He *broke in.* He got all dramatic about it and had to come back at night and make off with something he could just as well have stolen during the daytime. He *broke in*!"

"We regret this as much as you do—" Vanheul attempted.

"Oh no!" Monet shouted. "You'll come to regret this *much more* than I do—because you'll get me all over you, on top of losing that damn list. May I remind you, Mr. Vanheul, that that list of yours, the one that got stolen, contains all the names of . . . how many?"

"About three hundred," Vanheul said.

"Of about three hundred—*three hundred!*—company chairmen, managers, board members, and other people of note from nearly as many companies. And they may not be the real big names in the Netherlands, not the absolute top, but nevertheless they're important people who really matter to us, who've been willing to spend considerable sums on your organization, Mr. Vanheul. Money, really big sums of money. For which I personally have been the main intermediary."

"Mr. Monet," Van Tillo intejected.

Monet was breathing heavily and stared at her.

She'd known exactly when he'd run out of breath and had chosen that moment to speak.

"We are very much concerned with this affair. Of course we are. It's a terrible thing that could have been avoided, no discussion there. We've made mistakes. Which we admit. On the other hand, nothing is gained by shouting. There are solutions to be found."

"What will happen with that list?" Monet asked.

"We don't know," Van Tillo said. "Maybe the thief will take it to the press."

"Who is this thief? At least tell me you have some idea of his identity."

"We have his name and an address. Do you need more?"

"Ms. Van Tillo, I'm a businessman. What do you expect from me? That I'll solve your problems for you?"

"No," she said. "I don't expect that. But we're a political party. We can't solve this sort of problem on our own. But on the other hand, we do have his name and an address. That has to be sufficient to work toward a solution if professional help can be provided."

Monet said nothing. He didn't have to tell Van Tillo that he'd already made arrangements concerning the sort of professional help she didn't want to discuss. Some things he preferred to keep hidden from her.

"Perhaps you have a proposition?" Van Tillo said.

"I can't be bothered with these problems, Ms. Van Tillo."

"They no longer are just *our* problems, Mr. Monet," she said. "Not just those of the Party. This goes way beyond the Party. We're all in this together. We and you and the other contributors."

"*Contributors*," he said. "I always hated that word. It sounds so inno-cent. As if you give money and then that's it. No further involvement."

"Shall we look for a solution together? This is Amsterdam. There are strategies that are possible here . . ."

"Mmm," Monet said. "I may have something for you." Of course he had something for her. His plans were already drawn up. He had his troops ready. But he wanted Van Tillo and Vanheul to suffer first. Wanted them to panic, so he could freely abuse them. He enjoyed that. Dressing down a former minister and her secretary. Knowing he'd already arranged a solution. And while maintaining the upper hand. Everything under his control. That was important in critical moments.

He was, at that instant, quite taken with himself.

10

IT HAD RAINED BETWEEN seven and eight o'clock over a city that was preparing for an early night. Eekhaut had been eating in a snack bar close to his apartment, and the rain hadn't mattered much to him. People passed by with umbrellas, while bicyclists hurried past gleaming cars. The snack bar was Lebanese. He had ordered bread with a salad, chicken, hot sauce, hummus, a pâté of peanuts, and mushrooms. Nothing on the menu was expensive. He had drunk sweet, strong tea with his meal. No alcohol was served, even though none of these Lebanese were strict Muslims, if observant at all. Most of the other guests seemed to be from the Middle East: Lebanese, Turks, Syrians. And perhaps one Iraqi dissident.

He'd often encountered the same mix of people in Brussels. Cunning businesspeople, most of them. Small-time entrepreneurs, always with a keen eye on the bottom line. Hard workers, too. Kept their distance from anything illegal. On this level, crime was the preferred terrain of the Chinese and the Koreans. He didn't know how things worked in Amsterdam, though. He hadn't seen many Chinese.

He preferred not to think too much about Brussels. He'd left Brussels behind. He'd started working there ten years earlier out of necessity. It was after Esther had died. Her death had left him in a bad state. He'd neglected his job in Leuven, with the local crime squad. He'd neglected himself. He slid down an increasingly slippery slope. Although his colleagues in Leuven understood his grief, they had their jobs to do, as had he. But he was losing control. He understood what was happening to him, but it was as if he were looking at a stranger, to whom bad things had happened.

This state of affairs had gone on for half a year. By then he had lost the confidence of his mates. After a while, he'd been summoned to quit the local force and was transferred to the capital. The transfer was a relief to all concerned, him in particular. He'd worked hard for many years to earn his reputation, and then he'd thrown it out the window. Because of his grief. Without Esther, the world was an empty place with no future. He saw only empty days ahead. He saw an empty house.

He wanted to fill that emptiness.

But with what?

They'd never had children. Hadn't wanted any, had let the opportunities slide by, had never really taken the time to think about children. Esther was the one who couldn't imagine a life with kids. She had no maternal instinct.

And he had complied. Hadn't gone against her. And so an emptiness was created, which became even more pronounced after she'd died.

So the transfer to Brussels had been arranged. He wanted to fill that emptiness with new people and things and work. The capital seemed to provide the opportunity. It came down to working overtime most of the time, working unusual hours, taking on duties from other officers, taking the unpopular assignments, but in the process pissing off a number of people with his acrimonious attitude.

He quickly acquired a reputation. A reputation he didn't really want but couldn't get rid of.

He became a liability.

He wasn't often promoted—or not at all, because office politics were beyond him.

He sold the house in Leuven after his transfer but didn't want to live in Brussels, so he bought an apartment, still in Leuven, close to the railway station, and he commuted. The place was large enough for him, with less emptiness to fill.

His sparse holidays were spent at the seaside or deep in the Ardennes forests. In places with so few people he could endure life. He saw his family occasionally, but he seldom felt any need for their company. They couldn't tell him anything he didn't already know. That he didn't lead a normal life, or what passed for normal to them. He had no regrets. He didn't look back. He looked forward. The past was a story with details and premises that couldn't be changed. He didn't care for the sort of people who were constantly hashing over the past.

He folded his paper napkin and finished his tea. He looked at his watch. Ten past eight. Still early. He rose, nodded to the owner, and stepped outside. It had stopped raining. The rain had left puddles on the pavement. He'd worn a raincoat, out of caution, but he wasn't going to need it.

His first night in Amsterdam. What of it? He'd brought a compact city guide that he'd already studied on the train, searching for things to do in the evening. He walked along Utrechtsestraat, toward the center. He could go to Leidseplein, home to a variety of pubs and bars, but he wasn't really in the mood. He had no need for public entertainment. And too crowded, presumably. He wanted something much more intimate.

Two items in particular in the guide had intrigued him. He walked along Kalverstraat and passed the Dam at the Royal Palace. Then he strolled into Nieuwendijk. Around the corner from Gravenstraat was a pub, the Belgique. Belgian beers, said a sign by the door. Not that he was nostalgic for Belgian beers, but this seemed a starting place as good as any.

He entered. An old-fashioned pub, not large at all, welcoming visitors with the golden smell of beer. Busy, already, with people crowding the bar and sitting at the small round tables.

He took a position at the bar, attracted the bartender's attention, and ordered a Leffe Brown. Which came on draft, to his surprise, and not from a bottle. It was the sort of beer he drank in Brussels, after work. At the Mort Subite. The most typical of all Brussels pubs. The unofficial watering hole of part of the Brussels detectives. Where after a day of stakeouts, typing reports, filing, and clashes with superiors, a good pint—and, more specifically, an authentic Geuze—tasted like a product made in heaven.

Glass in hand, he looked around. The customers were mostly male, about his age. Two, three women. There was no smoking. Darkness had already descended on the city. It even penetrated the bar. The collection of beer bottles behind the counter was vastly impressive. He had heard seven hundred different beers were being brewed in Belgium alone, and most of them seemed represented here. He had no intention of trying them all.

He slowly sipped from the Leffe. Why did he come here? A Belgian pub in Amsterdam? Out of curiosity? The only thing he could do here was hang around and watch people. There wasn't enough light to read a book.

He left after he'd finished his beer. The air was crisp and fresh. Summer had already passed, after several months of nearly tropical heat. People welcomed the cool late summer weather. He preferred this season above others. Contours of people and buildings were sharp due to the rain. One could breathe so much more freely than during the summer. Even in a city this size.

He walked back south and passed Magna Plaza and the back of the Palace. To the right of the Nieuwezijds Voorburgwal, he knew there was a quietly hidden bar, Absinthe, which he'd read about in the guide.

He found the place and stepped inside. The bar was nearly empty. The owner had done up the place in mock Victorian, including heavy, dark furniture. It went well with the idea of the formerly prohibited green substance. Time folded in on itself here. Ghosts of former residents and artists seemed to live in the dozen or so bottles of green spirits, from a time when absinthe was the drink *par excellence* of poor artists and prostitutes, a vice along with other vices such as tincture of opium.

He ordered a glass of the stuff. It was poured as tradition demanded, over a cube of sugar. He took the glass to a table in a corner and sat down. Waiting for something to happen. In a place like this, things always seemed on the verge of happening. He kept an eye on the customers and took a sip.

The clientele was younger than that of the Belgique. Attired differently too. Urbane, maybe even sophisticated. As if the green spirit attracted people from a totally different walk of life.

He wondered what Alexandra—Chief Superintendent Dewaal to him when at the office—did in her spare time. What kind of person was she? A homemaker caring for a husband and three children? Or single and going to the opera every Thursday evening, inviting younger men to her bed afterward? Anything seemed possible. He knew nothing about her. On arriving here, he hadn't even known his boss was a woman. He had inspected her outfit and had judged her on that basis. Judged her wrongly, probably. She probably lived in some fancy suburb. He knew nothing about her. His conclusions would all prove to be wrong.

The clothes she had worn, however, had conveyed one simple message: she wasn't going to be analyzed by him, wasn't going to be judged. This had been her external side, and he wasn't going to get under her skin. She had worn the most perfect outfit for a meeting with a new colleague, giving nothing away but inviting speculation. And she had wanted to impress. Had succeeded. That's why they had lunch at Krasnapolsky: because she wanted to impress him.

More people entered the bar. People in their thirties, early forties. Loud, quite taken with themselves. One of the women lit a cigarette. Nobody objected. She was tall and slender, a natural brunette with wavy, shoulder-length hair. She glanced at him over her shoulder for just a moment. She didn't interrupt her conversation with the blond man at her side. They both drank absinthe.

Around eleven, he drank his second glass. It was the perfect drink for an evening when you wanted to forget all about the job. The brunette was still sitting at the bar. Her companions were on their way to total intoxication. Fourth or fifth glass. He had eyes for the woman only.

She didn't resemble Esther.

Let this be clear: she does not look like Esther.

And even if she did look like Esther, he wouldn't meddle with the ghosts from times past. He had better things to do. Make plans for the future, for one thing.

But in his mid-fifties, he had little future in front of him. And what was there was diminishing swiftly. Why not just concentrate solely on the present? Observing a woman at a bar drinking absinthe and ignoring him as if she knew he kept looking at her, even when he tried not to?

He did nothing more than look. His glass was empty. He could have it filled again, but then he would have had to approach the counter, where the woman was sitting. And her presence, her physical presence, would be more than he could endure. At least from close up.

So he waited.

He wasn't drunk after only two glasses of absinthe.

What he was waiting for, he didn't know. He couldn't explain. Not even to himself.

11

IT WAS AFTER MIDNIGHT when Breukeling drove into the street where he lived. His wife would chew him out for being so late, but he'd brought her a nice present—a manila envelope with a number of high-denomination banknotes inside. Enough for a trip to a very warm country and some clothes and things. And afterward, there would be more money yet, more than he'd seen in his life.

That would ease the pain of his being late.

He had no regrets. Not about what he'd done. Nobody would ever find out what he'd done. He would maintain that he had left the memory stick at the front desk in the justice department offices, with clear instructions for the stick to be delivered to the prosecutor. That had been the limit of his involvement. It would appear that they had lost the stick. It sounded plausible. Things always got lost at the justice department. In reality, he had given the stick to a young Russian fellow, as agreed. In exchange for the cash. Nobody the wiser. The money would allow him an expensive vacation with his wife. Far away from the dreary Dutch weather. He would grab some clothes and message the office he was taking some time off. He would claim he'd inherited some money. Or had cashed in his savings.

He was done with the whole thing, as far as he was concerned, and glad of it. Six months ago, the young Russian had promised to solve his financial and other problems. He had even been given an advance, also in cash. In exchange for a few small favors. Nothing spectacular. The young man had wanted some documents from the Bureau files. After which some people could no longer be prosecuted, for lack of those same documents.

Breukeling knew he couldn't play that little game for too long. People would get suspicious. Mistakes wouldn't be tolerated and couldn't be used too often to cover up what he was doing. He didn't plan on playing the game too long and risking getting caught. The Russian told him he would get a big opportunity and reap a lot of cash. Enough to start a new life elsewhere, with a new identity even. Which meant he would have to leave the Netherlands forever.

That opportunity presented itself two days ago.

The monitoring operation. The stakeout. He had gotten the job, and the Russian had told him exactly what to do with the recording. The other officer, the new one, Prinsen, had been an unwelcome presence and had nearly spoiled the whole thing, but Breukeling was too smart to let Prinsen foul up his business. He had put on a little act over the phone, and Prinsen had been easily fooled.

After that, it had been a walk in the park. Prinsen—the new chief's nephew, no less—had bought the story about the recording for the prosecutor. The fool. Considered himself smarter than the other officers. Nobody was smarter than a seasoned detective like Breukeling.

Freedom called. He felt the envelope. A lot of money for so easy a job. Enough money and more coming. A new life, for both of them. He wouldn't even have to return after the holiday.

What the young Russian planned to do with the recording didn't concern Breukeling. He would probably destroy it. In a matter of hours, he and Mrs. Breukeling would be lying on a white beach under a tropical sun, and he would tell her that the old life was behind them and a new one was beckoning. He'd send a note to the office, offering his resignation. They'd be surprised, but what could they do? He'd be out of their jurisdiction, and they wouldn't even have any real proof of his wrongdoing.

He closed the car and walked toward his front door.

Then he hesitated.

Something was wrong with the front door.

In the dark, he couldn't see what it was. Had somebody splashed white paint on the door or what? Had somebody been mucking around?

One of the neighbors who didn't like the police? A bit of vandalism? Wouldn't be the first time.

He stepped closer.

It wasn't a spot of paint.

Someone had hung a white plastic shopping bag on his doorknob.

What the hell?

He reached for the bag. He wanted to see what was inside.

A fireball rolled over him. The pressure from the explosion splintered the front door. The facade of the house was blown away. Windows of nearby houses were shattered.

Something that had been Breukeling a few moments before hung limply from a nearby tree.

TUESDAY

Amsterdam

12

EEKHAUT HAD SLEPT WITH the window ajar. The cool nocturnal air had been welcome. The absinthe had had no impact on the quality of his sleep. Maybe he had dreamt, but he couldn't remember.

In spite of his expectations, the city around him had been quiet when he went to bed. The occasional screeching from the trams and music from the neighbors hadn't even bothered him. He could have closed the window against the noise, but he hadn't. He preferred to have his bedroom ventilated. Although the outside air could hardly be called fresh.

His breakfast was a matter of pure improvisation. He hadn't been able to stock his kitchen with food. He had fetched some groceries from an all-night shop down the street run by an Indian youth, where almost everything that could serve as breakfast was exotic and spicy. So he made do with only a few biscuits and marmalade and a cup of tea. He needed to do some serious shopping but would have to get a more substantial breakfast somewhere in the vicinity first, in one of the snack bars that seemed open from very early in the morning. It would be a high-caloric breakfast, unfortunately. Probably eggs, ham, sausages, toast, and beans.

There would be coffee at the office. As bad as in any office, he assumed. Brussels had been the low point in coffee quality. Only the diehards drank the office brew. The others passed by a café first.

The sun heated his bedroom quickly now, which he liked. It would be wonderful waking each morning, even in midwinter, covered by that gentle warmth. He inspected the walls and the window frames and wondered if he shouldn't get some paint to freshen up his apartment. And perhaps buy a small bookcase in the process. With so many bookshops in this part of Amsterdam, he'd probably buy too many books for the currently available and actually nonexistent shelf space.

He had a look in the mirror. Summer trousers, pale blue shirt, dark blue jacket. Couldn't go wrong. He slid sunglasses in the breast pocket of his jacket, felt for his wallet, and realized something was missing. A holster and a gun. He would be handed a gun today.

He closed the apartment and descended the stairs. The shop was closed. It was half past eight. He was on time and even a bit too early. He preferred to start the day by being too early, although nobody would ask him to clock in.

The short walk from his apartment to the anonymous offices of the AIVD took him partly through Kerkstraat, which broadened, magically, into a sort of square with a church, and benches and primitive football goals constructed out of steel tubes. The local kids and the elderly seemed to be spending their time here, perhaps on quiet afternoons and on Sundays.

The AIVD building was a little farther down the street, cold, shuttered, official without looking official. He wondered if Alexandra—he still thought of her as Alexandra and not as Chief Dewaal—stayed here every evening, sleeping in a steel casket, to be awakened only when she was needed the next morning.

The Sleeping Beauty. Another fantasy he allowed himself privately. At least he had an attractive chief for once.

The entrance to the building consisted of a marble-floored hall with neutrally colored walls. The doorframes seemed made of steel and the doors of thick glass. Cameras were in the corners close to the ceiling. Behind a desk was a uniformed man who carried a gun in a very professional holster. Eekhaut presented his identification, attesting he was a Belgian police officer.

"Mmm, Mr. Eekhaut," the guard said, seemingly uninterested. "You have an appointment. Yes, you even have an office in this building. Just a moment. I'll provide you with a personalized access card."

The card was a red plastic affair with small black digits printed on it and a chip. "Hold it against the card reader next to the doors, and you can go anywhere you like. You have clearance for the whole building," the uniformed man said.

Clearance, Eekhaut thought. The man had used the English term.

Let's get this show on the road, he thought.

"Office zero one thirty-two, sir. One up. Elevator to your left."

The elevator was made of steel, no mirrors inside, as if claustrophobically inclined people were discouraged from using this building—or at least the elevators. He stepped into a wide corridor on the second floor. A fine stucco ceiling made it clear that at least part of the original interior had survived modernization. The detectors at the doors and the cameras on the ceiling spoke of Big Brother. The doors weren't original to the building and looked as if they could withstand a battering ram and even explosives.

Office zero one thirty-two happened to be not his own but that of the chief, who was already present behind a large but almost empty desk. Expecting him. Of course, she was expecting him. She gestured, and he assumed he could take a seat opposite her, in one of those modern steel frame chairs that didn't look capable of supporting human weight.

"This is officially your first day with us, Chief Inspector," she said. "We'll issue you a badge and a weapon in a moment." She didn't ask if the place had been easy to find and all the usual nonsense, or if he had slept well. There would be no time for idle chitchat between them, not today.

"And then we'll look at some of the dossiers. But before that, I'd like to go over some of our rules, the details of our collaboration. We don't have to be too stiff and formal about it, but we should at least have the parameters understood between us, right? The things that are expected of us. Well, from you, in this case."

He couldn't agree more, he indicated, while he quickly scanned the office. It seemed a bit grim, which was a letdown. The same neutral color on the walls as in the corridors, a framed van Gogh, a framed diploma, furniture in a combination of polished steel and black leather. Reminded him a bit of the shop downstairs from his apartment. No interior architect or designer had been allowed near these premises.

She, however, was a different story altogether. She looked as if she came out of a box, cleaned and pressed. Almost the same official-looking suit as the day before. No nonsense. He had expected something less formal today. Maybe he'd gotten her completely wrong.

"Let's fill out these forms first," she said. She pushed a cardboard folder in his direction. It contained about a dozen documents. Nasty white paper and fine print. A lot of fine print.

"There you are," she said.

"Right now?"

"Your office is next to this one," she said. "Shall we work on a first-name basis? That's easier."

"No problem."

"Good."

He left her office and entered his. It was somewhat smaller than hers but in every other respect almost a copy. Which he regretted. It was nothing more than an almost-bare cell with only a few pieces of furniture. He sat down on the multi-adjustable leather desk chair and opened the folder. He took his pen from his pocket and started reading.

It took him the better part of an hour to read and fill in all the documents. Had he been in one of the following countries (list of countries, some of which he'd never even heard of, probably all illegal for a Belgian or Dutch citizen to enter), how often had he drawn/discharged his handgun, did he have any ties to political organizations (which one, what sort of ties). And so on.

An hour. Twelve, no, thirteen documents. All of them attempting to ensnare him, to catch him in a contradiction, an outright lie. Forms he couldn't possibly fill out without at least two or three small untruths. He worked his way through the forms and gave free rein to his sense of whimsy, without really committing a serious lie to paper.

He finished, put his pen down, rose, slid the documents back in the folder, and carried the whole package back to Dewaal's office.

"Thank you," she said. "Take a seat again. We'll discuss your tasks."

"And these forms?"

"Oh, they go into the archives. Don't worry."

He said nothing. He'd committed half of his life to these forms. But they were going right away into the archives. Nobody was going to read them.

Dewaal said, "You're here, as you know, because we're investigating Adam Keretsky and the way his many companies operate. More specifically, his involvement with Fabna Bank. We talked about that yesterday. But that's just a part of your involvement with us. You're supposed to coordinate all information concerning international extremist and criminal organizations connected with Dutch and Belgian companies. That's quite a lot of work, actually, but it's what this Bureau does. We're part of AIVD. Here, however, in this building, we're our own boss. It's just us here, and our technical support teams. You'll spend time writing and editing reports, but you'll be active in the field as well. You're an experienced detective, and I want to use you as such."

"In the field."

"Exactly. Surveillance, analysis, intelligence gathering. That sort of thing. Real detective stuff, too. A lot happens in the field. We keep track of some five hundred organizations. That's a lot. We have a small team, about twenty-four people, no more, and that's hardly sufficient. But we get a lot of intelligence from the local police, customs, military intelligence, and others."

"A lot of information," he said. Twenty-four people covering five hundred organizations. It wasn't as if they were going to get one review each annually, these organizations.

"Our weak spot, exactly," she said. "And we're not even familiar with the Belgian situation, so we hardly work cross-border. Then there are the other adjacent countries to consider. You are fluent in both English and French, and that's interesting for us, when we deal with specific European countries. Like Ireland and France."

"Adjacent countries," Eekhaut said.

"Well, not really, but at least they're countries belonging to the European Union. With no additional borders between them. You know what I mean."

"I think I do," he said. "I'd be interested to see how this all pans out in practice."

"We've all heard about your methods," she said. "We're not going to use them, as we're not too keen on, well, the way you handle suspects, for instance."

"Methods?"

"I'd call them *intimidating*, these methods of yours I've heard about," Dewaal said. She used the word as if it concerned some nasty dental procedure.

"I see."

"I hope you do. We work by the book. That should be clear from the start. Rules. Suspects have rights. Everyone has rights."

"Those that are innocent and those that we think are guilty. They all have rights."

"Exactly," she said. "We're very careful with rights."

"We'll see how this works out," he said.

She looked rather unhappy. "I hope, Chief Inspector Eekhaut, that I made our commitment clear? Concerning your attitude?"

"Perfectly clear, Chief Superintendent. I understand I'll be first and foremost handling the Keretsky affair."

"Excellent. Now, I'll introduce you to the team . . ."

13

AFTER SHE HAD INTRODUCED Eekhaut and left him with the team, Dewaal retreated to her office and called Prinsen and asked him to join her. He came at once, assuming something was wrong. And something was wrong. "Where is the recording?" she asked. He was certain she already knew the answer. She was going to chew him out, or worse. She was going to make him regret there was a family connection between them. And make sure he understood there would be no favors from her.

Forget the family connection. He would have no reprieve. Until he really had earned her respect, on his own account. Till then he was going to have to prove to her he was better than the other detectives.

He tried to recall how she treated him when he was a child. But he couldn't. No memories came. As if his mind was blocked, the past stowed away, carefully hidden. He had heard stories about her from members of his family, in which she was—well, nearly—the Devil himself, or at least an apostate. But when he finally met her, as a kid still, she looked like any normal person. Or at least as normal as anyone in the village. In fact, *more* normal.

He had met her again a few times before he came to Amsterdam. She kept to herself, mostly, which was in itself suspect to the members of his large, fundamentally religious, reactionary family. She was a free woman, which was a greater sin still. His mother's younger sister, the problem child, the outcast. Didn't believe in church or God. Prinsen's mother loathed her, if only for that.

"The memory stick with the recording was delivered to the prosecutor's office on his demand," he said. That was what the report also said, the one he had filed earlier.

"And who ordered this?"

"Breukeling called the prosecutor in person on his phone."

"That's not an answer, Prinsen. I'll be clear, so there is no misunderstanding between us. Who ordered the recording to be delivered to the prosecutor and who asked that the original recording on the hard drive of the computer be wiped?"

"The prosecutor himself," Prinsen said. But more softly now, as if he was no longer certain who had done what and why. He had heard Breukeling discussing the matter with the prosecutor. Or had he not?

Dewaal leaned back and inspected him. She knew that look. It didn't bode well for him. He knew he was in trouble. "How good is Breukeling with computers?" she asked.

He didn't have any idea where the question would lead. What did it matter if Breukeling was a nerd or not? "About average," he said. "The usual things. Word, Excel, a few other applications. The utilities we use for—"

"Experts tell me you never really can delete a file from a hard disk. It can always be found. At least, if you act fast. Why would Breukeling follow orders from the prosecutor without consulting me first?"

"He's only a detective," Prinsen argued. He would defend his colleagues with logical arguments if needed. "He could hardly ignore an order from the prosecutor, could he?"

"Breukeling has been a detective in this Bureau for a considerable stretch of time. Long enough to know that the prosecutor has no right to interfere with an ongoing investigation of this sort. He didn't order the investigation in the first place. He isn't part of the line of command. Breukeling had only me to deal with. Can I get any clearer?"

"I'm sure—"

"But then I'm informed about what happened yesterday. The prosecutor is supposed to have the only recording of that conversation between Keretsky and Fabna Bank. A strange outcome and not something we agreed on. But I'm willing to let the matter slide. So I call the prosecutor this morning. The one Breukeling is supposed to have called yesterday. Because you heard him talking to the prosecutor, didn't you?"

"I suppose I did, yes."

"You suppose," she said. "Well, anyway, the prosecutor didn't know what I was talking about. He was even more surprised when I got worked up. I know we don't always see eye to eye, and we've had our differences of opinion, to say the least. But he knew nothing about this. He didn't speak to Breukeling. Not at all. He gave no such order. And Prinsen, this one time I'm inclined to believe him."

"But I assumed—"

"You assumed? Really? What did you assume? You heard Breukeling talking, and he told you he had been speaking to the prosecutor. And then, he did what?"

"He downloaded the recording to the memory stick."

"And after that?"

"He took the memory stick with him."

"Right. To give to the prosecutor. And he wiped the original recording, which we may or may not be able to retrieve, hopefully more or less intact. Unless Breukeling does *really* know his way around computers."

"Shit!"

"Are things becoming clearer? A memory stick destined for the prosecutor, who knew nothing of the whole business and wouldn't even care. In other words . . ."

"Shit," Prinsen said again.

"Breukeling didn't show up this morning. The recording is gone. The experts tell me it looks like it was never made. What Breukeling did, my dear Prinsen, was record the conversation directly on the stick, instead of on the hard drive—I'm sure I'll start to like this jargon—and then absconded with the stick while you were watching."

"Maybe he did . . ."

"And now for the really, really messy part of my story," Dewaal said. "Breukeling had a night out. He arrived at his house early this morning. Probably had been celebrating. Because he'd fooled all of us. We'll try to find out who he celebrated with, and where. Anyway. His wife was already in bed. Lucky for her, the bedroom is situated at the back of the house. That saved her life. She'll probably never hear anything again, but she's still alive."

Prinsen stared at Dewaal.

"Remember when Jaap van der Heiden was murdered in Alkmaar in, what was it, 1993? Same method. You hang a plastic grocery bag with explosives on your target's doorknob. His front door. The explosives are wired to a cell phone. From a distance, you keep an eye on the location. You dial the number of the phone in the bag, except for the last digit. When your guy walks toward his front door, wondering who left groceries behind, you punch the last digit. The phone in the bag acts as detonator. And that's that. The little that was left of Breukeling was brought to the teaching hospital. And he was not dead, can you imagine? All the more exceptional, since he had lost both his lower arms, and his right leg snapped off when they lifted him out of the tree he'd been flung into. His face was gone. They noticed he was alive because his heart was still functioning along with his brain. Luckily for him, that didn't last long."

"Jesus!"

"Jesus had very little to do with all this. And given Breukeling's past, he's not going to meet Jesus anytime soon. This is one of the very rare occasions an officer of the AIVD was killed on the job. I want this to be the only occasion, at least on my watch. Another thing I want is for no other officer to have any intention of betraying us. A considerable amount of cash was discovered in what remained of his clothes. Fragments of bank notes, actually, and not from his own savings. Somebody was prepared to pay Breukeling a lot of money so we would not hear the recording of the conversation at the Renaissance between Keretsky and Monet. And if you don't know who Monet is, you need to dive into your dossiers right away."

"Who is on this case? The murder, I mean."

"Internal Affairs has taken matters in hand. I'm pretty sure what will happen next. They'll discover that Breukeling had a lot of enemies, especially old ones. You know what the rumors say about him and his relation to certain obscure people in Amsterdam. Corruption is a word that might be used in this connection. Internal Affairs wasn't even surprised when they heard about the murder. They're analyzing the fragments of whatever was in the bag. As far as you're concerned, I'll add you to the group that's handling the Keretsky file. It seems you're already involved."

She'd given him her trust, he realized. But before he became giddy with joy, she added, "But I want you to work together with Van Gils on Breukeling. He was one of us, corrupt or not, and we don't let criminals murder one of our own."

"There are some other cases I have to—" These last few weeks he'd been investigating cases of human trafficking from the Balkans to the United Kingdom and Ireland. The many ways of the Lord were inscrutable, but it seemed those of traffickers were even more obscure.

"You can work on your other cases whenever you have some time left. This case gets full priority. If we cannot protect ourselves, how then can we protect others?"

Prinsen found it difficult to refute that argument.

14

THE SANDWICHES AND SALADS turned out to be of excellent quality, the coffee quite satisfactory. No buttermilk. No meat croquettes. No junk food. None of the clichés concerning Dutch food served at company meetings and at parties proved to be true. Clichés never are. They only tend to move about in packs and they are most often found where tourists congregate.

Eekhaut folded his paper napkin and made a mental note that he would have to ease up on the food intake during lunch, here in the Bureau's lunch room. He was no fan of sports—certainly not as a participant, and in spite of the choices of activities his former public employer in Brussels provided—and he had to be careful about his weight. Otherwise, he'd get fat and get in trouble with the cardiologist.

Two of his new colleagues walked past, offhandedly acknowledging his presence and sitting down at another table. The lunchroom was large enough for the two score people who worked here, airy, with pleasantly decorated tables and real plants. Two large TV screens adorned the walls but were not in use. Probably only when football was on. Some tables and chairs were arranged in cozy niches, as if people found it necessary to eat in secret.

He sat alone. And would be sitting alone for a while yet. He knew the unwritten rules of law enforcement units everywhere. You became one of the team only when you were one of the team. Or never at all. Few professionals were as exclusive as police officers were, and they had to be, since the man or woman sitting next to you could one day make the difference between life and death in a dangerous situation. So you were picky about making friends.

He was the newcomer. At his age! But at his age, he had more experience than most of the regulars here. Nobody looked over forty.

Alexandra Dewaal showed up, accompanied by a cultured yogurt and a small bottle of grape juice. He assumed she worked out. Or played tennis every day. Or whatever. Hours on end at a gym. Worried every day about having gained a pound. Religiously watching the scales every morning. Afraid of coronary problems.

She sat down at his table, alert and professional. "Walter," she said, "I see you have gotten acquainted with our amenities."

He smiled. Her choice of words. "There was a line. And I followed. The rest is history."

She grinned. He suddenly liked her more. He liked women with a sense of humor, above all other qualities. Did she have a sense of humor, or was she just being polite?

"You'll notice that cases will find their way to your desk easily enough. But don't assume you're here for the paperwork alone. We work at ungodly hours, often enough, like any police unit. And we go into the streets as often as not." She glanced away from him for a moment. "We've had our share of trouble this morning. You probably heard: one of our team members was killed last night. By a bomb attached to his front door."

"That's . . ." What was he going to say? Terrible? Fucked up? He couldn't find the appropriate reaction. "I'm sorry for your loss," he said, feeling dumb.

She shook her head. "It's complicated. The whole affair is a mess. We found out he stole material from us, which he probably sold to another party. And that same party didn't want to leave any traces."

"Are you saying that—?"

"I am. A traitor. Dramatic, isn't it? It means I'll have a lot of explaining to do to Internal Affairs and to my director. I'll have to explain myself in more than one report. They'll be all over me, and over us, for weeks if not more. The gist of it is that we've lost the recording of the conversation between Adam Keretsky and an associate of his,

Monet. That's a hell of a setback, but it also proves we're easily corrupted, at least some of us. And there isn't anything I can do about that. It means I'll have to watch the members of my own team."

"Even the ones that have been here for a while?"

Her cell phone vibrated. "Dewaal," she said. And listened. "The local police?" she asked. "Text me the address. You're sure it's him?" She listened again and then pocketed her phone. "I'm afraid I'll have to go. You're coming along? Finished?"

He wiped his mouth. "Finished. What and how?"

She frowned.

"What happened?" he clarified.

"A body. Shot dead. A neighbor stumbled over it. This morning."

"And you're concerned why?"

"I'm concerned because the body belongs to a rather well-known young dissident. Leftist circles, busy with sensitive material, extremism, and that sort of thing. Occasionally wrote pieces for radical papers."

"I see."

"I doubt that. His name is Pieter Van Boer. Thirty. Radical left wing, hated by anyone of the opposite persuasion. If someone like that is found dead and with a bullet through his head, we're interested. The local cops know it. They have my number. They'll probably be all too happy if we take this crime off their hands." She rose. "I'll have to get you a gun."

"I can live and function without a gun."

"I can't. And I can't live with the idea of sending my people out in the streets unarmed. The AIVD management has a different policy concerning packing weapons, but this is *my* department, so I do as I damn well please. Before we go see the corpse, we have something else to do as well. We have an appointment with the Big Man himself."

The Big Man? Capitals? Eekhaut wondered who that could be. Some important politician or a minister? A cabinet member? "Who?" he asked.

"Adam Keretsky. Who else? The man responsible for you being here. Are you eating that or can we go?"

Fifteen minutes later, he sat in the passenger seat of a black Porsche Cayenne. He had a brand-new SIG Sauer in a tactical holster on his right hip and two extra clips. Enough ammo for a small war. He felt uneasy with so much firepower. He also had a new police card in his wallet, which allowed him to operate on Dutch soil. Pretend to be a real police officer.

"Your card is a more important tool than the gun," Dewaal said. "And you'll need it more often, I hope. Otherwise, if the inverse proves to be true, we'll get in trouble with those bureaucratic assholes farther up the ladder who want a form filled out for every bullet you fire."

He too hoped he wouldn't have to use the gun. His last weapons training was four years ago, and he'd never fired a gun like this.

She drove through narrow streets, along canals, past bicycles, trams, and vans, past a gloomy church. Then she parked the car carelessly in a chaotic street, across from the entrance to the Renaissance Hotel.

"Can you behave?" she asked.

Eekhaut shrugged. "Isn't that what is expected of me?"

"You're here as the official representative of—" She shook her head. "Forget it. You have any ideological objections? Against Russians?"

"What's the difference between a Russian capitalist and a Dutch capitalist?"

She didn't answer that. He guessed he hadn't scored well with that remark.

Careful, Eekhaut.

A receptionist smiled at them, but he wasn't going to be impressed by a woman wielding a police card. "You have an appointment with Mr. Keretsky?"

"Yes," Dewaal said.

"I'll ring," the man said. After a short telephone conversation, he said, "You'll be escorted. In a minute."

"We'll find our own way," Dewaal said. "What room?"

"I'm sorry, ma'am. House rules. Mr. Keretsky's secretary will be along in a minute. He'll accompany you to Mr. Keretsky's suite."

Dewaal didn't want to cause a scandal, as that wouldn't be conducive to the relationship with Keretsky. A moment later a young man appeared. "My name is Tarkovski," he said. "Chief Superintendent Dewaal, ma'am, if you would care to follow me?" He spoke Dutch with a slight accent.

"You're Russian?" Eekhaut asked.

They stepped into the elevator, and Tarkovski slid a plastic card through a reader before pushing a button. "I am. Is it that obvious?"

"Not in the least."

Five floors up, they stepped out and found themselves in a corridor with thick dark blue carpeting, wooden paneling, a slightly vaulted ceiling, and discreetly concealed indirect lighting. The décor told Eekhaut this was not a floor for ordinary tourists. Not even for rich, ordinary tourists.

"Mr. Keretsky can spare you twenty minutes," Tarkovski said.

"Mr. Keretsky will have to oblige me by answering all my questions, no matter how long that takes," Dewaal said.

The young Russian did not reply. He held open the door to a suite. Keretsky waited for them in front of the large window. He wore a conventional gray suit but no tie. He stepped toward them and shook their hands. "Adam Keretsky, ma'am," he said. In English.

Dewaal introduced herself and Eekhaut. "Our visit and its purpose have been announced to you, Mr. Keretsky," she said. "Through regular channels."

"That is correct, Chief Superinendent. It should, however, be noted that I am complying entirely out of my free will. My visa is in order, customs has had nothing to complain about, I pay all my bills, and have committed no crimes in the Netherlands." He offered them a seat.

"We're aware of all that, Mr. Keretsky," Dewaal said after they'd sat down. "The question we want to put to you concerns your financial dealings in this country. That much has also been explained to you in our written memo."

"My financial dealings. And more specifically concerning—?"

"The reason for your visit to Amsterdam at this time."

"I'm a newly minted shareholder of Fabna Bank, Ms. Dewaal. That's no secret. The details have been covered thoroughly in the press. Quite thoroughly, actually. That's the price I pay for being somewhat infamous and wanting to do business in your country. Andreï, do bring coffee and tea. And please, madam, do proceed with your questions. I have no secrets, as I said."

"Thank you. What exactly are your plans as a shareholder of Fabna?"

Keretsky produced a winning smile. "I have money, of course, and I want to invest it. As does anyone who has money to spare. Some deposit it into a savings account, or they buy a yacht, but I want a piece of a bank. It seems a sound investment, even in these troubled times of bank failures. And their shares *are* a bargain."

"You're hardly *anyone*, Mr. Keretsky. You own considerable interests in many large Russian companies. Your name is connected with a number of takeovers and mergers and participations, some of which involve Western companies. You are now an important minority shareholder of Fabna. Yet you declined a seat on the board. Why?"

"It meant I would have to travel to Amsterdam once a month. I cannot spare the time. I have too many obligations elsewhere. I'm assured that the other members of the board are quite capable of running their bank, without me. Mr. Prins and his colleagues have my complete confidence."

"You're also involved in companies in several other sectors . . ."

"Of course I am. I spread my assets and likewise spread my risks. As any good Russian family man would do with his fortune."

Eekhaut leaned forward and deposited his cup on the salon table. "But," he said, ignoring Dewaal, "you do plan on influencing the policy of Fabna Bank?"

The Russian's attention was on him now. "In what sense, sir?"

"That should be obvious. Fabna is one of the largest Benelux banks. It's a considerable player in Europe as well. A stable and healthy company. Money is probably not your most urgent worry."

"Investing, that's what I do," Keretsky said.

"What my colleague has in mind—" Dewaal said, but she was interrupted again by Eekhaut. "What I mean, Mr. Keretsky," he said, "is this: let's assume that you might be in possession of funds of dubious origin. What better than a reputable Western bank to change the color of your money to something more agreeable?"

"Are you accusing me of money laundering? Of illegal activities?"

"I merely state a theoretical possibility," Eekhaut suggested.

Dewaal intervened. "Of course, this is not an official line of inquiry, Mr. Keretsky."

"Your colleague implies it is," Keretsky said.

Dewaal hesitated a moment too long. Eekhaut said, "It would be a perfect opportunity, would it not? A sizable chunk of a bank in your pocket and nobody would want to investigate your dealings with too critical an eye."

"Is that," the Russian said, "where this conversation is headed, Ms. Dewaal? In that case, this meeting is over."

"My colleague was simply stating a few possible developments, Mr. Keretsky—" Dewaal said.

"I take that as an insult."

"—while we have no intention of assuming any wrongdoing."

"And I must ask you to leave my suite, madam. I have out of my free accord consented to this conversation, but you are clearly misusing this opportunity." He rose. Suddenly Tarkovski stood at his side. Without coffee.

Silent and fast, that boy, Eekhaut thought. *Like a rapacious animal. Or a shadow.*

Dewaal said, "I am sorry if we —

"So am I, Ms. Dewaal. I had hoped for a civilized conversation with civil servants." Keretsky pronounced the last word with some clear disdain.

Servants, Eekhaut thought.

A few moments later, they found themselves in the elevator again. Tarkovski didn't shake hands when they left. The elevator door closed on him.

"If you want to chew me out," Eekhaut said, "I'd prefer you do that in the car."

Dewaal looked at him, surprised. "Do you think I expected anything else from you? With your reputation?" She proceeded toward the exit. He followed her. She remained silent, got into the car, and started the engine.

"Not even a reprimand?" he commented. "That's annoying. I try to live up to my reputation, and I don't even get reprimanded. How can I live with that?"

"I'm not going to reprimand you," she said. "I'm going to think about sending you back. But not right now. We're not finished. We still have a body to look at."

She drove off, a bit too fast. Maybe she was frustrated. He got the city tour again: canals, exotic shops, streets with bicycles, a few cafés, and restaurants. At last, she parked the Porsche behind two VW Golfs in police colors. Three uniformed officers were guarding the entrance to a house. Dewaal addressed one of them. Then she waved Eekhaut in. "Upstairs," she said.

The stairs were narrow, and a man in white coveralls tried to pass them, but he had to shuffle back. "What can you tell me?" Dewaal asked, showing him her card.

"Caliber nine mil, probably a silencer," the man said. "Two bullets. From no more than two meters. Killed instantly. No signs of forced entrance. Doors open, as far as we can see. No robbery either. Nothing of value was taken, although there is not much of value in places like these. There's a laptop, which a common thief would not have left behind. We've recovered the bullets, and I'll get them examined."

"Witnesses?"

The man shook his head and continued down the stairs.

The apartment was a mess. Clothes, books, newspapers, and some old furniture, probably bought secondhand. A sour smell. And something else too, something Eekhaut was familiar with. Death. The very particular smell of death.

The body lay on the bed, covered with a sheet. Blood on the bed and against the wall. Two uniformed officers, two men in coveralls, two plainclothes police officers. Too much of a crowd for such a small room. Dewaal addressed one of the detectives. "Joop, what do we have here?"

"And a good morning to you, Ms. Dewaal. Is this one from your archives?"

"If it's Pieter Van Boer, it is, yes."

"It's him all right. We've identified him."

"And?"

"He got an unwanted and unannounced visitor this morning. Two bullets, nine millimeter. Nobody heard the shots. They heard some racket, but that's about it."

"He defended himself. That sort of racket."

"No, he didn't have time to defend himself. There must have been someone else around." Joop pointed at a paper bag with breakfast rolls and croissants on the floor, next to a yellow number tag. "Somebody got him breakfast. His girlfriend, probably. Lived here with him, so the neighbors tell us. We're now looking for her. She probably walked in on the murderer, there was a fight, and we assume she managed to get away. Otherwise, we would have found two bodies."

"Who is she?"

"Eileen Calster. Twenty-one. From Groningen. Studies at the university. Lived here for a year or so. Do we contact his family?"

"Yes. And circulate a search warrant for her. If they hear from her, we want to know right away. Is there anything you can tell me about the killer?"

"Nothing. Nobody saw anything. Not in this neighborhood. People come and go. Nobody locks his door. Crazy, isn't it? In the center of Amsterdam? People not bothering to lock their doors? You wonder what sort of world they think they're living in. Not my world anyway. I always lock my front door."

"Nothing to steal," Eekhaut said. He looked around. Some things would be worth stealing, though. Drugs, for one. There would be drugs in a place like this.

"So it seems," Dewaal said. "Now it's our problem. No murderer and no motive."

"And why are you here, Dewaal?" the detective asked. "Because the kid was a member of the CPN and read Marx? He had quite a collection of Marxist literature. But that's hardly illegal. Not yet."

"He's someone we were watching, Joop. Part of the job."

"Well, someone lightened your load for you. You won't have to watch this one anymore."

"Let me know when something worthwhile turns up," Dewaal said. And to Eekhaut, "Come on, Chief Inspector. We have other things to do."

"Chief Superintendent," Joop said. "I heard about Breukeling. Really shitty business. But I also heard he wasn't completely clean either. Used to be one of us, Breuk."

"You heard correctly," she said. "Let this be a warning to the others. I personally would have wanted things to turn out differently, but here we are."

They walked down the stairs. Eekhaut had no more comments to make since he assumed she was unhappy about Joop's remarks. They got into the car and drove off. She parked the car around the corner, where a couple of pink dildos were featured as this week's sale item in a sex shop window.

She said, "How do you feel about this case? And try to forget Joop's comments."

"Someone had a problem with this Pieter Van Boer and solved it. Someone with a semiautomatic, a silencer, and just enough motivation to walk into a property in the middle of the morning and kill his victim in cold blood. He's a professional. And he gets paid well to do this. We can safely eliminate the usual motives, like jealousy or greed."

"My thoughts too."

"What do you know about Van Boer?"

"There's the problem. He was an informant."

"An informant? One of yours?"

She nodded. "Yes, one of the Bureau's. Occasionally, at least. If it suited him and when he had some sensitive information to share. We deal with the most unusual people, sometimes, Walter. We form unhappy alliances. But we have to. Some time ago, Van Boer told me he had an interesting lead. Some really sensitive info. And then, nothing. I didn't hear from him for weeks. I know he works—worked—with the PDN."

"CPN, PDN. Abbreviations," Eekhaut said. "I'm not a local boy—I don't know what they mean."

"CPN is the Dutch Communist Party," Dewaal said. "Small and toothless. Totally enthralled with the Marxist tradition but not happy with the excesses of state capitalism as in the former Soviet Union, which they call a deviation from the Marxist norm. They claim to be the real Marxists. They seem to have a very decent research center that at times reports on illegal and criminal dealings of government officials and the like. Van Boer wrote for their publications and magazines. Not under his own name. PDN is something entirely different. Partij Dierbaar Nederland, the Dutch right-wing party. Nationalist, anti-immigration, anti-Europe. Founded by Hendrika Van Tillo, former minister of justice, now without an official job. It used to be rather respectable a couple of years ago but then drifted to the far right. Speaks to a large audience nonetheless. The common man who fears his job will be taken by immigrants and who's against Europe and globalization."

"Like Vlaams Belang in Belgium."

"Oh, your average homegrown nationalist party, yes. About the same thing, but somewhat different approach. PDN does its utmost best to be respectable while it is also populist. Especially Ms. Van Tillo. She has a lot of supporters. Very outspoken too, that woman. On television, she isn't shy about silencing her opponents with cheap demagogic tricks and ideological, even racist slurs. Inflammatory speeches for the in crowd and supporters and provocative sound-bites for the news, especially the commercial stations. Dubious party financing too, but we can't prove that. She gets loads of money from certain parts of the business community."

"Is that what Van Boer was after?"

"I have no idea."

"Why he's now a corpse? Because he found out something he shouldn't have?"

"I really don't know. I have no leads. I hadn't seen him for a while. No idea what he was after."

"Because this kind of execution . . . this is no jealous girlfriend getting even. Few girlfriends walk around with a silenced nine mil."

"And yet the girlfriend or whoever she was managed to escape, it seems. That's less than professional."

"We all make mistakes. Just consider the risk this murderer took. Unknown terrain, unknown situation."

"You may be right."

"Someone who is familiar with the neighborhood, perhaps."

"The murderer? This is Amsterdam, Walter, not New York or Los Angeles. This isn't a city where you can hire a professional assassin just like that, in a bar or whatever."

"I guess you're right."

"And the PDN is certainly not into contract killers. They don't do that sort of thing. They're more subtle when it concerns their enemies. A little more subtle."

"But consider the possible point of interest. Party financing. It involves two sides: the one that receives and the one that pays."

She grabbed the steering wheel. "You're right. Let's think about that."

"What now?"

"The forensic lab will give us their results as soon as they're finished, but I won't hold my breath. A contract killer might leave traces we could link to someone in our files, but I don't expect much in the way of real results. We have to assume this was an outside job."

15

"I'M IN DEEP TROUBLE, Maarten," Eileen said into her cell phone. She stood in Kalverstraat, partially behind a wall, with the afternoon crowds passing by—tourists and the various bizarre figures who were so prevalent in the center of Amsterdam. She wanted to go into the McDonald's, hoping for invisibility among the young people, but maybe that wasn't such a good idea. She felt totally alienated from people her own age. And she wasn't going to eat anyway.

She had no good ideas left anymore. She was too visible wherever she went. The murderer could appear at any moment. She was sure he was hunting her, because she'd seen him and even more because she'd taken those documents. The center of Amsterdam wasn't very large. A tenacious hunter would find her soon enough. Or maybe not. On account of the crowds. She hoped.

Maybe she had more of an advantage than she expected. The man had been alone. And he had committed a murder. He'd want to disappear. Precisely what she also wanted to do. Hence her call to Maarten, her brother, who lived on Brouwersgracht in a single room. She hoped he would take her in for a couple of days.

Maarten. Who usually lived in some universe far from anything earthly and who'd forgotten why the hell he had moved to Amsterdam. Or why anyone would want to live in Amsterdam in the first place. And he was the one she called for help. Not a good strategy.

She didn't want to involve Maarten. It meant taking her problems to her brother. He wouldn't be able to handle her problems, since he couldn't even get his own life in order. But she was sure nobody had followed her, so they'd both be safe. Nobody knew where she was going.

She didn't want to put Maarten in danger.

He seemed to be having one of his rare clear-headed moments. He seemed to be able to parse her sentences and grasp their meaning. "What's the matter, sis? You don't sound happy. Something wrong with Pop or Mom? Where are you? Damn phones!" A noise as if Maarten was shaking his cell phone. Cell phones were inventions from a future world, as far as he was concerned, one too complicated for him to understand.

"Maarten, listen to me. I have to crash somewhere. I can't stay on the streets—"

"An argument with Pieter? Well, an argument with Pieter, why am I not surprised? That old fucker is just not right for you, sis. All that political . . . stuff. Communism, isn't it? Why didn't you leave him earlier? You should never have—What did you see in him, anyway?"

"Maarten! Pieter is dead!" She glanced up. Had somebody heard her? In the crowded street with people passing an arm's length away from her? No, nobody paid any attention. She was a girl on a street corner with a phone to her ear, in the most photogenic city on the planet, where tall, beautiful girls like herself were plentiful. "Pieter is dead, Maarten. He got shot. Shot, like, with a *gun*. By a man I have never seen before. That man was looking for something, a folder with documents. I took it. I got away. He would have killed me too."

"A folder?"

"Yes."

"What kind of folder?"

"That doesn't matter. Maarten? Are you—" *Lucid*, she wanted to say. But she couldn't use that word with Maarten. "Are you awake?"

"I'm . . . awake, sis. I understand what you're saying. Pieter is dead. Did he have problems with, like, an ex-girlfriend or what? Or is it political? Pieter is involved . . . was involved with those political things, and you often hear that they . . . I don't know."

"I have no idea." She managed to keep her voice calm, but she wanted to shout at him. Shouting wouldn't help, though. Shouting never helped with Maarten.

"Maarten, a man with a gun killed Pieter. I returned from the bakery. He wanted to shoot me too. I escaped. He wanted to steal—"

"Who? The murderer?"

"Yes," she said. Yes, she was talking about the murderer. Pieter had stolen something as well, but she wanted to keep the story simple. "The man had taken Pieter's documents. I have them here. Maybe Pieter had to die on account of those documents." No, she was certain of that. But she avoided explaining the whole story to Maarten.

Don't complicate things.

"You have to get out of there," he said, lucid for once. "Where are you?"

"In Kalverstraat. I'm staying away from the apartment. But all my things are there. Clothes and . . . the cops will be there, too. What can I do?"

And she thought, *That's the way things turn out. I end up asking Maarten for advice. He was always the one without any plans for the future, only living in the present. Today I want him to help me, although he can barely help himself. I'm asking him for help, and he was always the one who needed help from all of us.*

"What do you intend to do?"

Oh, she thought, *he's playing* that *game again. Reversing the question.* "Get as far away as possible from the apartment and the murderer. Somewhere where people don't know me. Somewhere safe."

"Where is it safe, Eileen?"

"Maarten!"

"I'm just asking. What has Pieter done? What was he involved in? One of his crazy schemes? And what about you? Are you safe? No, apparently not. I don't know what you should do. Go to the police. Give them those documents. Whatever it is, get rid of the problem."

You don't know anything, Eileen thought. If things were that simple, Pieter would have gone to the police. With that list. But he didn't want to. He must have had very good reasons not to involve the police. And his reasons, she thought, should be good enough for her.

Was she safe? She was not. The man crossing the Kalverstraat and walking in her direction could be the assassin, as far as she knew. Or a plainclothes police officer. The young woman at the other side, watching a shop window, could be stalking her. Behind that window, inside the shop, the murderer could also be observing her and waiting for a single instant of carelessness on her part.

No, she was not safe.

And why involve Maarten in all this?

She hadn't reached the end of her list of options. No, it wasn't that. There simply hadn't been a list. You go to your family first. It remains in the family.

16

"Mr. Tarkovski," Van Gils said in Dutch. "We'd like to ask you some questions concerning the details of your employment here in Amsterdam." Eekhaut, who was accompanying Van Gils, kept silent, as had been agreed between them.

"As you wish," Tarkovski said.

Both police officers had properly identified themselves. Tarkovski was familiar with one of them already. The one who had spoken with Mr. Keretsky, together with the female Chief Superintendent. The man who had asked Mr. Keretsky all those *wrong* questions.

They were meeting in the offices of Gilinski BV, on Keizersgracht, one of the many companies Tarkovski managed on Keretsky's behalf. It was, in a way, his favorite. The import of diamonds from Russia and Mongolia. Few people ever wondered if there were any diamond mines in Russia or Mongolia. It didn't matter—uncut diamonds didn't have serial numbers. All you needed was a collection of documents proving where they came from, and documents were plentiful in both countries. Even official ones. In Russian and Mongolian and written in Cyrillic script.

The company was also his favorite because it had a real shop window: twelve meters of street-level frontage from end to end, heavily secured, displaying the finished products of the diamond trade—necklaces, watches, tiaras, rings. Most of it was window dressing, although behind the window was a real shop in which three neatly dressed young Dutch men sold jewelry to actual customers at totally inflated prices.

But none of that had anything at all to do with the real operations at Gilinski BV.

Such was the world of Keretsky: glamor, pretense, and phony shop windows. Behind them, a shady world and real money, lots of money. But Keretsky was definitely moving into legal transactions after his money had been laundered. He was respectable, although he still occasionally traded in guns to embargoed countries that paid him with uncut diamonds, for instance.

"I am, how shall I put it, the manager of a number of companies owned mostly by Mr. Keretsky," Tarkovski said now. "I manage his interests. I am a businessman. You're probably aware of the sort of interests we have in the Netherlands. And you are equally well aware of our successes. We're very happy to be here, Mr. Van Gils."

"I'm sure you are," Van Gils said. He tried to loosen his tie a bit. He didn't care much for ties, which he considered a necessary evil that he got rid of as soon as he was no longer on duty. "Where have you been the last couple of days? You were probably very busy, with your boss around."

"He was around the whole time, yes," Tarkovski said. "And then your colleagues interrogated him, concerning things that were . . ." And then, in English, "He's here to protect his interests in some of his financial involvements. You do read the newspapers, I'm sure, Inspector? You do read your own files too, I would dare to speculate."

Van Gils replied in Dutch, "We're aware of a meeting, yesterday at the Renaissance Hotel, between Mr. Keretsky and a Dutch entrepreneur, Monet. Were you present, Mr. Tarkovski?"

"I was," Tarkovski said, in Dutch again. "Part of my job. Whenever Mr. Keretsky is in Holland, I am his personal assistant. It is a matter of trust. I also prepare the . . . these talks, yes? The circumstances. Renting a meeting room, taking care of catering, bringing people together."

"That conversation was strictly confidential, I assume?"

"You will not read a word about it in the papers, Inspector . . . would you care to repeat your name, please?"

"Van Gils."

"Ah, yes," Tarkovski said. "Van Gils. And your colleague here has a distinct Flemish accent, does he not? He seems a bit out of place, lost even. A bit like myself, I'd say."

"How many people work for you here in the Netherlands, Mr. Tarkovski?" Van Gils asked, not perturbed by the Russian's remarks. "For you and Mr. Keretsky."

"How many people? Hard to say. A considerable number of companies, doing very diverse things. How many people in all? Hundreds, I'd dare say. They come and go, you know how that is."

"No," Van Gils said, "I don't. Tell me."

"Hard to find reliable colleagues these days."

"You recruit Russians mostly?"

"Of course! We help our fellow countrymen find jobs. Not illegal, is it? Free market and all that. We take care of our own people. Even if they fled communism, Mr. Van Gils, they remain Russians. Some have lived here for quite a bit of time, have become as Dutch as any of you— well, except for your Flemish colleague here. That's why they work for us. After a sort of, well, an oath, really."

"An oath? To whom?"

"To the company, of course. A pledge of honor to their employer. Who did you have in mind? Putin?"

"Anything seems possible," Van Gils said. He quickly glanced at Eekhaut, who seemed to have no questions so far. All routine, Van Gils had told Eekhaut, although he knew that no conversation of this sort was ever routine. And he knew the Belgian had been a problem earlier with Keretsky. Now, however, he just listened.

"In Amsterdam," Tarkovski continued, "a large number of Russians originate from Moscow. There's this . . . tradition. People from Moscow move to Amsterdam. Those from Saint Petersburg choose Rotterdam."

"You're from Saint Petersburg. You're in the wrong city, then."

"I see you did your homework. You're right. Mr. Keretsky and I do come from Saint Petersburg, where he first employed me. We've been working together for a long time. There's a mutual trust—"

"You have no problems with the local Russians?"

"No. There's enough mutual respect. Do you have problems with Dutchmen from Rotterdam or from Leiden? You don't. You're all

Dutch. Same with Russians: we share the same culture and language. All brothers. Unless we talk football. Saint Petersburg has a better team than Moscow, although they dispute that."

"Yes," said Van Gils, "I'm sure they do. Where were you yesterday evening?"

"At a party. Here in Amsterdam. Plenty of people who know me. Why?"

"Just a routine question," Van Gils said while glancing in the little black book he used to jot down a few notes. The black book was purely for show. Generally, he just made doodles, nothing more, but no suspect knew that. Van Gils used his memory. His experience was that it made people nervous when you took notes.

Eekhaut leaned in toward the Russian. "Mr. Tarkovski, what are your chances of ever returning again to Russia?"

Tarkovski frowned. "Back to Russia, Mr. . . . Eekhaut? I travel to Russia whenever I please. I have a passport. I can travel tomorrow, today even. If I have a ticket. But getting a ticket is easy. Russian travel companies are very efficient."

"You may have a passport, Mr. Tarkovski, but I'm sure Mr. Keretsky decides if and when you make the trip. You're not really free to go, are you?"

Something changed in the Russian's attitude. He assumed a distance. "Mr. Keretsky has been a good employer, Mr. Eekhaut. He has employed me for a number of years now, most of them here in Holland. I like it here, and I like my job. Amsterdam is a most pleasant city to live in. Winters are most bearable here, much different from Russia. People treat me with respect, even the police. Is there a problem?"

"Oh, there's no problem. I just wondered if a Russian wouldn't want to return to Moscow at some point. Or Saint Petersburg, in your case."

Tarkovski shook his head. "You know nothing about the Russian soul, Mr. Eekhaut. Don't assume you will ever understand the Russian soul. You do not even understand your own." He sat up. "Can I help you gentlemen with anything else? Lists of people employed by our companies? You have a search warrant, I assume?"

"We'll leave it at that," Van Gils said. He rose. "Mr. Tarkovski. Thank you for your time."

"No problem, Inspector. Return whenever you seem fit. But do call in advance and make an appointment. I'm always eager to help the Dutch police."

"I'm surprised, though," Van Gils said, "that at no point did you ask us why we were here. You didn't seem interested to know the purpose of our visit."

Tarkovski frowned again. "Really? I didn't? Maybe I'm not interested in police business. I'm used to it. We're foreign, and so the AIVD is always on our tail. It's not a problem, though, gentlemen. You ask questions, I provide answers. Isn't that enough?"

"No, Mr. Tarkovski," Van Gils said, "that's never enough."

As they were crossing the street toward the car, Van Gils said to Eekhaut, "Arrogant little bastard. Laughing in our faces. I wanted to punch him. Really did. But I can't, of course. I'd get in trouble with everybody: Internal Affairs, Dewaal, the director, maybe even the public prosecutor."

"We didn't have anything sensible to ask him, did we?" Eekhaut said.

"And even so, he had nothing interesting to say. But it appears you know nothing of the Russian soul, do you? And what else did he say? Why was he talking about your soul?"

"Russians," Eekhaut said. "Always melodramatic. It means nothing."

"It doesn't? Then why do you look so preoccupied?"

17

"HE DIDN'T HAVE THE list," Adam Keretsky said, in English. And then again, as if he feared he hadn't been clear enough, in the same Cambridge English: "Parnow doesn't have the list."

Monet frowned. He had understood the Russian the first time. "And the young man?"

"Oh, he won't be a problem anymore," Keretsky said. "You can rest assured of that. But the list, that problem is not yet solved."

"He couldn't find the list?"

Keretsky consulted Parnow, in Russian. "He found the list," he then said to Monet, "but the guy's girlfriend returned unexpectedly and there was a fight, between her and my man here, and unfortunately she fled, taking the list with her."

Monet considered this. "This means the problem is not yet solved."

"It isn't," Keretsky said. "Well, it is solved in part. A main obstacle has been removed. The infamous and unfortunate young man is no longer a problem. That's what you wanted, didn't you?"

"We wanted the list back, Mr. Keretsky. That's what the whole thing was about, as you may remember. We wanted to avoid the list getting into the wrong hands and in the newspapers. What happened to the thief was less of my concern."

"I see," Keretsky said, not without irony. "You are a businessman. As am I. Plans and contracts matter to us more than human lives. That makes us successful. Now, as I assess the situation, it seems to me the list is hardly important or harmful as long as there's no believable messenger to back it up, so to speak. Are we not clear on that? No credible messenger to deliver this list to the authorities."

"Or the press."

"Or the police. I've had the police visiting me already. Some detectives from the AIVD. But not, it seemed to me, in connection with this affair. One of the detectives was very rude. He seemed unaware of the basic rules of diplomacy. Well, I'll deal with that later. Now, about the girlfriend. The one that got away with the list."

"Yes?"

"Parnow described her as one of those young people, so prominent in this decadent city, nurtured by godless anarchy and cheap drugs. She is, in simple terms, probably a junkie. Which makes her less than believable for, let's say, the authorities or the press. Question: what do we have to fear from her?"

You're an idiot, Monet thought. *I have more to fear from imported upstarts like you than from a hundred girlfriends of Van Boer et al. You're so shamefully careless because you assume nobody can touch you. You're a big player in Russia, where the police and politicians are in bed with you. But the rules are different here. And they sure are different from us.*

But he concentrated on the matter at hand. There was no point in getting angry at Keretsky. Keretsky had always been a problem, but of a different magnitude than the lost list. At some point he would have to deal with Keretsky, but that moment was not on the horizon yet. "So long," Monet said, "as that list can fall into the wrong hands— any hands but our own, that is—and as long as thousands of hands can make thousands of copies for any newspaper here or abroad, we have a major problem. I had hoped your assistant would have solved the problem, but it seems he didn't."

"My . . . assistant will leave no stone unturned to find the young lady, rest assured, Mr. Monet. But if she copies that list today, as you say, and distributes it, there is nothing we can do. I remain convinced, however, that she is a junkie with an unlikely story and as such is hardly believable. If she goes to a newspaper, she'll end up making a fool of herself and maybe finding herself in jail on a charge of libel. And that will be the end of your problem."

"I can try to find out where she's hiding," Monet said. Over the years, he had established a network of corrupt police officers and low-level servants within the department of justice. An old network of obligations and promises and money well spent. Keretsky needed no explanation. He knew all about that kind of network.

Monet glanced at Parnow. The Russian kept his hands folded like a mortuary assistant. *How apt*, Monet thought. *This man whom I wouldn't even notice in the street shot a young man dead but couldn't manage to subdue a girl.*

But Parnow wasn't his most pressing problem. His problem was the list. What would he do if it surfaced in a newspaper? He would deny its authenticity. He would call out leftist political parties trying to disrupt the prized political equilibrium. Trying to besmirch the business community, the backbone of Dutch civil society. He would threaten lawsuits for every last euro these newspapers owned.

There was one alternative, though. A risky alternative. He could point the finger at Van Tillo. He would incriminate Van Tillo and Vanheul and the whole PDN. Accuse them of blackmail, fraud, slander. He would deny ever having given a penny to the PDN. Nobody would find any trace anyway. There had never been any direct transfer of funds, not officially. The money had passed through a chain of companies and organizations, well hidden from view. Sometimes even through foreign banks. Occasionally, he'd even given cash. As far as he was concerned, there'd be no trace unless someone dug really, really deep.

There was only the list. And it didn't prove anything.

So why was he worried?

Because his reputation would be harmed anyway. Because part of the press and part of the public would associate his name and those of his companies with right-wing parties and illegal political financing. However popular Van Tillo's party was, financing it would not go down well with a part of Dutch society. People who mattered to Monet. People in circles where he wanted to appear ethical, as someone who wasn't averse to progressive ideas.

So by preference his choice was to cover up the existence of the list. He wanted a shot at being nominated as a board member in one of the big-seven Dutch companies at the top of the Dutch business world, but for that he had to remain untarnished. Even among people who, in private, were no strangers to Van Tillo's political ideas.

But that was Dutch society for you: based on illusion and deceit.

"My people are at your disposal," Keretsky told him. But it was clear the Russian wasn't very happy with the situation.

"We appreciate the sentiment, Mr. Keretsky," Monet said. And he wondered, *Why can't I find in Amsterdam, in the whole of Amsterdam, a single professional at least as effective as Parnow?*

Of course, he could. There were enough shady characters around who would, for a handful of cash, help him get rid of any problem. But then his name would be implicated as a contractor, even if he found an intermediary. There was always a risk. Parnow wouldn't spill the beans because of his relationship with Keretsky. Neither would the Russian. He was safe with both.

So they were going to have to solve his problem.

18

CHIEF SUPERINTENDENT DEWAAL WASN'T happy. "Pieter Van Boer, Ms. Van Tillo. This is his picture. Look at it. Taken in better times, I'll admit. But I'm sure you recognize him, don't you? He was murdered this morning here in Amsterdam. City center. He worked for you. Here, in these offices. And you tell me you have no idea who he is?"

Hendrika Van Tillo squinted at the picture. "Kees," she said to Vanheul. "Kees, we do know this young man, don't we? He works here, indeed, Chief Superintendent. He does. Or did, since you tell me he was murdered. I used to see him around here, but I didn't know him personally. You know how it goes in an organization of this size, don't you? There are a hundred or so people working here. Some just part-time. I know all their faces, but I don't necessarily know them all personally. I'm out often, on the road, meeting people, attending all sorts of public functions. Ask Kees. Mr. Vanheul is better acquainted with the staff. He's here more often than I. Kees?"

Vanheul leaned in, because his eyesight wasn't good and he wasn't wearing his glasses. "Van Boer? Yes. He wasn't here yesterday. Nor today, I've been told. Seems to have vanished all of a sudden. His colleagues had no idea where he was. He left no note, no message, as to what his plans were. Didn't call in sick either. Nobody was worried, because he's—was—the . . . how shall I put it, the artistic type, who couldn't always be bothered to show up on time, or even every day."

"When did anyone last see him? Friday?" Dewaal lowered the picture. Eekhaut remained standing by the door of Van Tillo's office as if he were merely a bystander.

"I guess so," Van Tillo said. "I don't remember seeing him at all last week. Can't say I did. Like I said, Chief Superintendent, I'm not in this office that much."

"Well, neither am I," Vanheul said.

"And there was no reason why his absence would cause somebody to worry about him?"

"Not at all."

Eekhaut was merely observing. But he knew they were lying, both of them, or if not really lying then not telling the whole truth either. Maybe just a very small portion of the truth. He kept his mouth shut and studied their body language. They felt more or less comfortable, not because they knew nothing or were innocent, but because they were sure the police had nothing on them. And would find nothing.

He finally decided on a change of role. He leaned in as if wanting to win her confidence and said softly, "Ms. Van Tillo, are you responsible for the death of Pieter Van Boer?"

Her head swiveled sharply in his direction, not unlike an antiaircraft turret on a battleship. Aiming right at him, hatred in her eyes.

Oh yes, he thought. *Hatred.*

Then she turned to Dewaal. "Chief Superintendent, could you explain to me why this individual is accusing me of involvement in the murder of Mr. Van Boer? Is he one of your people?"

Dewaal remained calm. "Chief Inspector Eekhaut is a new member of my team. He has been detached by the Belgian police to my department. So, ma'am, in that sense, yes, he is one of my people."

"Does that mean, Chief Superintendent, that I have to answer his ridiculous question?"

Before Dewaal could reply, Eekhaut intervened. "I think I posed a simple and very clear question, Ms. Van Tillo. I'm a police detective, and if you have any remarks concerning me or the way I conduct an inquiry, I would ask you to address me in person. Are you responsible for the death of Pieter Van Boer?"

Van Tillo breathed fire. Or she would have done so if humanly possible and reduced Eekhaut to ashes. "Mr. Eekhaut, in this country, politicians are treated with respect by civil servants, including the police.

I will let that slide, for now, on account of you being foreign. But the fact remains that you show considerable lack of tact and diplomacy. No, Mr. Eekhaut, we had nothing whatsoever to do with the death of Mr. Van Boer."

He looked her straight in the eye and said, "Thank you, Ms. Van Tillo, for this clarification."

Dewaal said, "We will have to talk to some of your colleagues. And we want to look at the office of Mr. Van Boer."

"You'll need a warrant for that, Chief Superintendent, as you well know. At least for the office. Kees will escort you and find Van Boer's colleagues for you. Feel free to ask them any questions you want."

"Thank you, ma'am," Dewaal said stiffly. She rose and gestured at Eekhaut to follow her.

Interviewing the colleagues gave them no new information. Van Boer was considered a quiet and hardworking assistant. Good with words but not engaged in social interaction. Nobody had expected anything like this. A murder? They didn't know anything about his private life, but who would want to kill such a nice young man?

19

OUTSIDE AGAIN, ON THE Herengracht, and while walking all the way back to the car that was parked a few hundred meters down the street, Dewaal remained silent. "Come on," Eekhaut finally said. "Get it out of your system. I know you want to."

She stopped and turned to him. Angry. Really pissed off. He hadn't expected otherwise. First with Keretsky, now with Van Tillo. He couldn't help it. He couldn't remain silent, couldn't keep his trap shut when he was faced with people he believed were lying through their teeth. He knew what would happen next: his boss would be angry with him. It had happened with all his bosses. And he'd given them plenty of reason for being pissed off at him. She wouldn't be the exception.

"Is this," she finally said, "some personal tactic, your way of getting on everybody's nerves? And embarrassing your colleagues in the meantime? Twice in one day, that must be a personal record. Not for you, but for me."

"Yes," Eekhaut said, "that's what it is, my successful personal method for making people like Keretsky and Van Tillo uncomfortable. It's one of the reasons I'm here. The main reason, actually."

Dewaal managed to contain her fury. "Keep in mind that I can send you back anytime I want. Tell me why I shouldn't."

"So you said earlier. But there's little you can do. They don't want me back. And they lied."

"They lied? Who did?"

"Van Tillo and her secretary. They were lying."

"Of course they were! That was clear even to me. They know something. I don't need your Flemish genius for that! And even less your boorish manners!"

"So you know. When I put the question to her, I knew for certain. They know something about Van Boer they don't want to share with us."

"Do you really think you can accuse one of Holland's most famous politicians of murder? Because they're holding back on something?"

"Did I? Accuse her of murder?"

"You did."

"Can't remember . . ."

"You said—"

"I know what I said." He turned his attention to the canal. A passing postal van got in his way. Since his arrival, he had seen almost nothing of Amsterdam. But he had been here for only two days. Two days and already disliked by his boss. "I asked Van Tillo if she was responsible for the death of Van Boer, not if she killed him herself. I wouldn't expect that. Can't we have a drink somewhere? Corruption and lies make me thirsty."

Dewaal wanted to object but changed her mind. "Let's find a terrace. But no alcohol."

He looked at her. "As you wish, ma'am. I'll do with a soda."

She looked up at him. He was nearly a head taller than she. Standing next to each other forced her to look up at him at all times. He found that interesting. She in her fashionable clothes and he in his much less glamorous suit.

"Or a sparkling water. Anything. Any kind of water without a fish in it."

He followed her. They found a café with a terrace and sat down. A blond girl in jeans and a sweater asked them what they'd like to drink. Dewaal looked at the girl, then at Eekhaut, and all of a sudden started to snicker. The girl looked at her, surprised. Eekhaut intervened: "Two coffees, please. Or a cappuccino, Chief? No, just two plain coffees."

The girl left. "Damn it," Dewaal said, wiping tears from the corner of her eyes. "So much for my reputation. Damn you, Eekhaut."

"That's all right," he said. He knew where that was coming from. The sudden hilarity. Nerves. Tension. And him on top of that.

She said softly, "Asking Van Tillo if she had something to do with that murder. You wouldn't do badly on a talk show, confronting her like that."

"I'll pass if you don't mind."

Her smile disappeared again. Instead, she looked grim. "I don't want you to tell the others about this. At the office. I'm very serious. Not a word."

He knew what she meant. "Isn't that what you ask a suspect, under these circumstances? If they're involved in the matter?"

She frowned again at him. "Van Tillo isn't a suspect until I say otherwise. Or till the prosecutor says otherwise. Till then, she is merely somebody we interrogate in relationship to an ongoing investigation. Only because Van Boer worked for her."

In his opinion, all politicians were suspect. He'd gotten to know a lot of them in Brussels. Most of them were disreputable and dishonest, focused on their career, their popularity. "I wanted to see her reaction. People are most vulnerable when you attack them unexpectedly."

"Well, you managed that all right. You got your reaction. She almost killed you with that look."

The coffee arrived. Eekhaut paid the girl. "She clearly has absolutely no sense of humor," he said.

"You haven't seen anything yet. You got out alive. She usually eats her opponents, skin, bones, and all. Till nothing is left of them. You were lucky. You should watch one of her television debates. Pure entertainment. She's capable of anything once she's cornered."

"I don't watch TV," he said. He added cream and sugar to his coffee. She drank it black. *Your stomach will be grateful for that, in a couple of years*, he thought. Black coffee, yogurt, fruit. No wonder she was skinny.

"What, no television?"

"Not if I can avoid it. And I always manage to avoid it."

"How do you keep tabs on what happens in the world?"

"Whatever is on TV is badly informed entertainment, at best. Spectacular news and the most provincial items. Waste of time. Whatever is really happening, I learn through other means. And even then, I'm careful about drawing conclusions."

"You mean the internet?"

"Books, reputable magazines, and talking to informed people. And yes, sure, the internet. Television will very quickly become the medium of the past. People aren't taking it seriously anymore, not even for entertainment. Full of junk, really."

"So you do watch."

"Occasionally I'm tempted to watch, to see if it's all that bad. And then I discover time and again that it is. But let's talk about our investigation."

"We haven't gotten far yet."

"A body, a bullet, a missing girlfriend, no motive, no murderer, no witnesses," Eekhaut said.

"We have a possible motive."

"Do we?"

"Van Boer's political connections," Dewaal said. "Left-radical, engaged, and occasionally dangerous to the conservatives."

"That's rather vague. Won't get you far. So he had a lot of friends, and he had a lot of enemies. It seems he did something much more dangerous than simply writing left-wing stuff and pointing the finger at the capitalists. This cannot be merely ideological."

"You're right, I guess," she admitted. "We're nowhere still."

"Why was he working for the PDN?"

"We don't know. He didn't tell me anything about working there. He was busy, as always, and now it appears he was engaged in writing propaganda exactly contrary to his political beliefs. That doesn't make sense."

"He wasn't there because he shared their beliefs. On the contrary."

"Apparently not, no," Dewaal said.

"And he wasn't there because he needed a job and couldn't find anything else, either. Working there ran counter to everything he believed in."

"He would have had difficulty finding a job anywhere, but nevertheless—"

"He was there," Eekhaut said, "because he was spying on them."

She shook her head but said nothing.

"You don't agree?" he asked.

"He wasn't working for us, if that's what you're thinking."

"No, I wasn't thinking that at all."

"So he was working alone. Solo. That's what you're implying?"

"Probably. He discovered something that made it worth sacrificing—what, a year? Working in that place for a whole year? And now he's dead. If we find out what he was looking for and what he was probably doing there, we might find out who killed him."

"Maybe he found something he could use against Van Tillo," Dewaal said. "Something he found just before he was killed. Which made killing him such an urgent matter that a contract killer was sicced on him."

"That's possible. But then, why didn't he surface with that information? He could have contacted you."

"If that's what happened, Van Tillo and Vanheul are part of the cover-up. And maybe they even ordered the murder."

"So my question wasn't entirely—"

She wasn't going to spare his feelings. "That wasn't your call to make, Walter."

"If you want to play around in politics, then it was. I grabbed the wrong end of the stick, that much I'll agree to. But I never intend to play fair when politics are concerned."

"And where do you stand, when politics are concerned? I need to know."

He looked at his hands, not because he didn't want her to see his eyes when he answered her, but because he needed time to consider the right formulation. "I stand on the side of the little guy whose life is fucked up time and again by all those who are richer and bigger and faster, the sort of people whose only intention is to get even faster and richer. I don't care what color that little guy's skin is or where he or she came from or what god he or she believes in. I care only for justice and in decency. Does that suffice as an answer?"

"I would guess that's a good description of a police officer."

"It seldom is. Most police officers see crime as a personal deviation from some socially accepted norm—a norm decided by those same rich and powerful people I was talking about. They hardly ever see the broader picture, of a society run wild. What kind of police officer are you, Ms. Dewaal?"

"I liked you this morning. For a moment, I thought, There's a man I would want to follow down some dark and dangerous alley. There's a man who would protect me, without considering his own safety. There's also a man who can and will make the same assumptions as I do."

"I try to stay away from dark alleys."

"But now, in this moment, I realize you're much more dangerous than anything that might lurk in one of those dark alleys."

"Am I?"

"Yes, you are. You're an idealist. And that's unacceptable in a police officer, because an idealist will always ask those same questions of people like Van Tillo. But, on the other hand, that may be a good thing too. I shouldn't have been angry, just because you did what you do best: denounce the untouchables." She sipped her coffee. "You may also have understood by now that you're not functioning along the lines of your assignment, as it was originally intended. Russians and Keretsky and communication between neighboring countries. Don't fret about that, as I'm sure you won't. I need an assistant I can trust absolutely, someone who asks questions no one else dares ask."

"That won't be a problem."

"All right," she said. "But why *do* I trust you? I don't even know you. You come here, from Belgium, spat out by your own hierarchy, and I decide to trust you at once."

"I have that effect on women. Almost exclusively on women."

"Keep that sort of talk to yourself. I want to involve you in this investigation because you're an outsider. You know nothing of Dutch politics. That's why you're not bothered by people like Van Tillo. Nobody has tried to bribe you, you have no past in this country. That puts you one step ahead of my colleagues in the office. And I want everything we're discussing here, on this terrace, to remain between us alone."

"You take your whole life with you, Chief Superintendent Dewaal," Eekhaut said. "Everywhere you go. That's what I learned. Every time a human being ends up dead in a gutter, a child gets raped, a woman's body is dredged from a canal, each time you take your life and your experiences with you. And nothing stays behind on this terrace."

"That reminds me of Breukeling," she said. "A lugubrious idea, isn't it? He too took his life everywhere he went. And that killed him in the end."

"How is that investigation progressing?"

She made a face. "Internal Affairs is occupied with scrutinizing what was left of the bomb. I got a call just before coming here. The bomb was put together with bits and pieces that you can buy anywhere—exactly the sort of device our friends on the other side of the fence go wild for. Whenever they want to close the deal on blackmailers and smugglers and people they in general don't like."

"But why Breukeling?"

"Internal Affairs isn't concerned about that question anymore. So they tell me. Look, Walter: Breukeling was a street cop for most of his career. Like many of his generation. When you walk the beat day in day out, it's difficult to keep your hands clean. He probably didn't. But he was never caught doing anything irregular. Made a lot of enemies, though, probably because he accepted money from the wrong kind of people and didn't return the favor often enough. Internal Affairs assumes he was still doing that, collecting an extra income. And then someone wanted to put an end to that collaboration."

"And the memory stick? No sign of that?"

"No."

She fell silent and looked at her empty cup.

He knew their conversation wasn't finished. Not by a long shot.

20

"The nerve of that Belgian!" Hendrika Van Tillo said. Her bosom heaved out of pure frustration. "Kees! We can't allow this to happen. We have to take measures. Who do we know in the police?"

"This is AIVD, Hendrika," Vanheul said stiffly. "This isn't some local cop. These aren't ordinary police officers. This is AIVD, and we have to be careful."

"AIVD, my ass! We know somebody there as well. Call the ministry. Who else is there? Anyone from the old team? Anyone we can rely on to keep these cops in check?"

"I'll make the call. But I don't think it's a good idea."

"I'll tell you whether it's a good idea or not. You do trust my judgment, don't you? A Belgian, on top of that! Comes into my own office and accuses me of murder!"

"Strictly speaking he didn't."

"No? Are you out of your frigging mind? What did you think he was doing?"

"He asked if you were responsible for the murder of Van Boer. That is, legally speaking, entirely different. He knows very well you didn't shoot that boy yourself."

"How do we know he was shot?"

"We read it in the newspapers."

Van Tillo thought about this.

"Furthermore, his question isn't that absurd, Hendrika. After all, Van Boer did work here."

"The chief prosecutor of Amsterdam," Van Tillo said. "We have met professionally. I'm probably the one who got him his job in the first place. A man without any redeeming qualities, but he'll listen to us. Call him, Kees."

"I will." Vanheul knew when not to contradict his boss.

21

UPON THEIR RETURN, ALEXANDRA Dewaal disappeared into her office, and Eekhaut began sorting through the mountain of files and folders that had suddenly materialized on his desk. He felt obliged to do his duty and read all of it, which hadn't happened in a long time. He began surveying the intimate relationships between extremist organizations on the European front, a subject he wasn't at all familiar with.

Just as he was not familiar with Russian oligarchs.

What he found was an intricate labyrinth of the most diverse ideologies and people inspired by different religions. Most of them could be discounted as brainless extremists and the fundamentally maladapted. About ten percent of them were important in an international context and thus potentially dangerous. Some of them seemed democratic on the outside. Partij Dierbaar Nederland was one of them. But their file contained not much more than a few short biographies and a list of points of view.

Half an hour later, Dewaal was at his desk. "A second body has been found by local police, a young Surinamese," she said. "Possibly the same weapon. There seems to be no connection with Van Boer, except this remarkable fact: the address Van Boer gave to the PDN as his own was a fake. It was the address of this young man who now is dead."

"Which goes to prove again that Van Tillo is connected with these murders," Eekhaut said. He spoke quietly, so nobody but Dewaal would hear him. He leaned back, his arm over the backrest of his chair.

"Too weak as evidence as yet."

"What's the victim's profile?"

"The Surinamese young man probably knew Van Boer personally, but we don't know that. No witnesses, I assume, as earlier. And no leads. The police are canvassing the neighborhood, but first reports say nobody noticed anything. They'll keep me informed."

She left him alone again. He returned to his documents, read for a couple of hours, got more confused owing to the sheer abundance of material, looked for and found some coffee that came in a plastic cup and was barely drinkable, and observed some female officers working in the common room. Nobody talked to him; nobody bothered him. At four thirty he called it a day, stored the files in a locker, and left the building.

He slowly walked toward Utrechtsestraat. He tried to remember what he had had for lunch, remembered it consisted of a sandwich from the cafeteria, and went looking for something more substantial. For a restaurant that promised decent food at a decent price. Lebanese fast food again? No, that would become a bad habit. Today he wanted more quality for his money.

Maybe he would have to cook in his apartment like he'd done often enough in Leuven. The apartment came supplied with the necessary kitchen utensils. But it wouldn't be the same as eating out.

Not tonight anyway. He still hadn't bought any groceries. He remembered the fridge from the morning. It had been almost empty.

Slowly, he strolled in the direction of Rembrandtplein, crossed at Muntplein, and walked into Kalverstraat, where tourists were calling it a day and retreating to their hotels. He realized he should let a few people know he'd arrived safely in Amsterdam. Esther's parents, perhaps, whom he hadn't seen in months. His two nephews, with whom he had even less contact. A phone call would be enough. Or he would send a postcard, why not? That's what a common tourist would do. But his family, what was left of it, was a vague presence on his horizon. Things had been different when Esther was still alive. She'd kept the family together. Even during those last weeks, when she'd been ill. After that, he had no longer bothered.

Finally, he arrived at the Spui, where he found a large Indonesian restaurant. It was almost deserted. He sat down at a table.

A young man brought the menu. "English?" he inquired. Eekhaut shook his head. "Dutch," he said. He received a Dutch menu that turned out to be complex. He remembered having dinner here in the past and knew he had to order meat and vegetables separately. And not order too much, given the large portions they served.

The food came almost at once. A small Indonesian *rijsttafel*, with all the ingredients on one plate and only a side order of veggies. He needed the better part of thirty minutes to get through it all, accompanied by a beer. At the table next to him, a couple of young Americans had ordered dinner for two and couldn't figure out who was going to eat all that food.

Afterward, feeling satiated, he walked over the Spui again and looked at the Athenaeum bookshop and then at the American Book Center, both closed. His first day off he would spend here, but he'd have to buy a bookcase first.

Pieter Van Boer was on his mind. He thought about the boy's girlfriend, who was now probably on the run from a killer. Her clothes still in the apartment, her life disrupted, her future stolen from her. Maybe she'd be found in one of the canals tomorrow or next week. Maybe she wouldn't be found at all.

There was nothing he could do about that. He had to wait this one out, hoping she would turn herself in.

He sat on a bench and took his phone out of his pocket. Punched the number on the business card Dewaal had given him.

"Yes?" she said.

"Sorry to disturb you," he said.

"Oh, it's you. No problem."

"I was thinking."

"Good initiative. Keep that up. We'll go a long way if you keep on thinking. About what?"

"We may need to have another look at Van Boer's apartment, maybe tomorrow. We ought to be able to find the girlfriend."

"I had that in mind too," she said. "That's why you called me?"

"Yeah," he said.

"All right. Then let's do it tomorrow. Have a good night."

He couldn't remember why he really wanted to phone her.

22

ONLY WHEN HE ENTERED the Absinthe did he remember. He'd wanted to ask Dewaal why his presence earlier that day had been so important. Why had she taken him along to the scene of the murder? He had entered her professional life only just recently, coming out of nowhere. She had no idea what sort of police officer he was. She'd read his file, and there was nothing favorable in it. She didn't know whether she could trust him. Moreover, she had a dozen people in the office she could just as easily have brought along. All of them experts. Why had she picked him? And in connection with a case that had very little bearing on his function in the Bureau.

Had she chosen him because she feared the case would be a bit too sensitive for her colleagues, as she'd suggested earlier? Did she have a private agenda? Or privileged information? Did she have professional secrets he wouldn't even know to recognize? He had wanted to look into her head, but that was a privilege she hadn't yet allowed. It was much too early for that.

Or had she chosen him because he really was the one who could be trusted in that dark alley, because he was an idealist who never doubted himself?

Whatever the case, Van Boer might have been her personal informant, and perhaps she knew very well what his project had been.

No, that much she had denied. And he believed her. She had confided in him, and so he was sure he could believe her. She hadn't known what Van Boer was up to. His death wasn't her fault. He couldn't imagine why she would want to keep the other members of her team away from the murder scene.

There was nothing unusual about detectives having their own informants and networks. If you wanted information, anything at all, you needed them. It was always a matter of personal trust. Or loyalty. Sometimes things went south. An investigation got fouled up by information from an untrustworthy source. Sometimes the detective got hooked on the promise of information. He assumed none of that was true here.

He ordered another absinthe. It was a foul drink, disappearing much too smoothly down his throat. And guaranteed to obliterate his past. As if he needed that. As if he needed anything to separate him from his past.

Yes, there was a past he wanted to obliterate.

He looked up toward the counter.

There she was again, the woman. She was clearly not an incidental tourist. He was glad about that. He would speak to her. But not yet. Not at once. He couldn't. Tired, and one drink too many. He would make a fool of himself if he attempted a conversation. He would talk nonsense and mess up the approach. He knew he would.

And she was with somebody. With two men, even. Were they the same men as before? He didn't know. He had hardly looked at them the other day.

His attention was more focused now. A glass of absinthe, a woman. That was enough.

And then, suddenly, she sat in front of him at his table. She was alone. She wore black. The only color about her was her lipstick. And she spoke to him as if they'd been friends for some time. "The only thing wrong with this bar," she said, "is that there's no decent jazz. I prefer that old southern jazz, Louisiana-style. You don't hear that much anymore."

"Something can be done about that," he said. Or at least, that's what he thought he said. "Can't you ask the bartender if he could play some jazz?"

"I'm Linda, by the way," she said. But she didn't extend her hand. "You were here before, weren't you?"

That made him smile. She had noticed him, after all. She had remembered him. "Is it so remarkable when people return?"

"Yes," she said. "You don't see many regulars here. Except for me and two, maybe three people, all of whom I know personally. This is no ordinary bar. What we drink here is not beer. It's *absinthe*. An accursed drink." She smiled. Her hair was dark brown but her eyes pale blue. He very much liked that combination.

"I'm Walter."

"You from Flanders?"

"Is it that obvious?"

"The accent. I like Flanders. Love going there. Bruges, Ghent, Antwerp, Ostend. I feel much freer in Flanders than in Holland. In the sense of . . ." She snapped her fingers and glanced upward as if looking for meaning. "You know what I mean."

"You probably know more about Flanders than I do about Holland. I've been to Amsterdam twice, maybe three times before."

"I only go there on holidays. I don't travel professionally."

"What is your non-traveling profession?"

"I'm a management assistant for a large company here in Amsterdam. You?"

"Government," he said.

That smile again, telling him she accepted the banality of that description without reserve. But she seemed genuinely interested in what he did. "Government? That sounds ominous. A diplomat? A spy? Or do you collect taxes?"

"Police."

"That's odd. Here in Amsterdam? As a Belgian?"

"Collaboration between Belgium and the Netherlands concerning international crime prevention."

"Oh," she said. "Then it's political as well."

"More or less."

She looked at him, more serious than a few moments ago. "Politics."

"It's mainly about extreme political parties, religious extremists, that sort of thing. Troublemakers, really. But troublemakers with a considerable and possibly dangerous political agenda. And the organizations who pay their bills. And the usual suspects: neo-Nazis admiring Hitler a bit too much, or sects with a tendency toward megalomania."

She eyed his drink.

He followed her gaze to his almost empty glass. "Can I offer you one of these?" he asked. "Or anything else?"

"I don't want to stay out late."

"Have to get home on time on account of the parents?"

She grinned. "A policeman with a sense of humor. Where will this end? We only see them on TV. And you're not in uniform. Do you occasionally wear a uniform, Walter?"

"Never."

"Good," she said. "I'll have another absinthe. Against my better judgment."

He got the drinks at the bar, paid, and walked back. "Are we here because we have something artistic in common?"

"No," she said, "because we are both into self-destruction. Isn't that what was said of drinkers of absinthe in earlier days? Poe, Baudelaire? That their addictions destroyed whatever creative gifts they had? Addiction to drink, opium, women, literature?"

Nice, he thought. A dark, intelligent woman in a bar in the heart of Amsterdam telling him something interesting about dark poets like Poe and Baudelaire. Things could have turned out much worse this evening. He was most intrigued by her long, slender, tawny hands. As if they had seen a lot of sun this summer, like her face and arms. Maybe she'd been on a boat, somewhere in Spain or Greece. Maybe she had a garden. He opted for the former. She looked like she knew somebody who had a sailing yacht in some subtropical country.

He felt warm because of the alcohol. It was a dangerous feeling. It told him the world and he were at peace with one another. That nothing would disturb that peace. It went counter to his knowledge of how the world functioned.

"How long have you been in Amsterdam?" she asked.

"Second day."

"Oh. And already out in the night on your own? Quite an adventurous spirit."

"I don't live far from here. And not far from my office either."

"That's nice," she said. "Most places in the center are expensive. A lot of nuisances as well. Drugs, prostitution, rowdies. Not during the day. The rats come out at night. But to you that's not a problem, I assume."

"You live around here too?"

"Yep. But I wasn't born here. I'm from Utrecht. That separates me from the typical citizen of this city. And by God, they make sure you know it! Well, whatever. I've been living here for the better part of three years."

She looked around. "I had hoped to find a friend here tonight, but she didn't show up. Instead, I get to meet you. Funny how things turn out, isn't it?"

"Is it?"

"You believe in coincidence, Walter?"

"I only believe in people. In their bad and good qualities. Anything else is metaphysics. There might be something like a coincidence, as I occasionally witness in my job, but it doesn't have any deeper meaning."

"So there is no higher plan, no real meaning in life?"

From Poe and Baudelaire to deeper meaning and metaphysics. Maybe this was the absinthe speaking. "In what sense?"

"In the sense of something that inspires and gives meaning to life and existence," she said. "A creator, maybe."

"I prefer not to believe in a creator."

"You prefer to disbelieve."

He smiled. "Yes. You could say that. The meaning of life is life itself, that's what I believe. There is no deeper meaning. Assume the contrary—there's something after life—and chaos would ensue. And fear. I prefer finality. A final and unique life. A random universe, without meaning or any sort of master plan."

She rose. "I would like to discuss this more deeply and so on, but I need to get home. And God or whatever deeper meaning there is to life is not going to wait for me. And neither is he going to do my job in the morning."

"I can find a taxi and take you home if you want."

"No, that won't be necessary."

He looked at his watch. "You're going to take the tram? At this hour?"

"No, I meant, I'm old enough to get a taxi on my own, Walter. Do I get to see you again tomorrow?"

"Of course," he said. "I'll try to be here."

"I'm sure you will," she said. She had brought an elegant woolen overcoat with her, he noticed. And then she was gone, after a last glance over her shoulder. A meaningful glance. One of those really meaningful glances.

The short walk to his apartment helped clear his head a bit. He had no trouble finding the keyhole and ascending the stairs. He forgot to turn on the lights, but the stairwell wasn't all that dark, with light coming in from what appeared to be a roof window. Then a shadow closed in. He reached for his gun and felt ridiculous at once. Toon, his neighbor, stood on the landing. "Sorry to scare you," the old man said. "Can I offer you a drink? Or is it too late? No, it is never too late to have a drink with a neighbor."

Eekhaut wanted to go to sleep, but he couldn't just ignore the man, who was old and probably lonely and wanted just a little company. *I'll be that man in a couple of years,* Eekhaut thought. "All right," he said. "Let's have a last drink."

"Good! I have some jenever like you never drank before. Not where you come from, anyway."

Toon's apartment was what Eekhaut expected: sad and messy and at the same time cozy. The furniture dated probably from before the war. Toon gestured toward an old horsehair coach, and Eekhaut hoped the man had neither dogs nor cats. He didn't see any anyway. "Be right back," Toon said. He disappeared in the back of the apartment and returned almost immediately with a tall brown earthenware bottle and two small glasses.

"Taste this first," Toon said.

Eekhaut imitated his host and emptied the glass in one gulp. It stung in his throat for a short moment, but it was a gentle sting, a smooth caress, followed by a warm feeling.

"Well?" Toon said.

"It is . . . very special," Eekhaut said. The jenever tasted like nothing he had tasted before, almost like a clear liquid honey.

"Tears of the Bride," Toon said. "I don't know where they get those names: *Tears of the Bride*. Made by Wynand Fockink. Have a look at his shop if you have the time, Mister . . ."

"Eekhaut."

"Mr. Eekhaut, I am an old pensioner, but I bought this apartment fifty years ago, which allows me to remain in the heart of Amsterdam. I don't need any luxuries, but I allow myself a bit of this heavenly drink, now and then. Why shouldn't I?"

The apartment needed redecorating and a touch of paint, and perhaps a new carpet, but none of that would happen. Toon was the sort of man who was content with living in his past. And Eekhaut did not begrudge him his freedom. He noted a small plaque on the sideboard. A golden shield. Toon noticed his attention. "Yes," he said. "My badge. Got it from my colleagues when I retired."

"A policeman?"

"Yes, a policeman. A cop. A *pig*. That's what they said to your face on the streets, some of the fine and upstanding citizens of Amsterdam. It may have been a bit of an honorary title for me as well. This is my life. Amsterdam. On the beat for so many years."

Eekhaut couldn't find the appropriate words. Toon ignored his silence and poured another glass.

"Tears of the Bride, you said?"

"Yes. Remember the name: Wynand Fockink. In Pijlsteeg. Close to the Damrak. Heart of the city. Known only to ghosts of my past. Drink up. There's more where this came from. And somebody should drink it besides me."

Eekhaut knew he wasn't going to get to bed for a while.

23

NICK PRINSEN RESTED ON his bed and looked at the ceiling. It wasn't remarkable, even though he had painted it white himself when he came to live in this apartment. Painting it white had been difficult because the previous tenant had applied a dirty dark gray, or perhaps it had become dark gray on account of a succession of tenants who hadn't bothered to paint or clean anything, least of all a ceiling. Nevertheless, whatever the case, it had taken him two buckets of paint and four coats to disguise the gray and return the ceiling to a dignified white.

Not that it mattered in any way. He liked a white ceiling, that was all.

Prinsen had also painted the walls. Not white, but a soft yellow— because that particular color had been cheap. The Pakistani who had sold it to him assured him this paint was of excellent quality, which Prinsen hadn't believed. Not at that price. But it also didn't matter if the paint started to fade after a couple of months. Its patina would add to the apartment's charm.

The apartment had two rooms and a bathroom and a toilet. It measured fifty square meters in all. Which was considerable, in the center of Amsterdam. And at such a modest rent. People with jobs in the center of Amsterdam had no choice but to live small, unless they preferred to commute for an hour from the suburbs. The suburbs would be green and quieter, certainly better for families, but they didn't offer the excitement of living in the center.

His choice had been easy. There was no reason for him to move out of the city.

This sort of problem had never existed in the village where he grew up. When he was a child, he had never known people who had to live in confined circumstances because they needed to be close to their job. In the village, people lived small because they knew themselves to be modest under the gaze of an all-seeing God. Under that gaze, you wouldn't do anything spectacular or exceptional. You didn't build a house larger than your neighbor's. You didn't want to belittle or anger them. You didn't build a house with more windows than your neighbor's. Didn't add anything frivolous to your house, like a pergola. You did nothing that distinguished you from other people.

As a child, however, he had mentioned the large houses he had seen pictures of in books. He had been wondering aloud, as children do, about the wonderful things people did, like traveling to the moon or climbing mountains. "Nobody goes to the moon," his parents told him. Chastised him. "Those are all made-up stories. Vanities. These modern times, they make you crazy. Make you believe in fairy tales. It is impossible to travel to the moon."

His mother had taken him to the rector, an old and frail man who always dressed in black, whose voice was sharp as a razor. He was whatever came closest to a religious leader in the village. "The boy has too much imagination," his mother said. The rector let him sit on an upright chair. The room the rector lived in smelled stale, of old paper and old cigar smoke and old clothes. That air had been lingering in the house for a very long time. This was also how the rector smelled. Everything in the house was dead or reminded Nick Prinsen of dead things. The rector was old. The world he represented was old. What could such a man tell him?

"Why does he have that name?" the rector asked in his razor-like voice. "His Christian name. Nick. *Nick*, isn't it? That's not a Dutch name! Not a name of this people!"

"His father's idea," Prinsen's mother said. "He said it was Dutch."

"His father!" the rector said.

"Yes," said Prinsen's mother. "His father wanted him to be called Nick."

"Nobody in the village is called Nick."

"This is unfortunate," Prinsen's mother said. "Maybe I can have it changed."

"Nothing changes in the world," the rector said. "The things that were and have been will remain so till the end of times. Till this world disappears. Till God's final judgment. He will always be called Nick. And he will bear the shame—"

"It's not a shame to be called Nick," young Prinsen had said, in his sudden anger. You were not supposed to get angry. That was a sin. And certainly not around the rector. Who would have been called a vicar or a *dominee*, but who wanted to distinguish himself from other so-called men of God.

Even children could sin. That's what the rector said. Even children were not innocent. Nobody was innocent. Original sin had all of them in its grip. It *defined* all of them.

The rector said, "This is a shameful thing because nobody is called Nick. It is a name from the modern world, and therefore it is not suited for anyone here. But now it cannot be changed anymore. We understand how difficult it is for a child to have such a name, but that will make the child strong." He leaned toward Nick Prinsen. "This will make you strong, boy," he said. He spoke in a condescending way, but to Nick it sounded like a condemnation.

Prinsen had bought most of the furniture for his apartment from street markets or from people who wanted to get rid of old junk. Things they considered junk but were still usable. He had bought a bed and a wardrobe. Only the mattress on the bed was new, as were the sheets. That sort of thing, he bought new. In the other room, he had a round table and four mismatched chairs. And a cupboard and a bookcase. Everything was free or secondhand.

He didn't care much about furniture. But he spent money on other things that, in a way, could be labeled frivolities. A widescreen TV on a small table in the corner. A laptop on the old desk, attached to a steel ring mounted on the wall, for safety. A compact stereo in the bookcase.

He had entered the twenty-first century. He had left the village behind.

"On Judgment Day," the rector had said, "the Lord Jesus will return and call each and every one of us by his name. But how will he do that with you, Nick, with your strange name and you being such a strange boy? But do not fear. The Lord Jesus will call on all children of the Word and will forgive all of them for their sins. You too, Nick. You too. So be prepared for that moment. And consider yourself warned from now on: you must prepare for the mercy of the Lord, and sin no more."

He had been nine or ten perhaps at the most. There had been no calendar anywhere in the village. Hadn't been for a century or more. Nobody told Nick what a century meant. Nobody told him anything about history as it happened outside the village. The rector was the sole teacher. The rector only taught the Bible. It was the only book children and adults alike had to read.

There was a town close by, but people from the village seldom went there. Sometimes they went and bought clothes or tools or visited the pharmacist. But the village and even the town were a long way from any other part of the country.

Later, after he had fled the village, he couldn't understand how people managed to remain ignorant of the world in the midst of the richest country in Western Europe.

But that was later.

He rose. He no longer wanted to look at the ceiling. It was a morbid habit. He had to get out and live.

He went to the window. His apartment was on the fourth and highest floor, under the roof. The street was crowded as it usually was, except in the first hours of the morning. Even when he closed the window and the curtains, he could hear the continuous sound of the city.

A city. A real city.

There had been only silence in the village. Cows and pigs in the stables and sheep outside, and occasionally a truck or a tractor. But there had been mostly silence.

He didn't miss that silence at all.

WEDNESDAY

Amsterdam, and Then to Leuven

24

EILEEN CALSTER HAD SPENT the night in Maarten's bare and absurdly empty room. It contained no more than a bed, a wardrobe, a small table under the window, and two chairs. The fact that he had two chairs was absurd: he never received visitors. The walls were unadorned. Not even a calendar. The place was devoid of any personality. But to Maarten, this was where he felt at home.

She stretched her skinny arms above her head and watched her brother sleep on the other side of the room, on top of an extra blanket. He had offered her his bed in an offhanded way, not out of kindness, but because it was a logical choice. He had to protect his sister, and that meant giving her shelter. And the bed. For now.

She wanted a shower. There was a shower on the landing. She would have to borrow one of his towels. She would have to buy new clothes later. Returning to her apartment was out of the question, as she realized all too well.

Either the killer or the police would be waiting for her there.

She sat up. Maarten was still asleep. He slept soundly. Had always slept soundly, even as a child. Almost nothing would wake him. She rose. The bed smelled musty, and not because of her. The room smelled unpleasant. She opened the window. The room was situated at the back of the building. It looked out over a collection of ill-kept little city gardens, rooftops, chimneys, walls, and some windows. She wore the T-shirt from the day before, and yes, she needed fresh clothes.

She had her debit card and money in the bank. She would be all right for the time being.

Did the police know who she was?

Of course they knew. All her documents were still in the apartment.

She borrowed a towel and a bottle of shower soap from the wardrobe and went into the corridor for a shower.

Fifteen minutes later, she was back, more or less refreshed. More or less clean. Maarten was awake, sitting on his thin blanket in a Zen-like position, eyes closed.

"You're leaving again today," he said, not opening his eyes. "That's your plan, right? You're not staying."

"I can't stay here, Maarten. That would put both of us in danger. I shouldn't even have come. That was stupid. I should get away from here as fast as possible. Also for your safety."

He said nothing. Just sat there, at some great distance from the world.

"Can't you understand?" she insisted. "These people who were after Pieter, they're no amateurs. They *will* find me if I stay here."

He opened his eyes, focused on her. "And where will you go?"

"To Annelies."

He shrugged. "That's stupid." Then he added, "Why her and not me? If they can find you here, why not there as well? Does that make sense, sis?"

Eileen arranged the sheets on the bed. "I'm sorry I came here, Maarten, that I interrupted your life and all. It was an emergency."

She could have said, that's what family is for. But she didn't. Not under these circumstances.

25

RESTAURANT ZEEDORF IN AMSTERDAM South had an excellent reputation for good French cuisine and an elaborate menu. It served seafood in a traditional Mediterranean fashion, eschewing the use of animal fats. The kitchen staff was of Italian and Sicilian origin, which meant that portions tended to be somewhat bigger than what the pure French cuisine prescribed. The chef came from Flanders, where he had received two Michelin stars. The staff was well-trained and well-paid. Service never disappointed nor failed. You sat in armchairs, and the tables were larger than in the average restaurant. And you didn't have to sit too close to your neighbor. It was cozy, and it was discreet.

So, all in all, a nice upmarket restaurant. But in spite of that, it had a bad reputation, which had nothing to do with its inherent qualities but merely with the fact that the whole of the Amsterdam crime world made it its favorite hangout. It wasn't uncommon to see at its tables a number of people whose mostly unflattering portraits adorned the mug-shot books of the city's criminal division. On occasion, they could be found in the newspapers, where their exploits—recent or past, depending on the zeal of the writer—were commented on in hostile terms. If you needed a "who's who" of Amsterdam crime, you just had to show up here on a regular basis. You would know at once who was talking to whom, and you'd just as easily find out who was in conflict with whom.

The department store adjacent to the restaurant belonged to two brothers of Iranian descent. The restaurant did nothing to attract clients for them, but the brothers couldn't care less. They made most of their money on the underground parking garage beneath the store. Not that they demanded unreasonably large sums from the regular store customers. Their interest lay in the patrons of the restaurant who came in the evenings, after the store was closed. The sort of clients who would want to park their Bentley, Maserati, Porsche, or Hummer somewhere safe. Where it wouldn't be damaged by vandals. Or fitted with a bomb while no one was looking. The Iranian brothers provided safety, for an appropriate sum. So the guests of Restaurant Zeedorf could enjoy their meal in tranquility.

Only on special occasions did Adam Keretsky dine at the restaurant, discreetly, and outside the circle of influence of criminal Amsterdam. In that sense, the restaurant was a sort of free zone. He came here to enjoy his meal quietly. This time would be an exception, however. He was to meet with a number of Russian gentlemen. Tarkovski was good at fitting such events into his boss's busy schedule. Keretsky didn't know of Zeedorf's reputation and didn't care, as he often frequented similar establishments in Moscow and around Russia. The local Russians preferred to meet him here, even if they knew their arrival might be registered by the unavoidable cameras down the street, courtesy of state security. What did it matter? They often waved at the cameras and then enjoyed spending considerable amounts of ill-gotten money on food and Zeedorf's famous wines.

The proprietor of the restaurant guaranteed his customers that there would be no surveillance by outside forces inside the restaurant. No unwanted eyes or ears. And he had set rules. No weapons were allowed inside, you couldn't threaten another customer, and your safety would be guaranteed on the premises. A safe haven for crime lords, as it were. Someone on a disreputable internet forum had once suggested that a heavy bomb in the cellar would rid Amsterdam—and perhaps the whole of the Netherlands—of all organized crime. But until now, no one had come forward to execute this daring and probably suicidal plan, most likely because anyone who could do it successfully was already in the employ of people who patronized the restaurant.

Tarkovski couldn't prevent the proprietor from displaying his knowledge of the French and Italian cuisine, but the young man had insisted on vodka being served. Vodka as aperitif and vodka with the meal. The restaurant, used to complying with the extravagant demands of its upmarket clients, had bought a special stock. And they had managed to acquire several bottles of Yat, surprising even Tarkovski. When the almost frozen bottles arrived on the table, everyone was thrilled. "Keretsky," one of the men said, "this is astonishing. Are you planning to import this divine beverage into this dreary country?"

Keretsky smiled but said nothing. He wasn't here for the vodka. He had other ideas concerning what he wanted to do with Holland. He sat at the head of the table, raised his glass, and wished everybody good health. Glasses were emptied at once. All of them spoke Russian, even those who had been living in the Netherlands for a long time and had become uncertain about the finer points of Russian grammar.

"To Russian friendship," Keretsky said.

Tarkovski looked at his boss after he had drunk the vodka. He knew Keretsky didn't drink all that often. Tarkovski would fill both their glasses with water from a bottle—one exactly like the Yat—that stood on the table between them. Let the others drink, Keretsky had said. Russians who drink too much tend to talk too much as well, often without thinking. That would suit Keretsky well.

"Let's also drink to Holland, this congenial country we like so much," Keretsky said. "And where the Russian hospitality knows no borders." Again, glasses were emptied. Plates with smoked salmon and caviar appeared on the table, accompanied by bread and salted butter.

"And to our new ties with the Dutch financial world," said a man sitting at Tarkovski's right hand, a balding, stout, and badly dressed Muscovite whose name was Osip Bender. He was an expert in car export. "Always been a capitalist, haven't you, Adam," he said. "And now the unashamed co-owner of a Western bank, no less. If that's not Russian irony."

"'Owner' is a bit too grand a word," Keretsky said. "Four and a half percent, that's a long way from ownership. You never fully or even halfway own such a big bank. But the fun thing is, when ownership is a matter of small shareholders, power is diluted. Consequently, when you have around five percent of the shares, you're already a member of the inner circle. It means you can influence the bank for a rather modest sum."

"A modest sum!" someone at the other end of the table said. "How many rubles have you really been spending, Adam?"

"You will read all about it in the newspapers," Keretsky said. "But it is no secret. The money is owned by my companies, by the way. And it's not rubles. It's all in euro, my friends. Exactly what our friends in Holland want."

"That's the way the world is turning, Adam," said a younger man with smooth black hair at the other side of the table. Tarkovski made it his business to know each of the men around the table, but he assumed Keretsky was not much interested in them and would surely not care to remember their names.

"The world," Keretsky said, "is doing us many favors. Or better still, we *will* it to do us many favors. Look at where we came from and where we are now. What kind of place was Russia in the past?"

"A republic," someone said, foolishly.

"An idea," said another. "Something invented by revolutionary Marxists."

Keretsky raised his hand. "Russia was many things, but mainly it used to be a backward country. And it remained a backward country for most of the twentieth century, governed by a perverse ideology and boorish, paranoid leaders. Gentlemen, let's not forget that. It was a country where entrepreneurship could not flourish, unless practiced by corrupt members of the *nomenklatura*. And what is Russia now?"

"The future world leader!"

"Absolutely. Well said. We were feared during the Soviet period, but for the wrong reasons. Our tanks managed to invade Hungary and Czechoslovakia, but that was as far as they would ever get. Even then, they ran out of parts. Our army was cumbersome and corrupt and couldn't even defeat a bunch of Afghan farmers with outdated rifles. Our government only served to suppress the creativity of its citizens and squander the inherent riches of our nation on people who didn't want to work."

"While we—" the black-haired young man started.

"Today we have become a proud nation!" someone shouted.

"A nation that will export its power," Keretsky concluded. "But not like the Americans have been trying for decades. Not by military force. Russia does not need to use military force. It does not have to invade Iraq, not anymore. It does not need a firm fist. Russia is creative. Russians want to work hard and have ambitions. Russia will dominate the economic sphere. With oil, commodities, energy. But also with its financial power."

"Keretsky's utopia!" someone joked. More vodka was consumed. Keretsky remained sober. "But what do I see today?" he bellowed. "What do I see here in Holland? I see a flock of idiots who still trade drugs as their primary means of economic activity. Who think in terms of extortion as a means of regular income. Who prefer to trade in stolen cars. Who trade in illegal arms with third-world countries. Who still dabble in prostitution. As if they still are small-time shopkeepers!"

There was a sudden silence, even among those who had been drinking heavily. More food was brought in. Roasted fish, pasta, vegetables. Bottles of French wine. And more vodka.

"We have to make a living," Bender said. He was sweating profusely and not only because of the vodka. "You cannot blame us for still doing what we have been doing well in the past and what our fathers did before us."

"That is exactly right," Keretsky said. "The same thing your fathers did. That was in the good old days, when they were people of limited means and few dreams. Now we are big. We are one big nation, and we must stop thinking small. The world will be at our feet soon, gentlemen. We must start thinking big. This is no longer about a boatload of nearly new luxury cars that your men can sell at rock-bottom prices in Moscow, on account of every *nouveau riche* in the capital wanting to be driven around in a large BMW or Mercedes. BMW and Mercedes are already importing these vehicles themselves into Russia, and their customers only want new and officially delivered cars. Price is not a problem anymore. And guns? Everybody deals in guns these days. You want a Kalashnikov? The Chinese man on the street corner will sell you one, a new one, *made in China*. Is this the sort of operation that will guarantee us a future?"

Around the table, men remained silent.

"Eat!" Keretsky said. "This divine food must not go to waste. Eat. But meanwhile listen to my words." He took a bite from a portion of fish on his plate.

"While you were thinking small, the world has caught up with you. Gentlemen, today I bought a significant portion of a large Dutch bank. Today I'm offered a seat on the board of directors. I refuse. Why do I refuse? Because I play my own game. Not the bank's game. Not the game of the Dutch. Tomorrow I exchange large quantities of dollars for euros. The exchange rate of the euro drops by two percent. That is what I do. That's how I make money. Same thing with oil. Why does the price of oil go up? Is there suddenly less oil than a year ago? Than ten years ago? Has it become more difficult to get the oil out of the ground? Yes, but that is merely a technical problem. The costs go up a few percentage points. But the price goes up a quarter. Why? Because I want it to go up a quarter. Because people like me want it to rise."

The men around the table ate. They drank the wine and the vodka. They listened to Keretsky and learned his lesson, because that was why they were here.

"And what do I see here? I will tell you what I see here. Just the other day, a Dutch police officer was killed by a bomb. He worked for the AIVD. The AIVD, which monitors my activities. They have a very big file on me. They have big files on all my companies here in the Netherlands. Am I worried? No. I am not worried. That's what the police are for. To fill files with documents about me and my companies.

"But I am worried about a police officer who is killed by a bomb in front of his home. He did something he was not supposed to be doing, and he knew too much. But I did not order that killing. I would never order such a killing. Because that is not the sort of thing I do, gentlemen. You would, gentlemen. You would arrange for a police officer to be murdered, but not me."

Empty plates were taken away by efficient waiters. New hot plates were brought in with more food: meat, mostly, Italian style.

"Eat, friends," Keretsky continued. "And consider this: the difference between you and me is that I do not dispose of people. That is not what I do. I am a businessman. Police officers are not an obstacle on my path. Remember that."

An hour later, after conversations had returned to the commonplace subjects that people talk about when they eat and drink, and after the men around the table had said goodbye to Keretsky, he and Tarkovski sat in the Bentley. "What lesson did you learn today, Andreï?" Keretsky asked.

Tarkovski was no longer certain if he could still talk with his boss in confidence, not after tonight. Because he'd realized that the truth was a tool Keretsky was able to bend and distort any way he wanted. Even worse: truth was nonexistent in the Keretsky universe. "I assume you want us to distance ourselves from criminal activities."

Keretsky patted Tarkovski's knee. "You understood perfectly well, Andreï. Very well. You keep your distance from criminal activities. That is what you tell everybody. Finally, when you say this often enough, people will tend to believe you. They will believe that you are a respectable businessman. That you can be trusted. The banker I saw yesterday knows I am respectable. Why does he know that? Because that's what he reads in the newspapers, and that's what his analysts tell him."

"But the police officer?"

"Who? Oh, the police officer. Let me tell you, Andreï: there is one thing you have to be perfectly clear about. Never let your reputation stand in the way of important and difficult decisions at a certain point in your life. Even when you have to make unpleasant decisions. You are a righteous businessman, but at the same time you make decisions that will end a human life. Because that too is a part of business. The Russian way. That is the lesson I want you to take home tonight." He gestured toward Amsterdam, outside the Bentley. "Do you like it here, Andreï? I think you do, but do you really?"

"Of course, Mr. Keretsky. I see no reason to complain."

"You managed that situation with the police officer very well. Do not worry about it anymore. It was a bit too spectacular for my taste, but then, there should be a bit of spectacle now and then."

"The bomb was the idea of our Ukrainian friends, Mr. Keretsky."

"Ah, I understand. A flashy, garish people, these Ukrainians. But good at what they do, I'll admit. True to their word as well. The officer had no idea the money was counterfeit?"

"It was dark," Tarkovski said.

"And he was greedy. Good. What happened with the recording?"

"I had it destroyed, as you asked."

"I knew I could count on you, Andreï," Keretsky said. "I knew I could count on you. The recording, we could not permit that to exist."

Tarkovski looked out at the city. He had lied only once, today, but the lie had come easily. He did not want to look his boss in the eye, however. He had heard people notice when you lie. They watch your facial expression and know you lie. He was not going to take that risk.

26

"Her name is Eileen Calster and here are some recent pictures of her, a few of which we got out of the university computer."

Keretsky didn't have to know where Monet had gotten the photos and information. He was familiar with the power of money. He knew what the hunger for money did to most people and their motives. In a society geared for consumption and consumption only, money was the ultimate motivator.

Or was it not? Power was, maybe. Power might be an even stronger motivator than money. Power over the life of others. But finally, after all other factors were weighed, it was not about money or power but about recognition. It was about receiving the appropriate recognition for your actions and for what you were. That made people tick. That's what made them work twelve hours a day on impossible projects.

"Mr. Monet," he said, "I notice that this affair is important to you, but I have to leave very soon, unfortunately. I need to attend to urgent business in Moscow. Things that cannot be postponed. Both my assistants are at your disposal. Mr. Parnow, unfortunately, doesn't speak English or Dutch, but Andreï does, and he will help you."

Andreï nodded as if the current arrangement suited him fine. Keretsky, however, had failed to talk this through with him. He had hoped to accompany his boss back to Moscow with a permanent position in the capital by way of promotion. He had hoped to get out of rainy Amsterdam.

But now Keretsky was returning alone. Tarkovski would need to talk with him about that. But Keretsky had no time planned for his assistant anymore. Why not? Had Tarkovski not earned his return? Had he not been Keretsky's servant for long enough? In the Netherlands, a country he had no affinity with? How long had that been? Two years, nearly three? He had even learned the language in a short time. And served the interests of the Keretsky empire. Tended to the business side of the empire, and occasionally a few illegal matters as well.

Earlier arrangements had been made concerning Tarkovski's tasks and his return to Russia. He had been made to understand that an end would come to this exile. He had repaid his debt. He wanted to return to Russia. But he wouldn't. Even then, he wouldn't contradict Keretsky or refuse to help this fellow Monet. He would follow orders, once again.

The worst thing was that he had to babysit Parnow. The man loathed him, saw him as an effeminate bureaucrat. Or so Tarkovski assumed. Parnow knew better than to express his feelings. But his face tightened every time he saw Tarkovski, who couldn't help noticing the man's disdain.

"Thank you, Mr. Keretsky," Monet said stiffly. He too knew that Keretsky's departure wasn't to his advantage. Now he would be first in the line of people responsible for the whole affair with Van Boer. If something went south, the cops would call on him first.

He gave the photographs to Andreï. Monet glanced at the Russian secretary. The young man didn't seem the kind of person who would act swiftly and decidedly—he didn't look up to the job. Monet didn't know what to do about the whole matter. Parnow would be the right man in a tight situation, but Andreï would be useless.

The meeting was taking place in the Renaissance Hotel after dinner. Downstairs, Keretsky's Bentley was waiting. Coffee had been served in the room, which was much too large for just the four of them.

Monet was familiar with these Russians. The hard marble hand in the velvet glove. *No*, he thought, *not hard as marble, but dead.* They were all dead. Emotionless and dead. The Russians wouldn't hesitate to kill him if they thought he would damage them. *These are the sort of allies you have chosen*, he thought. They were one step up from the rabble of Amsterdam South, somewhat more civilized than the people who traded guns in the harbor, but only just. They would deal with problems in exactly the same way as the rabble. He didn't doubt that would be Parnow's main mission.

Andreï Tarkovski was even less happy with the way things were going. He had wanted to speak to Keretsky about the ongoing business, but the Russian had ignored him. He would be left behind in Amsterdam with a limited budget to run Keretsky's affairs. For one thing, he wouldn't have the funds to organize a large-scale search for the missing girl and the list.

Why did Keretsky want to help those Dutch? The list had his name on it, but why would that matter? Keretsky supported dozens of parties in nearly as many countries. And he sometimes supported different parties with contradictory interests in the same country. Right-wing nationalists, former communists, mainstream socialists. It didn't much matter to Keretsky, as long as he could influence the decision model in that country.

Keretsky had his own interests to consider in Holland. Dutch criminal society—the men he had seen earlier—would remember whatever assistance they had received from him over the years. That was how he worked. He would visit Amsterdam again in a year or so, bringing along new expansion plans for his companies. He would call in his debts and renew old friendships like the one with Monet. He now owned a decent share of Fabna Bank, and in a year, he would convince other people to invest in that same bank, strengthening his own position. At some point, he would take over their shares, ending up with more than five percent of the bank's assets.

That was why Andreï Tarkovski would have to recover that famous list: because establishing obligations was a part of Keretsky's strategy, and he needed an untarnished reputation. If more people got hurt during the process of retrieving the list, it wouldn't be Keretsky's problem. Maybe Tarkovski could earn his way back to Russia that way.

Tarkovski had taken his own precautions, however. He hadn't destroyed the recording he had bought from Breukeling because he assumed he needed some sort of life insurance. Because he might need it as leverage against his boss. He knew it would be dangerous to play this sort of game with Keretsky—who was far better at such games than Tarkovski—but he still hadn't destroyed the recording.

He furtively glanced at Parnow who, as usual, was ignoring him. The man reminded him of the pictures he had seen of Egyptian statues. Or Chinese. He was unapproachable. Tarkovski knew the man had been a soldier. Spetsnaz, in the Soviet era. Or even later. Not just any unit, he heard, but one belonging to the Ministry of Defense, the GRU. Afghanistan, probably. And other hot spots where Russian interests had been defended with guns. You didn't make it into one of those special units if you weren't a hard-ass. And you needed a link with organized crime too, so Tarkovski had heard. But he was sure a lot of professional and dedicated soldiers were part of the special units as well, because they were tough and liked the adventure, not because they were criminals. Most of organized crime recruited their own soldiers from ex-military who had done active service abroad.

Andreï didn't have to know where Parnow came from. The man was dead. He had no feelings. There was no life left behind those eyes. And now he, Andreï Tarkovski, the son of a philosophy teacher and a musically gifted mother, was teamed up with a murderer.

Not that he had much of a choice.

A long time ago, this choice had been taken from him.

Keretsky had almost total control over his life. That was his privilege.

Saint Petersburg, seven years ago. Keretsky had been able to take over Tarkovski's life then. It had been inevitable. His parents had asked for Keretsky's help and protection against a vicious loan shark. His father, a common teacher with few financial prospects in a struggling economy, had been foolish. He needed a car to commute, and he had borrowed the money. Public transport had been degrading rapidly after the end of the Soviet era and had become the battlefield of mobsters, rapists, and other scum. The car was a wreck, and the money had been loaned at a rate of 12 percent. Per month. The ruble was devaluating rapidly, and it would never rise again from its abyss. The loan shark wanted his money back, threefold, after three months. He sent two men in leather jackets when Tarkovski senior was unable to pay. They broke both his wrists.

Father had gone to Keretsky, a man more powerful than the mayor or the chief of police. Had promised him eternal loyalty. Keretsky intervened. The leather jackets did not come back. Keretsky returned the money but not threefold. The loan shark disappeared six months later, never to be seen again. Everybody knew what had happened to him, more or less. Keretsky didn't like too much competition in his city. The message had been clearly understood by all.

"Give me your son," he had said. "I'll give him a new life." He wanted the young Tarkovski on account of his intellectual capabilities. "He's a brilliant young man," Keretsky had said to Tarkovski senior. "But here, he has no future. He has no future in Russia. I'll give him a future."

Andreï's parents lived in a small rent-controlled apartment. They had little money. They had no choice. Andreï went to work for Keretsky, on account of his parents. Keretsky paid Tarkovski decent enough wages as well as all his expenses. He had him settled in Amsterdam. Andreï hoped he would earn enough to buy a cottage in the countryside for his parents.

But Keretsky had bought his soul. There was no way around it. The man remained civil and never treated Tarkovski as a slave. The young man became a trusted and well-paid employee. Keretsky had been headhunting.

And now Tarkovski would be left with a problem he dreaded solving: Eileen Calster, a young girl, close to his own age. She would have to die, he assumed. She knew too much. He didn't like that.

Tarkovski wondered how Parnow had been recruited. Not that it mattered much. As he looked at Parnow, he knew Eileen Calster wouldn't stand a chance.

27

EEKHAUT LOOKED AROUND, TRYING to find meaning in what amounted to chaos. In the messy room, only a few bloodstains on the mattress reminded him that a human life had ended here in an unfortunate way. This was the essence of a human existence: a few stains of precious circulating fluid, spilled by a careless killer. A life definitely wasted. Van Boer's life.

"What do you hope to find?" he asked Dewaal, continuing to observe the room, in search of that one revealing small detail that would lead to the murderer. He knew that, in reality, it didn't happen too often. "The technical people have been going over this place, haven't they?"

Not that he was familiar with the routines of the Dutch. But he also wouldn't object to a second or even a third thorough search of a crime scene, knowing that things were occasionally overlooked by previous investigators.

"We return time and again to the same question," Dewaal said. "Why was Van Boer executed?" She took some of the books from the shelves, flipped their pages, and looked at the text on their backs. "Well? We know about his political affiliations and his urge to go work for his enemies, which in itself is a conundrum, isn't it? I like that word. I was sure I was going to need it at some point. There's a connection, surely, but what? I hope at least there's an identifiable reason for his murder. Otherwise, we're completely in the dark. If it's, well . . ."

"Random," Eekhaut offered.

"Yes, random."

"These political backgrounds," Eekhaut said, "would that be the only option?"

She folded her arms. "I see no motive beyond that. The technical boys found nothing for us to work with. Actually, there were too many traces. These young people seldom bother with cleaning their apartments. What you see is what you get. Clothes, both Pieter's and the girl's. Books, again both of theirs. Heaps of documents, mostly clippings from newspapers and magazines and printouts of websites—he seemed to have collected everything. We could read through all that, but I'm sure we'll be none the wiser."

"Let us assume Van Tillo and her party are in on this, somehow. Then we must assume Van Boer had sensitive information on them. Would make sense. Something they would rather not see in his hands, or anywhere else. Something that made him potentially dangerous. You don't hire a contract killer because your employee is absent from the office."

"No, we can assume that doesn't happen here."

"So we're left with an unknown factor. Big bloody unknown factor."

"Several unknowns," she said, offhandedly looking in some drawers. She found two large notebooks and flipped through them, again hoping for secrets suddenly revealed. She knew she would probably have to ask one of the team members to go through all these papers. "A sort of diary. It will take days if not more to sift through this. We don't have that luxury. Meanwhile, we'll get nowhere, not even with Van Tillo."

"And what about Breukeling's murder?"

She seemed annoyed by that question, he noticed. "Internal Affairs has questioned his wife. Looked into his accounts, gone through what was left of the house, questioned his friends. Made a thorough nuisance of themselves. All that in a burst of totally unusual activity, Walter. What can I tell you?"

Nothing he didn't already know. That Breukeling at some point had been seduced by the dark side. Had taken the wrong path and gone off the reservation. And in the process had met someone who was not going to let the detective live, not with the knowledge he had.

He stood by the dirty window, looking out. Amsterdam seemed careless and without much concern for the suffering of people. From where he stood, it seemed hopelessly provincial and small. Neglected and even a bit derelict, this city, as if it had realized, long ago, that its golden age was passed and would never be retrieved. People, he assumed, felt at home in this city without ever being home. "Something I wanted to ask you, Chief," he said. "Why have you brought me along on this investigation?"

"You have a problem with that?"

"I mean, you have a complete team over there. All of them experienced people, many of them younger than me, all more familiar with the situation in Holland than I am. And then you drag me along, though you have no idea what I can contribute. Seems strange to me. Not the sort of thing I'd expect you to do, I mean."

She kept looking through the notebooks—searching for hidden meaning, for confessions. Not interested in answering him.

"Don't get me wrong," Eekhaut continued. "It is not a reflection on your intentions or anything. I appreciate your attention. And I completely understand if you don't want to talk about this. You already mentioned that—"

"No," she said.

"No?"

"I mean: I want to talk about it. I certainly do. And I have very good reasons for bringing you along. But I'm sure I already explained these reasons to you. You're the odd man out. The new face on the team. The unknown factor. That's what this is about."

"I understand. The odd man out with the terrible reputation."

"Exactly. The odd man out, with a clean slate." She looked at him. Amused, it seemed, for a moment. "This is the thing. For some months now, strange things have been happening to my crew. It started when I became their boss. And maybe some of it was going on much longer than that. There is at least one mole in the office. Maybe more. Confidential information is leaking from my team to the outside world. I'm not talking about Breukeling, that's something else entirely."

"Leaks to the press?"

"If only. The press is sometimes made aware of what we do, but they never get the details. It's much worse: information is being leaked

to people and organizations we don't want to have any intimate kn
edge of our investigations. And as a result, they're often one step a
of us."

"So there's a mole in your office."

"Yes. Maybe more than one."

"So you prefer to work with the odd man out. Me."

"At least I know you cannot be implicated in any of those l
You arrive here out of the blue, with your annoying attitude and
even more annoying habits, but at least you're clean. Even if you w
clean in Brussels—and I'm not asking, not even interested—you
no connections with Dutch crime."

"I'm glad I passed the test."

"Happy to oblige," she said. "And that's why I want you to tag a
When I heard Van Boer was dead, the alarm in my head went off.
loud, that alarm. I knew he worked for PDN but had no idea
he was after. Suddenly things started to get complicated." She (
the notebooks. "There's not much to find here, I assume. I'll rea
whenever I'm in a romantic or philosophical mood but not now."

Eekhaut kicked a cabinet. "Do we take the room apart?"

"Would that make sense?"

He crouched down and lifted the sheets and then the ma
Looked under the bed.

"You can't be serious!" she said. "You're not going to crawl
the bed!"

"No, I don't need to," he said, retrieving two pieces of pape
sure your technical people are good at what they do, but in thi
they were a bit careless. Never underestimate what you may find (
a second or a third search."

"What is it?"

"A list." He handed her the papers.

"Shit!" she said. Looked at him sharply. "Maybe this is what w
looking for."

"It is?"

"A partial list of donors."

"Donors? Like an offering in a church?"

"No, in a general sense. Isn't that the term used in Belgium too? People and organizations that give money. To a political party, in this case." She held the sheets in front of him. "To the PDN."

"Aha!"

"Yes, indeed. And if this is what Van Boer stole, a complete list, we've found a motive for murder."

"A complete list? This isn't complete?"

She looked at the papers. "No. Pages eleven and twelve of twelve."

"The murderer has the other pages then."

She thought about that. "Not necessarily."

"The girl."

"Exactly. The murderer, if he was worth his money, would have made sure he had the complete list and made equally sure Van Boer hadn't made copies. But that probably didn't happen. The girl walked in on him, and somehow she took off with the list."

"That sounds plausible," Eekhaut said, although he felt Dewaal was drawing conclusions much too quickly.

"You think?"

"The girl took off with an almost complete list of the contributors to Van Tillo's party. The killer went after her. We have her name, but we don't know where she is at this time."

"We'll have to contact her family. Maybe they know something."

Eekhaut shook his head. "If she's smart—and I assume she is—she won't approach her family. She knows they can easily be found." He kept looking around the room, searching for leads. Even with the windows open, the place didn't smell civilized. "Looks like we're going to have to turn the room inside out after all."

"Not something I look forward to."

He stood by a bulletin board. Pieces of paper with telephone numbers, Post-its, clippings from local newspapers, three postcards.

"I'll get more people in from the team," Dewaal said. "We need more hands and eyes."

"She would want to get away as far as possible," Eekhaut said.

"I assume so," she said. "I would."

"Like, for instance, Belgium."

"That's an option. An easy option. Not quite far enough, I suppose, but easy. Same language, for the most part. She wouldn't stand out in a crowd either."

"Leuven, for instance."

She frowned. "Why the hell would she go to Leuven?"

He took a postcard from the board and showed it to her. The picture was of a Gothic building with little turrets and statues. "Leuven City Hall," he said. "The historic building."

"Oh," she said. "That's where you come from."

"That's why I recognized it at once." He flipped the card. "And her sister's name is Annelies." He handed the card to Dewaal. "I am not clairvoyant either."

On the back of the card was written, in a neat hand: *Dear Sis, Greetings from Leuven, Annelies.*

"Now we're getting somewhere," she said.

"Yes," he said. "And she's getting somewhere as well. It seems I'll have to return home."

28

"This doesn't amount to much," Dewaal said.

Prinsen and Van Gils would, under other circumstances, have agreed with her. They were equally convinced that their investigation into the murder of Breukeling amounted to almost nothing. They knew their boss, however, and judging from experience, they knew they'd have to listen to her opinion on the matter. What she said was more for her own benefit than for theirs.

"No witnesses, no clues. No rumors circulating as to who made that bomb and why. And the motive? Revenge on a dirty cop? One of our own? Are you sure that's going to be enough to solve this case?"

"This was a professional hit," Van Gils said. "Not many people can make this sort of explosive device. At least not in Holland." Everything he said Dewaal already knew. So she ignored him.

"Take apart his private life," she said. "Piece by piece. Every person he spoke to in the last year, every pub where he had a pint, each and every drunk he had a talk with, everyone we know and don't trust. Each time he cheated on his wife or she cheated on him. Every time he drove over the speed limit. Did he cheat on his wife, Van Gils?"

Van Gils pursed his lips and held his head at a slight angle, as if he didn't want to tell on Breukeling. To him that was, even now, a form of professional courtesy. Part of the tradition of police officers. Dewaal would have to understand. She wouldn't, he feared. "You know how these things work, Chief," was all he said.

"No, Van Gils, I don't know how these things work at all. Please elaborate. I keep my private life as far removed from work as possible. I'm not concerned about my colleague's hobbies. I hear things, I hear rumors, but I'm only concerned when and if your private life influences the way that you function on my team. My team, Van Gils. Breukeling is a case in point. He was involved in a number of matters—and long before my time—that he shouldn't have been involved in. And somebody was pissed off by something he did. You can work that out. The recording of the conversation between Keretsky and Monet has disappeared, and I want to know why. I want to know who fixed that, and I need to know urgently what these two gentlemen talked about. I want to know why Breukeling was killed. Can you live with that? And I want you to work this case yourself, because I don't really expect much from Internal Affairs."

Van Gils nodded. Dewaal looked at Prinsen. "And you, Nick? I'm not hearing all that much from you."

Prinsen hesitated. "Why did Breukeling say the prosecutor called?"

"When was that? Oh, while you were at the Renaissance."

"Yes. He could have sent me away just like that, taken the recording, and had it disappear. He could have invented an alibi, something about the equipment malfunctioning."

"Under other circumstances, he would have been alone at the Renaissance," Dewaal said. "He wasn't expecting you. Maybe he had to improvise. Too little imagination, who knows."

"We all know you and the prosecutor—" Van Gils started.

"Leave the prosecutor out of this," Dewaal snapped. "We have our differences, and he has little sympathy for this department, mainly because we tend to operate independently. But I don't think he's involved."

"Keretsky," Prinsen said, warning her.

"What do you mean?"

"The prosecutor and Keretsky. Isn't there a connection? Maybe something less obvious?"

"There's no connection we could prove," Dewaal said. "And I forbid you to delve into it. Don't go there, Nick. That's a warning. I don't want the leadership of the AIVD having this whole investigation carted off to the archives on account of your foolishness. There are other . . . well, regardless. Try to find out who's behind the attack. Stick to that."

"Looks like we're going to take a stroll in Amsterdam South," Van Gils said.

"It's a nice neighborhood," Dewaal said, "with a lot of wealthy people living there. People with the sort of background we always find fascinating. Question is whether they'll want to talk with you."

Van Gils looked at his watch. "It's still early morning, boss. Some of those boys are having their coffee now. They discuss the weather, women, their next job. Maybe this is the right moment to drop by at their favorite café, shoulder up next to them to enjoy their company, and chat about whatever's on their mind. The usual, really."

"Good," Dewaal said. "I'm relying on you."

"Boss," Van Gils said, rising. "What about the new guy? The Belgian?"

"What about him?"

"The boys here, they wonder why he's already involved in such an important inquiry as the Keretsky case. You know how they feel. They haven't had a chance to get to know him. He didn't join us for a drink. First day at the job, you'd expect—we've hardly even seen him. Always out with you. People talk, which you could have expected."

"We'll all get to know one another better once this ongoing and urgent inquiry is behind us, Van Gils. I have more urgent things than a drink on my mind at the moment. But we'll come to that. I'll speak to him about buying you all a drink."

Van Gils beckoned Prinsen. "Come on, kid. We've got work to do." They went into the parking lot, chose a dark blue Ford Mondeo, and drove off toward the south. "I understand you want to play down your relationship with her," he said. "But it must be difficult, having your aunt for a boss."

"Yes," Prinsen said.

"I mean, you meet under other circumstances as well, family matters and so on, and what do you talk about then, eh? 'How are the kids?'"

"She has no children," Prinsen said.

"She doesn't? Funny, how little we know about her. Is she married?"

"No. Not anymore."

"Happens a lot among police officers. And you? Any social life at all?"

"Not very much, no," Prinsen said.

"Are you close, as a family? Parents, your aunt, grandparents, that sort of thing?"

Prinsen shook his head. "We're from a very traditional milieu. My parents and my aunt don't speak to each other, haven't for a long time. She's younger than my mother. Much younger. She left home to study in Amsterdam. She has almost no connections anymore with the family."

Van Gils kept quiet.

"I assume she . . . she has more in common with me than with her sisters and brothers. Or with the rest of the family."

"Traditional, eh?"

"Strict religious," Prinsen said, wondering how much he could tell Van Gils about his family. If Van Gils would at some point use that information.

"Yeah, I know. I come from the north. Totally different from Amsterdam. But we've lived here for thirty years now. You get away from that religious crap after a while. It stops haunting you."

"Some people never get rid of that religious crap."

"I assume some don't," Van Gils said. "Yes, I've noticed that. Question is: how does somebody like you, with your background, get into the police? Maybe not that surprising—a strong sense of what's right and wrong connected with your religious upbringing. Stronger than for other people. See what I mean?"

"Mmmm."

"You don't like to discuss this. I understand. A man carries the weight of his past. Look at those Russians that live here. Some of them have been here since the sixties or seventies. They're still Russians. They're not Dutch. I wonder if their children feel Dutch. Some of them have completely adapted, though. They've become Dutch through and through, language and all. Maybe because there's no great divide between the Dutch and the Russian soul. Maybe not. But make no mistake: a Russian is not a Dutchman."

"Do you know many of these Russians?"

"This is Amsterdam. This is where all sorts of nationalities congregate. Serbians and Albanians—those are the worst criminals, some of them real psychopaths. Seem nice when you happen to run into them, but they've been oppressed for so long and have known little else but war and hardship, and when they end up here—the ones that end up here—they're dangerous beyond belief. Often enough, they've been subjected to torture by their own countrymen. Or by their neighbors. And there are the Moroccans, who form a tight, closed society and keep to themselves. The Italians, with their long criminal tradition. And certainly not least the Asians, but you'll find more of them in Rotterdam, on account of the port."

"And we, in the middle of all that . . . ?"

"The AIVD occupies a specific terrain, so to speak. We don't have the resources to investigate all of them, all of these groups, or we'd need at least five times the workforce. So we pick our favorite victims. Today it's the Russians, because they have loads of cash."

"And because they do a lot more than just smuggling drugs or weapons."

"Who did you have in mind?"

"Keretsky. The man doesn't deal in those things. He deals in money. Buys influence and power. And that's more dangerous than just a few containers of illegal weapons, I guess. The other things, they leave clear traces."

"Well, if you launder money, you can also leave a trace."

"It's not about laundering, Van Gils. The money in Keretsky's pockets is clean enough. He wants to do something useful with it."

"Gas and oil."

"Yeah, that too. But he mainly buys power."

The Ford came to a stop in a street bordered by trees and with squat brick buildings on either side, no more than four stories high. As far as Prinsen could see, there was nothing else but these buildings, rows and rows of them. Dating from the fifties, or so he presumed, neat buildings in a classical style, with pointed roofs, shops and restaurants on the ground floors. A neat neighborhood, where apartments would cost quite a bit of money.

"This is it?"

"Never been here?" Van Gils asked.

"No. Looks nice enough."

"Oh," Van Gils said, "this is a respectable neighborhood all right. This is where a better class of people lives. No unemployed kids hanging around, no drugs in the streets, no hookers. No pimps and no police cars. All you see here has been developed by the city council. But whatever goes on inside these apartments is for you and me to figure out. Only discreet people live here. Mostly middle-class pensioners. Tidy old people who mind their own business. IKEA furniture or antiques inherited from their grandparents. The younger generation is discovering this area as well. People in their thirties and forties who have money but no wish to live in a villa in the suburbs, on account of the distance to their job."

"Why are we here then?"

"Criminals, specifically those who have done well for themselves, tend to move into these well-to-do neighborhoods. They make sure they have some sort of official income, and they pay their taxes promptly. They stay under the official radar. Respectable citizens, every one of them."

"Oh."

"And the local amenities are better than average. A number of good restaurants and not too cheap either. People who live here can afford the occasional dinner out in a fancy place."

"And then we drop in and talk to some of them."

"Of course we do. Isn't that what we usually do? The main thing we do? Interesting people over here, in this part of Amsterdam. You'll see. Won't be too happy to see us, but we're not supposed to care about their feelings."

"You haven't always worked for AIVD, have you?"

Van Gils smiled. "You're a smart kid. I was a regular cop first. In the rougher parts of Amsterdam, learning the ropes. In Warmoesstraat. Infamous area. Not bad for experience with street life. Then I ended up here, another local police station. Civilized people, even the hardened criminals. Talk freely about their family, their dog, the cottage in Zealand, their legal affairs. They're your best friend, once they get to know you, even if you're a cop. But if murder is the only way out of a problem, they'll pay someone to do it for them. That's the way they operate. If you're in their way, or you insulted someone, you may end up as a corpse in an incinerator. Under the foundations of a building site. Unless they want your body to be found, as a message to others. And if your body needs to be found, it won't be a pretty sight. Because the message must always be clear to the ones concerned."

"Right. And we're going to have a chat with that sort of person."

"I've done it all my life." Van Gils got out of the car. "And will continue to do it for a while yet."

29

"THIS IS NICK," VAN GILS said. "Our most junior colleague. He's from way north but now is a proud Amsterdamer."

"You don't just *become* an Amsterdamer," said the bald man at the other side of the table. He was way up in his fifties and had the arms and neck of a professional wrestler. If you wanted the caricature of a bouncer, this would be it. "You're born in Amsterdam or you're not."

"As if you, Carlo, were born in Amsterdam."

"No," Carlo said, "but my children were. I'm Italian. Even better, I'm from Sardinia. I've lived here for thirty years. I don't speak like I'm from here, but I feel at home. My children are as Dutch as they come. Want to see their rooms? Soccer and more soccer. Holland national team. Orange!"

The proprietor of the café approached them and brought the coffee and cakes Van Gils had ordered. He gave the man a ten-euro note and received some coins in return. Prinsen noticed that it was exactly five two-euro coins. That's how it went. Nobody the wiser, he assumed. Except for Carlo. Carlo knew the score.

"And what about the Russians?" Prinsen asked Carlo. "Do they all feel at home here? Or have they remained Russian?"

Carlo looked Prinsen over. He wasn't a tall man and hadn't shaved properly that morning. His eyes were dark and glanced in irritation at the young man, who resisted their implication. "Why would I want to talk about the Russians?" Carlo asked.

"Because," Van Gils said, "one of our people is dead, on account of a bomb. A bomb detonated from a distance, in a shopping bag affixed to his front door. He came home and *wham*! The bomb went off."

"Why?"

"Why? What does it matter, Carlo? What is it we cops do? We investigate crimes. We pursue criminals. Some of them get nervous when we do that. It comes naturally. And then, sometimes, bad things happen. We try to avoid it, but they happen nonetheless."

"I am no criminal, Van Gils. You know that. I'm not the one you want."

"I'm not implying you're a criminal, Carlo. That's not the point. Still, you've been involved in a number of shady affairs, some even plainly outside the confines of the law, and that could be interpreted by certain people as—"

Carlo waved the whole thing away. "Ah, the law! The law says many things. Maybe the law ought to change. Some laws are ridiculous."

"Car theft and the unlawful export of funds to certain African countries? And what happened with that truck full of cigarettes we stopped at the border, with you behind the wheel? It wasn't your truck or your cigarettes. You don't even smoke."

"Stupid things I did when I was young."

"That was four years ago, Carlo. You had put your youth behind you for some time by then. But that's not why we're here. A bomb. Someone who is good with bombs. Someone who can attach a mobile phone to a bomb without blowing himself up. Not something everybody can do."

"I guess I know a few guys who can handle that sort of equipment. Mirko, to name one. The Serbian."

"Yes, I had him in mind. But he's in jail."

"Oh? I didn't know. Bad luck. He'll be missed, the psychopath. Don't tell him I said that."

"Who else?"

"Who else? Why are you asking me?"

"Because I can have a word to customs and detectives, and you'll need my support whenever you fall asleep behind the wheel of a truck again."

Carlo looked at him disdainfully. "Always making trouble, Van Gils. Fucking up hardworking people like myself. If not the cops, then your boss."

"You're still alive, and the last time I saw you, you had a nice house and a family. You seem to be doing well for yourself. What's with the complaining?"

"Because," Carlo said, "things go downhill. Margins are getting smaller, and clients are getting choosier. As if you didn't know." Carlo looked up. "Now what's that about?"

Prinsen glanced over to where Carlo was looking and saw three men enter the pub, take off their coats, and sit down at a table. They ordered something and looked around. One of them eyed Carlo and the two police officers. The other two ignored them, but it was obvious they hadn't wound up here by coincidence.

Van Gils threw them a quick glance. "A concise explanation would be all we need, Carlo," he said. "Because business may go downhill even further."

Carlo shook his head and toyed with his cup. "There's this Dutch fellow. They call him Mick. I don't know his last name. He's into explosives. You want to open a safe against the owner's will, then he's your man. Learned his trade in the army. Nobody said what army."

"Mick."

"But a lot of people are handy with the stuff. The explosive stuff. After that war in the Balkans, there are plenty of people around who can handle all sorts of weapons and explosives. And brought a bit of stock with them. That's why so much of the stuff is around and for sale at basement prices. Even automatic weapons, and do tell me, Van Gils, who in my profession would want to use an automatic weapon?"

"Makes you nervous, doesn't it?"

"I read the newspapers, Inspector. And I read about your man and the bomb on his front door. I look out for suspect packages."

"What do you have to fear?"

Carlo whispered, "Those Russians take the best parts of the market. They have plenty of cash. You sell your business, or they pay you with an unannounced visit. You know Bernardo? Who had a hardware shop two streets down? Well, he sold his business—"

"Including his dealings in stolen electronics in the harbor, you mean."

"Well, yes, that too. He got paid all right, but now he's at home, doing nothing, and that's driving him crazy."

"But all that's small change, Carlo. The people we're looking for don't get involved in minor stuff."

"I couldn't care less who you're looking for."

"Back to the bomb. Who can have done that?"

"I hear some Russians have the same problem. They're asked to sell their business to one of their countrymen, someone with a lot of money. There are some new players around, Inspector. Big players. No financial limits. They're not in the market for a hardware store. They don't need a hardware store. That's all I know. All I'm saying as well."

Van Gils rose. "Well, thanks for the chat, Carlo. See you around."

"I prefer not," Carlo said. But it didn't sound unfriendly.

Van Gils and Prinsen left the pub and walked back to the car. "I didn't hear the name Keretsky," Prinsen said. "But it was close."

Van Gils shook his head. "Carlo probably never heard of Keretsky. Nor of his colleagues. This is another level of operations. But people are nervous. Something is happening. New players, yeah, tell me about it."

Three men appeared in front of them. Black leather coats over black suits and sweaters, like a uniform. The men from the pub. "Gentlemen," the first man said, "you are far from home." He had no accent. But he wasn't Dutch either.

Van Gils inspected him. "Is there something we can help you gentlemen with? A charge of illegal possession of a firearm maybe?"

The man shook his head as if deploring Van Gils's statement. "You still happen to have some friends, Inspector Van Gils. Even in this part of the city. There aren't many of them left, though. These friends don't want anything happening to you. That's why we're here."

"Like a bomb on my front lawn."

"Something of the sort, yes. Very annoying if it should happen, for all parties involved. Nevertheless, some things can't be avoided. Like when people talk too much or ask too many questions. Or annoy some-body. You know how it works. An overzealous assistant, someone mis-understanding a suggestion, and accidents are bound to happen."

"I'll take you off the street, gentlemen, any time one of your ugly mugs shows itself to me," Van Gils said. "So stay off my turf. We won't be told off by scum like you. Imported scum, on top of it. Ragheads from the Balkan. Goat fuckers. Worse: bastards of Balkan goat fuckers."

The man's face showed no emotion. He didn't seem to take the insults personally. "I'm just informing you that you still have friends around here, Inspector. Have a nice day." They turned, all three of them, and stepped away.

Van Gils toyed with his car keys. "Don't ask me what's going on, Prinsen," he said.

"I'm not asking."

"Good. Because I'm not in the mood to answer stupid questions."

30

EILEEN HAD MANAGED TO get money out of an ATM. A couple of hundred euros, in twenties. It would get her through the coming days, even if she weren't living frugally. She didn't have to go hungry or be out in the cold and could even spend a few nights in a cheap hotel.

And she had been careful. She'd taken the money from a machine with a long line of customers. Not that it mattered much. Even if someone were checking up on her account, they wouldn't be much the wiser. She'd gone to Central Station and bought a ticket, in cash, leaving no trace. She had become careful and paranoid. She didn't lack for motivation: that frightful man and Pieter's body were stuck in her memory.

She was sitting in a corner of the train carriage, watching the other passengers, at least the ones she could see from her position. She felt relatively safe. It would have been nearly impossible for the murderer to have followed her this far. And even if he had, he wouldn't take any action on a train, not with so many witnesses.

She didn't have much in the way of luggage. She'd quickly bought some underwear and toiletries, two T-shirts and a pair of jeans, and a small duffle bag. Whatever else she needed she would get in Belgium. There would be plenty of cheap clothes in Belgium. Her immediate goal was to create as much distance between herself and the murderer.

And she'd need to be invisible. There was the problem. She would have to learn many tricks. Always using cash, only using public telephones (both would be a problem in practice), no credit cards or anything that could pinpoint her on a map. Pieter had taught her about these tricks. Techniques for disappearing under the radar of the networked society. She had hardly listened then, but a few ideas had stuck nevertheless. And now they'd come in handy. Where had Pieter learned them? Had he ever needed them? She knew almost nothing about his previous life. Maybe he'd left her out of it on purpose because his past contained potentially dangerous things. And dangerous people.

Nobody knows where I'm going, she thought. *Nobody can know.* The advantage of Holland was the anonymity of its crowds, at least in the big cities like Amsterdam—no individual stood out in the crowd unless he or she wanted to.

She had bought a cellophane-wrapped sandwich and a Coke from a stall in the station and started to eat a late lunch. She wasn't hungry, but she had to eat. Otherwise, she would be in trouble with her glucose level and maybe even her blood pressure. She could do without that sort of trouble.

It would take her three hours to go all the way to Leuven. Her first time in Belgium. She had no idea what the country looked like, nor did she know what to expect from Leuven. A medium-sized university city, Annelies had written her on one of the all-too-rare postcards she mailed to her sister in faraway Amsterdam. Seemed a nice enough place, judging from the pictures on the cards. Not that it mattered much. She had crossed the border now, in both senses, an invisible but nonetheless real divide between fear and hope. Let's not get too comfortable, she thought. Her life would never be the same again, not after this.

The papers that the murderer wanted were tucked away in her bag. Pieter's list. What should she do with it? Keep it as a form of insurance? Something to barter with, for her life perhaps? *Don't be naïve, girl*, she told herself. *You've seen how Pieter was treated and how much his life was worth. The price of a bullet. That's what your life is worth to these people. The ones now hunting you. Your life is worth less than that list.*

She fought the urge to grab her bag and take the list out, to have a closer look. The information it contained didn't mean much to her. That had been Pieter's area. He'd given his life for that information, and so it was important to her that she put it to good use. Although she had no idea how.

Because anyone who had anything to do with that list would be in danger.

31

DEWAAL REMAINED A MYSTERY to Nick Prinsen. Aunt Alexandra, who had fled the family long before he did the same—fled from the awful village she was born in to build a new life in Amsterdam, on the other side of the world, or so it seemed to everyone in the village. She had been punished by God because her marriage had remained childless; her husband had divorced her soon enough. God knew how to punish the apostates, the sinners. That's how the family saw it. After the divorce, the rector struck her name from the village's official records. Although this was no more than a symbolic gesture, it meant that she no longer existed for his community.

How old had Nick been? Twelve, perhaps. Maybe going on thirteen. He had been impressed by the cold, dark church and the sinister rector who threatened the community with punishments so dark and far-reaching that everyone knew their immortal soul was at stake. Aunt Alexandra, who no longer existed, had committed many sins, and she had been punished accordingly. She wouldn't be one of the Chosen at the end of days. The outside world lived in the latter years of the twentieth century, but this isolated village saw no reason to leave the Dark Ages behind.

But young Nick Prinsen had followed his aunt. Not immediately. He left the village when he came of age, was probably struck from the records as well, and he worked his way through a decent schooling in almost no time and through university afterward. He managed to get into the AIVD only by chance. He happened to enroll in the police academy by chance as well. He had studied law at university, but he grew tired of archaic legislation. He managed to graduate, and then his aunt phoned him one day. Would he like to enroll in the police academy? And come work for her after that?

He'd been surprised to hear from her. She worked for the AIVD, which explained how she got his phone number. She didn't speak of her motives in bringing him into the AIVD. He got through police training in two years. The day after his graduation, he stepped into her office.

Later, he understood that she wanted him to work for her because she needed new faces and new ideas on her team. She wanted to partially replace the older guard, who had done too much time on the beat before joining the AIVD and whom she believed had been tainted by what they'd done before. She accepted the older guard for their experience and their ideas about running an investigation, but she needed new people as well—people integrated into the twenty-first century.

People like herself.

But then, after he'd joined the team, she mostly ignored him. Or only spoke to him formally, about cases and methods. She occasionally took one of the detectives out to lunch, for a personal talk, but never him. It was as if she wanted to isolate him to show people that there would be no favoritism between them.

Maybe she wanted to spare him.

And she never inquired about the family, his parents, grandparents, her sister, her home.

Where she no longer existed.

He wanted to ask her about all these things. About her past in the village, the way she'd escaped, what she felt now.

But there were more pressing things to deal with. He had cases to work. With Van Gils, among others. She never said much concerning the older detective. She'd only warned Prinsen that some people on the team could never fully be trusted, as had been proven by Breukeling. What about Van Gils? Could *he* be trusted? Close to his pension, always kept his hands clean. And he knew a lot of people from all walks of life, most of them from the criminal milieu. Which was to be expected: his work was that milieu.

"Three men," he said, into his cell phone.

"What sort of men?" Dewaal asked. The connection wasn't very good. Prinsen wondered where she was.

"Judging from their outfits, they could have been Russian mob. Somewhat southern types. Balkan. Mediterranean. Something like that."

"You see them in all shapes and sizes these days," Dewaal said. "Van Gils messaged me about this. He doesn't take it seriously. Me, I'm inclined to be careful. That bomb, that was not good. It can't get worse. It's supposed to be a warning for all of us. Such things should not happen between criminals and the police. It's bad for relations and mutual understanding."

"Carlo seemed to imply that a new breed of Russians had entered the picture," Prinsen said. "People with money. With a different approach, non-criminal even."

"It's still a crime when you take over a Dutch company with foreign funds that originate from criminal activities, Nick. Politicians and the business world aren't happy with the way things are drifting. On the other hand, some entrepreneurs won't mind a capital injection, with no idea where the money comes from. Hard times, Nick. Fallout from the banking crisis and all that. They need funds, and many of them have cash-flow problems."

"And then Keretsky has an intimate conversation with the president of Гabna," Nick said. "He wasn't shy about it either. Four and a half percent of stock. That's a lot of stock. A lot of money too."

"Not a secret, exactly. We're worried about that conversation. The question is obvious: what did he talk about with Monet? He's certainly not going to provide Monet's companies with new capital. Other ideas have surely been worked out, over there in Saint Petersburg. And in Moscow. It's precisely this sort of operation that we're interested in."

"You're working this case with the Belgian, I hear?"

"That's right. I'm keeping him separate because I want him to concentrate on this matter, which is extremely sensitive. So I need an outsider to take a look at it."

"People talk. About him."

"They always do. There will always be talk and gossip in the office. If I park my car in a different spot, they'll talk about it. If I wear a pair of pants instead of a skirt, they talk. It keeps them busy. And it keeps them at a distance from the more sensitive cases where I cannot allow their interference."

"We're not getting anywhere."

"With the Breukeling investigation? I don't expect us to. That's a dead trail. At least for now. Internal Affairs understood that much, so they're doing nothing. I asked Van Gils to have a look at his files, to see if anything worthwhile pops up. Strictly speaking, that's Internal Affairs' backyard. And some people are getting nervous."

"What do we get out of it?"

"I don't know yet. But stay focused. I need to go now. I'll be in Belgium for a day or so. I'll see you tomorrow. You and Van Gils keep working on the Breukeling investigation."

"Will do," he said. *Breukeling investigation*, she called it. As if it didn't concern a colleague. As if it were nothing more than a manila folder that could be filed away, maybe forever.

This felt like the most intimate conversation he had had with her since his arrival. It didn't amount to much, as intimate conversations went, but he was glad they'd spoken.

"Oh," she said. "Before I forget. You do carry your gun with you, I assume? At all times?"

"Yes," he said. "At all times."

"Take it home as well. I insist. Will you do that?"

"I'll think about it," he promised.

"Good," she said and was gone.

He remained at his desk for a bit longer. He stared at the screen of his laptop and then gazed outside for a while at the narrow stretch of world he could see from where he sat. Then he unearthed a key from his pocket and opened the top drawer of his desk. He had kept his SIG Sauer in there. The weapon was new and hadn't yet been used, except for target practice. He took the weapon from the drawer and inspected the empty magazine. He found the box of cartridges and started loading them one by one.

32

"LET'S GO," DEWAAL SAID, looking glum. It didn't suit her very well, Eekhaut thought, but he wasn't going to comment. She slid her phone into her handbag. It looked like an expensive handbag, but Eekhaut wasn't an expert in the matter. He assumed that Dewaal didn't buy cheap stuff. The phone looked expensive too. It was one of those devices that could do anything except brew coffee. Was she a nerd, in that sense? Permitting herself the most cutting-edge technological gadgets? What else would there be in that handbag? Her gun too?

"Right away?" he asked. He didn't like these sorts of surprises. He preferred to plan his day in advance. Most surprises that had happened to him had been bad. Life wasn't generous with positive surprises.

She clearly wasn't in a great mood. "Of course, right away," she told him. "What did you expect? Keep up, Eekhaut. This isn't Flanders. We have a reputation to maintain. We like to be punctual. I'll always expect you to be ready at any time. And I keep an overnight bag in my car. You?"

An overnight bag? As if he would be carrying an overnight bag with him, and clean underwear. He didn't even have a car. Not here. "I have an apartment in Leuven where I keep some things. Would that do?"

She looked at him as if he had just committed an unforgivable faux pas. A suggestion not appropriate for their formal relations. But that couldn't have been the reason for her mood. Something else was going on. "I have a spare bedroom," he said. "You can sleep there if we don't make it back in time." As if he could have meant anything else.

She ignored his remark. "We'll take my car. It's in the parking lot."

He closed his computer, rose, and followed her. Suddenly, he wasn't looking forward to a quick trip to Belgium. He had reconciled himself to his exile, however temporary. And with the exile, he'd been granted time away from his former problems.

She strode down the corridor, looking different from the day before. She took on an aggressiveness in the way she spoke and held herself. She bore a distinct purpose, and people had better get out of her way. She didn't look back to see if he was following her. He could have simply ignored her, let her go by herself. But that didn't seem like such a good idea.

They took the elevator in silence. The underground garage was a steel and concrete affair, with the smell of ozone and new cars. It was essentially a nineteenth-century building, but he assumed AIVD had enough money to convert any building into a modern fortress. Perhaps with deep subbasements, safe rooms, and passageways to other government buildings.

But before they reached the garage, there was a door, probably reinforced with steel. Dewaal stopped in front of it. A voice said, "Identification, please."

"What?" he said. Nobody was around.

"Identification, please," the voice repeated. "First warning."

It came from a small grille in the doorframe, under a small red light.

"Oh," Dewaal said, "that's Basil. He guards the perimeter of the building. Does a full-body scan and reads your card as well." She stepped back and waved her card in front of the grille. "Dewaal," she said. "And one visitor."

"Identification complete. Unidentified visitor noted. Please use your access card." The door slid open.

"Will comply, Basil," she said. She grinned at Eekhaut and motioned him into the parking area.

"Basil?"

"Yep. Basil Fawlty."

"What?"

"*Fawlty Towers*. The British TV comedy. Never seen it? God, you've never watched *Fawlty Towers*!"

"Oh, yes. I did."

"Good. Well, remember. Basil won't let you in without your badge and a full-body scan. We're very serious about security."

"I'll think about that."

The Porsche Cayenne awaited them, black and shiny, as if straight from the showroom. She got in, he slid into the passenger seat, and they drove off. She switched on the navigator, which showed them a map of the surrounding area. "Punch in the destination," she said. He did, although he knew exactly where they were heading. She wanted the reassurance of technology, he assumed.

"There will be a lot of traffic," he warned her. He had driven to Amsterdam and back a couple of times, as a tourist. He had parked his car somewhere around the RAI, close to the terminus of Tramline 4.

There they were, in the middle of what looked like the whole of the Dutch nation driving on the highway between Amsterdam and the south.

"Why don't we contact the local police in Leuven?" he proposed. "We wouldn't have to drive all the way."

She ignored his request. Stubborn, he assumed. She wasn't going to deviate from her plan, not because he had other ideas. "What do we know about this matter?" she asked. "The identity of the fugitive but not of the murderer. We assume we know where the girl went, but it's just your guess. If you're wrong, we'll be back in Amsterdam by tomorrow. Empty-handed. It isn't fun, but I'm willing to take the chance."

"Call the local police and ask for protection. For the girl's sister," he repeated. He couldn't envisage going to Leuven and not involving the locals.

"I spoke with the prosecutor just before we left. He mocked the idea. No proof of anything, he said. Where would this murderer have come from? Who would have sent him? Why would the girl be in danger? We're chasing ghosts, that's what he implies. Somebody's been talking to him. Somebody told him he shouldn't bother."

"Somebody? Who?"

"Jesus," she said, angry now, "you're slow, aren't you? Is this the famous and feared detective from Brussels? It's a given that the prosecutor and certain high-level members of the political class occasionally have dinner together. Members of a right-wing political class. Need I fill in names, Walter? It's the same politicians you like to offend."

"Oh," Eekhaut said. He was slow all right. But he knew nothing of this particular prosecutor's leanings, did he?

"Which is the main reason this particular prosecutor slammed the door in my face. And the door will remain shut. He'll be on the phone with the interested other party, and he certainly will tell them we're going to Leuven. I was careful enough not to mention any names, but rest assured the other party isn't stupid and can connect the dots."

"Shit."

They drove slowly along the ringway, with trucks in a long row to their right and two cars in front of them, not making any speed. They had several hundred kilometers ahead of them. "Yes," she said. "Shit. We have to hurry, and we're not allowed to involve local police. If we were the FBI or whatever, we'd be in a chopper all the way." They'd reached the exit to the highway toward Rotterdam, which had three lanes instead of two, and Dewaal accelerated at once, steering the Porsche to the left lane. "And so we drive. Nice car, isn't it?"

Eekhaut searched for his cell phone. "I'll call somebody."

"No, you won't. We keep this strictly to ourselves."

He could be as stubborn as she could. "I know a detective on the local force who can help us. Without making this official." He dialed a number.

She glanced at him but had to concentrate on the road and the traffic, with the Porsche now doing over eighty. Then traffic became congested again near Schiphol.

Eekhaut's call was answered. "Albert!" a tiny voice on the other end announced.

"Alberto!" Eekhaut said joyfully. "Been a while. How are you?"

"Eekhaut? You still alive? I assumed they'd buried you over there in Brussels. What's going on, buddy?"

"They tried to bury me but found out after a while they couldn't shut me up even six feet under. I'm in Holland now, but that's a long story."

Dewaal looked his way, ignoring the traffic just long enough to warn him with her eyes. He ignored her.

"I need your help for a thing that's both urgent and confidential," he continued.

"Aha. As if it would be any different. I assumed you didn't call to ask about my health."

"I'm willing to discuss your health all right, and we can have a pint at the Domus when I'm in Leuven. But I have a name for you: Annelies Calster, C-A-L-S-T-E-R. She's a Dutch student. She has a sister Eileen, E-I-L-E-E-N, who will most probably be traveling from Amsterdam to Leuven. And she'll meet up with her sister. You need to keep an eye on both till we arrive. And this is a serious matter: we have good reason to believe both their lives are in danger."

"No shit! You just touched down in Holland and already you're dealing with international human trafficking. And murder? Any good reason why you can't talk to us officially?"

"Local prosecutor—the one in Amsterdam—refuses to do the paperwork."

"That's annoying. Good, I'll see what I can do. You got an address?"

"No, I'm afraid not. But you can find her through your contacts at the university. Throw her name at the computer."

"Of course. And unofficially."

"That's it. Nobody hears about this. There's also politics involved."

"As it always is. Human trafficking. Dirty business. Count me in. I'll jot down your number and call you back ASAP."

"Thanks, Alberto," Eekhaut said, cutting the connection.

"Can he be trusted?" Dewaal asked. "Because I don't want any trouble with these off-the-books deals."

"Absolutely trustworthy."

"You seem sure."

"I saved his life once. That means something, I guess. And we worked together for a dozen or so years. Can't do better than that. And if it's enough for me . . ."

Dewaal said nothing.

The traffic got thicker. They hardly made any progress. "Shit!" she said. "I'm going to use the siren and lights."

"Why didn't you do that before?"

"Because of the speed cameras. I'll be asked what the urgency is. And will have to fill out a bunch of documents that will have to be signed by four different civil servants."

"And what we're doing isn't urgent business?"

She gave him a look, reached for the dashboard, and flipped two switches. Sirens and lights: suddenly cars started to make room for them. They advanced more rapidly but not yet at full speed. They drove along the Rotterdam ringway, after which they managed to speed up again. For a few minutes, another police car followed them while they were doing ninety in the left lane, but then it disappeared again.

"They checked our registration," Dewaal said.

Eekhaut's phone vibrated. Alberto again. "Walter. I found her address. Note it down: Vanderlindenstraat 8, Leuven. You know where that is?"

"I think I do. Student rooms?"

"Yes. I'm in my car down the street, and I'm keeping an eye on the house. Nothing to see at the moment. What does your Eileen look like?"

"Short dark hair, punk, bit unkempt, skinny, tall."

"Like about half the female student population of Leuven. I see. This can't be hard. When are you here?"

"In another two hours, maybe three. We're passing Rotterdam. And traffic is—"

"I hear a siren."

"That's us."

"Right. Well, I'll stick around. See you later. What if your girl turns up?"

"Follow her. We want to speak to her. And make sure that she isn't already being followed."

"By who?"

"We don't know."

"You're no great help, Walter. So I hunt for ghosts. Like in the good old days. Well, see you."

Thanks to the sirens, they managed to speed all the way to the Belgian border. Antwerp would be their next problem. Eekhaut checked his watch. Late afternoon. They had been on their way far too long. He calculated that they would need about forty-five minutes to Leuven. He was hungry, but there was no time to eat.

Dewaal kept on speeding. She only slowed down on the Antwerp ringway. They took the exit to the E19.

"Don't go all the way to Brussels," he said. "Too long a detour and too much traffic at this time of the day. Take the Hofstade exit and drive to Leuven from there."

She didn't comment but followed his instructions. He switched off the navigation system. They drove the distance to Leuven at high speeds along a two-lane provincial road.

Leuven, finally.

It didn't feel like coming home.

But then, he had been away for only a couple of days.

33

"She has a brother and a sister," Monet said. "Did the brother enlighten us?"

Andreï Tarkovski managed to keep his hands from shaking. They would shake not because he was confronted with Monet again but for what had happened during the last hour, which had been one hour too much in his life. He wanted to forget that hour, but couldn't.

He sat opposite Monet in the man's office, deep in a labyrinthine old building close to Central Station. The vague smell of machine oil and decrepit electric machinery hung in the air. From a distance, the rattle and drone of trains could be heard. This looked like a temporary office, with hastily gathered furniture and new, expensive computer equipment.

No secretaries in sight, no evidence of any administration, no security guards, and no windows. A day later, this office would again be a storehouse or an empty lot. A day later, this whole operation would have become virtual, a company consisting of nothing more than a mailbox and an internet site. Monet probably ran a number of these companies. Sometimes they would do something real, like exchanging money and spending money and in fact laundering money. Not that Tarkovski cared.

Monet had given him the address of Eileen Calster's brother over the phone. A little visit, he had suggested. Surprise the young fella with a little visit and listen to what he had to tell about his next of kin.

"There was very little the brother could tell us," Tarkovski admitted. His soul felt hard as ice. Monet expected a report. He got a report. He got words. What he did not get was the pain and the fear.

"Let's return to the heart of the matter," Monet said succinctly. He didn't want to be informed about the methods the two men had used to extract information from Calster. "Does he know where his sister is?"

Andreï was reminded of Parnow. He thought about Parnow all the time now. Parnow's face was in his mind all the time, his immobile face. He had wanted to stop Parnow, but he knew the man wouldn't have let him. There was no way back. That much Tarkovski had understood. Parnow could have arranged for a way back, but he had closed off that exit the moment he put his strong, ugly hands around the boy's throat.

The boy hadn't wanted to talk. He had a specific air about him, Tarkovski had noted, angry and careless at the same time. He didn't seem to appreciate the urgency of the situation. "Where is Eileen?" Tarkovski had asked him. The question seemed to have no meaning to the boy. He could even have asked him—

Oh, it didn't matter anymore.

And now he too, Tarkovski, was implicated in murder.

A senseless, cruel murder. Because the boy had told them where Eileen was. Once he understood the question, he just replied.

Parnow's eyes. And his hands. That seemed to be the only thing Andreï remembered. The boy had died in silence. He had hardly resisted, as if he welcomed death. Strange boy, living in that cell-like room of his. Had died with no more fuss than a quiet sigh.

"The other sister, Annelies, lives and studies in Belgium," he said.

"She must be easy to find."

"She is," Tarkovski said. He did the brain work. Parnow would do the brute work. He was the one who asked the questions. He knew which of them was more esteemed by his Russian master. He had no illusions.

"Why are you still here, then?" Monet asked.

"Because I wanted to keep you informed."

"You could have done that over the phone while driving to Belgium."

"The phone might be tapped."

"So what? You don't have to name names. Two words would have sufficed. Where's the gorilla, by the way?"

"Parnow? He's waiting downstairs."

"And the Bentley?"

"We had it brought back, along with the driver."

"Good. In the garage of this building, you'll find a new 3 Series BMW. A black one. Clean and registered. Keys are in it. Paperwork is in the glove compartment. Take the car and drive to Belgium."

"To Leuven."

"Wherever she is. I don't give a shit where you end up. Find Eileen Calster and bring the list back to me. Whatever you do with her is not my concern. But make sure she doesn't talk about this anymore."

34

Van Gils cursed and turned the wheel sharply to the right. The Mondeo came to a stop against a green waste container. Pedestrians stepped back. The Mercedes came to a screeching halt behind the police car. Prinsen threw open his door and rolled onto the ground. He thought of only one thing: how to draw his weapon as quickly as possible.

Three, four loud bangs sounded in the street accompanied by other noises: breaking glass, screaming people, car alarms.

And the stench of oil and guns.

He got to his knees, drew the SIG Sauer from its holster and chambered a round in one smooth move, and pointed it upward. He took cover behind the rear of the Mondeo.

They teach you a car won't necessarily stop bullets but slows them down, and you stand a better chance of survival with a slower bullet, with less energy. He kept the car between him and the assailants.

The Mercedes backed up again, wheels spinning and rubber smoking. A man wearing a ski cap hung halfway out of the rear passenger window. He held a sawed-off shotgun. He wasn't looking at Prinsen. His attention was on the front end of the Mondeo, where he expected trouble.

When he noticed Prinsen, he turned the barrel of his rifle in the direction of the detective.

Prinsen fired. Two shots. He hit the Mercedes. The driver shifted gears. The heavy car spun round. The shooter lost his bearings on Prinsen.

The vehicle disappeared from Prinsen's sight. He rose. The Mercedes turned a corner. Other vehicles were halted chaotically in the street, with the drivers kept out of sight.

He stepped around the Mondeo and opened the dented door on the driver's side.

Van Gils hung over the steering wheel. Glass and blood. This didn't look good.

Prinsen tucked his gun away and took out his phone.

35

VANDERLINDENSTRAAT WAS A QUIET street in the southern part of the city. Eekhaut was familiar with it, since he grew up around here. Even after thirty-five years, little had changed. The whole neighborhood had been built in the fifties and early sixties and consisted mainly of large multistoried family houses, occasionally interspersed with small apartment blocks that were added in the seventies.

"Park the car in a side street," he told Dewaal. "This is Bayostraat. Park here, where it's less visible. There aren't many cars around here with a Dutch license plate."

Dewaal parked. They walked around the corner to Vanderlindenstraat. A silver Ford Focus was parked halfway down the street. The man behind the wheel opened his window. "Hello, partner," he said to Eekhaut.

"Appreciate this," Eekhaut said to the man. "This is Chief Superintendent Dewaal of the Dutch AIVD."

"Good afternoon, Chief," Albert said, still from behind the wheel. "Come and join me."

They joined Albert. Dewaal sat in the back, Eekhaut in front. He showed a picture to Albert. "Eileen Calster. Have you seen her yet?"

"No, don't think so. Nobody has entered or left the house since I arrived here. This happens to be my day off, by the way, partner. Just so you know. Doing you a big favor—so you know that too."

"There's never a day off for a dedicated policeman, but I appreciate your efforts," Eekhaut said.

"Never a day off for a policeman?" Dewaal cracked. "I'll certainly remember that when you ask me for a vacation, Walter."

Albert glanced in the mirror. "What's all this about?"

"Murder," Eekhaut said. "Break-in, theft, conspiracy to commit. Political, all of that. You can easily imagine the mess we're in."

"Arrest warrant?"

"Not yet. We can't arrest the girl. She doesn't have to know that, however. We prefer—"

"You've already been working too long for the Dutch, mate," Albert said. "No offense, ma'am."

"We prefer," Eekhaut continued, "that she'll return with us out of her own free will."

"But you don't have that piece of paper. Be careful," Albert said.

"I'm always careful."

"Yeah, that's why you were so popular with everybody." He glanced in the mirror again. "But maybe I'm saying too much."

"I'm aware of his reputation, Albert," Dewaal said. "I know what he's worth. Nothing you say can surprise me anymore."

"This isn't about me," Eekhaut interrupted. "Thing is, what do we do? We don't know if Eileen is coming here."

"But that was your bloody idea," Dewaal said. "You were sure she would come to her loving sister in Leuven."

"And you could have involved my colleagues," Albert insisted. "Even without your prosecutor backing you up."

"We're not supposed to operate outside of the Netherlands," Dewaal said. She looked out. "Who's that?"

A girl was coming down the street. She was blond, slender, in jeans and a sweater. She carried a white canvas bag. She stopped at number eight and opened the door with a key, went in, and closed the door again.

"Annelies?" Eekhaut asked.

Albert shook his head. "No idea. I noticed there're four bells on that door. You don't have a picture of her? You have no idea what she looks like? Does she resemble her sister?"

"We don't know."

"Then we'll have to wait. I can't stay here, though. My wife will wonder what I'm doing on my day off."

"We'll take it from here, Albert," Dewaal said. "I'll park our car here so we have a better view."

"What, with the Dutch tags?"

"Can't be helped."

"Good thing your emergency lights are invisible. They would completely betray us."

"And so Albert can still enjoy the rest of the day," she said. She got out and went to the Porsche.

Eekhaut said goodbye to Albert.

"Peppy little lady you got there," Albert said.

"She sure is."

"Better than your previous boss?"

Was she? Better than any of his previous bosses? Teunis, for one? Yes, he was sure of that already. She could handle a Porsche Cayenne in heavy traffic. She endured him, had done so for several days already. A good start.

"We only just met," he said. "The thing is, she's already aware of my reputation, and she has seen what I'm capable of."

"But still . . . Holland!"

"My opinion wasn't asked, Albert. They told me to get as far away from Brussels as possible. Even so, new people, new challenges."

"As if you still need challenges. Couldn't you just spend those last years in some rustic village, as the local cop or whatever?"

"Nothing was working anymore for me," Eekhaut said. "Certainly not Brussels. Not with the social diseases I saw there. And local politics being worse than anywhere else. They offered early retirement, what could I do? Spend the next twenty years or so in my apartment? There are only so many books you can read. Holidays? Soaking up the sun in some third-rate holiday resort, with what pension I would get?"

The black Porsche parked behind them. "Yeah, partner, I understand," Albert said. "There's your boss now. I'll leave you to it then. Success. And you have my number, in case you need help. You know you can call me. You do, don't you?"

"I do. Thanks again. I owe you one. Here, or in Amsterdam."

Eekhaut changed cars. He was glad the Porsche wasn't the sports version. That would have been a bit too cozy, he and Dewaal in a small sports car.

She was on the phone. She listened. Then she said, "Nothing can be done about that, I'm afraid. I'll be back by tomorrow evening at the latest." She listened again. "Yes, very well then." She closed the phone. Eekhaut didn't look at her. He didn't want to talk about her personal problems.

"We'll need food and something to drink," she said. "You know the neighborhood. Can you get us something? Sandwiches, that sort of thing?"

"There're a few places in Naamsestraat where we can have a bite. It's only a few streets from here. But that's mainly student territory, so I'm not sure if the culinary standard is high enough. Or do you want me to get something to eat in the car?"

"Yes, Eekhaut," she repeated. "This is what we specialists call a stakeout. One of us stays here. The other fetches food and coffee."

He shrugged. He wasn't in the mood for irony. And perhaps Eileen would not show up, or not right away, so they might have a long night ahead.

"Take your time. I'll call you if anything happens."

He got out again and walked in the direction of the beltway. Then he went downhill toward Naamsestraat. What would she want to eat? Choices were limited. A sandwich bar and a pita restaurant. He chose sandwiches. Having no idea of her preferences, he took two large sandwiches with cheese and ham, two cans of soda, and four bottles of water. He took everything with him back to the car.

"Ham and cheese," he said. "Hope you like it." He deposited the water on the back seat. Dehydration was sometimes a problem during long stakeouts. "No coffee?" she mumbled around a mouthful of sandwich. "We must get coffee as well. I have an empty thermos in the trunk for occasions like this."

"There're a few pubs around, but I'm not sure if they'll sell me bulk coffee," he said. "I'll give it a shot."

36

"You pissed somebody off big time," Veneman said. The officer filled the doorway with his presence, and this was a larger door than most—this was a hospital, where doors were large enough for beds to pass through. Veneman wore a navy-blue suit but no tie. The suit seemed a bit tight around the shoulders. He looked and talked like a police officer, as if each word were expensive.

"Yes," Prinsen said simply. Yes, they had pissed somebody off. But was that sufficient reason for an attack on two police officers in the streets of Amsterdam? Did they really piss somebody off that much? This was the stuff of movies. Not something that happened regularly to Dutch cops.

But Prinsen knew that organized crime had become more ruthless over these last few years, as much in Holland as anywhere else. The smallest provocation warranted an all-out reaction, with excessive violence. These people were mostly short-fused and would not be fucked with.

He had already been warned at the police academy. Organized crime was a hotbed of psychopaths and freaks, and most came from areas of conflict or countries with a strong antisocial tradition. The Balkans, Russia, Georgia, Serbia, Middle East, South China, Korea. Mostly—but not entirely—people who had known only repressive regimes and poverty. Dutch criminals had always been bad enough. They fought over lost territory, over a missed opportunity, over matters of personal honor. But they also talked to each other. They made deals, divided the territory. Divided the business. Occasionally somebody got wasted, maybe spectacularly. But that was the exception. Now some veterans had left the business because it had become too bloody.

"Van Gils will be all right," Veneman said. "He'd be dead if they had wanted. A couple of small holes that can be fixed."

Van Gils had been in surgery for some time now, or possibly was still in recovery, Prinsen didn't know. He had driven his partner directly to the hospital, at full speed, sirens and all. With a car that had more holes in it than the man did.

"They got the pellets out of him, gave him blood, gave him tranquilizers, and now they're sewing him up. Tough guy, that Van Gils." Veneman was rarely in the office because he usually worked on the Bureau's legal affairs. Not in the streets, but in the courts. "And don't let your aunt say different," he continued. "There's a whole generation of policemen, people like Van Gils, who made the force what it is today. Even the Bureau. And they, well, they're wary of young people like yourself, with academic degrees but no street cred."

"She never said otherwise," Prinsen said. "I'm sure she has nothing but respect for him." As if he could know what Dewaal really thought. But he wanted to appease Veneman.

Veneman entered the room. "Let me tell you something about Van Gils. When he was still working as a detective with the Amsterdam force, he was in the office when a patrol brought in two Moroccan boys. Real dickheads, the worst. Sociopaths up to their eyeballs. They had stabbed an old woman after they'd taken her handbag. Stabbed her just for fun and laughs. There was no need for that, they already had her money. See the sort of animals I'm talking about? So Van Gils and a colleague question them. 'What do we care about the old bitch,' one of the boys said. Van Gils jumped at him and whacked him over the head. One blow. You know the size of Van Gils. So, broken jaw, concussion, hospital, a lot of fucking trouble, of course. Even a lawyer. Team leader covered up the whole thing. Suspect had tried to escape. Who believes a kid like that anyway? Van Gils sat at the woman's hospital bed for three entire days, made sure her cats got taken care of. Even organized a fundraiser for her medical expenses. But maybe nothing of this means anything at all to you, I don't know."

"Is that what all of you liked best? The beat? Working the streets? Old women and Moroccan thugs? Stabbings? Vandalism?"

Veneman shook his head, a bit sadly, it seemed. As if he regretted having to be here, in a hospital room with a colleague in surgery while criminals roamed the streets. "We knew nothing else, at that time. It was useful work. Keeping the scum off the streets. But things evolve. Van Gils understood soon enough. Crime changes and so does the police. We both transferred to AIVD because they needed hardened cops like us. But the new chief has never known the sort of situation we came from. I'm sure she understands and appreciates us, but she'll never have that same relation with crime that we do."

"I'm sure she appreciates Van Gils."

"Oh, she does. But at some point, she wanted to get rid of him. Talked to him about taking an early retirement and all that. Well-meant, I'm sure, but not what Van Gils needed. He didn't want anybody else to decide when he was going to leave. And maybe he can't go yet. Has a daughter in college. Maybe, after this—"

"What am I supposed to do now?"

"You'll be working with me for a couple of days, I guess," Veneman said. "There are three people working on the incident. You and Van Gils made enemies, that's for sure. Which is unavoidable, given the current climate. These criminals know who you are, what you look like. Between crooks and cops, it's a small world, even at our level. The advantage is that we'll soon know who they are as well. Did you have a clear look at one of the assailants?"

"Black ski mask, I'm afraid. And things happening much too fast."

"And what about the three men you saw earlier? They could have been the same men."

"I don't know. Why would they first show themselves and then shoot at us? Makes no sense."

Veneman inspected his hands and then observed the place where Van Gils's bed had been before he was taken to surgery. "You woke somebody up, that much is certain. With your questions, with your presence. This much violence means that somebody really took offense. Russians, I'm sure. These new Russians, very unlike the ones that have been here for years and kept quiet. Different ethics, new rules. Perestroi-ka-capitalism. This is taking an ugly turn."

"But why shoot at us? Van Gils and me?"

"You came too close, I guess. They don't fear regular police, but they know we're their real enemy. You show your face in the neighbor-hood, and they'll react. We can expect more of this to come."

Prinsen remained silent.

"And what happened to you today," Veneman said, "is going to affect you much more than you can imagine, kid. Van Gils got hit, but in a way so did you. Not by a bullet. You were shot at, and you escaped unharmed, but it's going to be in your head for a long time."

"Of course it will."

"And you'll ask yourself, why was Van Gils hit and not me?"

Prinsen looked at his hands. They were stable. Had been for the whole time. He was all right. He was going to be all right.

"And your weapon? Did you give it to the tech boys?"

"Yes, I did."

"Get it back right away. Get another one if you can't get it back soon. You shot twice at the assailants, even if you don't remember. But you did. You used your gun in a street, in public. You probably hit the Mercedes, because we didn't find any impacts. But you may not remember. That's all right. That's shock. No, your hands aren't shaking, but it's in your head. You need to deal with that."

37

Parnow and Andreï Tarkovski drove the black BMW all the way to Leuven. Traffic had been dense. Parnow, at the wheel, didn't utter a word, didn't complain, didn't object. He stared in front of him and occasionally at the side mirrors, focused on driving. A machine driving another machine, that was Tarkovski's impression. A machine that had been given an order and executed that order without deviating for one moment from the preprogrammed path. Not even thinking about the sense of it all.

Exactly the sort of people Keretsky needed for special operations like this. *Ah*, Tarkovski thought, *special operations*. As if that meant anything other than more murder.

That would be the jargon Parnow's companions used in his former military units. Tarkovski couldn't remember all that much about Afghanistan; he had been too young then. But he assumed Parnow had gotten familiar with the local population on a very intimate level. Presumably from behind an automatic weapon. Like all Russians, Tarkovski knew about the shameful retreat of the Russian army. That had been under the Soviets, but it remained a stain on the uniform of many military. Like the Americans in Vietnam.

Was Parnow really just an intelligent killing machine? Tarkovski suspected not. There had been moments of hesitation, short ones, but still. The man's eyes sometimes seemed to express emotions that contradicted the cliché of the cold, dead soldier. But finally, when it came down to it, Parnow would do exactly what was expected of him. And Tarkovski knew full well that included killing in cold blood.

He dozed off against the side window and woke with a sour taste in his mouth. He wanted something to drink. He wanted to freshen up. He couldn't help dozing off, although it annoyed him. But he had never signed on for operations like this. He was supposed to be behind a desk, managing Keretsky's affairs, not going on a search mission with a murderer. He was a diplomat, not a special forces commando.

They passed the border and continued toward Antwerp and then on to Brussels. Finally, they arrived in Leuven. It had taken a seemingly endless four hours.

Tarkovski inspected the piece of paper with the little map he had drawn himself, based on information given him by telephone that morning. He had then consulted Google Maps for a map of Leuven. He guided Parnow into the city. Finding the right street didn't take them long. Parnow slowed down and wanted to turn onto Vanderlindenstraat, but stopped the car at the intersection. He nodded toward the street. A black Porsche Cayenne was parked halfway up the street. With Dutch tags.

"Police," he said.

38

ANNELIES WAVED GOODBYE TO her friends and crossed Ladeuzeplein. It wasn't cold, thanks to a weak sun. The square in front of the university's main library was no longer the student gathering place that it was during spring and summer, when they mostly sat on the low, long stairs and talked and ate. There were some tourists now, gaping at the impaled giant beetle on what looked like a magnified needle—an artwork by Jan Fabre—but they didn't stay long. Most people were just passing by. Annelies sort of liked the beetle, a postmodern work of art that had so many locals scratching their heads when it was installed. It was, she found, sort of ironic.

She was on her way to the Appel, where she would drink another coffee. After that, she would walk back to her room, eat a sandwich, and study. There had been a couple of parties the last two days, parties she couldn't avoid, and she was now behind with her work. Too much fun in Leuven, too many occasions for not working. A city filled to the brim with seductions. For students away from home, some for the first time in their life, this was a recipe for disaster. Too much freedom. Few were able to ignore these seductions.

But in the end, there would be exams. Now, at the end of September, the academic year hadn't even properly begun, so there was still room for distractions. For now, she needed a few hours to wrap her head around a history text, and later she would go out again, not too late, but enough to feel part of the world at large.

Yet nothing like that was going to happen, because Eileen just stepped out of nowhere, in jeans and a T-shirt and carrying a bag. She didn't look happy. Something was wrong.

"God, Eileen, what are you doing here, girl?! Why didn't you—?"

Her sister fell into her arms, weeping. Eileen, all skin and bones, her arms thinner than Annelies remembered. Eileen, always the strongest of the three. Now, however, she was a terrified, desperate little creature who held on to her sister as if they would never again be separated.

"Hey, kiddo, what's happening?" The last time they'd met, Eileen had been full of plans for a future with Pieter Van Boer. That had been ten months ago. Plans, ideas, adventures—everything seemed possible at the time. "Tell me, why are you here?"

"Pieter is dead, Annelies," Eileen said. She wiped her nose on her wrist. Her eyes were red. She had been crying and had missed sleep recently. And it looked like there was more to it than just Pieter's death.

"Come on," Annelies said. "Let's sit somewhere and have a drink, and tell me everything."

Annelies guided her sister to a table on a terrace in front of the library building and ordered two Leffe Blondes. Maybe not what Eileen needed, but it wasn't going to hurt either.

"Now, tell me."

"There was a man in our apartment, and he shot Pieter. Yesterday morning. Like that, with a gun. And he wanted to kill me too. But I ran away."

"You're not serious! Why would anybody want to kill Pieter?"

Eileen drank the Leffe.

"Well?" Annelies insisted. "I know he was into politics, but people don't get killed for that."

"He stole some documents from that party, Van Tillo's party, where he worked. You know, I told you about that. That's what the murderer wanted. Those documents."

"And that's why Pieter had to die?"

"Yes. Seems that way."

"Have you been to the police?" Which sounded like a stupid question, but Eileen was here. She was no longer in Amsterdam.

Eileen shook her head. "No."

So, Annelies thought, not really a stupid question after all. "Why not?"

"Pieter didn't trust the police. He said there were too many right-wing police officers connected with PDN. And some of them were a bit too close with Van Tillo."

"But now we're talking murder—

"All the more reason not to approach them. And I have those documents!"

"Documents?"

"A list of names of people who donated money to the PDN. Pieter wanted to give the list to a sympathetic journalist, but that didn't happen. I'm sure Van Tillo and her gang are behind the murder, but I can't prove that."

"And now you're here—"

"Yes, with the list."

"Which means you're in danger as well."

"I tried to disappear, Annelies. I tried to get as far away from Amsterdam as I could."

"You're not safe here either. Not with that list."

"Then what should I do?"

"Make it public. That's what Pieter would have done."

"Make it public? Where? With whom? I don't know who Pieter would have given that list to. He never told me any names. I know very little about the stuff he was doing. And I left everything, all his documentation, in the apartment."

"And you can't go back there. I can give you a place to crash for a while. I have a room. Nothing grand, but we'll manage."

"Just for a couple of days. Until I've worked out what I should do."

"You should go to the police, kid."

Eileen shook her head and finished the Leffe. It made her light in the head, what with not having eaten enough the whole day. And then the excitement.

"As you like," Annelies said. "I have no good advice to give you. But Pieter . . . dead!" She had met Pieter only a couple of times. To her, he seemed charming but absent. Older and experienced and a bit of a mystery. Too much of a mystery, as it now turned out. Annelies understood what her sister saw in him. She had seemed happy. Whatever it was they had, it had gone beyond mere infatuation.

"Did you speak to Maarten?"

"Maarten. Yes. I stayed the night in his room. Maarten hasn't changed. He can't help it. That's why I came here. And I needed some distance between myself and Amsterdam. I shouldn't have gone to him, but I had nowhere else to go."

"Nobody was following you?"

"Don't think so. But I'm not really sure."

"How did you get here?"

"By train."

"Train. Good. Well, you can stay as long as you need. You have money?"

"Enough for a couple of days."

Annelies went over the options. She couldn't do much. "Money will be a problem. I'll ask our parents . . ."

"No. No way. Keep them out of this."

"Maybe I can find you a job."

"Yes. A job. That would be a good idea."

39

"AND NOW WHAT?" TARKOVSKI asked Parnow. The BMW was parked around the corner from Vanderlindenstraat, out of sight of the Dutch car. The goddamn Dutch car that fouled things up completely for Tarkovski. It couldn't be anything but a police vehicle. This was not some lost tourist. This was the Dutch police—and probably the AIVD, with a car like that—observing what could be Eileen Calster's hideout. How did they get here? How did they find out? Why didn't things go his way? The whole affair could have been settled with a kidnapping or just a retrieval of the list. He hated complicated situations.

Parnow was impatient in his own fashion. He bit the nail of his thumb, something Tarkovski hadn't expected he'd ever witness. Parnow was supposed to be the alpha male who could deal with any situation. Abduction, break-ins, a bit of rough violence. Whatever. *And murder*, Tarkovski thought. *Let's not forget murder.*

He should be the one biting his nail.

Parnow turned to him. "What now, comrade?" It sounded ironic. No one used the term anymore. Except some die-hard communists, those who thought lovingly about Stalin. "Our assignment is to get the list. And we can do whatever we want with the girl, as I seem to remember."

Tarkovski shook his head. "Retrieving the list is enough, Parnow. I don't want another murder on my conscience. I can do without that." He could do without a stretch in a Dutch prison, that was for sure, which was where he was going to end up if things got out of hand. And he could do without a Russian prison even more. The things he'd heard about Russian prisons. He knew Keretsky would make sure nothing untoward happened to him, but he would be in prison nevertheless.

But Keretsky's anger, that would be worse than prison. They couldn't afford to mess this up.

"Hmmm," Parnow growled. Almost literally. "Violence is unavoidable when you work for Keretsky, mate. You know that." He glanced out of the side window.

Tarkovski could physically feel the enmity. "I prefer not," he said. "We keep strictly to the terms of the assignment." *And I make up the rules while we're here*, he thought. *If that's no longer possible, then we'll drive back to Amsterdam.* But he realized he had little say in that. He couldn't overpower Parnow if it came to that.

"We have nothing," Parnow said. "No girl, no list."

Tarkovski considered the problem. He knew all too well they couldn't return without results. But there it was—with the police around, it would be difficult to kidnap the girl.

He needed fresh air. Sitting with Parnow in the confines of the car was suffocating. He opened the door and stepped out. Parnow didn't react. Tarkovski stretched his limbs. Four hours in a car. He needed room. The air was cold. The streets were quiet. A quiet neighborhood with large houses. Rich people, he assumed. He admired these Belgians. They lived in bigger houses than the Dutch did. They had more space to themselves, it seemed.

Two girls approached from the other end of the street. They walked in the direction of Vanderlindenstraat. One of the girls was Eileen Calster.

He jumped into the car.

40

"THAT'S HER," DEWAAL SAID.

"And probably her sister," affirmed Eekhaut.

The two girls walked down the street, hanging on to each other as if afraid of the walls or open spaces. Two frightened but equally spirited girls. Who together would take on the big, bad world by themselves, if need be.

"What now?" Eekhaut asked. "Assume we pick her up for her protection. We assume she is in danger. We don't need an arrest warrant for that. She won't even resist, I guess."

"Yes, why don't we?" Dewaal said and stepped out of the car. "But it seems highly uncertain that we can convince the prosecutor that she's worth listening to. Oh, whatever. Let's do it."

Eekhaut fell into step behind her. "I didn't come here with the prosecutor in mind," he said.

"Miss Eileen Calster," Dewaal called.

Both girls turned. They eyed the well-dressed woman suspiciously. And then the less well-dressed older man.

Dewaal produced her card. "Chief Superintendent Dewaal, Dutch security services. My colleague Walter Eekhaut. We've been looking for you, miss. Do you mind accompanying us?"

"You can't arrest me," Eileen said. Defiantly.

He sister held on to her as if she wanted to prevent Eileen being taken by force.

"No," Dewaal said, "we can't. But we would like to protect you."

"I don't want that!"

"It's for the best, Miss Calster. Other people are looking for you, and they may not have any favorable intentions at all concerning your person."

"Pieter didn't trust the police. Why would I?"

"Pieter is dead," Eekhaut said, without mercy, just stating a fact. "And it wasn't the police who did that."

Eileen looked at him. "We all know who ordered that murder. What are you going to do about it?"

"We can only go after whoever ordered the murder," Dewaal said, "if and when we have a clear-cut case. The information in your possession, Miss Calster, is important to our investigation. Either you come with us out of your free will or I'll have you arrested for obstructing the investigation and withholding evidence." It sounded professional and impressive, but she was bluffing. Eileen didn't know that, though.

Annelies said, "This isn't your jurisdiction."

Smart-ass, Dewaal thought. "Let's not get too technical, miss," she said. "This is about the safety of people, not about legal details."

"I'll scream if you touch me," Eileen said.

Eekhaut knew the situation warranted a very radical approach. He took two photographs out of his pocket and showed them to the girls. The pictures left nothing to the imagination, which was why he'd brought them. Sometimes—usually—photographs were more convincing than words. He said, "This is what remained of Pieter Van Boer after he was shot from close range with a 9mm pistol. It's the kind of gun that makes for nasty wounds. Don't you think so? And how will you look after the assassin has finished with you?"

Dewaal shot reproachful glances at him, but he ignored them. She was predictable under these circumstances, and he made good use of that predictability.

The girls looked at the pictures.

Annelies said, "Fuck!"

Eileen looked paler than before, as if she might faint. Annelies held her.

Eekhaut grasped the girl's arm. "It is entirely up to you, but there's a choice to make, Eileen. If you want Pieter's murderer to be punished, then you'll come with us."

"Yes," she said. "Yes, I'll come with you."

41

It was difficult for Eileen to say goodbye to her sister. They had a long cuddle, and there were tears and whispered words that weren't meant to be overheard by the detectives. Eileen produced the famous list from her bag and unceremoniously gave it to Dewaal. For her, it was as if she were taking leave of her life, or what was left of it, as if she were giving the last part of Pieter away. Then the girl stepped into the back of the Porsche.

"We won't drive back to Amsterdam today," Dewaal announced. "I don't feel up to it. And the traffic isn't getting any better, even this late. I propose we spend the night here, somewhere in Leuven, and drive back tomorrow morning."

"I can live with that," Eekhaut said. He didn't care. "Finding a hotel can't be a problem." He turned around, toward the girl. "Did you bring things for at least one night?"

She nodded. On the seat next to her was the bag she'd brought from Amsterdam. Her face was still wet from her tears. She wanted to disappear into a corner of the seat. He was sorry for her—she had become involved in a conspiracy much larger than she could ever have imagined. She had been gulped down the throat of a very big and nasty whale. He'd known other people in her shoes. People to whom the same sort of thing had happened. And most of them were left with what little remained of their life. Except for those who were dead.

"I'd like to freshen up," she said.

"Let's go to the Novotel," Eekhaut proposed. "Nice rooms, you can take a shower and then eat something. From there we have almost immediate access to the highway tomorrow morning. If we start early, we'll be in Amsterdam by ten."

"You'll have to explain to me where I can find that hotel," Dewaal said.

He pointed. "Take the beltway here, and just drive on. I'll tell you where to turn off."

She followed his instructions. She didn't notice the black BMW that followed them. She was used to seeing Dutch tags, and she had other things on her mind. Her mind was already in Amsterdam, where more trouble was waiting for her.

They reached the hotel, opposite a large brewery. "There's a parking garage on the left," Eekhaut said.

"Shall I let you out first?" Dewaal suggested.

"No," Eekhaut said. "We'll get out once we're in the garage. It seems safer. And less obvious." He'd contracted the paranoia virus a long time ago, and it remained with him. You never underestimated your opponent. That was a major rule if you wanted to survive the virus. And you stayed one step ahead of your opponent. There would always be a conspiracy, invisible but all too real. And everyone was after you. Yes, you.

Dewaal drove into the underground garage and parked the car. The parking spaces were narrow, suited for midget cars only. Midget cars, midget people, Eekhaut thought. But Dewaal nevertheless managed to slide the Porsche in between two other cars. They got out, with some difficulty. "I need toiletry things," he said. "Maybe I'll drop by my apartment."

"We'll book the rooms first," Dewaal said. This was her operation. She made the decisions. They took the elevator to the ground floor. "A twin room and a single," Dewaal announced to the girl behind the desk. She produced a golden credit card. "For one night. Adjoining rooms."

The girl consulted a screen. "Second floor, ma'am," she said. "Two rooms." She started filling out forms. They were given their keys. Dewaal gave the single room key to Eekhaut. Looked at him. "What else did you expect?" she said. She seemed amused by his momentary confusion, as if she had caught him in a reverie about cohabitation with his boss.

"Oh," he said, "No." His attention had been elsewhere. Things from the past. He had been here before, in this hotel. Had long conversations in the bar. With suspects and informants and other police officers. But also with a woman who at some point had confided in him, had told him—and only him—about her present and her past. She had clearly wanted more than just a talk. That had happened when Esther was still alive. He had lunched with the woman in the restaurant on the ground floor but had made it clear that their relationship was not a relationship.

"Can I take the car?" he asked.

The woman had come by car, a bright red Italian sports model. It was a telling detail. It said too much about her temperament and her expectations in life. And her expectations of him. She was married, but it wasn't much of a marriage, as she was keen on telling him.

She wanted him as a trophy.

He had pitied her, one way or the other, which was why he'd rejected her offer.

Dewaal threw him the key to the Porsche.

"We'll sleep in the same room?" Eileen asked.

"Yes, girl, we will," Dewaal said. "I'll stay close. Don't worry. And I don't snore."

The girl shrugged. She was in no position to complain. The presence of the self-assured and authoritarian police officer seemed to reassure her.

"You want something to eat?" Dewaal asked.

She nodded. "Please."

"And you?" Dewaal asked Eekhaut.

"Not right now. I want to collect a few things. See both of you later." While they went to their room, he took the elevator back to the garage and unlocked the car. He reached for his holster. Yes, he had his gun. He didn't know if he was permitted to carry a weapon in Belgium, but he didn't care—it seemed irrelevant.

He started the car and drove off into town. Ten minutes later, he parked again, next to the building he had left only a few days ago. It seemed ages now. He glanced around. No, nobody was paying him any attention.

His apartment was dark and quiet. His furniture was covered with plastic sheets. He had switched off the fridge. There was nothing to eat or drink in the place.

He went into the bedroom and pulled the plastic from the wardrobe. In the drawers were his extra sets of underwear, a few shirts, razor blades, toothpaste, and two pots of the shaving cream he ordered from London. Things he hadn't intended to take with him to Amsterdam and that he would need whenever he was in Leuven for a couple of days.

He didn't need to convince himself of the obvious. This apartment was going to be his real home, probably for the rest of his life. He was born in Leuven and he was never going to leave, at least not for any real length of time. He would have to leave behind too much personal history if he did.

He grabbed a small bag from the wardrobe and stowed some items in it. He closed the wardrobe and replaced the plastic sheeting. Then he hurried out of the apartment again. He had already spent too many long evenings here. That's why he hadn't minded the move to Amsterdam. Teunis had done him a favor.

He parked the Porsche in the hotel garage and took the elevator to the second floor. His room was nice, airy, modern, and practical. He stowed his gun under his pillow, undressed, and took a long shower. Then he went to bed. He hadn't eaten but didn't care. He slept almost immediately.

42

DARK CLOUDS HAD FORMED over Amsterdam. It started raining by 7:00 p.m., indicating it would rain all night. Prinsen left the hospital, looked up, took off his jacket, and draped it over his head. He never bothered with an umbrella. But then, of course, he would get wet all over. He observed the street, people scurrying past him like characters in a shadow play. They all seemed hurried. Shoulders hunched. He hoped to find a taxi, because it was a long walk back to his place. Veneman had left earlier, after their conversation. By then, Van Gils had been returned to his room, drowsy and weak but more or less fixed up. Prognosis, so the doctors said, was good. No vital organs were hurt. He would be spending a bit of time in the hospital, which Van Gils started complaining about right away.

"We'll keep an eye on him," the doctor said. Prinsen left as soon as he felt he could. He wasn't good at speaking to doctors.

The investigation would be temporarily suspended, Veneman told him. Too few leads and no information from contacts. Other things were happening. Things that needed urgent attention more than an armed assault on two police officers.

"You be ready when I call, even tonight," Veneman had told him. "Anyway, you need to report to the office tomorrow morning."

"And what about the Keretsky business?"

"There is no Keretsky business. Not at the moment, there isn't. The man returned to the motherland, and we let the case rest. It's frustrating, I know, but there's not much we can do at the moment. We'll tackle Keretsky some other time."

He noticed Prinsen's reaction. "What? Did you assume I wouldn't want to get that scum behind bars? We won't allow our people to be shot at. So we'll get them later."

No taxi in sight. Prinsen walked down the street and ended on a small square with a coffee bar. He stepped in, ordered an espresso, and took out his cell phone. Van Gils was always on his mind, Van Gils who had been shot. And the possible link with Keretsky. And whatever else. It seemed every criminal activity was linked. He told himself he was overreacting.

He called a taxi and drank his espresso. The taxi arrived. He was home twenty minutes later.

The only sound he heard in his apartment was the dripping of water. The neighbors conspired to keep him surrounded by silence. He unfastened his holster and tucked it and the gun away in a drawer. It felt strange to have a weapon in the apartment. It would need cleaning now that he'd used it. He would do that with the usual care, but not tonight. He couldn't bring himself to handle the gun now. He feared his hands might still shake. Too many bizarre thoughts went through his head. The gun might have an all too fatal attraction.

He sat at the table. These sorts of thoughts would have to be kept as far away as possible. He sat in the dark apartment listening to the rain. A rational part of his mind told him it would be a good idea to leave the weapon at the office. That same part told him to rationalize what had happened to him and Van Gils. But this dark mood of his wasn't about the life-threatening situation they'd experienced. It wasn't about Van Gils in the hospital.

He had no idea, however, what it really was about.

Even during his schooling, he had been warned: it is difficult to deal with sudden, extreme violence. People will say they're all right, but they aren't. It's mainly about reflexes: heightened adrenaline level, tensed muscles, increased heartbeat, and so on. The body knows how to deal with a sudden threat. The mind doesn't. The mind can't cope.

They tell you what to do about the voices in your head, the rational and irrational ones. *You should see a specialist about that.* So much for their advice.

I shouldn't sit in the dark, Prinsen thought. *That's not a brilliant idea. I should switch on the lights. Nobody can cope sensibly in the dark. People aren't meant to live in the dark, wear dark clothes all the time, and see nothing but the unnatural straight lines and corners of a city around them. People can't live with the idea of being damned forever on account of something like original sin, cast out by a vengeful God and awaiting eternal punishment in hell.*

That was exactly what people do to each other: convince each other that they're doomed, that humankind is rotten to the core, that there is no salvation except in death.

He got up and switched on the lights.

The apartment looked dreary even then. Chilly, lonely.

Especially lonely.

People fled loneliness, usually for the company of others, with friends, with family, in a pub. At work. He had fled from precisely these things because all of them confronted him with his past.

And he couldn't handle his past. He couldn't handle the insistent voice of the rector, the hands of his mother, the eye of God, and the eternal punishment. None of these would ever be out of his life, never. Not as long as he permitted them to linger on.

As a child, he'd been convinced that the eye of God and the hands of his mother guaranteed a fair life. Sinners were punished, the guilty condemned. God saw everything. Even his mother seemed to possess a supernatural power. She knew everything he'd done, saw through every little lie. She called him the black sheep of the family, and he never could understand why. No sin of his was important enough to have any adverse effect on the family.

When he glided from childhood into adolescence, his biological urges became urgent, then unbearable. He allowed himself erotic dreams while strolling the dense fields during the summer, or lying about doing nothing. He learned how to masturbate and enjoyed what must have been the most heinous sin of all. Girls were strange, distant creatures, only to be observed in the wild, sometimes naked in the deep pools hidden in the woods, but mostly fully clothed and withdrawn. Fear and sex were constant companions.

The rational part of his mind told him that nothing he did was a deviation, a sin. Already at that time, he saw through the lies, the religious inventions that chained people to a heavenly despot. But his experiences precluded a regular and normal sexual relationship. And a deeper, darker part in him warned him: even in adult life, you will never experience love or normal sexual relations. You were not conditioned for either.

And so he would leave the gun in the office next time. Because of what that older, deeper part of his mind whispered.

Maybe he fell asleep after that thought. He woke and found his watch. It was four thirty. And then he realized he had been woken by his phone. He answered. It was Veneman. "Sorry to drag you out of bed at this hour, kid, but the boss needs us. And urgently. Grab your gun and put on some clothes. I'll wait for you at the office. We're going on a hunting trip!"

43

TARKOVSKI CLOSED THE DOOR of the BMW. He looked worried. He tried to hide his emotions, but he knew he sometimes could be read like an open book. "They've taken rooms in the hotel," he said.

Parnow ignored him.

"But I don't have their room number," Tarkovski continued.

"Ask at reception," Parnow suggested as if it was obvious.

"They won't give us the room numbers."

"Of course they will. It's how you do it." His Russian was short and to the point. A military man's Russian. He didn't need diplomacy in dealing with Tarkovski.

"No violence," Tarkovski warned. "We can't have that. We're not in Amsterdam."

"I don't speak English," Parnow said. "You have to ask."

Tarkovski looked at him. "Aren't you listening? They don't give room numbers to strangers just because they ask. Maybe they do where you come from but not here."

"Where I come from, people treat me with respect. I expect the same from you."

Tarkovski shrugged. *You'll be finished*, he thought, *after I've talked this through with Keretsky. When I tell him you fucked up this case, he'll have no respect for you anymore. He'll kick your ass back to Russia where you'll end up as the bodyguard of some third-rate mafioso. Or with a gunshot wound in a dirty, rotten city, somewhere far away from any decent medical help. That's your fate.*

But he kept these thoughts to himself. Sharing them with Parnow would not be a good idea. He was afraid of the man. He was the sort of man who had no interest in the quality of other people's lives. Parnow would strangle him on the spot. Or shoot him, except that it made too much noise.

Parnow reached into his pocket and produced a card, which he handed to Tarkovski. It was a Dutch police card.

"How did you get this?"

"You're an idiot," Parnow said. "Go to reception, show them the card, tell them you're a colleague of Dewaal, and ask for the room number. It is simple."

Tarkovski got out of the car again. "They'll hear I'm not Dutch."

"Do you speak Dutch or not?"

"A little. But maybe not enough. They won't believe I'm Dutch."

"Doesn't matter. Just ask."

They walked into the hotel and turned left toward reception. A young man with a minimalist hairdo smiled at them.

Andreï showed him the police card. "Dutch police," he said, trying to sound formal. "I have an urgent message for Chief Superintendent Dewaal, who's staying with you. This is important. What is her room number?"

The young man looked at the card, wide-eyed. "I really don't know if I can give you . . ."

"Quickly," Tarkovski snapped, trying to embody the role of an impatient police officer on an urgent mission. "We have no time to lose."

"Twenty-five, second floor," the young man said. "Shall I—?"

"No, you don't call her. You don't do anything at all. We will wake her. No phone."

He and Parnow turned toward the elevators. The young man remained behind the reception desk, immobile. The elevator doors opened and both men stepped inside. Tarkovski pushed a button. A moment later, they exited on the second floor. The corridor was empty.

"Left," Parnow said. In Russian. It sounded ominous.

Room twenty-five was at the end of the corridor. Tarkovski hesitated. Parnow drew his gun and screwed the silencer on. He nodded at

Tarkovski, who looked unhappy with the situation. It was all too clear what Parnow's intentions were. And he didn't agree. "Please," he said. "A Chief Superintendent of the AIVD. We can't do this. Mr. Keretsky will be furious."

"We want the list," Parnow said. "Nothing more. After that, we leave."

Tarkovski knew that wasn't going to happen. He knew Parnow wouldn't hesitate to shoot, even if he wasn't provoked.

Parnow produced a small metal object from his pocket, slid it in the lock and pushed, and the lock opened. He pushed against the door. Dark inside. A short corridor, door to the bathroom on the left.

Parnow held his gun in front of him. He stepped over the doorstep.

Two flashes accompanied by two loud bangs welcomed him from inside the room. Bullets struck the wall next to Parnow.

He stepped back. Cool and efficient. And fired his gun. Two, three times.

He banged into Tarkovski, who backed down the corridor. A new shot from inside the room. Plaster shattered.

"Parnow!" Tarkovski said. "Let's go!"

Parnow squatted down, aimed again, and fired two more times. The muzzle fire from the gun lighted up the room. Tarkovski was too far away to see details.

He stepped back some more. "Parnow!" he warned again.

Another door opened. A man stepped into the corridor. He wore slacks and had a gun. The gun pointed at the Russians.

Parnow fired at the man. Splinters and plaster exploded. The man stepped back, finding cover. Tarkovski ran down the corridor, toward the elevator. Parnow followed him, shooting once more in the direction of the man with the gun. No fire was returned. The elevator door opened. The Russians stepped in, went down, and exited the hotel. The lobby was deserted. There was nobody outside the hotel either. A moment later, they drove off.

THURSDAY
And Back Again to Amsterdam
(with Some Difficulty)

44

"AND ONLY BECAUSE THE kid at the desk felt something was suspicious and phoned my room," Dewaal was explaining. "I guess he saved us. We would have been dead. They would have shot us in our beds, just like that."

It was crowded in the room and the corridor. Much too crowded for so little space. The air smelled of sweat and of people who had gotten up in the middle of the night and hadn't had time for a shower.

Dewaal and Eekhaut were both dressed. All told, three plainclothes detectives and seven uniformed police officers were in attendance, along with three men in white coveralls. And a police photographer. And then, finally, the local prosecutor, also fresh out of his bed and not happy. He was a tall man, balding, large-nosed. He frowned deeply. He didn't appreciate when foreigners made so much trouble in his city. He didn't appreciate them bringing hired killers.

"So you tell me, Chief Superintendent," he said, "that you've been conducting an investigation over here without having formally contacted local law enforcement. Without even a warrant from your own prosecutor. And then you have a shoot-out with two gangsters in a hotel, endangering other guests. All this to protect a witness and recover documents."

He cast a quick glance at Eekhaut but didn't comment on his presence at the scene. He wasn't going to say anything concerning firearms and permits. At least not for now. Eekhaut assumed the matter would be discussed later. There would be a long stretch of discussions later.

"That is more or less the gist of the matter, Prosecutor," Dewaal said, professional and to the point. She was not going to make excuses. "The investigation suddenly evolved so quickly that we weren't able to obtain the necessary permits. And we had only the safety of the witness in mind. She wasn't arrested, by the way."

"Which means there's going to be even more paperwork in the wake of this," the prosecutor said. "Post-factum, so to speak. And I don't wish to add the fact that you've brought firearms into the country without a permit."

"We have been lax concerning certain details," Dewaal said. "And a few things have gone wrong. But a life was at stake. A young life." Eekhaut hadn't seen that side of her: the way she suddenly moved her body and nearly fluttered her eyelids, and the graceful movement of her slender hands while speaking. It was almost hypnotizing. She was trying to influence the prosecutor, who suddenly seemed less assured of himself, less severe.

"Local police could as easily have protected the witness, ma'am," he said. But his heart wasn't in it anymore. "Right, we'll straighten things out one way or another. At least there were no casualties."

Dewaal kept her mouth shut. Her strategy had worked. She had given him the full treatment, and he had backed off.

"But what about the damage to property?" the prosecutor asked. "The management of the hotel isn't going to be happy with all these bullet holes."

"I will see to it that compensation is arranged," Dewaal said.

"More paperwork," he complained. "My people will be very busy with this, Chief Superintendent. And why is there a Belgian officer on your, eh, team?"

"He's been seconded to my team as an international intermediary, through Belgian Federal Headquarters," she said. As if this were merely a detail. And it was, her eyes said. A detail. "And I like having him around, as if that would matter to anyone. He is familiar with this city."

"Oh, well, everything matters, ma'am. Certainly, the presence of Chief Inspector Eekhaut, whom we know well." He looked at his watch. Three uniforms were left. The technical people were ready.

"I'll talk to the management," Dewaal offered. "It's my responsibility."

"They're your rooms, so you better do that," the prosecutor said. He turned to Eekhaut. "Chief Inspector, it's been a while. Really, I had hoped never to meet you again in any official capacity."

"The pleasure is mutual," Eekhaut said. But he wasn't going to antagonize the prosecutor.

"And certainly not under circumstances like these. Your use of a firearm: I'll let that slide, but only because you work for them, not for us. You realize this could have been much worse?"

"It could have," Eekhaut admitted. "But my objective was to protect the witness."

"Well, that's clear then. Take your precious witness back to Holland and be so kind to send me a full report later on. I'm sure it will be read over here attentively. And, by the way," he said to Dewaal, "do you need further protection on Belgian soil? I don't have to remind you that the aggressors got away. They'll try again, I assume. Or am I wrong?"

"Your conclusion is correct," Dewaal said. "But the chief inspector and I are capable of getting the girl safely back to Amsterdam. Nevertheless, I appreciate your concern."

"Good. Well. We can close up here, then."

45

Parnow plucked the wood splinters out of his lower arm. His face didn't betray any pain, only concentration. He was clearly familiar with wounds. They hardly meant anything to him. Painful, probably, but nothing compared to what he might have endured before. He dabbed the wounds with a piece of cotton drenched in alcohol from the car's first aid kit.

They sat in a truckers' restaurant along the highway. Three men in jeans and work shirts leaned against the counter over coffee and rolls. They were interested in nothing but their breakfast. Behind the counter, a woman of about forty in a dark blue outfit was occupied with a space-age coffee machine. Apart from them, the place was deserted. The sun was rising over the highway. A slight fog was traveling west, across some old and gray trees that looked as if they were made from ancient paper. The world itself looked old and discarded, mainly because the restaurant had known better times, in spite of the new coffee maker. It looked like a remnant from the 1958 World's Fair and probably had been built in the fifties.

"Holy shit!" Tarkovski said in Russian again. He would have used the name of the Lord, but normally he refrained from doing so, at least this early in the morning. He never talked to God or any other deity. He only believed in the stupidity of people and not in their illusions. "That went as badly as it could have," he said. He whispered even though none of the people present would understand Russian. But he didn't want them to hear the two men speaking in a foreign language. They were trying to keep a low profile.

"Go to hell, intellectual," Parnow said. He was clearly pissed off, although he didn't sound as if he was angry. "Go to hell with your stupid ideas on how to run things. Next time we'll wait for them in the street and shoot them. Clean and easy and without all that hassle."

"We won't," Tarkovski whispered angrily. "No way are we going to shoot people in the street. This isn't Moscow. Nor is it Saint Petersburg. You don't shoot at the police in this part of the world. And you don't do that at home either. No longer."

"It's the only language they really understand. Take it from me. I know how they think. You have to handle them my way. That's what we did in Russia. Dutch police are kid stuff compared to Russians. You just have to show them you mean business."

"Tonight we went too far!"

"You know nothing! Just because you speak Dutch and English and you've studied, you think you know about the world. The world means nothing. A strong hand is needed to govern the world. And violence is necessary if you want to prove you mean business. Otherwise, you are nothing and nobody."

Tarkovski leaned forward. Parnow had his weak spots, like everybody, probably without knowing them. They were hidden, but he had them. "I know enough about the world we live in," he said. "More than enough to handle my life. The war is over, Parnow."

"This is not a war. This is a problem. We do not have the list: that's the problem. And we came for the list."

"No, we didn't get the list, and we're not going to get it either, not this way."

"You have a better plan. I'm sure. I'll listen."

Tarkovski didn't have a better plan. He had no plan at all. He wasn't into this sort of thing. And he seriously lacked experience in the field. He was like a cross between a lawyer and a diplomat.

Parnow wasn't going to let him get away with it. "Well? Do you have a better plan? I didn't think so. So I say we catch them under way. On the road. They have to return to Amsterdam. While they are in the open, we'll have our chance. I'll call some friends, and we'll wait for them."

"Some friends?"

"Yes. People I can trust. Who know what to do in a case like this. Mr. Keretsky will gladly pay. A telephone call and these people come to help."

"Fuck, Parnow! What do you want? Start another war, on the road this time?"

"Yes," Parnow said. "If it has to happen, it will happen this way."

"You're mad!"

"Yes," Parnow repeated. "I am mad enough for this sort of operation. But I get results. And you don't. I make sure the work gets done. Yesterday evening it did not work. But it would have if we had gone into the hotel unannounced. But you wanted to play nice."

"You were the one who wanted to use the police card," Tarkovski said.

"Well, from now on we don't play nice anymore. We play my way."

Tarkovski sat back. *Piece of shit*, he thought. But he knew he had no choice.

46

PRINSEN WAS SITTING IN the passenger seat of the armored black Mercedes, with Veneman at the wheel. Behind them was a second similar vehicle, with three more detectives from the Bureau. Both cars were in a parking area along the highway, pointing north, ready to go. They were waiting for a signal, Prinsen assumed, from Dewaal. The Belgian border was only ten kilometers south of them, in the opposite direction.

Veneman stroked the steering wheel, almost lovingly. "Nice car, isn't it? Aptly suited for the heavy work. But usually they stay in the garage. There's little need for them. We occasionally use them to transport politicians and diplomats, or criminals we need to keep alive between prison and court. Beautiful machines. A bit of weight on them, three tons or so, but with enough power under the hood for speed. Can easily go up to hundred eighty kilometers an hour. That's enough for a country this size."

He sounded proud, as if talking about his personal car. As if he had saved his money and bought himself this nice piece of technology. Prinsen had witnessed this attitude before with cops. They were usually unhappy about the way the organization was run but in awe of the equipment that came with it. It was probably a guy thing. And it was always *their* equipment. They were very possessive about it. Like these cars.

"Where is Dewaal?" he asked. Someone had given him a plastic cup with very strong black coffee, strong enough to replace his feeling of drowsiness with one of nausea. But he was awake now, at least. "Is she in Belgium?"

"We received a message," Veneman explained. "We're supposed to wait for her at the border. She's bringing a witness and needs protection. Something happened in the hotel where they stayed last night, and she assumes more trouble will be ahead."

"And what happens now?" Prinsen sat against the door and longed for a second coffee. Or perhaps breakfast. Breakfast would be good. Breakfast would be most welcome. There was a shop next to the gas station where they were waiting, but Veneman kept everyone in the cars. "Do we just wait till we get a second call or what?"

"We do," Veneman said. "We wait. The life of a cop is nothing but waiting. And hoping you reach your retirement without anything serious happening to you. Like a bullet."

Prinsen admired the car's interior. Tan leather, neatly stitched, and mock wood paneling on the doors and dashboard. A car like that was likely to be expensive. Someone would have to have had a considerable budget.

"Sleep well?" Veneman asked.

Prinsen failed to understand the question, simple though it was. "Did you sleep well last night?" Veneman repeated.

"Oh. Fell asleep without taking my clothes off, it seems. But for how long, I have no idea."

"Sleep helps. Talking too. You have to talk about what's bothering you. Important rule for any of us in this profession. If you see a colleague who stops doing that, talking I mean, then you know he's in trouble. And trouble usually starts at home. Wife gets beaten, children run away or take drugs. That sort of thing. It leads to divorce, and the cop ends up alone. I've seen it happen too much. What about you?"

"I'm living alone," Prinsen said. He hoped it didn't sound querulous. Or melodramatic and lost. *Poor little boy alone in the world* sort of thing. "I'm single and live by myself. Not much to show for it, but I'm taking care of myself."

"Alone. Well, I guess we're all alone in the end, even the ones who've been married for twenty years. Who can tell?" Veneman didn't take his eyes off the road in front of them. "We're alone even when you need to trust others. Know what I mean? No lone wolves in this outfit. We can't afford that. And you? No girlfriend?"

"No."

"You should get out more. Mingle with people, other cops if necessary. The lads say they never see you in the pub. They talk about that. Why don't you join them on occasion? Drink a pint, smoke one of those awful cigars, celebrate some mate's success? Be part of it all, that's what matters."

"I'll think about it," Prinsen said. He tried to imagine Aunt Alexandra in a pub, holding a beer. He couldn't. He could only see her in her official capacity, when she wasn't a member of his family. Which was painfully ironic, since she was the only member of his family he cared about.

A beep sounded from the dashboard.

"They're coming," Veneman said. He started the car. Behind them, the engine of the second Mercedes came to life as well.

47

THE HOTEL STAFF HADN'T made any remarks, not during breakfast and not when Dewaal checked out, as if nothing at all had happened last night. As if the hotel hadn't been turned into a battlefield, a room and corridor hadn't been shot up, and guests hadn't been rudely awakened by gunfire. The young woman behind the desk didn't even seem aware of the nocturnal troubles, or else she was successful in hiding her curiosity.

During breakfast, some of the other guests eyed them conspicuously and exchanged remarks, but Eekhaut and Dewaal ignored them. They fetched their rolls and coffee and fruit juice while one of them stayed with Eileen at all times and watched the surroundings. Eileen looked as innocent as before in her T-shirt and jeans. People would speculate about their individual roles in this little drama, as to who was the convict or whatever, but neither Eekhaut nor Dewaal cared much for what people thought.

Dewaal—again in that nice suit of hers and very official looking— made two phone calls, but not when Eekhaut was around. He didn't ask who she called. He had a vague headache, and that boded a difficult day ahead, so he was glad she didn't share her problems with him.

Then they left. Dewaal stopped at a gas station somewhere between Leuven and Antwerp and bought food and bottles of water and soda for all. It was obvious that she didn't plan to stop again, given the risk of another assault. As the sun rose, they drove on toward Antwerp, having passed Brussels, braving morning rush-hour traffic. Eekhaut would have suggested using the siren and lights again, but perhaps discretion was the better option.

After an hour, they reached Antwerp. Eileen remained silent, all by herself in the back of the car. As silent as both detectives. All three realized their enemies were still at large. Eekhaut and Dewaal each carried their guns, with two extra clips.

Beyond Antwerp, traffic lessened. Dewaal sped up. She switched on the navigator but hardly looked at it. Her cell phone was on the dashboard, ready for use.

They passed the border. She said, "We're being followed."

Eekhaut didn't look back. "Yes? What do you see?"

"A black Mercedes followed by a black BMW model 3." She pushed a button on her phone, but nothing seemed to happen.

"Why don't you use the siren and light?"

"Why would I?"

"We'd be able to go faster. See if they could follow us."

She glanced in the mirror and flipped a switch. "There we go. Sound and lights. Eileen, stay down. Walter, I'm going to the left lane at top speed."

She pushed the pedal. The Porsche immediately responded with a mighty purr. Eekhaut saw the needle of the speedometer climbing. Fast.

"And?" he asked. But he knew what the answer would be.

She looked in all three mirrors. "They sped up too. I see three cars chasing us now. A large silver four by four as well. A Land Cruiser."

"Shit!" he said.

"No problem."

"No problem? Three cars? How many people is that? At least six. We don't have that much ammo."

"This is an AIVD car," she said. "We have enough ammo. We even have enough firepower. There's a Heckler & Koch MP5 and a shotgun in the trunk."

He looked in the back, where Eileen was sitting. "We can't get into the trunk while we're moving."

She cast him a quick look. "So you think. Climb in the back."

"Can't get there," he said. But he managed, with some effort, to squirm between the two front seats and join Eileen on the all-too-narrow back seat. The girl smelled of sweat. She was afraid. Of course she was.

"And now what?" he asked.

"Pull down the middle section of the seat. There's a strap."

He did. And uncovered a black and padded space behind the back seat, which probably was part of the trunk.

"Now pull down the part of the back of the seat where you are," Dewaal said.

He complied, leaving even less space for him and the girl.

Behind his seat, he found both guns, two extra clips for the machine gun, and a box of shells for the shotgun. "Your secret stash?"

"This is an intervention vehicle. Those weapons are kept loaded at all times. What do you think our business is? Traffic control? Come back up front where I need you."

He managed to crawl back into the front seat with both weapons. "Which one do you want?"

"Neither of them for the moment," she said, concentrating on the road in front of her and on the pursuing vehicles. He noticed she was doing a hundred sixty kilometers per hour. Vehicles ahead hurried out of the way. He glanced back. Through the window, he saw the black Mercedes. It was almost on them.

"Tailgating incurs a fine of five hundred euro," she said. "The BMW is coming up on our right."

These were no more cars in the center lane. Only a few trucks on the right.

The BMW closed in from behind them.

Three, four shots were fired, with the Porsche hit in several places.

Dewaal yanked at the wheel. Eekhaut bumped into her. Eileen cried out. The Porsche veered right. Behind them, the BMW braked hard, tires screeching. Dewaal hit the brakes as well. The Mercedes passed them on the left. Open window on the passenger side. A gun. Two shots that missed.

"Let's get off the highway," Dewaal said.

She opened both windows of the Porsche.

"Use the shotgun first," she ordered over the racket.

Eekhaut aimed the gun out of the window and to the back, but there was no target he could see, except for an enormous truck close behind them. He could clearly see the angry head of the driver.

He didn't see the BMW.

Dewaal hit the accelerator again.

Eekhaut was thrown back in his seat. He pulled the gun back in again.

The Porsche gained on the truck and went to the right lane. Behind them, the truck braked hard.

Dewaal steered the car, much too fast, to an exit ramp and from there to a parking area. Lots of cars and trucks. People were looking at them.

The Porsche passed the parked cars. Dewaal hit the brakes again at the other end of the parking area, where there was plenty of open space.

"When I stop, you jump out and find cover. Use the shotgun. Leave the HK for me."

The Porsche came to a stop close to a small brick building.

A family fled away from the approaching vehicles.

Eekhaut slammed open the door and waved the shotgun around, looking for a suitable target. Eileen tumbled out of the car and fell behind him on the grass.

The Mercedes came to a stop in a cloud of earth and dust, about thirty meters from where they were standing. The BMW followed and stopped close to the building. Men got out of both cars and opened fire at once, but randomly and without aiming too carefully.

Eekhaut shot at them four times, forcing them to seek shelter behind their cars.

He counted his shots. He had four shells left in the rifle, he assumed. Or was it only two? And there was a box in the car with more shells. On the front seat, where he couldn't get at it, because he was flat on his belly in the grass, between the Porsche and Eileen.

Where was Dewaal?

There she was. On one knee, hiding behind the front of the Porsche at the other side, shooting single shots from the HK toward the black BMW.

Shots fired back.

These people meant business.

Windshields were shattered. Tires punctured. Bullets penetrated car bodies and engine blocks. Some of these cars would not drive again anytime soon.

He called to her. The silver Land Cruiser had probably missed the exit and now came driving backward from the other side. Its back door was open. A man with an automatic rifle started shooting at them. Eekhaut aimed his shotgun and fired three times. Dewaal followed with the HK. Two men jumped out of the Land Cruiser and ducked away. Eekhaut didn't see the man with the automatic rifle anymore.

He turned again. One of the men from the Mercedes was running in his direction. Eekhaut fired at him, forcing him to seek cover. He pulled his pistol.

Eight bullets. And two extra clips.

This did not look too good.

He imagined crawling back to the Porsche and fetching the box with the shells for the shotgun. But he would be too much of a target if he did.

Where was Eileen?

He couldn't see much. Sweat dripped into his eyes. There was movement from the Mercedes. He shot twice, more or less at random. He shouldn't do that. He should make sure every bullet counted. He heard Dewaal's HK again. At least she was still alive.

Then she shouted.

Two other cars approached at speed. Two black Mercedes. Blue flashing lights. They stopped, and several men and women jumped out of them.

Eekhaut aimed his pistol but didn't need to fire anymore.

The cavalry had arrived.

48

"Our very own mobile unit," Dewaal said. "Two armored cars we acquired some years ago. A steal, at that price. Served with the Foreign Office in the past, but they weren't using them anymore. Big-time criminals enjoy their ride to and from the court more in one of our rides. Safer, too. Bit of gas guzzlers, but they're worth every nickel."

"And they happened to be around, just like that," Eekhaut said.

"I called Veneman this morning—oh, you haven't met him yet—when it looked like we were going to be in trouble even before reaching Amsterdam. He started the thing, the procedure, the intervention. It's more or less automatic. GPS trackers in our cars and a radio alarm on my phone. Fun, isn't it? Technology? Especially when you don't need to fill in forms in advance or wait for someone's say-so before going into battle."

She was flushed, he noticed. It was the clean, crisp air. It was the action. She enjoyed it.

"You could have warned me that things were going to be all right," he said. "I would have been . . . prepared." His shirt was drenched in sweat, he stank of it, and of cordite (or whatever was being used as a propellant in munitions these days), and of tension and relief. He needed a shower. He wanted, most of all, a cold beer. It looked like he was not going to have either on short notice.

"What did you expect? That I was going to let these people stop us from delivering our package?" Even Dewaal looked a mess. Her clothes had dark patches and were torn in a few places. She had scratches on her arms and legs. He was glad he had no mirror because he would look just as bad.

Eileen was being looked at by two medics who had flown in with a chopper. She was shocked but seemed otherwise OK.

"You did deploy the whole army," he said.

"Some in the Bureau badly needed the exercise," Dewaal said. But she didn't sound so casual anymore. He noticed her hands were trembling slightly. She was brave, he knew, but the stress got to her anyway. She looked up at him, assuring him that all this was routine at the Bureau. He knew it wasn't. This type of action would be rare. "And I wanted to be in Amsterdam by this afternoon. Looks like it will be later."

A man in his fifties, hard-faced, with short gray hair, walked over to them. A big and sturdy man. He wore a bulletproof vest over his white shirt and tie. On his hip, he had an oversized black holster with an equally big gun. "Chief Superintendent?"

"Yes, Veneman? What have we caught?"

"Three dead. Could have been worse. The others are a nice collection of rented scum. There's this guy, Tarkovski, who pretends to speak only Russian. Your Miss Calster has recognized one of the others as the murderer of her boyfriend. Parnow is his name, but that's all we know. Not in our files, it seems. We'll ask Interpol about him."

"Good catch. We'll interrogate this fellow Parnow about his employers. In Russian if needed."

"Can't do, ma'am. He's dead. Not a big loss, all in all. But there's this Tarkovski. He looks interesting."

"Yes, we know all about him. Isolate him. He doesn't talk to anyone; he doesn't get any news from anyone. And he certainly doesn't get a lawyer anywhere near him."

"Right, Chief."

"He's Keretsky's little helper. I wonder what he's doing with an outfit like this."

"He wasn't carrying a gun," Veneman warned her.

"Doesn't matter. He's at least an accomplice. Thanks, Veneman. Now on to the cleanup."

"Towing service is on its way. You want all these cars taken to Amsterdam?"

"Yes. I want all of them in our garage. And the tech people have to comb through them. A full review."

Veneman nodded and walked off.

"Is this what you had in mind when you came to Holland, Chief Inspector?" Dewaal asked Eekhaut. "This sort of adventure shoot-out, a war on the highway? Is this what went on in Brussels?"

"Not at all, Chief Superintendent. It's been a long time since I used a weapon. And all that for a stupid list."

"This isn't finished, I'm afraid. Paperwork, interrogations, answering questions from higher-ups. And you won't escape any of that, Walter. I want a full debriefing. Eileen Calster has to be questioned. Not today, but it will have to be done tomorrow, and I want to see you in my office by ten. Washed, dried, and ready for the really hard work."

She wasn't joking.

He didn't expect a joke. Certainly not after this experience. Was this how things went down in Holland between police and criminals? In that case, he needed to dress accordingly and not risk a good suit. He would need one of those bulletproof vests at least. And more ammo. And an extra weapon.

A pale black-haired young man approached. "Prinsen," Dewaal said. She gestured in the direction of Eekhaut. "Inspector Prinsen, Chief Inspector Eekhaut. You haven't met yet, I assume. Well, now you have. You'll work together in the future. Why are you here, Prinsen?"

Prinsen indicated Veneman. "He brought me along. I wasn't getting anywhere with the Van Gils case."

"Pity," Dewaal said. She rubbed her face with her hands, but all that did was make it dirtier. "I want to get out of here, gentlemen. Get this whole affair back on track. And I want to have everybody in the office tomorrow."

She started calling people on her phone. Eekhaut went off to inspect the cars. Their Porsche had holes in it but not in any essential parts. It would take them back to Amsterdam, he assumed. A man in shirtsleeves was changing one of the tires. The window in the back was shattered.

Close call, he thought.

The BMW had been reduced to scrap. It had been rammed in the flank by one of the police cars, which had sustained only minor damage and was missing only its front grille and one headlight.

One of the ambulances left. The bodies were being taken off in a black van. The rest of the assailants had already been escorted back to Amsterdam in an armored bus. Dewaal had been able to call in a lot of cavalry, it seemed.

He glanced up at a helicopter hovering over the area. A man with a camera hung on the open door. They would be on the news. Behind the police tape, a couple of hundred meters in the distance, more press had gathered. He didn't like being in the news, but that's what you got when you shot up a lot of people and cars in a public place.

49

ALEXANDRA DEWAAL KNEW THAT one cliché about hospitals was no longer true: they didn't smell of disinfectants or death. Modern, well-run hospitals had no smell. They were very careful about that. And so the VU Medical Center on De Boelelaan, where Van Gils had been brought, was as odorless as humanly possible. The public was welcomed in almost neutral surroundings. The receptionists didn't wear white smocks or lab coats. The place was more like a hotel.

Nevertheless, people died in here, she knew. A hospital was a place for people to heal but also to die. Medical science had its limits, and the main one was death. Van Gils was improving, however. Others had fared worse in this same building. She was thinking about her mother, who currently resided in another, almost similar institution. An institution where every professional wore a lab coat and a name tag, where the smell of death was prevalent. Dewaal had decided she would never end in such a place. Not if she could help it.

She asked for Van Gils's room number. "Visiting hours have ended," a kind middle-aged woman told her. White coat or not, she guarded the entrance to the place. "Maybe you could come back tomorrow?"

Dewaal looked at her watch. Half past eight. "I am Inspector Van Gils's superior," she said. "He was shot doing his duty. I need to talk to him urgently. You will understand if I ask for an exception."

The woman looked at Dewaal, at the state her clothes were in, and then consulted a list. "Please follow the arrows for unit three thirty-four, ma'am," she said. "Explain to them again why you're here."

And she would. She would talk herself into Van Gils's room.

One floor up, she walked down a corridor. A nurse came out of a room. "Ma'am?" she asked. "May I help you?"

Dewaal explained, again, the urgency of her visit. She spoke in her official voice. She insisted.

"Yes, ma'am," the nurse said. "Please follow me. Mr. Van Gils may be asleep. He's been given a mild sedative, so I don't know if you can talk with him."

"Well," Dewaal said, "If I only could see him and make sure he's all right. It's just a—" *A personal thing*, she wanted to say but didn't.

"He's all right, under the circumstances. Lost a lot of blood, but he's stable now. The bullets have been removed."

Buckshot, Dewaal wanted to correct her. *Pellets*. "He'll probably want to keep some of it as a souvenir. You think that can be arranged?"

The nurse frowned.

"It's a . . . a thing with cops," Dewaal explained. "Superstition, really. The bullet—or buckshot in this case—that doesn't kill you becomes a sort of a talisman. We don't expect people to understand."

The nurse smiled. "Superstition. Yes, I get it. I think some of it was left at the nurses' station. Or given to the gentleman that was here earlier."

Oh, Dewaal thought. The tech people would probably have collected it. "Doesn't matter. We'll sort it out. Can I see him now?"

"Of course, ma'am," the nurse said. "Call me when you need me. I'm at the station."

Dewaal sat down next to the bed. Van Gils was asleep. She wasn't going to bother him. There were no get-well cards, no flowers. There had been no visitors. What did she know about Van Gils? Not much. He had been married. But she hadn't been at the office long enough to get to know him personally.

And she knew that was wrong. Should have been her first job. Get to know your people. Know all about them. See if you can trust them but also get to know the little and insignificant details of their life. She probably wouldn't have found out what sort of trouble Breukeling had gotten himself into. Would not have caught that. But nonetheless.

She needed to change a lot of things at the Bureau.

50

PRINSEN CLOSED THE DOOR to the apartment behind him, deposited the key on the cabinet next to the entrance, and switched on all the lights. Then he opened the front window. A light rain was falling, and a few fresh drops hit his face. He pulled off his jacket, his shirt, his shoes, and his socks. Everything smelled bad. He walked into the bathroom and turned on the shower.

He waited till the water was hot enough, pulled off his pants and underwear, and stepped into the shower stall. He soaped himself thoroughly, washed his hair, rinsed, and left the stall. He welcomed the fresh outside air. He dried off and wrapped himself in a bathrobe. Then he stepped into the living room.

He realized he had left his gun at the office, in his locker, and that it needed cleaning. He hadn't even considered taking it home. Not for a moment.

He switched on the TV. A political talk show he didn't want to see. He recognized a face or two, but his interest in politics was very limited. He had learned about politics and ideology at the university, but he couldn't grasp why people got upset about it. The commercial stations had even less to offer him—stupid game shows and soaps. It all looked and sounded the same to him.

He was vaguely hungry but not enough to warrant action. He had missed lunch. A few hours ago, somebody had given him a cheese sandwich, which he had eaten without tasting it. There had been coffee.

After the wrecks and the people had been carted off to Amsterdam, he had helped the traffic police clear the area.

Afterward, back in Amsterdam, there had been forms to fill out.

At no point did any of the five agents on the team—Veneman, the three others, or he himself—discuss the operation. No stories were swapped, no congratulations, just people doing their job. Like it had been nothing more than a trip to the zoo.

Not even that.

He knew why. He had had the same feeling after the assault on him and Van Gils. You had to deal with it by yourself. Talking about it wasn't part of the culture. It wasn't considered professional.

The only thing you did was write it down in your report. Dead language, dead words. Dry, to the point, businesslike. Sentences, no feelings.

He was glad he had left his gun at the office.

51

The woman in Absinthe.

Linda.

As if she was waiting for him.

But first Eekhaut had to get rid of what had bothered him during the day. Alcohol would be most useful in this process. It offered oblivion but not reassurance. After a day like this, he should have gone to his apartment, taken a shower, gone to bed. Tried to sleep away the tension. But it would probably have been a sleepless night. Instead, he had gone to his apartment, taken a shower, dressed in clean clothes, and left again.

As if that had been a better idea.

As if alcohol would help answering the questions and evading the answers. He knew better. Ten years ago, he had learned that lesson. Alcohol had no answers to give, and the questions became all the more painful to deal with. You poured the junk down your throat, and the poison remained in your head.

But he had promised the woman—Linda—that he would come back, and yesterday he hadn't been around.

No phone number. No address. Only her first name.

Absinthe. Not that he had gotten used to the taste. Foul drink, still. But it proved to be forgiving. It forgave him his shortcomings. He now better understood those Victorian outcasts and their efforts to get away from the parochialism of their contemporaries.

He sat at one of the tables with a glass of the green spirit in front of him, the taste of danger and violence still in his mouth. And she sat at the other side of the same table, holding her glass with both hands, leaning over to him as if they had secrets to share, as if they had known each other for a long time. As if they had become familiar and were likely to share the most shameful secrets.

"What have you been up to?" she asked. "You look like you . . ." She left whatever she was thinking unspoken. Maybe he had fallen down some stairs, or a hooker had been rough on him, or whatever.

"Small misunderstanding with some people who disagreed with the law," he said. "That's why I wasn't here yesterday. Short mission abroad. Your abroad, not mine. And this morning we had a problem with people who needed to speak to our witness urgently. Of course, we wouldn't let them."

"Oh," she said. Then it dawned on her. "The incident on the highway, down south. I saw it on the news."

"Yes."

"Why didn't you say so? What did you do to get the mafia behind you?"

"It wasn't the mafia. Not that it matters, though. We're investigating a matter of political corruption."

"Tell me all about it," she said. She wanted the unadorned truth.

They all wanted to hear the real story whenever they got to talk to a police officer in private. It had happened to him before.

"I can't say much about it. A very sensitive matter. Some well-known people are involved. People in the business community and politics. And I'm already saying too much."

So much for discretion: he bared his soul to a woman he had met in a bar, told her what he did for a living, told her too much already about an ongoing case. This wasn't good. But at least he seemed to have found an interested soul, and she made him forget all about Esther and twenty years of marriage and hot summer afternoons in the garden and a trip to Seville and long conversations about having children.

She smiled. "I understand. I work for a large company that shall remain nameless. I often see and hear things that will never leave those offices, and I close my eyes and plug my ears. If I'm not discreet, I can't do my job. At least not for this employer."

"I know," he said. "Keeping eyes and ears shut. We're all weak, in the end, and potentially corrupt." He thought of Breukeling.

"Are you?" she demanded.

"What? Corrupt?"

"Yes."

"I am each time I'm not able to solve a crime because I let my actions be dictated by others. I'm corrupt because I let people who have no moral or ethical values dictate my future. Or very few morals and values, at least. Isn't that the common definition of corruption?"

"There is only so much we can do," she said. "And after that, well, it's out of our hands. But it doesn't have to mean you're corrupt. I think you're being too harsh with yourself."

"No, sometimes we can do more. And that's why I'm not satisfied. Another drink?"

"A fruit juice, if you please."

He got two fruit juices. "We can always do more," he repeated.

"Yeah, and risk being spat out by the system. After which we can do nothing anymore, not even the little things that might make a difference."

She knows exactly what I'm talking about, he thought. "Is that your experience?"

She shook her head. "I too have secrets, Walter. I too need a sense of security. And I can't find it anymore in the place where I work. If I ask you direct questions, will you answer them? Without holding back or without conditions?"

"Without conditions?"

"Yes."

"Depends on what these questions are."

"Without conditions, Mr. Policeman. Which means: any sort of question. Don't bullshit me."

"In that case: no. No, I won't answer your questions. Not without conditions."

"The same goes for me."

"Our situations are different."

"In what sense?"

Eekhaut said, "I defend public interests. At least that's what I am supposed to do. You don't. You defend the interests of private capital, I assume. The interests of stockholders. Private shareholders, and not public. That's the difference."

She thought about that. "Maybe you're right. But we all need a sense of security, even if we don't know where to find it. Maybe I'm not looking in the right spot." She seemed amused. "What a random meeting in a bar can lead to! To really deep thinking!"

"Sometimes it's easier to talk to a stranger because there's no risk in damaging . . . a relationship. That's why there are help lines for people who consider suicide. Talking to strangers. It's sort of therapy."

"It is? But it precludes serious relationships."

"It does. But then, serious relationships are always on the brink of disaster, aren't they?"

"You're always this serious when you drink absinthe? Good thing we switched to fruit juice."

"Do I sound sentimental? Or just plain desperate?"

She smiled. "Both, really."

She broke the spell by looking at her watch. A small, elegant, and clearly expensive watch. A gift from a friend? "I have to go, Walter. Will you be here tomorrow?"

"I might," he said.

And then, a few moments later, he was back in the street.

He wasn't drunk but he felt a bit dizzy. Probably on account of the long day. At his age, he needed to be careful with too much stress. Shoot-outs on the highway, things that would get him in the papers and on TV. His life was supposed to be boring. Boring wasn't good, but it would be better for his health. He was supposed to be working at a desk. Doing research, for one thing. Not shooting at people and—even worse—being shot at.

He had drunk four or five absinthes. And he had spoken to a most attractive woman. He would see her again. Now he walked along Utrecht-sestraat, careful, avoiding objects and people. The alcohol meant nothing.

Arriving at his apartment, he looked into the store for the punk lady, but the shop was closed. Of course, it was late. Inside, Toon showed up. It seemed the man had been waiting for him. "A drink," Toon offered. And then he said, "You look terrible."

"An accident," Eekhaut said.

"Two drinks then, to forget those troubles I see behind your eyes."

"Best not tonight, Toon. What I need is rest."

Toon looked at his clock. "Twelve thirty," he said. "I hope you're not coming directly from work? What do you do for a living?"

"I'm a detective with AIVD. Today we had—"

"On the highway! You were on the news. Tell me all about that!" Toon ushered Eekhaut into his apartment. "A colleague," he said, and he sounded delighted. "Small world. What is a Belgian doing with the AIVD?"

This was going to be a long night.

Tears of the Bride, he noticed. A new bottle.

He made a mental note to buy his own bottle of the stuff. For Toon. As a gift. The man would run out, one day. "Because they wanted to get rid of you," Toon concluded after hearing Eekhaut explaining his personal exodus. "Not surprised. Same with all these management types everywhere. They can't have people thinking for themselves, can they? But if anyone ought to think for himself, it's a detective, isn't it?"

"Probably so," Eekhaut said. Toon had filled his glass with Tears of the Bride again. Things were getting worse. He had never drunk as much as he had tonight. Not in a long time, anyway.

"You look like you were once married, but you obviously aren't anymore."

"That's correct. And you?"

"Never crossed my mind to take the step. Saw what happened to the colleagues. Children and all. All well if you climb that ladder quickly and can avoid street duty and nights out. I mean, sitting behind a desk and ordering people around allows you to have a decent family life. Otherwise . . . well, anyway, here I am. To love!" They toasted. "Because without love there's no marriage that can hold."

"My wife died," Eekhaut said. "Ten years ago."

"Oh," Toon said. "That's bad. Maybe it had . . . was it a good marriage?"

Was it a good marriage? Eekhaut needed to think that over, even now. Stolen glances at young female team members at his office, some attempts at seduction on his part, furtive talk, but never anything serious. He suspected she had had a lover at some point, and vice versa. There had been good years and bad months. He fought evil because she was in the same world as that evil, and he needed her to be safe. That was more or less his metaphysical excuse for working long hours. He had lacked attention. He had lacked feelings for her. He saw children being exploited and killed by family members, even by their parents. He saw addicts committing unspeakable acts of cruelty upon vulnerable people. He saw old folks tied up and beaten to death for a bit of money.

Esther couldn't have understood. And he didn't want to explain the persistence of evil in the world around her. He wanted her to remain ignorant of all that.

It took her time to understand, but by that time, a distance had come to separate them. And then another kind of evil started to spread in her body. One he couldn't fight.

FRIDAY

Amsterdam

52

EEKHAUT'S MIND WAS STRANGELY clear when he woke up the morning after. Even after four drinks with Toon.

Though it wasn't easy to get out of bed, take a shower, and fix breakfast. Breakfast was a hastily bought box of cereal that he finally decided to eat, with added soy milk, coffee, and some biscuits with jam.

Man's wealth is mirrored by the extensiveness of his breakfast, still supposed to be the main meal of the day. In his case, he made do but didn't care much.

Anyway, he would have to buy groceries and stock his kitchen. But when? In between chasing criminals, protecting witnesses, and arguing with Dewaal? Not likely. Not that he would have trouble finding food in this part of Amsterdam—although there seemed a distinct lack of supermarkets or greengrocers. Everybody seemed to cater to exotic clients, hungry tourists, and the hurried office slaves. *Later today*, he promised himself. And he would stay in his apartment tonight, although he had made some sort of promise to Linda.

Although not really.

While his mind was in perfect working order, his body seemed to refuse service. Joints aching, soft bluish spots on his arms and legs. He had to shave and did, but even that proved difficult. He combed his hair. Discovered more aesthetic damage, but nothing that wouldn't fix itself naturally.

Dewaal had said she wanted him in the office at ten o'clock. She had left him a bit of a margin, maybe because she knew she would have to fix herself up in the morning as well. Ten o'clock. Did he have anything to report? The case solved, or nearly? Pieter Van Boer's murderer caught and tried at the same time? There would be more reports to file and forms to fill out.

Entering the Bureau's offices, Eekhaut was greeted by the guard. But a problem arose when he tried to open the door with his card.

"Biometrics unsupported," the tinny voice from the speaker said with a sort of triumph, as if it didn't expect his biometrics to be in order. "Entrance refused."

"He's been doing that all morning," the guard said. He seemed to be resigned to the problem.

Eekhaut was taken aback. "What are you talking about? What biometrics?"

The guard indicated some abstract space behind him with a slight movement of the head, as if his dark alter ego was in attendance. "Basil."

"Basil? The security system?"

"Even the boss wasn't allowed in at first."

"What did she do?"

"She proposed pulling the plug. She said that loud enough."

"And then?"

"What do you think? Basil got really mad. He hermetically sealed off all entrances. We almost had a nationwide alert."

Eekhaut couldn't suppress a smile. "Really? What then?"

"Boss called tech support. They came right over. They'll cart him off to the garbage dump if he does that again."

"Second try," Basil announced.

"Can I get in or not?"

The guard shrugged and pushed a button. Nothing happened. He pushed the button again. "Manual override, you idiot," he called. Not at Eekhaut.

"Control delayed," Basil said, reluctantly. Eekhaut wasn't sure where exactly the voice came from. The system was probably all over the building. But now at least he was granted access.

"Andreï Tarkovski isn't talking," Dewaal said. She was drinking her coffee black. Four detectives had spent all night interrogating the men they had captured the day before. "The other three assailants pretend to speak only Russian. That was last night. An interpreter was called in—in the middle of the night, mind you—but they kept mum. Maybe they only speak a very rare dialect, an almost forgotten language. Or they're keeping their mouths shut because they know what'll happen if they talk. Whoever ordered this whole thing must be someone with a lot of power. You can't bring together an army like that if you're not a heavyweight."

Eekhaut glanced to his right. The young detective, Prinsen, sat in the other chair in Dewaal's office. He kept his distance as if he didn't trust Eekhaut yet. He, too, was drinking coffee from a plastic cup. He didn't look like he'd had a good night's sleep recently.

Dewaal continued, "I had a chat with the minister. Yesterday evening." It didn't sound as if the conversation had been a pleasure. Eekhaut knew why the man had wanted to talk to her right away. The disaster on the highway had been front-page news in the papers and had been on the late-night TV news as well. When that happened, the minister of the interior couldn't avoid having to give a press conference.

"Yes," Eekhaut said. "Ministers." He knew about them. Politicians. Always ready to criticize the police if that gained them votes. He had no illusions concerning the political class. "And what did His Excellency tell you?"

"He was delighted—his words—the team solved the case—as if he had any idea what case we were working on—but he was disappointed we had made such a show of ourselves. Discretion, he mentioned. Something about being more discreet. And, of course, he mentioned the list. Told me he hoped it would be restored to its rightful owner without any delay."

Eekhaut frowned. "In other words—"

"You understood me perfectly well, Walter. You're not even allowed to make a copy of that list. It has become something like a state secret, and we're supposed to give it back to Van Tillo."

"That tells us a lot about who's playing games with whom."

"Bugger off with your games. Our reputation and autonomy are at stake here. I want you to get that into your head. Public displays like yesterday are bad for our reputation. Discretion, Walter."

She leaned back, and Eekhaut noticed she avoided looking at Prinsen.

Who had not yet said a word.

"Is it my fault . . .?" But then he stopped. Because he had nothing to add. The presence of the young detective annoyed him. He tried to remember what Dewaal had said the day before about Prinsen, who was now part of the investigation.

He looked at Dewaal again. She wore a long skirt and gray blouse and a pearl necklace. Not the same woman who had braved a bunch of killers yesterday. "No," she said. "I didn't mean it that way. I'm not happy with having to hand over the list either. I badly want to catch the people behind this matter. Parnow wasn't operating on his own. Neither was Tarkovski, who is on the payroll of an infamous Russian oligarch. But beyond Tarkovski, we have no real proof of any involvement."

"Can't we question the Russian on that involvement?"

"Tarkovski?"

"No, his employer. Can't we bring him in?"

"Keretsky? Are you mad? The man who needed one signature to become one of the main shareholders of Fabna Bank? Imagine the influence he has and his impact on the economy, Russian or otherwise. You're not going to question such a man concerning organized crime. Anyway, he's in Russia again. Don't expect the local police to help us."

"We wait till he returns to Holland."

"That could be a long wait, and it won't change his situation or ours. He remains untouchable. Walter, I want you to have a look at Tarkovski's things. Two technicians are working on his apartment right now. They'll bring back anything that seems important. His computer, documents, whatever."

Prinsen said, "We can do something about that. Keretsky, I mean. We have his local representative in jail on charges of conspiracy, maybe even murder, and a few other things we can pin on him. Either Keretsky needs a new man or he'll try to keep Tarkovski out of jail."

Eekhaut said, "I'll wager he'll return to Holland soon."

Dewaal shook her head. "Even then we can't touch him. Didn't you hear what I just said? The man is like a diplomat. He can't be touched."

"Because the minister will intervene if we try anything," Eekhaut said. "And you'll get a slap on the wrist for being a naughty girl."

"Something like that. And I have the whole of the AIVD on my back, on account of the war we waged yesterday. I have to report about everything: use of firearms, number of bullets fired, damage to external property, overtime, pathology exams on the victims, and so on. Two other people and I will have nearly a full-time job on our hands for a couple of days."

Maybe I should have taken my coffee black this morning, Eekhaut thought. *Black and strong. To rinse my mouth. Get rid of the disappointment.* He glanced at Prinsen, who seemed calm as he slurped his coffee. As if he weren't concerned.

"What are the plans for Tarkovski?"

"We try to get something useful out of him," Prinsen proposed. "A confession. That would be something at least."

"He speaks Dutch?"

"A little. A lot, actually, but he refuses to speak it. Seems to have forgotten it, suddenly. We use English. Neat trick though: later he can always pretend he was misunderstood."

"And he's not talking?"

"Nothing so far," Dewaal said. Her phone vibrated. "I have to take this. Yes, Dewaal." She listened intently. "I'll come over right away. Yes. Yes, at once. I'm in a meeting." She sounded annoyed and closed the connection.

"Duty calls," Eekhaut said. "And it always calls very loudly."

She eyed him angrily and shook her head. "It's nothing," she said. "Family problems." A quick glance at Prinsen, communicating something that Eekhaut couldn't make out.

He knew they had a previous history.

"Oh, family," he said.

She got up. "That's it for now. Do follow up on Tarkovski, will you? Take over if needed. We need to know who paid for the murder and the kidnap. I'm not interested in the boy himself." She let her gaze drift for a moment. "Another thing. We haven't told Eileen her brother is dead. I don't want her to hear that by accident. I'll talk to her tomorrow. Maybe I'll get psychiatric help for her."

"Really? A shrink? Can't we—"

"No, Eekhaut," Dewaal said. "You can't."

He rose and walked back to his office, where he opened the window that looked over the buildings behind the Bureau. The air was moist. He had a lot to think over. Dewaal. Family. Tarkovski. Calster. And Prinsen. Then he took out his phone, looked at a piece of paper he had been given, and punched a number. He got a man on the line. *Good*, he thought, *so there's a guard present at least.* "Chief Inspector Eekhaut," he said, for once using his official title. "How is Miss Calster?"

"She doesn't speak much, sir," the guard said, "but she's safe in her room back here."

"I'll come around," he said.

"Yes, sir."

Eekhaut pushed his gun in his belt holster and locked his office behind him. Tarkovski could wait. Eileen Calster was the victim, and he was more interested in victims than in criminals. Victims had their own story to tell. Often it was a fascinating story. But the details were too often overlooked by other people. He had always made it his business to listen to victims. They needed a good talk with an understanding police officer.

Eileen had been tucked away in a safe house a few hundred meters down the same street. A house with cameras and other extensive security measures. On the ground floor was a desk with a female officer. On the second floor were another desk and another officer. Both armed, both wearing vests.

Calster had her own room in the house. For now.

He signed the register after having his card checked. He also filled out a form titled *Use of Quarantine Facilities*. An extensive administration would be required to deal with all these forms. It didn't add to the real police work, however.

He knocked on her door. She opened it and let him in, almost casually, as if he were a visiting uncle. As if nothing had happened the day before but a pleasure trip to Belgium. Her bed was made up, and clothes hung over the chair.

"Did they bring you new clothes?" he asked. She wore white cotton slacks and a sleeveless blouse she probably had not chosen herself.

She nodded. "Yes. Not my style, but I have other things to worry about."

"You'll have to stay here for a while. Till we're sure you can safely walk the streets again."

Which would be, in his opinion, not soon.

"They caught Pieter's murderer, didn't they?" She stood by the window, waiting for her life to start again.

He remained by the door. The room was like a prison cell. On the wall hung a poster of a Swiss mountain landscape, snow and all. The window was open, but there were bars. And there would be some sort of alarm. She was safe but not from the police, and not from whoever controlled the police. There were a lot of people who would make her life hell. This hadn't happened yet because she didn't seem to know anything about the PDN or Van Tillo, about Pieter's intentions, the Russians, or criminal money. She knew a few things but not the whole picture. She was still alive because of her ignorance.

"They have caught the murderer," he said. "But not the people for whom he worked. So you're not in the clear yet."

She acknowledged the problem only with a slight nod. He hadn't come here to warn her. He came to avoid an intervention by a shrink. He was going to tell her the bad news herself.

"Something I have to tell you, Eileen," he started, knowing that there was no right or wrong way to do this. "About Maarten, your brother."

"Maarten? How do you know I have a brother?"

"We didn't, but the people who wanted that list knew it, apparently. I'm sorry to bring you bad news, Eileen, but Maarten is dead."

He looked her in the eyes while saying that. Nothing in those eyes seemed to change, but neither was she still the same person anymore. She had been annoyed, angry even, and now those feelings were wiped away. Then her face changed. The expression in her eyes changed. Her features tensed. She brought her hands up, covering her mouth, covering a cry. Then she closed her eyes, and a single tear rolled down one cheek.

He put his hands on her shoulders. She stepped back and blindly sat down on the bed.

Eekhaut squatted in front of her.

"I'm really very sorry," he said.

"Do my parents know?"

"No, probably not. We can't let the details of the investigation leak out. So no, they have not been informed yet. When the prosecutor allows it, we can talk to them, as soon as possible. For what it's worth, the murderer is dead. He was killed in the shoot-out. And we're concentrating on the real conspirators."

"You'll never get to them," she said. "These people . . . Pieter knew them well enough. These people will never be caught. You saw what they're capable of."

"Did Pieter understand the position he was in? The danger?"

"I think he underestimated them. He didn't assume he was in mortal danger, or that my life would be in danger. He didn't. Would he have stolen the list if he'd realized what they would do? I don't think so. But I'm not sure."

"We still have the list. But we're under pressure to hand it back over to Van Tillo."

"Of course you are," she said. "That's how it works, doesn't it? All those murders, the dead people. Evidence must disappear from your files. These are people with real power and influence."

"The world doesn't belong to people like you and Pieter," he admitted. "On occasion, we're brutally reminded of that."

"What will happen to me?"

"You know nothing. Almost nothing. That may keep you in the clear. The only one you can testify against was Parnow, and he's dead. You have seen nothing, and you know nothing of his employers."

"Then why do I have to stay here if I'm not in danger?"

"Just for a couple of days. We need to talk to you some more. Fill in more details."

"We are talking right now."

"This isn't an official visit."

"Oh."

"What would Pieter have done with the list?"

"Given it to a journalist."

"I assume so. Who?"

"A newspaper that is critical of Van Tillo."

"I'm Flemish. I don't know much about Dutch newspapers and their ideologies."

She wiped her face with the back of her hand. "Like *Vrij Nederland*, I guess."

"He knew somebody there?"

"Pieter knew a lot of people."

"So he kept their coordinates on his phone."

"Didn't need it. He knew who to talk to. He always knew where to find the right people. He didn't need an address book."

"But you know nothing."

She shook her head. "I was with him for only a year. He often spoke about politics and his ideas and the things he was working on. But he used first names when speaking about his friends. If you want to make that list public, Inspector, you can make it easy on yourself. Take it to all the newspapers in this town, and enough people will want to publish it. Many of them are not happy with Van Tillo or the PDN."

"Except that I can't make the list public."

"Of course you can. Things are always being copied. Enough machines to do that. Nobody knows anything. Nobody sees anything."

"And you?"

"What about me?"

"What would you do if you had the list?"

"Oh," she said. "I would know what to do with it. I just told you."

53

"Where have you been?" Dewaal asked. "You were supposed to interrogate Tarkovski. Or did I get that wrong?"

"I'll question Tarkovski right away," Eekhaut said. He had passed Dewaal in the corridor by their offices. "I've been to see Eileen Calster."

"Really? In an official capacity? Did you file a demand for that, in triplicate and through the correct channels?"

Eekhaut shook his head. "No to all those questions." He wasn't sure if she was serious.

She snorted. "Way out of line! Again, I need to fill in a stack of forms, all about you. You have no idea how much trouble you cause. Witnesses are only to be questioned officially, with a second officer present. By the book, Walter. By the goddamn book. I thought you had understood that much by now, didn't you?"

He was going to say *take it easy boss, no harm done*. But he didn't. He insisted, "She really needed to talk, nothing more. She needed human contact. Jesus, I can't believe I'm actually arguing with you on this subject."

She raised her voice. "You seem to be the one who's in need of a real conversation. But that's no excuse for what you did."

She looked angry, but not because of his little indiscretion. Not because of the paperwork. He was sure it had to do with her family. Something that was bothering her personally. She was the one in need of an intimate talk, unburdening herself. But that wasn't going to happen.

Or was there another problem, an official one? Had she been reprimanded?

He gazed at his watch. "Lunch?" he proposed. It was still early, but a longer lunch break would be a good idea. She had earned it, he felt. They both had.

She seemed surprised. "Lunch? Here?"

"No, bloody not here. Somewhere outside. It's not raining, we can sit on a terrace somewhere. These are probably the last remaining nice days before winter arrives. And a talk, that will do both of us a lot of good. Trust me."

Yes, she had to trust him.

She shrugged and gave in, but not without effort. "Let's do it, then."

They left the building and walked down the street and found the terrace of an Italian restaurant with little cloth-covered tables on the sidewalk. A sign displayed the menu and the specials.

"There should be more of these terraces in Amsterdam," he said. "Large enough terraces for tables and chairs. In Leuven we have—"

"I've seen enough of Leuven."

"You've seen nothing. A street, the interior of a hotel, and the face of the local prosecutor. We have to go back, on our own time. It's a great little town in the right season with lots of beautiful young people. With pubs, restaurants, terraces, small streets with people drinking and eating, all spring and summer long. The true Burgundian life Flanders is so famous for."

"Oh," she said, "that's what we hear all the time about your people. Your leisurely *mode de vie*. Your famous laid-back atmosphere. Good food, beer, and wine. People enjoy life, much more than we here in the north. Me, I'm not buying it. There's no place comparable to Amsterdam. Excuse my chauvinism."

She peered at her phone.

"Expecting trouble?" He wanted to know everything about her problems, but a white-aproned waiter approached and asked to take their orders. They both chose seafood salads and beer.

"My mother," she finally said. "She's dependent on me, and in an advanced state of dementia. Sometimes she remembers who I am, but most of the time I'm just another face to her. She thinks she's twenty and the war just broke out."

"How old is your mother?"

"Eighty-two."

"She can't remember the war. How come your mother is that old?"

"My mother was six when the war broke out. She was ten by the time Holland was liberated. That much is still very clear to her. She lived in a small village in the north for her entire life. Never went anywhere. Now she lives in an institution just outside Amsterdam. She remembers things from during the occupation. She gets things mixed up. She also has these . . . delusions. The doctors tell me it's irreversible. And about me having an older mother: she was forty when I was born. None of your business, by the way. My sister—she had two daughters—is a lot older than I."

"Oh," he said. He was saved any further embarrassment by the waiter, bringing the beer.

"Sometimes she doesn't recognize anybody at all. Not me, not the nurses. She doesn't know where she is, doesn't know who the other patients are. Can you imagine? Living in a world that has no meaning anymore. Where every experience is absolutely new. Would you be able to live like that?"

"And you take care of her."

"I would, but I can't. The staff at the home she's in is too small, so they occasionally expect family members to help out. I can't. Not with my job. I can't make time for her. Sometimes when there's a crisis— when she's having a crisis—they call me."

"Any other relatives?"

"None. Except my sister, and she still lives in the north, with her husband. Young Prinsen's parents. My father died a long time ago. Any other member of my family is very distant, in all meanings of the word."

"So you're alone in the world."

"Yes, in a way I guess I am."

"And frightened every time your phone rings."

She looked at him, probably wondering if it was a good idea, confiding in him like this. About her family and her personal affairs. But she had already come this far. "That's about it, yes. I even have a separate ringtone for the institution. I feel like I'm awaiting her death. She's eighty-two. This should not have happened."

Time to change the subject, he felt. Something else had been bugging him for a while now. Something he had to bring to her attention. "Are you still convinced there's a leak in your department?"

She put down her knife and fork and wiped her mouth with the paper napkin. Then she took a drink of beer. "Yes," she said. "Too much confidential information finds its way into the world. It's spooky, sometimes. And even while we're eating and chatting here, I'm not sure we're not being recorded or anything. There's a lot of things going on I seem to have no control over."

"And your office?"

"A lot of security measures were taken right after I arrived, but who guards the guards? There's all the other organizations that concern themselves with bits and pieces of national security, up to and including military intelligence. They usually have technology equivalent to ours, if not better. I can't guarantee that all my people are trustworthy. I can't guarantee they're not corrupt. Sometimes a politician inquires about details of an ongoing case, details he's not supposed to know anything about, and he won't tell me who whispered in his ear. Yes, we've got leaks."

"It is entirely possible that Van Tillo—"

"You'd do better not to use that name in public, Walter. Not even on a terrace in Amsterdam. Some subjects are taboo. Not long ago, she was minister of justice. She still has friends in that department. And elsewhere. A lot of people think as she does. Holland is no longer the friendly, open country it once used to be. Hasn't been for some time now."

"Neither is Belgium."

"No. The score isn't good."

"Question is, can you trust me?"

"We've been here before. This question, I mean."

"Yes, but has the question been adequately answered?"

"You need that in writing? Well, here it is. You wouldn't be here if you were corrupt. You would still be in Belgium, and you'd be a commissioner yourself. They wouldn't have sent you off to Holland if you had many good friends in high places."

"That's your norm? I'm a failure, and so you can trust me?"

"Yes, that's about it."

"You're weird, boss."

She smiled. And he didn't know what to think of that smile.

When he got back to his office, someone had dropped all of Tarkovski's material on his desk. A MacBook, a dozen memory sticks, an external hard drive, and three cardboard boxes with paper files.

He had expected more paper, but even these Russians had entered the digital age.

"Do I have to go through all this?" he asked.

But there was no one to answer the question. So he sat down. Opened the MacBook and switched it on. Someone had left him the password on a yellow Post-it. Nice set of icons at the bottom of the screen, ready to play games with him. He entered Tarkovski's virtual space and encountered at once the main problem: everything was in Russian.

Of course it was in Russian.

He had a look at what was on the sticks.

More Russian.

Graphs, images, lists.

All in the unreadable Cyrillic alphabet.

He needed a translator. But that would take forever.

He grabbed the phone. He was going to ask some technical expert to have a closer look at the innards of the computer and look for hidden files.

54

HENDRIKA VAN TILLO LOVED meetings. She loved encountering her supporters, people with similar ideas to her own, people who would follow her blindly. That's what the whole political circus was about: manifesting herself in public. She didn't like closed meetings with her staff, and she certainly didn't like the political arena of the Parliament. She loved the street, and the street loved her back.

People shouting, the intensity, the rush, the crowds, the smell of sweat. She *loved* it. It was something animal. It told her things would be OK for Holland, as long as people wanted to see her, listen to her. Listen to her ideas.

A few journalists had posed critical questions. About immigration and about citizens of foreign descent. About the political solutions the PDN stood for. What to do with those people of foreign background who had been here for so long, who had a Dutch passport, or those who had assimilated, even if their papers weren't in order? What to do with problems in the ethnic neighborhoods and with unemployed youngsters? How to deal with the economic problems, unemployment, the chasm between the poor and the very rich? Would she want to be a member of the government again? What would she do at the next election?

She didn't like that. Those questions.

She could handle the press. She had her answers ready. Stock answers, mostly. The journalists were never happy with those answers, but so what?

Who is the main financier of your party, Ms. Van Tillo? Why does your party not publicly discuss its funding? How much money does your party have?

Those questions she would *not* answer. Or she would become angry. *Don't get angry,* Vanheul had warned her, *because when they see your reaction, they'll want to know more.* They knew when something interesting was in sight. But she would ignore Vanheul. Who was chairperson of the Party after all? *She* had to deal with the answers. In her own way.

"Did we finally get that list back?" she asked him. It was the only real question on her mind right now. At least none of the journalists had asked about the list.

"The AIVD has it," he said. "That's the latest, as far as I know. A lot has happened after the business on the highway. A lot of people are worried. Still, no one has connected the dots. Nothing points to us yet. We'll deal with the AIVD if need be, Hendrika."

"I want to see Monet, Kees. Set up a meeting. At once."

He had expected that. She wanted to speak to Monet. Monet, on the other hand, was not interested in speaking to her. Not after the botched abduction. But he would speak with her. He had no choice. There were obligations. Mutual obligations.

And, of course, his name was on that list.

55

TARKOVSKI'S ENGLISH WAS ACCEPTABLE. Neither his grammar nor his pronunciation was very good, but it would do.

Problem was, he didn't want to talk. Not in English and not in any other language.

This time, Eekhaut mused, *I'm going to do this by the book.* As Dewaal wanted. A second officer present and a sound recording made. Prinsen was the other officer. The young man stood by the door, patient, arms folded, giving Eekhaut the space to develop his strategy.

Develop his strategy. This was what Eekhaut had in mind.

Although he didn't have much of a strategy.

"Who was Parnow?" he demanded. He sat in front of the young Russian, whose face had been marked by the incident on the highway. *I don't look undamaged myself,* Eekhaut thought, *but at least neither do you.* One of Tarkovski's eyes was more or less completely swollen shut, he had cuts on his cheeks and forehead, and one hand was bandaged. The cavalry had been a bit rough with him.

It didn't matter. It did for Tarkovski, but Eekhaut didn't give a damn.

It offered him the opportunity to play the Good Cop.

"They didn't exactly treat you nicely, did they," he said. This time a reaction came. Tarkovski blinked.

Good, Eekhaut thought. *The subject is alive. We're getting somewhere. Not far yet, but it's a start.*

"As I see it, you're here only to handle your boss's finances. You're a glorified bookkeeper, that's all you damn well are. You lead his Dutch office. You are a graduate of Saint Petersburg University, you're from a decent family, no criminal background. How did you get involved with these gangsters?"

Tarkovski said nothing. He didn't even look at Eekhaut. The wall and the ceiling held more interest for him than the somewhat damaged police officer.

Eekhaut observed the young Russian's body language. He had used the voice of reason. Some fell for that. The really hardened criminals did not, of course. They laughed at him and his reasonable voice. But Tarkovski was no hardened criminal. He wasn't any kind of criminal. Not in Eekhaut's book.

He had, however, chosen the wrong friends.

"I'm returning to my previous question. Who's Parnow? One thing he's not: a friend of yours. Clearly not. I refuse to believe you have friends like Parnow. That you mix with that sort of company. At least not voluntarily. A young fellow like yourself shouldn't have that sort of friend."

"He is no friend," Tarkovski said, and he cast a quick glance at Prinsen, by the door.

Good, Eekhaut mused. A reaction. Four words. Conversation would be a bit easier after this. "Your name is Andreï, isn't it? Do you mind if I use your first name? Makes talking easier."

Tarkovski shrugged. "Whatever."

"That's right," Eekhaut said, "whatever. I can do whatever I want in here. You, on the other hand, can do nothing at all. You're under arrest. For a number of crimes. You can do nothing but wait for your trial and hope the judge hears a few arguments in your favor and doesn't give you a long sentence. Not something like, for instance, ten years. Imagine ten years in the presence of the likes of Parnow. The whole time, day in and day out. I don't want to think about it. Neither do you. You won't be safe, not for one minute. And certainly not when they find out who you work for. As for me, that's an entirely different matter. I'll walk out of here and go to a movie or the park, and I'll meet my girlfriend. And we'll go to my apartment and fuck our brains out. Maybe after that I'll enjoy a long vacation, somewhere without a winter. All of the things that you'll have to do without. For ten years. Or for a shorter period, depending on what you tell me."

Tarkovski said nothing.

Maybe he didn't like those places without a winter. He was Russian, after all. Maybe he didn't want to fuck a woman. And so on.

But Eekhaut knew the message had hit home. Hard.

"I'd really like to know a bit more about Parnow. We don't know all that much about him. He's a blind spot. A void. And he's dead. It means he can't go to trial. And he can't be a witness either. He can't go to prison for the rest of his natural life for multiple murders. You wouldn't care anyway, since he was no friend of yours. At least I assume he wasn't. At least that's what I understand so far. What was he, then?"

"Ex-military."

"Mmmm. That explains a lot. Ex-military. But not the type that spent his time behind a desk. No, he was the operational type. Boots on the ground guy. And a murderer as well. The girl recognized his face. He killed Pieter Van Boer. Case closed. A murderer. Like the rest of the scum that was waiting for us on the highway. But I'm sure they were no friends of yours, Andreï. I'm very confident of that because they had guns, and you didn't. But, you know, a judge won't make that distinction. You were part of an armed assault against police officers, and that's the same as carrying a gun."

"They weren't friends of mine."

"Exactly. They all worked for Keretsky. Like you do. Well, there's the catch. Keretsky is safe in Russia. Keretsky doesn't have anything to do with common criminals. He's a very nice man and completely clean. And when he comes back to Holland, there's no reason for us to arrest him. Even the thought that we would want to arrest him would be ridiculous. He has a lot of friends, all in the right places, too. I can't even blow my nose when he's around for fear of getting suspended."

Tarkovski said nothing.

"And so he's untouchable, your big chief. But I'm not interested in Keretsky. What I'm interested in, Andreï, is the man who asked Keretsky to clean things up here in Amsterdam. Don't tell me Keretsky is the man who gave the orders about Van Boer and Eileen and the list and everything else. There's somebody else. And you know who I'm talking about, don't you, Andreï?"

Tarkovski's one good eye spoke whole chapters. He clearly didn't like the direction this conversation was going, even if it wasn't a conversation. This suited Eekhaut best. Tarkovski was beginning to feel the heat. Eekhaut would keep up his side of the conversation. *Time is on my side*, he thought. For this once, it was.

"You're faithful to your boss, aren't you, Andreï? Too bad your boss is in Russia and I can't get to him. But you're aware of all this. I'm not asking you to betray him. I want to know the name of the man behind the operation. Your operation, Andreï. The man so intent on recovering the list that Van Boer and others had to die."

"You know very well who you're talking about," Tarkovski said.

"Help me refresh my memory, Andreï." Eekhaut waited for a moment. Then he said, "I'll make you a proposal. You tell me the name of the man in the background and sign a confession. And I make sure you're out in a week or so, so you can return to Saint Petersburg or wherever you choose."

Tarkovski inspected him intently. His one eye spoke of a longing for Russia, home, parents.

"Your parents will be happy to see you again," Eekhaut said. "In good health and as a free man."

Prinsen, against the wall by the door, didn't react. He probably didn't know what to make of this proposal and the unusual terms the Belgian was concocting. The proposal wouldn't become reality, not in a hundred years. But that wasn't his problem.

"You can guarantee that?" Tarkovski said. He was whispering now, as if he wanted only Eekhaut to hear him.

"I can."

"Can I think this over?"

"No. The moment I get up and walk out of that door and somebody else takes my place, you will be questioned the rest of the day and night until you're willing to confess to anything they can think of, but by that time the deal is off."

Tarkovski hung his head.

"I want to go back to Saint Petersburg," he said.

Eekhaut pushed a writing pad in his direction. "And now," he said, "we'll do this by the book. Go ahead, refresh my memory."

56

PRINSEN WALKED OUT. ANOTHER detective took his place in the room with the young Russian. He didn't know what to think of Eekhaut. Or perhaps he did. He knew exactly what to think of Eekhaut. The Belgian was mad. He was bonkers. Making promises to a suspect, knowing he wouldn't be able to keep them—that was not supposed to happen. Not here, not in the Bureau. Here the game was played correctly. If you were a cop working the streets, you didn't bother about the promises you made. Nobody expected you to keep them. But in this operation? This was the AIVD, and your opponents were of a special breed. Not the sort of people who take a broken promise lightly.

As for Tarkovski, he would soon have a top lawyer at his side, a Dutch lawyer of Russian descent, probably. And the man would get Tarkovski out of here, on bail, if he was any good.

Prinsen returned to his office and looked at Van Gils's desk. The empty desk. Which would probably remain empty for a while.

His own desk wasn't empty. New dossiers continued to pile up. New information, things he would have to read. Was this what he had in mind when he came to work here? When Aunt Alexandra asked him to join her department? How had that happened? A phone call, an invitation, a job description. Had it happened because he was brilliant or had his aunt selected him for personal reasons? But she hadn't been interested in their blood ties. She wanted somebody to confide in.

It meant that he was here because she knew she couldn't trust the rest of the team.

And these others were aware of the reasons behind her choice. Or at least they'd made assumptions.

And the Belgian had been brought in for nearly the same reason.

So he and Eekhaut had at least one thing in common.

57

"Politics is your problem," Monet said furiously into his cell phone. He had been called away from a works council, where he'd wanted to bring down his wrath on the union representatives. He didn't like meetings with the works council or the boards of any of his companies. And he surely didn't like unions. Furtively, he glanced around. There was nobody in the vicinity. He could vent his frustration unhindered.

"I'm fed up with this bullshit, Kees," he continued. "I see on the late news there's been a *battle*—I have no other word for it—in a parking lot by the highway, and three people were killed. Bloody hell, Kees, in Holland! The press is all over this, blames it on organized crime, but you and I know what's really going on. I didn't order this! I didn't sign on for a full-fledged war with the AIVD or whatever. This was that young Russian's idea, Andreï, whatever his name is. He had to go all out on this and bring in an armored brigade . . ."

"We're not sure if this is connected to Andreï, Mr. Monet," Kees Vanheul said. "We don't have any details yet. Tarkovski was supposed to arrange matters in connection with—*you know what*—but that was all he had to do. Make sure the thing was settled."

Vanheul sounded frightened. *Good*, Monet thought. *I hope you shit your pants, Vanheul. That will teach you to think twice before calling me again on an open line.*

But Vanheul had plenty of reasons to sound scared. Calling Monet and talking openly about the matter was one of them. They both knew their calls could be monitored. But he was sure the likelihood was slight.

Any demand for a tap had to pass through the office of the prosecutor, and Vanheul had his man in that office. He would know if his own phone or Monet's had been tapped.

At least, he hoped.

And they hadn't implicated themselves anyway.

He hoped.

But Monet didn't seem to care who was listening in. He said, "Let me spell this out as clearly as possible for you, Vanheul. The list is now out of our reach, as long as it's in the hands of the AIVD. And I don't trust those people. I'd like to have them taken off the investigation and have it in the hands of people who are more . . . sympathetic to us. But that's not going to happen. My political enemies have given special privileges to Dewaal and her Bureau, and they're out of control. *Your* politicians need to do something about that. Why can't they? Why not limit the power of the whole AIVD? Do we live in a police state or what?"

"The AIVD is directly accountable to the department of justice and to the minister. There's no way to change that."

"Then why don't you call people in that department? Why did you call me? Doesn't Hendrika still have connections? It's her former ministry, isn't it? Oh, I know what her problem is. She's more interested in her current political career. She wants to concentrate on her supporters. As if that will help her save her career when the list goes public."

"That won't happen, Mr. Monet."

"I sincerely hope not, Kees. Because if that happens and I get implicated, a lot of other very nasty things will suddenly surface. I want you to understand that. I want Van Tillo and the Party to understand that. It's time to stop this, Kees. Make that list disappear."

"I can assure you that this is exactly what we all want."

Monet broke the connection. *The day when you and the witch you work for disappear from the face of the earth, I'll be truly happy.* He hated Van Tillo. Giving her and her party money had been a good investment, nothing more. He occasionally needed her support, back when she was minister, and even now. He needed export licenses that were sometimes hard to come by, especially for products that were on somebody's blacklist. And he occasionally needed work permits for what he officially called "foreign nationals."

Having a few politicians around always proved handy. How had Holland become rich? Because entrepreneurs had been given a free hand to do what they did best: trade. That's what it had done in centuries past. These days, unions were making up the rules. Always demanding higher wages, which meant companies could no longer compete with foreign rivals. He was against a guaranteed minimum wage, as he was against the whole idea of unconditional basic income. Where was the sense in that? Giving people money to do nothing? What society had ever done that before? And why was this country giving free rein to drugs and pornography? Society needed rules, his rules. Those of Van Tillo and her ilk.

58

"The Commission of Internal Affairs will suspend you for this," Dewaal said. She looked unhappy.

"The Commission of Internal Affairs can get buggered, or whatever it is you say here in the north," Eekhaut said. "This is a signed confession by Andreï Tarkovski, in English—or at least in his personal version of English—accusing Dirk Benedict Monet of conspiracy to commit murder. What's going to be the problem? This Monet fellow too big for you?"

"Big enough. If we take him on, the newspapers are going to have a field day. But will I get the prosecutor to sign a warrant for his arrest? Based on this confession, by a Russian without any credibility? And I'm not even mentioning the way the confession was obtained. So really, no, I don't think I'll get my warrant."

"It's a confession, boss. It doesn't say how it was obtained. This is about murder. Several murders and conspiracy to commit a kidnapping. And illegal political financing. And connection to criminal activities. If this doesn't weigh enough for the prosecutor, what will?"

Dewaal leaned back in her chair. She had been angry, but that anger left her now. She calmly considered the situation. "Implicating Monet and Van Tillo," she said. "Seems unlikely we can pull this off, but it is not impossible."

"Of course it's not impossible. But Monet first. We bring him in first, and we find the link to Van Tillo afterward. Soon enough."

She sat upright again. "But there's only Tarkovski's confession, Walter. A suspect who himself has been part of the aforementioned criminal activities. Any lawyer worth his fee could reduce this case to kindling."

"And so what? Monet gets his moment in the spotlight, he loses all public and private credibility, and—"

She pointed her finger at him. "No! We can't do that. The political implications of this case go way beyond Monet. Do you think I care about Monet?"

"I know enough about police work to know politics always lurks around the corner."

"You knew that before you led Tarkovski to this confession, Walter. And you got him to confess without his lawyer present. One deadly sin after another!"

"I didn't force him to confess."

"Oh, Jesus. Right! You made him a promise you knew wasn't going to happen. He'll go to prison, and you know that. What will you do? Help him escape and put him on a plane to Russia?"

"We're the police, Alexandra. And they are scum. We owe them nothing. I'll lie and I'll steal if I have to, as long as I get the scum behind bars. And that includes Monet."

"I'll have you sent back to Brussels, Eekhaut!"

"You could have done that right away. From the first day. But then you'd have to fill out thirty-seven forms and sign them all. That takes a while. *If* they want me back."

She calmed down. "Fine. You can stay. For a while. Let's step back a minute and see what we have."

"Not much. A confession, a motive."

"Monet has no motive. He has no reason to have Van Boer killed."

"His name is on the list."

"Along with a few hundred other names, all indirectly implicated in this matter. They don't want the list to become public either. Monet had no more motive than any of them. Have you seen the list? The names probably mean nothing to you, but there are a lot of midsize Dutch companies. And we can't use the list anyway."

"We can't?"

"We have to give it back to Van Tillo. She has too much influence. And she wants our promise that no copies have been made."

"So we lose exhibit A."

"That's right."

"And Tarkovski's testimony? What about that?"

"Not much value on its own. We send a few people to prison because of what happened on the highway, but they're mere soldiers. They'll do time and get paid for it. It really does look like your friend will to be on a plane back to Russia soon, but not because you promised him."

"I wanted to keep him, actually. Started to like him. And that seemed mutual. I'm not going to let him walk just like that."

"Can't say I'm sympathetic, Walter. Keep that in mind when you mete out loyalties."

"Still, it felt like we had a moment there, Alexandra, back there behind the car with bullets flying all around."

"That's exactly the sort of moment I'd prefer to avoid. Much as I want to avoid damage to my Bureau."

"Does that mean some crimes go unpunished?"

She nodded, slowly. "Some crimes will always go unpunished."

"Do I tell that to Eileen Calster?"

"You've said too much already to Eileen Calster. I suggest you keep your distance."

She knew he was right, but she wasn't going to admit it, he thought. "And what's the story she tells her parents? About Pieter's murderer, and the murder of her brother for no reason at all, only because some Russian psychopath was given free rein? That the psychopath, Parnow, killed their son because that's the sort of thing he does? And we couldn't catch him, and now he's dead, and that's the story Eileen will have to tell her parents?"

"That will do, Inspector! That will bloody well do! I can't solve all the injustice in the world, and neither can you. Now leave me. I have a lot of work to do."

It pleased him to hear she was using his rank again. The affection had been short-lived. Police matters took the upper hand.

The phone on her desk buzzed. She answered it and signaled to Eekhaut, who wanted to leave. "Send him to my office," she said into the phone.

"What now?" Eekhaut asked.

"Tarkovski's lawyer is on his way. Stay for a minute."

"Really? I'm not very good at handling lawyers. I can't even stand to be in the same room as them. I certainly have no problem with lawyers defending victims. But otherwise—"

"In this case," Dewaal said, "you're going to conduct yourself like this man's best friend. Because I need you to witness this conversation."

"Oh," he said.

"That's right: *oh*!"

A knock on the door interrupted them. Eekhaut opened it. A man in his forties with a fashionable crewcut inspected both officers for a moment before entering the office. "Chief Superintendent Dewaal?" he asked Eekhaut, who made a slight head movement toward the real Dewaal, while enjoying the confusion.

"Oh, excuse me," the man said. "My name is Siegel. I'm a lawyer, and I assume my client, Mr. Tarkovski, is in one of your cells?"

Dewaal shook his hand. She didn't ask him to sit down, indicating the conversation would be brief and to the point. "Interrogation room, actually. We hardly use those cells. Criminals go straight away to Amsterdam CID or prison. But we have Mr. Tarkovski as our guest, on account of some details we wanted to straighten out."

"And what is he accused of?"

"You know very well what he is accused of, counselor. The prosecutor must have talked you through this. Murder, possession of a firearm without a license, conspiracy to commit an abduction, conspiracy to commit murder, resisting arrest, attempted manslaughter of a police officer. Quite a busy bee, your man."

"He didn't have a gun," Siegel said. "You can't pin that one on him."

"Whether he used a gun or not isn't clear at the moment, counselor, and the technical report isn't complete as yet, but we're holding him on that point as well, to be sure. There are sufficient indications."

"When the report is finished, Ms. Dewaal, you will see that my client didn't handle a gun, nor did he own one. He was present in a car with criminals, but he was the involuntary witness to a crime. That's as much as you will get with him."

Dewaal snorted. "At the very least, he ordered the assault on police officers and the abduction. We'll get him for the murders as well. Don't hold your breath, counselor."

"You have no reliable witnesses, only malicious gossip."

"Yes, we have witnesses, even if they're not talking yet. But they will. They're looking at ten or fifteen years in prison. And you of all people should know how easily people start to talk with such a prospect in mind."

"You can hold my client for a very short time, and you're running out of time now."

"Did you bring a release form?"

"I deposited it with the prosecutor's office. By the book, ma'am. Tomorrow morning my client will walk out of here a free man. I hope he'll be spending a comfortable night in one of your cells. Now, can I speak with him, if it isn't too much to ask?"

"It is too much to ask, counselor. We're not the regular police. You know that. We have special privileges and powers. Keeping a suspect in isolation to safeguard the inquiry and all that. Also by the book."

Siegel grinned maliciously. "Yes, ma'am, I am aware of your privileges. Tomorrow then, let's say at ten sharp?" He cast a quick glance at Eekhaut and left the office.

Dewaal remained silent, but it was a meaningful silence. She probably had expected how the conversation would turn out.

"Let's sleep on it," Eekhaut finally said. He left the office.

He looked at the time. It was still early, but he had worked overtime on the previous days, so he felt he was allowed some time off. He left the building. He still needed to stock his fridge, but again he had other things on his mind. He walked to the Bijenkorf department store and bought a pair of tan chinos, two blue shirts, underwear, and two white T-shirts. He admired a dark blue woolen sports jacket but didn't buy it.

He then walked along Kalverstraat and entered the American Book Center, where he bought three hardcovers of authors he knew by name.

Only then did he buy groceries. He stowed everything away in the apartment and made something to eat. A microwave dinner, actually, but he didn't care. He read a newspaper while eating but skipped the local crime section.

59

This time Eekhaut asked for her phone number. In case he couldn't make it next time, although she probably wouldn't wait for him. "I'm afraid I've let you down," he apologized.

"Is this a sort of friendship we're experiencing here?" she asked, not without glee. She tore a page from a small planner, wrote down her number, and handed it to him. "And I want your business card. Which I will then show to all my friends."

Friendship. "I only have one of the cards issued by the Belgian police, I'm afraid," he said. "The cell number is still valid, though. You should be aware that it's a foreign number for you."

"Well, why not?" she said. His card went into the planner after a quick glance. "You told me last time you were, like, corrupt."

"In a special sort of way. Not in the real meaning of the term. At least I hope not."

"In that special sort of way, a lot of people are corrupt."

"Because I'm not able to stop evil. But like most people, I don't do it on purpose. I just . . . well, I let it happen."

"*Evil*," she said. "Capital letter. Sounds good. *Cool*, the kids would say, because they don't know what evil means. What it brings about."

"It doesn't have to be anything big. It could be all sorts of little evils, mini-evils, small daily corruptions. People who evade taxes, undeclared work-time, faked invoices, petty theft, all the casual forms of corruption that make us immune to the bigger frauds. The things the really rich do, and companies and government as well."

"While we all pay the bill for corruption. Society ends up paying the bill for any sort of fraud."

"Oho," he laughed, "the role of cynic has already been taken—by me. I'm the cynical policeman. That's me. Drinking in a bar, approaching an innocent lady. And trying to forget whatever there was between them the next morning."

"Oh? Will you have forgotten me by morning? I hope not." She was teasing him, but it sounded like she was also worried about him.

"No," he said, "I won't forget you. But I'll regret that I may have been too frank."

"I'll accept that," she said. "Imagine I'm a good fairy. A green fairy, which would be appropriate, considering what we're drinking here. Please feel free to share your troubles with me."

"Let's keep the roles clear, Linda. I'm the alpha male policeman, and I help you out of trouble. That's the way things work best."

"Now, I don't know about that. Tell me, since you're the alpha male, what happens to people who, within the framework of their job, are forced to go along with . . . I mean, have to assist in Evil? I'm being a bit over the top now, I know, but I mean—"

"What?" This sounded interesting.

"I mean . . . imagine you're doing a job you like. You assume you work for a decent company. And suddenly you discover improper dealings of some sort. Things that are immoral and even criminal. Your company and your boss are, well, immoral."

"Depends on what you call immoral."

"Things you cannot condone personally. Worse: actual crimes. You're not involved directly but are in the background . . . and you've been a witness to these criminal dealings."

"You could go to the police," he said. "As long as you haven't committed a crime yourself."

"And what if you're, I mean, implicated?"

"I don't know, Linda. I've dealt with hundreds of people who wouldn't have wanted to commit a crime, but they still did. They didn't want to sin or go against their moral principles, but at some point they crossed the line. On only a few occasions have I met someone who knew perfectly well he was committing a crime. And did so knowingly, without any remorse. And, of course, there are the psychopaths, but that's another story."

"I see. No, I don't. Not completely."

"Is there a reason you ask?"

"So, it's all about people making choices," she said. "Isn't it funny: we met here some evening, just passing time, now we're talking like we've known each other for ages."

"At least we're not discussing the weather."

"That would be a less dangerous subject."

He said, "But then we wouldn't get to know each other, either."

She sat up. "I'd like something else to drink. Who drinks this stuff, actually, unless it's out of curiosity? Can I have a fruit juice?"

"No problem." He got her a fruit juice and a Canada Dry for himself.

"And your job?" she asked "How about that, accepting the unavoidable corruption?"

"I have to look people in the eye who I know are guilty, but I have to function within a framework that sets these same people free as soon as possible. I'm not saying we need an American system of social punishment. But too often, I meet with the parents of murdered children, family members of a rape victim, and the victims themselves, and I wonder about a system that lets psychopaths run free again after, what, five years? And without treatment. And then there's major economic crime, which often goes unpunished."

"I see," she said. "Well, no, I don't, but I get it." She touched his arm. "I'm here to comfort wounded policemen, Walter. I'm the green fairy. I see a police officer between alcohol and his dreams. What a dreary little cliché. How about your future?"

That made him smile. "You're right. I need to leave my work at the office. Sleep the sleep of the innocent, even if other people can't. May I see you again? Can we have dinner soon?"

"No. I'm a fairy. I'm enchanted. Without these bottles of absinthe, I turn to flesh and blood."

"I'll take my chances."

SATURDAY
Amsterdam

60

"The prosecutor isn't likely to share your enthusiasm," Dewaal said the next morning. A chilly morning announcing the new season, the inevitable onset of winter. People had started wearing leather coats and scarves, but still casually, as if they weren't afraid of the cold yet. "We need a new prosecutor, Walter. One who doesn't shit his pants every time he gets a call from a politician. One with balls." She watched Eekhaut with glee. "You're not supposed to take that literally. I would welcome a female prosecutor anytime."

"Is some powerful politician we won't name responsible for the lack of enthusiasm?"

That got her worked up again. "That kind of talk will get you crucified, Walter! I'm warning you. Don't take this too far."

The morning hadn't started well. Not with a prosecutor who wasn't going anywhere with the Tarkovski matter. And the weather had gotten to Eekhaut as well. It had been raining earlier, and he wasn't keen on spending fall and winter in Amsterdam. He was glad his apartment was close to the office. He would walk anyplace else only if strictly necessary.

"What are our plans with young Tarkovski?" he asked.

"He can expect an elaborate indictment."

"And Monet? What will happen to him?"

Dewaal shook her head. "I'm not sure I know who that is," she said, in mock confusion. "Let me see . . . Monet. No. No one by that name figures in the files." She looked at him intently. "And I'm sure I don't need to warn you not to show any personal initiative concerning this person." Her expression told him she was more than serious.

He leaned toward her. *To hell with that*, he thought. *We've been shot at and nearly killed. We risked our lives for this. We deserve this.* "We're civil servants," he said, although he wanted to say something different. "And we serve the people. Don't we always?"

"I know what you're going to say, Chief Inspector. I know what your little speech will be. I've heard it often enough, here in this same office. You're not the first one to appeal to my conscience. But I'm not going to be dragged into that discussion. Not with you. I avoid having ideological discussions with my colleagues. I talk tactics and I talk procedures. Leave politics to politicians."

Oh yes, he thought. *Politicians. They're well suited to dealing with conscience.* "I try to do the right thing, Alexandra."

"I know. Eileen Calster's parents, Eileen herself, Van Boer's family, I know. They all need the truth to come out. And we owe that to Pieter Van Boer as well, though he knew the risks."

"There shouldn't have been risks. Not even for him. Citizens have the right to know what their politicians do. That sort of information doesn't have to come with capital punishment attached."

"All right," she said. "All right. So I arrest Monet on what we have today. Which is next to nothing. I arrest Van Tillo and her secretary on what we don't have today. Then their lawyers arrive. An army of lawyers. And they drag the prosecutor and the minister and other politicians in with them, because we touched people in their own class. A lot of problems for all concerned, but especially for us. I'll get fired. The Bureau will be shut down. The files burned. Van Tillo will be even more popular afterward, because this boosts her public image. Eileen Calster will have to move to Argentina and end up in a community of devil worshippers. Tarkovski will go to jail for ten years, where he'll be raped on a daily basis by addicts and maybe commit suicide. You'll be fired and live in a cabin in the Ardennes with a gun under your pillow. That's how the story plays out. Is that what you want?"

He knew she was right. She was right in every single detail. He didn't want to end up in the Ardennes with a gun under his pillow. And he didn't like the rest of the story either.

And because she was right, he was angry. He was angry because, after so many years, he still had to play along. Here, in Brussels, everywhere he went he had been obliged to play the game. Often enough he hadn't, but then he'd paid a personal price. And nearly as often, he had seen innocent people on their way to prison.

"You're not to make any sort of deal," she warned him.

"A deal? Me?" As if she'd accused him of beheading baby chickens with his teeth. Him, a deal? As if he'd do anything without her knowledge and agreement.

"Yes, you. I know how you tick. You don't like the way things turned out, and you want Van Tillo and Monet behind bars. I respect that, and I want them behind bars too, but I accept reality." And then she said, "My hands are tied."

He sat up. "And mine aren't, you mean."

She shook her head. "Yours too. Of course they are. I must see to it that you follow procedures. By the book, again. Our book. Our Dutch rules. Make you fill in the correct forms and get permission for every step along the way. That sort of thing. And if you don't follow these procedures, you get a slap on the wrist. From me. Actually, there is little else I can do to you other than slap you on the wrist."

"You're not completely in control, you mean."

"I'm not?" she inquired.

"No, you aren't. To mention one detail: I'm still paid by the Belgian government. So you can't fire me. You can send me back, but that's all you can do."

"No, not really. I can't send you back. That would mean a hell of a lot of red tape, as you yourself pointed out recently. And nobody wants red tape. What's more, they don't want you back. Again, as you were so kind to point out to me. Remember, Walter? You're so unpopular that I seem to be stuck with you indefinitely."

"Too bad," he said. "Red tape. We must avoid that by all means."

And he knew he had made a decision. Or, better: decisions.

61

HE SIGNED IN AT the safe house. Wrote his name in the book, filled out a form, walked up the stairs. As far as he was concerned, this would be his last visit to this place. Because he had made his decisions.

Eileen stood by the window. Her upright posture told him she wasn't going to be defeated. *Good for her*, he thought.

She leaned against the windowsill. "I am going mad in here," she said. It didn't sound desperate. It sounded like she was challenging him. She wore a short skirt of brown cotton, white sandals, and a yellow top, as if it were still summer. It had stopped raining, but water was dripping nearby, an annoying sound. A Chinese water torture.

"They'll let you go soon," he promised.

"And where do I go? I can't go anywhere. Can I return to the apartment? Pieter's apartment? I'd like to, for just a little while. I want to collect my things."

"I assume you can get your things. But do you still want to live there?"

"No, I don't. I'll leave Amsterdam and go back to Groningen. What else can I do with my life?"

"Finish college?"

She shrugged.

"You're disappointed," he said.

She sat down on the bed. Skinny, but well-muscled. Pale, lacking sun, lacking a healthy lifestyle. She clearly wasn't the sort of girl who would spend summers on a beach. In the library, maybe. "Yes, of course

I'm disappointed," she said, "but that word doesn't even begin to convey my feelings. Pieter has disappeared from my life. People want to kill me. What will happen now?"

He sat down on a chair. *She could be your daughter,* a little voice told him. The little voice that influenced many of his decisions. The little voice he tried to overrule with his rational mind. More disappointment was coming for Eileen Calster. Life would see to that. Because nothing would ever compensate for her loss. Because life would treat her badly later on. She expected justice, which she wouldn't get. In the end, she would turn into a cynic. A bit like him. Maybe too much like him. If he could, he wanted to help her avoid that.

So he was going to help her. By finding justice.

He took the folded sheets of paper out of his jacket pocket.

She frowned deeply.

Already, he thought, *there is mistrust. She mistrusts even the people who are committed to her.*

"It's a copy," he explained, "and it's not supposed to exist. We weren't allowed to make copies. Not even for our own files. But, you know, today, there are copying machines everywhere. It's unavoidable. Someone makes a copy of everything at some point."

"And you expect me to run off to the press with—"

"No," he said, softly. "No. I don't want that. Because you'll be in danger again. Someone might come after you again, maybe just out of spite. And there might be nobody to protect you this time. I won't be there to protect you."

He tucked the list away again.

"Who knows of this?"

"You. And me. That's enough. For the moment, it's enough."

"But they'll suspect—"

"Yes. Of course. They will have suspicions. But it'll be too late anyway."

"You can't take that risk."

"Of course, not," he said. "Of course, I can't take that risk. Neither can you. The difference between us two is that I'm in a better position to run the risk than you. But I have to be careful. That's why I'll wait."

"For what?"

"Till you're safe in Groningen. Till I get a postcard with a picture of some local landmark and your personal message. At least that."

"Oh," she said. She didn't show her feelings.

"And then again I'll wait."

"Yes?"

"There is always the perfect moment for showing your best cards."

"But you'll have to show them sometime, at least."

"Of course. I will. But you must be out of the picture first. You have nothing to do with this."

He rose. "I wish you the best," he said. "I hope to see you again sometime, but not here."

She stood up and embraced him.

He hadn't expected that.

62

DEWAAL AND EEKHAUT HAD to wait for fifteen minutes in a small room on the second floor of the PDN headquarters. A slim and artificially blond young woman had let them in and asked them to be patient.

Eekhaut thought, *This is Van Tillo making sure we understand she's still calling the shots.* He assumed Dewaal thought the same. She looked worse for wear, her face pale and tense and her lips thin and almost bloodless.

The magazines on the table had one thing in common: they all had some item on Van Tillo and her party. Van Tillo visiting and meeting important people and speaking at conferences. Neither he nor Dewaal bothered reading them.

The secretary opened the door again. "Ms. Van Tillo will see you now," she said.

They both rose and were ushered into Van Tillo's office. The politician rose from behind her desk, visibly tense. She wore too much gold for Eekhaut's taste. Vanheul stood by her, dressed in an ill-fitting beige suit.

"Chief Superintendent, Inspector, please take a seat," Van Tillo said.

"My colleague is a chief inspector," Dewaal said, "if you insist on using our ranks. We want the correct ranks being used, ma'am."

Van Tillo smirked at them as if to say, what does it matter? A chief superintendent and a chief inspector, as if either of them would have any impact on the situation. She had ministers and captains of industry behind her. She met with board members of important companies face to face. She was intimate with important politicians.

"You have come to return the list that was stolen from our offices," she stated.

"That's correct," said Dewaal. She produced a brown envelope from her purse. "This is it. The original list."

"A shame so many people had to die for it," Eekhaut remarked, like he wasn't really addressing anyone in the room. "Pieter Van Boer in the first place, who worked here, in this building. He worked for you, Ms. Van Tillo, and he probably did you a lot of favors, professionally, I mean. Giving you his all as a writer of your purple prose."

"Van Boer," she said, hatefully.

"Hendrika," Vanheul warned her. "Don't get carried away."

"I'm not getting carried away, Kees. But let's not talk nonsense. He was here to spy on us, Mister . . . whatever your name is. *Chief Inspector*. He was here to damage us. To destroy us, even. But I'm not getting carried away."

"I read some of your brochures. Well written. His work? Or yours?"

"Doesn't matter. As long as he worked for us, he had to—we would not have kept him if he wasn't good at what he did. But he spied on us. He lacked the most common decency."

"And who was he really spying for, in your opinion?" Dewaal asked.

"I can only guess, Ms. Dewaal. But we have our list of suspects. We are aware of the reprehensible communist anarchy these sorts of people promote."

"You loathe people like Van Boer?" Eekhaut asked.

Van Tillo turned to him. "I know what you want to achieve, Inspector. You want me to speak my mind about . . . but we have nothing to do with the murder of Van Boer. That's not the sort of thing we do. We're into politics, not into crime."

"Someone is," Dewaal said.

"Chief Superintendent, if you want to question me formally in connection with this murder, you'll have to do that through regular channels. I wanted to meet you today because you told me the problem with the list is solved. Now you arrive here, with this . . . gentleman, and you start to question me. If that's the case, I want our lawyer present."

"This is not an interrogation, Ms. Van Tillo," Dewaal said, speaking softly now, even surprising Eekhaut. As if she were sharing intimate information with Van Tillo. "If this were an interrogation, we would be in *my* office now, with your lawyer present, and we would have a really *formal* conversation."

"Which is not the case," Van Tillo said. "So I don't have to listen to you anymore. Thank you for coming and for the list. Vanheul will escort you out."

"I'm afraid a few details still need to be attended to," Eekhaut said.

"There is nothing more to discuss," said Van Tillo.

"There is, ma'am. But before I continue, Chief Superintendent Dewaal will leave this office and wait for me in the corridor."

Dewaal got up, left, and closed the door behind her.

Neither Van Tillo nor Vanheul moved.

"What kind of freak show is this?" Van Tillo asked. "What are you up to?"

"Any document can be easily copied today," Eekhaut said.

Van Tillo flushed. Deeply. Angrily.

Before she could reply, Eekhaut continued, "And there is no limit to this copying capability. No limit. Copies of copies and so on. Endless numbers of copies."

"The deal was—"

"That was a deal between you and the Dutch police. Dewaal kept her part of that deal. I, on the other end, have made no deal, not with anybody."

"You should also—"

"I do not belong to the AIVD, the Dutch police, whatever. I am a Belgian citizen and a Belgian police officer. *Chief Inspector*, by the way. Please feel free to complain to my superiors, but they care little about Dutch politics. This makes me something of . . . a free agent, if you see what I mean."

"If you've made copies of the list and you pass them on to other parties, we'll have your head on a platter, and very quickly too."

"You will find, ma'am, that in order to have that head on a platter, you'll need to go through an impossible amount of red tape. During this investigation, I've collected evidence against the murderer of Pieter Van

Boer, Maarten Calster, and another young man. That's three murders. It's very painful to abandon a trail of dead people in exchange for a few sheets of paper. But I propose a deal. A deal you can't refuse. A very attractive deal."

"I don't make deals with corrupt Belgian cops."

"That really hurts, ma'am. Calling me corrupt. But I'll let it slide for now. Maybe you'd better listen to my proposal."

"No way!"

"Hendrika!" Vanheul warned her. "Listen to what he has to say."

"Shut up, Kees. You were supposed to solve this. That's what I'm paying you for. First the lack of security and then the Russian who could not even—"

"Hendrika!"

Eekhaut calmly said, "Ms. Van Tillo. My proposal is simple."

She kept her mouth shut.

"First, I keep a few copies of the list for myself and you make sure Eileen Calster is left alone and is safe."

"Calster? Oh, Van Boer's girlfriend. And?"

"Maybe she's no longer in danger, but I want to make sure of that. And second, I want the name of the person who ordered the murders."

"You caught the man. It's in the papers."

"We caught the people executing orders. I want the man who ordered these murders. That, and the list. Someone has to pay."

"And we . . ."

"You stay out of sight. I personally regret that, but I'll take the other trophy for my wall. And make no mistake, Ms. Van Tillo: where I come from, I have the reputation of always getting my trophies."

"This is unacceptable."

"I will step out of here in a moment with your promise and a name. Or I will walk right into a newspaper office and hand them the list and my story on background. The choice is yours."

"Hendrika, listen to me," Vanheul said. "We have to do this. Give him the name. It means nothing. He still has no proof." He turned to Eekhaut. "You understand that you still will have no proof, right?"

"The name is enough. The rest of the investigation is our business. You see, I don't ask for much. Two small favors. And total confidentiality in return."

"And what about the Chief Superintendent?" Van Tillo asked.

"She has no part in this," Eekhaut said. "That's why she left the room."

"But she knows what we are discussing here?"

"She has no part in this," Eekhaut repeated. "I have nothing to add."

Van Tillo looked at Vanheul. "Can we think this over, Inspector?"

"No," Eekhaut said. "I want your answer right away."

Vanheul said, "It means nothing, Hendrika. We have other relations we can depend on. Give him what he wants."

Van Tillo inclined her head. "Very well, Inspector," she said. "I want your formal promise the list will never surface."

"That promise you have."

"And we assure you we have no intentions regarding Miss Calster. She knows nothing, and so she means nothing to us."

"And the name?"

Van Tillo took a deep breath. "The man who ordered the murders is Monet. Dirk Benedict Monet. I hope you're satisfied, Mr. Eekhaut."

"Excellent. It was a pleasure dealing with you both. I hope the feeling is mutual. Oh, and I assume you'll call Mr. Monet as soon as I've left your office."

"Of course."

"Please convey my regards. Tell him I will do everything in my power to find proof against him."

63

THEY WERE OUT IN the street again. Eekhaut was studying the capricious clouds. It would rain again soon. That seemed appropriate. Amsterdam in the fall and rain. This wasn't a city for summer or sun. It needed a cover of dark clouds, people rushing home in anticipation of rain, chaotic traffic, and department stores that were much too large as safe havens against the hostile elements. The young people who made the city their second home during the summer season, looking for cheap drugs and interesting sex, didn't belong to the real Amsterdam.

Dewaal lit a cigarette. He didn't remember she smoked. But it made sense: she ate little and smoked. He would have to lecture her about her health. It was in his personal interest that she remained healthy. Soon, she would be his only ally in Amsterdam.

She exhaled a cloud of smoke. Her hands shook a bit. "I'm completely mad," she said. "Giving you that much space to do your thing. I must have lost my mind."

"You gave me the space because you wanted to. Because you need a way to solve this problem, however improper."

"No, I want a clean case without any legal hassles."

He shrugged. "There are always hassles. And by the way, this time the victims win."

"Really? Is that what you think? I see no winners in this game."

"Yeah," he said, thinking this over. "Yeah, maybe you're right." He was silent for a moment. Then he said, "I haven't figured out yet how to address you properly."

"Keep it simple, Walter. Who gives a shit? I'm your boss for as long as you're here in Holland. You address me using my rank. In the presence of others, you call me 'Chief Superintendent.' That's the way things go from now on. Simple."

"Right. As you wish. What now? Do we get to question Monet?"

She wiped her forehead with the palm of her hand. "First, we build a decent case against him. What do we have?"

"Seems better not to discuss the details here, in the open. I feel the infernal stare of Van Tillo on my back. Don't you?"

They walked into a side street and found a pub, where it was quiet. "What will you have?" she asked.

"Not one of those Dutch beers. I'll have a Leffe Brown. I'll stick to my home brew if you don't mind."

A moment later, she returned with two Leffe Browns. "Item one," she said. "We cannot link Monet with the murders and the assaults."

"We can."

"Oh? Can we?"

"Consider our dear friend Mr. Tarkovski. He gave us a written statement to that effect."

"Which is useless and will not be permitted in court and certainly cannot be used against Monet. Walter, you have no idea—"

"But I have."

"We would need Monet's fingerprints on a murder weapon, and even then we're not sure that he won't just walk away." She drank from the beer. "And you promised Tarkovski he could return to Russia. Remember? How would that sound in court?"

"Yes, you're right again. Funny you should remind me. But now we have two witness statements. Van Tillo and Tarkovski."

"Neither is usable! We won't get Van Tillo to testify in public to what she told you, and as for Tarkovski . . . well, you know what he's worth."

"But surely Monet doesn't know that."

"Van Tillo is calling him at this very moment, and they're having a good laugh. They know we don't have the shadow of a case. There is no happy ending. Eileen Calster can return home, that's one thing at least.

Maybe we send Tarkovski to Russia. And that's the end of it. Live with that, will you, Walter?" She drank from the beer again. Then she asked, "Did you find anything useful in the junk we got from Tarkovski's apartment?"

He shook his head. "Lacking a Russian translator, I asked the tech boys to go through his stuff. His computer files. I still hope they'll find something. And I'm hoping for a team of translators—"

"Don't count on it. No budget."

"Then let's hope he left some sensitive information in Dutch or English."

64

Dewaal called Prinsen on the phone. "Nick," she said, unaware that she was using his first name. "You should go to the safe house and pick up Eileen Calster. Do it now. You'll find the forms you need on my desk in a yellow folder. Take a car and drive her to Groningen. To her parents. No detours, no objections on her part. The only thing she's allowed to do is pick up some things from her apartment. She has already been informed. And take your gun with you."

"I'm on my way," he said.

He ended the call. *Messenger boy*, he thought. This was what having family at the AIVD meant: proving to everybody that you had no privileges. Driving a girl all the way to Groningen and having to come back as well, which meant he would be on the road for the better part of the day. And evening.

So he drove a Honda to the safe house. The car was midsize, dark gray, and as good as new. He parked it in front of the house and walked in. He passed security after the inevitable checks. The guard phoned to the second floor. "There's a detective down here for you, miss," he said. He listened and then indicated to Prinsen that he could walk up.

In the room, a lean, tall girl was waiting for him, a red nylon duffel ready on the bed. It seemed she had quickly packed her life in that bag, with still enough room for an extra life.

"Eileen Calster?" he asked, unnecessarily.

For a moment, she said nothing, as if she were still thinking about trusting him. Then she said, "I'm ready. Have they told you I want to pass by the apartment first?"

"Yes, I've had my . . ." *Instructions*, he wanted to say, but that sounded too official and much too unfriendly. As if her life were totally subjected to instructions.

She had very clear eyes, he noticed. "Shall I carry the bag?"

She smiled but preferred to carry the bag herself. He took the lead, down the stairs and into the street. He opened the passenger door to the Honda. She kept the bag on her lap.

He started the car and looked at his watch. After four already. And he had to drive all the way to Groningen. About one hundred and eighty kilometers. That would take two hours.

He drove a couple of blocks, remembering the address she had given him earlier.

"Turn right here," she said. She pointed. He parked the car.

"I'll go in with you," he said. "I guess the apartment will be locked."

"They gave me a key," she said.

Of course they had given her a key. "I'll accompany you anyway," he said. "I'm not supposed to let you wander off on your own."

"Whatever," she said. She got out, leaving the bag in the car. A moment later, they stood in the apartment. It was in total disarray, worse than before because of the searches. The mattress had been removed, thank God. So had the sheets and blankets. No blood in sight anywhere. The disposal team had done a good job. Traditionally, it had been left to family members to clean up after a crime, but these days the city paid for a specialized disposal team.

She didn't look at the bed but opened a large wardrobe, found a travel bag, and started to go through her possessions. It took her ten minutes. She collected a few things from the desk and finally looked around.

"What happens to the apartment?" she asked.

"I don't know. Did Pieter own it?"

"No, I don't think so. He rented it."

"Would anybody want his possessions?"

She shrugged. She didn't want to think about it. She clearly wanted out of the apartment as soon as possible.

"The family will see to it," Prinsen assured her. "It'll be all right."

She glanced at him. What did he see? Gratitude? Because he cared?

"Take me home," she said. And that was all that was needed to be said.

Driving was difficult, with the evening rush. Everyone wanted out of Amsterdam. It took Prinsen almost an hour to get away from the city, and then suddenly they left the traffic behind them and were driving past level fields with large farmhouses and sheep behind fences. She wasn't in a hurry and seemed to enjoy the view.

"So you're a policeman," she said. It wasn't a question.

"I work for the AIVD," he said. "State security," he explained.

"Really?"

"Yep."

"To what do I owe the interest of AIVD?"

"On account of that list and the political implications of—"

"Oh, I remember you now. I saw you in one of those other cars, on the highway."

He drove carefully, not exceeding sixty. He had a girl in the car with him, and things could have been worse. And she remembered him at his most heroic moment.

"You're probably not going to a happy homecoming," he said.

"My parents have already been told about Maarten. He was . . . very special to them. I don't know about—how do you cope with such a loss? How do you help people cope? You're right, it won't be a happy homecoming."

"I don't know how I can help you."

"What is your name?"

"Prinsen. Nick Prinsen."

"Nick. How do you cope with loss, Nick? I had plenty of time to think about that, in my room. I was allowed two calls, to my parents. But I couldn't . . . I couldn't really talk over the phone. Not about Maarten. My mother didn't want to speak to me. She's not angry, but she simply could not—"

"Eileen?"

"My father had to take the phone. Their son is dead. Nothing is ever going to change that. Not the death penalty for the murderers. Not angels descending in the garden. Not prayers."

"Eileen?" he said urgently.

"What?"

Softly, he said, "I don't know how to handle grief and loss, Eileen. I don't. There surely are people who can help you, but not me. I'm sorry."

She was silent. He'd betrayed her, one way or another. He was a police officer and was supposed to protect her. Not against criminals now, but against herself. Against sorrow and fear and loss.

But there was nothing he could do.

She looked at him. Her eyes were dry. He would have been at a loss had she cried. But she didn't.

"I'm sorry, Eileen."

She turned toward him. "It's all right, Nick. You can't help me, I understand. And that's all right. I can cope. It's my parents I'm most concerned about. Not for their loss, but for the days and nights I'm going to have to spend with them. Afterward, I'll leave them again. I can't live with them. They know I can't. They knew their children aren't going to accompany them into old age. But death, that's rather radical."

"You're not staying with them? Later on, I mean?"

"No. I've chosen to lead a different life, and that's what I'll do. In spite of the thing with Pieter. I'll be back in Amsterdam in a couple of weeks. Things will be all right for me, don't worry. Now is the time to comfort my parents, and afterward is the time to say goodbye again. Isn't that ironic?"

He didn't know how to deal with that.

And yet, he did.

She's like me, he thought. She'll live in Amsterdam in a tight little room if need be, or in another lonely city. She'll live alone because living with somebody will remind her of Pieter. And that may be suffocating for her. So she'll create the biggest possible distance between herself and her past. It's banal, but it's life.

It was much like his own story.

"If you ever come back to Amsterdam, Eileen," he said, "please call me, won't you? You know where to find me."

She smiled, but her smile was almost invisible to him in the growing dark.

65

EEKHAUT HAD BEEN LOOKING forward to this moment. First, a hot shower and a careful shave, then clothes better suited for the evening—even if nobody in Amsterdam cared about the sort of clothes he wore. He combed his hair and left the apartment. He got money from an ATM. He was a bit tense but he also felt a sort of casual freedom; at the same time, he told himself he was a fool. What did the woman in the Absinthe see in him? And what did he expect from her?

She had a name. She was called Linda. He would have to get used to that name. She would only become a real person when he used her name.

The evening chill took him by surprise. He wore a jacket but no overcoat. His body told him not to dress too warmly. Not yet. What would he wear in the middle of winter? How many overcoats would he need then if he already wore one now?

He crossed Rembrandtplein—the terraces were almost deserted—and walked in the direction of the Dam, passing Japanese tourists who were probably looking for the red-light district off the canals. German tourists, of another age group, seemed on the hunt for food. Elegantly dressed young men on the lookout for each other. Surinamese families with plastic carrier bags looking for a tram. Everybody was looking for something. All he needed was a quiet bar and a good conversation.

When he entered the Absinthe, jazz was playing. The better kind of jazz: smoky, lived-in jazz, not too much swing but a lot of blues. A grumbling tenor sax, a piano, and percussion in the background. All this on excellent sound equipment. At least this proprietor cared enough about music. He ordered his green drink and confiscated a table that would be his till the end of the evening. The bar wasn't crowded, with about a dozen men and women, mostly in their forties. In one corner, Cuban cigars were tried out and nobody protested. It was that kind of bar.

She entered a bit after eight. They hadn't settled on a specific time but had assumed the other would, at some point, arrive. She cast him a glance, got an absinthe from the counter, and sat with him at his table. She wore jeans, a dark blouse, and a short leather jacket, which she took off.

"To excellence," she said and raised her glass to him.

He smiled. "Today I want to drink to excellence," he said. "Today. This is a day for optimism. About the human race."

"Good," she said. "I'd hoped you weren't the pessimistic type. I can do without that."

"I'm not. Not as a rule. Not by nature. But in my profession, optimism is always a challenge. By nature of my job, I'm constantly confronted by the downhill race of humanity. People never come to us with an uplifting story."

"And then you end up in a bar with a woman." She held the small glass gracefully, her elbow on the table. He admired the gentle curve of her wrist and arm.

"Precisely. And then my confrontation with the world dissolves into, well, nothingness."

"I don't want to sound like I'm in a philosophical mood," she said.

"What will we talk about then, if not philosophy? Not the weather, I hope."

"No. No, not the weather." She grinned. "Although we Dutch jabber all the time about the weather. It's in our blood. The battle with the elements and all that. We talk about it even more than politics. Go figure. I'm fed up with those conversations."

"Let's talk politics, then," he proposed. "You'll have to explain Dutch politics to me. I'm in need of enlightenment."

"I don't know all that much about politics, except what the parties stand for and who's leading them. Most boring subject after the weather."

He raised his glass. "About absinthe?"

"Yes. What do you need to know? That it isn't poisonous, or any more addictive than other alcohol, as was once was thought?"

"I'm not in the least worried."

"And that the most important ingredient is called wormwood, which is also used as a basis for vermouth? It's a Swiss invention, actually. Can you imagine, those slow, peaceful Swiss are responsible for a drink that was banned a century ago."

"Really? Chocolate, discreet banking, watches, all good things seem to originate in Switzerland. What was wrong with absinthe?"

She smiled. "No, you don't want to know."

"I do. It's fascinating. Why was it forbidden?"

"Because at the end of the nineteenth century the settled bourgeoisie considered the drink a poison, only fit for progressive artists, bohemians, you know. Criminals and prostitutes. The kind of people who didn't hold a job, refused to be controlled by society, boozed all day, chased women—"

"I know a few of those—"

"Baudelaire, Oscar Wilde, Verlaine, Rimbaud, all enjoyed the green devil."

"And you wouldn't want to be seen in their company."

"Precisely." She folder both her hands around the glass, which disappeared completely. "Why am I trying to educate you?"

He grabbed her hands, suddenly serious. "Educating me is a necessary evil," he said.

"Really? You're too old to need an education. You're too old for me. You're an old, old man." There was a smile in her eyes. He hoped she was teasing him. Then he held her hands, and she let him.

"Even this old, old man can still be taught a few tricks," he said.

And suddenly she was serious again. Her hands slid out of his. "You lectured me on responsibility," she said.

"Well, I wouldn't call it lecturing. I have no lessons to teach you."

But she remained serious. "I'm younger than you, but I have a past."

"Ah," he said, "a woman with a past."

"Be serious for a moment, Walter. A past, which means a mix of good and bad experiences."

"Haven't we all had those?"

"Yes. And so it isn't easy to . . . Things were easier when we were twenty and didn't yet have a past."

"Today, kids already have a weighty past by the time they're twenty. Some, at least."

She smiled again. "It's not a coincidence, Walter; us meeting here. Us liking each other."

"No, it's the way life turns out, I know. You miss one opportunity, a mere second of inattention, and your life goes in a completely opposite direction."

"Is it the music?"

"What?"

"Us being so melancholic? Is it the music?" She smiled again at his confusion. Then she searched for something in her handbag. She produced a small device, shiny black, a digital recorder. She slid it across the table toward him.

"What's this?" he asked.

"A digital speech recorder," she said, matter-of-factly. "That's what we specialists call it." She was clearly teasing, again, but nervously at the same time. He thought: *This was a big decision, giving me the recorder.*

"I'm in sync," he said, "with the twenty-first century. I know what it is and what it does."

"It records speech," she said. "Like when you're in a meeting and you need to record what you and the other party is saying."

"Like taking notes."

"Taking notes is so twenty-first century."

He didn't want to react.

"I told you that I work for . . . people who are less than scrupulous, less than moral in their dealings. So, whenever I can, I take precautions. I don't want to be involved in the affairs they conduct. They pay me, and I work for them, but I'm not going to be dragged into their dirty business."

"Dirty business," he said, hoping for her to continue.

"There was a meeting between two parties. I was supposed to, you know, attend, as a secretary, which is what I basically am."

"All right."

"But they asked me to leave. I wasn't supposed to hear what was going to be said. I had brought along this recorder. I had it switched on in advance. Something I usually do. I left it in the room. They didn't notice. Who notices one of these things, today, eh? They sweep meeting rooms for hidden bugs, but they never look twice—or even once—at a recording device brought in by one of the staff."

"So you recorded a conversation. Should I be interested?"

"We met here by accident, Walter. Later, I realized who you are. I realized what case you were working on. I realized the connection between my job and yours."

"Fascinating, I'm sure, but what—?"

"I work for Dirk Benedict Monet. I'm his staff liaison and occasional secretary. I accompany him. Like when he meets with a certain Russian gentleman. And then he asks me to leave the room. I'm not supposed to hear what my boss has to say to the Russian. I'm not stupid, but I am curious by nature. So I leave my recorder in the room, as if by accident."

"Monet."

"And a certain Russian fellow. I'm sure that you will be very interested to hear what is on the machine. I found it enlightening, anyway. It helped me decide to quit my job soon. You didn't get this from me. You can voice-test the recording, establish who is talking. As to the context of their talk, well, you'll find that extremely interesting as well. I'll no longer be working for Monet. But neither will anybody else, except for some stooges he might recruit while he's in prison."

She rose and closed her handbag. "I hope you still want to see me again, Walter? I may not have any more surprises of this nature for you, but at least we'll have something to talk about, apart from the weather."

SUNDAY

Amsterdam

66

"You promised me I could return to Russia. You said that I could."

Eekhaut looked up. It was Sunday morning. He didn't work on a Sunday. No sensible person worked on a Sunday. He had worked all week. His first week in Holland. Then why was he here? "Tarkovski? Like *the* Andreï Tarkovski? I've been wondering, are you related to the famous filmmaker?"

"Same family, no direct relation," the young man said sourly. "And my parents were movie buffs, hence the first name. It could have been worse." He wore the same outfit as the day before, his chin unshaven and his hair unkempt. Maybe he hadn't taken a shower out of spite. He seemed to lack focus and didn't know what Eekhaut wanted.

As if Eekhaut knew where he wanted to go with his questions.

"You understand that even this, I mean you having a famous name and so on, does nothing for what will happen to you?"

Tarkovski shook his head. "What is the value of your word, Mr. Detective? Before we talk any further, I want to know. I want to know what your word is worth. What is it worth?"

"Nothing," Eekhaut said. "My word is worth nothing when given to a criminal. Let that be clear. On the other hand, I doubt that you're a criminal. Hence my dilemma."

Tarkovski kept his mouth shut, but not without effort. He hadn't slept well. Eekhaut assumed those cells lacked any comfort. And there wouldn't be many facilities for the temporary inmates. But he wouldn't advocate for better cells. If you were guilty, you needed to feel misery.

"You're Keretsky's assistant, and that's all you are," he said. "You take care of your boss's projects. Keretsky asks you to find an assassin, and you comply. He asks you to chase a girl and shoot her, and you do that. You don't pull the trigger yourself. You're too careful to do that. We can't pin murder on you. But, have no fear, we will pin other crimes on you. Enough for a long stretch in prison."

Tarkovski shrugged. He had already signed a confession. What else could he do?

Eekhaut leaned forward. "Should I allow you to return to Russia, Andreï, to return to the world of your lord and master, Keretsky? Where he decides life and death. Where there is no distinction between power and crime. Is that what you want?"

"It's easy to talk about morality, Officer, when you're on that side and not at the center of the game. Because if you're in the heart of the game, that distinction is less clear. What you call a distinction between power and crime is a distinction between a question and an order. It is the distinction between the life you lead and the life you would like to lead."

"Yes," Eekhaut said. "You're right. You're right about a lot of things. But then, I'm not paid to sit in the center of your game. I throw you in prison, that's what I get paid for. I get paid to send people to prison. And the life lesson is thrown in for free. Sometimes. Not always. Some people aren't worth the bother. In your case, you're worth it, and the lesson will change your life."

"How long?"

"How long what?"

"For how long do I go to prison?"

Eekhaut kept looking at the man. Things had to be made right, but not by him. "I'm not the judge, Andreï. The judge decides how long you go to jail. At least for a year or two. Maybe just that, and not more. Maybe you'll get out early. We can say you weren't directly implicated in the murders. You know we can."

"And after that?"

"After that?" Eekhaut shrugged. "You won't stay in Russia for long. That much I am convinced of."

"No?"

"No. Take it from me. You'll be back here. And maybe, if you like, we'll have a beer in a quiet bar somewhere in this city. And we'll talk about the Russian soul. I look forward to that occasion."

Eekhaut rose and walked out of the room without further comment. He looked at his watch. Whatever the day, time moved on. Tomorrow it would be Monday. Tomorrow Monet would be indicted.

And he still needed to get his apartment in order. Because, after all, it seemed he would be staying a while in Amsterdam.

Afterword

Some organizations mentioned in this book are genuine, and the abbreviations of their Dutch names are used. Some are fictitious. AIVD stands for *Algemene Inlichtingen-en Veiligheidsdienst* (literally, General Information and Security Service). The *Bureau Internationale Misdaad en Extreme Organisaties* (Bureau of International Crime and Extremist Organizations) is, to my knowledge, fictitious. The Partij Dierbaar Nederland (PDN) is also my invention, although there are plenty of right-wing parties in Europe that could serve as a model. Fabna Bank does not exist but could, for the Belgian Fortis Bank could have merged, sometime in 2007, with the Dutch bank ABN Amro. This did not happen, however, because Fortis Bank probably ran out of funds, and then there was the international financial crisis. The Ford Mondeo that figures in the book is the Ford Taurus for American readers, of course, but Ford insists on giving its models different names in Europe.

As to me using my own name as that of the main character, well, there's a long story behind it, which I save for public readings and book presentations. Anyway, the short version is that *Walter Eekhaut* also happens to be my grandfather's name. Since British and American readers might not know how to pronounce his (and my) name, I've found this simple trick: *Eekhaut* rhymes with *stakeout* but without the first two letters. If we ever meet, try to get it right.

I'd like to thank a number of people (and I may be forgetting some, for which my apologies). Jürgen Snoeren was the publisher of the original Dutch edition of the book, and his careful work assured me winning the

Hercule Poirot Award in 2009. My agent, Peter Riva (of International Transactions Inc.), supported and encouraged me, as a firm believer in the qualities of this book. Cal Barksdale is my editor at Arcade, who oversaw the birth of the American edition of this book with professional grace and quite a bit of patience. Leigh Kennedy and Joanne DeMichele are, respectively, my equally patient and astute proofreader and copy editor.